SECOND CHANCE WITH HER GUARDED GP

KATE HARDY

MILLS & BOON

For Vicki Ward Hibbins,
with love and thanks for the seal lightbulb!

SECOND CHANCE WITH HER GUARDED GP

KATE HARDY

BABY MIRACLE FOR THE ER DOC

KATE HARDY

MILLS & BOON

Published in Great Britain 2021
by Mills & Boon, an imprint of HarperCollins*Publishers* Ltd,
1 London Bridge Street, London, SE1 9GF

www.harpercollins.co.uk

HarperCollins*Publishers*
1st Floor, Watermarque Building,
Ringsend Road, Dublin 4, Ireland

Second Chance with Her Guarded GP © 2021 by Pamela Brooks

Baby Miracle for the ER Doc © 2021 by Pamela Brooks

ISBN: 978-0-263-29773-7

08/21

MIX
Paper from
responsible sources
FSC™ C007454

Kate Hardy has always loved books, and could read before she went to school. She discovered Mills & Boon books when she was twelve, and decided that *this* was what she wanted to do. When she isn't writing Kate enjoys reading, cinema, ballroom dancing and the gym. You can contact her via her website: katehardy.com.

CHAPTER ONE

OLIVER LANGLEY TOOK a deep breath.

This was it. His new start. Not the life he'd thought he'd have, six months ago: but that had been before the world had tilted on its axis and mixed everything up. Before his twin brother Rob had gone to work for a humanitarian aid organisation in the aftermath of an earthquake and his appendix had burst. Before Rob had ended up with severe blood poisoning that had wiped out his kidneys. Before Ollie had donated a kidney to his twin.

Before Ollie's fiancée had called off their wedding.

Which had been his own fault for asking her to move the wedding. 'Tab, with Rob being on dialysis, he's not well enough even to be at the wedding, let alone be my best man.' He'd been so sure his fiancée would see things the same way that he did. It made perfect sense to move the wedding until after the transplant, giving both him and Rob time to recover from the operation and meaning that Ollie's entire family would be there to share the day. 'Let's move the wedding back a few months. The transplant's hopefully going to be at the beginning of June, so we'll both be properly recovered by August. We can have a late summer wedding instead.'

'Move the wedding.' It had been a statement, not a question. She'd gone silent, as if considering it, then shaken her head. 'No.'

He'd stared at her. 'Tab, I know it'll be a bit of work, changing all the arrangements, but I'll do as much of it as I can.'

'That's not what I mean, Ollie.'

He'd stared at her, not understanding. 'Then what do you mean?'

'I—I've been thinking for a while. We should call it off.'

'Call it off?' He'd gone cold. 'Why? Have you met someone else?'

'No. It's not you. It's me.'

Which meant the problem *was* him and she was trying to be nice. 'Tab, whatever it is, we can work it out. Whatever I've done to upset you, I'm sorry.' He loved her. He wanted to marry her, to make a family with her. He'd thought she felt the same way and wanted the same things. But it was becoming horribly clear that he'd got it all wrong.

Her eyes had filled with tears. 'It's not you, it's me,' she said again. 'You're giving Rob a kidney—of course you are. He's your brother and you love him. Anyone would do the same, in your shoes.'

'But?' He'd forced himself to say the word she'd left out.

She'd looked him in the eye. 'What if something goes wrong? What if *you* get ill, and your one remaining kidney doesn't work any more, and you have to go on dialysis? What if they can't find a match for you, and you die?'

'That's not going to happen, Tab.' He'd tried to put

his arms round her to comfort and reassure her but she'd pulled away.

'You're not listening, Ollie. I can't do this.'

'Why?'

'You know how it's been with my dad.'

'Yes.' Tabby's father had chronic fatigue syndrome. He'd been too ill to do much for years.

'Mum stuck by her wedding vows—in sickness and in health. I didn't realise when I was younger, but she worked herself to the bone, making sure my brother and I were OK, and keeping us financially afloat, and looking after Dad. Obviously when we got older and realised how ill Dad was, Tom and I did as much as we could do to help. But my mum's struggled every single day, Ollie. She's sacrificed her life to look after Dad. And I can't do that for you. I just *can't*.'

He'd frowned. 'But I'm not ill, Tab. OK, I'll need a bit of time to recover from the transplant, but I'll be fine. Rob will get better and everything will be back to normal soon enough.'

'But you can't promise me you'll always be well and I won't have to look after you, Ollie. You can't possibly promise something like that.' Tabby had shaken her head. 'I'm sorry, Ollie. I can't marry you.' She'd fought to hold back the tears. 'I know it's selfish and I know it's unfair, but I just don't love you enough to take that risk. I don't want a life like my mum's. I don't want to marry you.' She'd taken off the engagement ring and given it back to him. 'I'm so sorry, Ollie. But I can't do this.'

'Tab, you've just got an attack of cold feet. We'll get through this,' he said. 'We love each other. It'll be fine.'

'No, Ollie. That's the point. I do love you—but not *enough*. I'm sorry.'

He hadn't been able to change her mind.

She'd got in touch to wish him and Rob luck with the transplant, but she'd made it clear she didn't want him back. He wasn't enough for her. To the point where she hadn't even wanted him to help cancel all the arrangements; Tabby insisted on doing it all herself.

Ollie had spent a couple of weeks brooding after the operation, and he'd realised that he needed some time away from London. So he'd taken a six-month sabbatical from the practice in Camden where he was a salaried GP, lent his flat to a friend, and had gone back to Northumbria to stay with Rob and their parents. The open skies, hills and greenery had given him a breathing space from the bustle of London and time to think about what he wanted to do with his life.

Though the enforced time off after the transplant, once he'd untangled the wedding, had left Ollie with the fidgets. Much as he loved their parents and completely understood why their mum was fussing over her twin boys, Ollie liked having his own space and the smothering was driving him mad. He was pretty sure that doing the job he loved would help him get his equilibrium back and help him move on from the mess of his wedding-that-wasn't.

Then he'd seen the ad for a three-month maternity cover post at Ashermouth Bay Surgery, which would take him nearly up to the end of his sabbatical. He'd applied for the job; once the practice had given him a formal offer, he'd found a three-month let and moved into one of the old fishermen's cottages near the harbour, within walking distance of the practice.

And today was his first day at his new job. He might

not have been enough for his fiancée, but he knew he was definitely good enough as a doctor.

The building was single-storey, built of red brick and with a tiled roof. There were window-boxes filled with welcoming bright red geraniums, and a raised brick flower bed in front of the door, filled with lavender. The whole place looked bright and welcoming; and next to the door was a sign listing the practice staff, from the doctors and nurses through to the reception and admin team.

Ollie was slightly surprised to see his own name on the sign, underneath that of Aadya Devi, the GP whose maternity leave he was covering, but it made him feel welcome. Part of the team. He really liked that.

He took a deep breath, pushed the door open and walked in to the reception area.

The receptionist was chatting to a woman in a nurse's uniform, who had her back to him. Clearly neither of them had heard him come in, because they were too busy talking about him.

'Dr Langley's starting this morning,' the receptionist said.

'Our newbie,' the nurse said, sounding pleased.

At thirty, Ollie didn't quite see himself as a 'newbie', but never mind. He was new to the practice, so he supposed it was an accurate description.

'Caroline's asked me to help him settle in, as she's away this week,' the nurse added.

Caroline was the senior partner at the practice: a GP in her late fifties, with a no-nonsense attitude and a ready laugh. Ollie had liked her very much at the interview.

He didn't really need someone to help him settle in,

but OK. He got that this place was a welcoming one. That they believed in teamwork.

'And, of course, he's fresh meat,' the nurse said.

The receptionist laughed. 'Oh, Gem. Trust *you* to think of that.'

Ollie, who had just opened his mouth ready to say hello, stood there in silence, gobsmacked.

Fresh meat?

Right now, he was still smarting too much from the fallout from the wedding-that-wasn't to want any kind of relationship. And it rankled that someone was discussing him in that way. Fresh meat. A slab of beefcake. Clearly this 'Gem' woman made a habit of this, given the receptionist's comment.

Well, he'd just have to make sure she realised that she was barking up completely the wrong tree. And he didn't care if his metaphors were mixed.

He gave a loud cough. 'Good morning.'

'Oh! Good morning.' The receptionist smiled at him. 'We're not actually open yet, but can I help you?'

'I'm Oliver Langley,' he said.

The receptionist's cheeks went pink as she clearly realised that he'd overheard the end of their conversation.

Yeah. She might well be embarrassed. Fresh meat, indeed.

'I'm Maddie Jones, the receptionist—well, obviously,' she said. 'Welcome to the practice. Can I get you a cup of coffee, Dr Langley?'

'Thank you, but I'm fine,' he said coolly. 'I don't expect to be waited on.'

The nurse next to her also turned round to greet him.

'Good morning, Dr Langley. Nice to meet you,' she said with a smile.

Surely she must realise that he'd overheard what she'd just said about him? And yet she was still being all smiley and sparkly-eyed. Brazening it out? That didn't sit well with him at all.

'I'm Gemma Baxter,' she said. 'I'm one of the practice nurse practitioners. Caroline asked me to look after you this week, as she's away on holiday.'

'That's kind of you, Nurse Baxter,' he said, keeping his voice expressionless, 'but quite unnecessary.'

'Call me Gemma. And, if nothing else,' she said, 'I can at least show you where everything is in the surgery.' She disappeared for a moment, then came through to join him in the waiting area. 'It's pretty obvious that this is the waiting area,' she said, gesturing to the chairs. 'The nurses' and HCA's rooms are this side of Reception—' she gestured to the corridor to their left '—the pharmacy's through the double doors to the right, the patient toilets are over there in the corner, and the doctors' rooms are this side.'

She gestured to the other corridor. 'If you'd like to follow me? The staff toilets, the kitchen and rest room are here, behind Reception and the admin team.' She led him into the kitchen. 'Coffee, tea, hot chocolate and fruit tea are in the cupboard above the kettle, along with the mugs. The dishwasher's next to the fridge, and there's a rota for emptying it; and the microwave's self-explanatory. We all put a couple of pounds into the kitty every week and Maddie keeps the supplies topped up. If there's anything you want that isn't here, just let Maddie know.'

She smiled at him. 'I need to start checking the out-of-hours notifications and hospital letters before my triage calls and vaccination clinic this morning, so I'm going to leave you here. Your room's the third on the right, but obviously you'll see your name on the door anyway.'

'Thank you for the tour,' he said. That 'fresh meat' comment had rubbed him up the wrong way, but he was going to have to work with her for the next three months so it'd be sensible to be polite and make the best of it.

'I'll come and find you at lunchtime,' she said. 'As it's your first day, lunch is on me.'

'That's—' But he didn't have time to tell her that it was totally unnecessary and he'd sort out his own lunch, thanks all the same, because she'd already gone through to the other corridor.

Ollie made himself a coffee, then headed for his consulting room. It was a bright, airy space; there was a watercolour on the wall of a castle overlooking the sea, which he vaguely recognised as a local attraction. A desk; a couple of chairs for his patient and a parent or support person; and a computer. Everything neatly ordered and in its place; nothing personal.

He checked his phone for the username and password the practice administrator had sent him last week, logged on to the system and changed the password. Then he put an alarm on his phone to remind him when telephone triage started, and once his emails came up he started to work through the discharge summaries, hospital letters and referrals from over the weekend.

Gemma knew she was making a bit of a snap judgement—the sort of thing she normally disapproved of—but Oliver Langley seemed so closed-off. He hadn't responded to the warmth of her smile or her greeting, and he'd been positively chilly when she'd said she'd show him round. She sincerely hoped he'd be a bit warmer with their patients. When you were worried about your health, the last thing you needed was a doctor being snooty with you. You needed someone who'd listen and who'd reassure you.

Yes, sure, he was gorgeous: tall, with dark floppy hair and blue eyes, reminding her of a young Hugh Grant. But, when you were a medic, it didn't matter what you looked like; what mattered was how you behaved towards people. So far, from what Gemma had seen, Oliver Langley was very self-contained. If he was the best fit for the practice, as Caroline had claimed, Gemma hated to think what the other interviewees had been like. Robots, perhaps?

Hopefully she could work some kind of charm offensive on him over lunch. She intended to get a genuine smile out of him, even if she had to exhaust her entire stock of terrible jokes.

She took a gulp of the coffee she'd made earlier and checked the out-of-hours log, to see which of their patients had needed urgent treatment over the weekend and needed following up. Then she clicked onto the triage list Maddie had sent through, before starting her hour and a half of phone triage.

The system was one of the things the practice had kept from the Covid days. It was more efficient for dealing with minor illnesses and giving advice about coughs and colds and minor fevers; but in Gemma's view you could often tell a lot from a patient's body language— something that could prompt her to ask questions to unlock what her patient was *really* worrying about. That was something that telephone triage had taken away, since the Covid days. And trying to diagnose a rash or whether a wound had turned septic, from looking at a blurred photograph taken on a phone and sent in low resolution so it would actually reach the surgery email, had been next to impossible.

At least things were a bit easier now. They were all adjusting to the 'new normal'. She worked her way through the triage list until it was time to start her vaccination clinic. Even though the vaccination meant she had to make little ones cry, it also meant she got a chance for baby cuddles. Gemma would never admit to being broody, but if she was honest with herself her biological clock always sat up and took notice when she had this kind of clinic.

It had been twelve years since she'd lost her little sister—since she'd lost her entire family, because her parents had closed off, too, unable to deal with their loss. Gemma had been so desperate to feel loved and to stop the pain of missing Sarah that she'd chosen completely the wrong way to do it; she'd gone off the rails and slept with way too many boys. Once her best friend's mum had sat her down and talked some sense into her, Gemma had ended up going the other way: so determined not to be needy that she wouldn't let her boyfriends close, and the relationships had fizzled out within weeks. She'd never managed to find anyone she'd really clicked with.

So the chances of her attending this particular clinic rather than running it were looking more and more remote. It was a good six months since she'd last had a casual date, let alone anything more meaningful. The nearest she'd get to having a real family of her own was being godmother to Scarlett, her best friend's daughter. She was grateful for that, but at the same time she wondered why she still hadn't been able to fix her own family. Why she still couldn't get through to her parents.

She shook herself. Ridiculous. Why was she thinking about this now?

Perhaps, she thought, because Oliver Langley was precisely the sort of man she'd gone for, back in her difficult days. Tall, dark-haired, blue-eyed and gorgeous. And his coolness towards her had unsettled her; she was used to people reacting to her warmth and friendliness in kind.

Well, tough. It was his problem, not hers, and she didn't have time to worry about it now. She had a job to do. She went into the corridor and called her first patient for her clinic.

CHAPTER TWO

'I'VE BEEN DREADING this appointment. I really hate needles,' Fenella Nichols confessed as she sat down by Gemma's desk, settling the baby on her lap.

Gemma could've guessed that, because the year-old baby was fussing, having picked up on her mum's stress. 'A lot of people do,' she said with a smile. 'But you're doing absolutely the right thing, bringing Laura here to protect her. Meningitis is nasty stuff, and so are mumps and measles and rubella. And you've dressed her perfectly, so I've got easy access to her thigh and her arm and it won't cause her a lot of worry.' She stroked the baby's cheek. 'Hello, gorgeous. Do I get a smile?'

To her relief, the baby gurgled.

'You've got her red book?' Gemma checked.

'Yes.' Fenella produced it and put it on the desk.

'Great. How's everything going?' This was the point where Gemma knew that if there were any real worries, Fenella would unburden herself and Gemma could start to fix things.

'My husband thinks she's a bit behind. I mean, I know she's a bit on the small side, but I thought she takes after me.'

Fenella was slender and just about five feet tall, a

good six inches shorter than Gemma. 'You're probably right. I'll measure her and look at her centile chart,' Gemma promised. 'And I can hear for myself that she's starting to get chatty.'

'Dada, dog and duck are her favourite words,' Fenella said with a smile. 'And she's pulling herself up on the furniture.'

'It won't be long until she's walking, then. You'll be seeing the health visitor about her milestones,' Gemma said, 'but from what you're saying there's nothing to worry about.' Gemma waved at the baby, who waved back. Then she took a picture book from the tray on her desk, opened it and held it in front of the baby. 'Can you see the duck, Laura?'

The baby cooed and pointed at the picture of a duck.

'Can you help Laura find the lamb in the book, Fenella?'

With both mum and baby distracted, it was easy for Gemma to prepare Laura's thigh for the vaccination and administer it. Laura cried for a moment, but was soon distracted by her mum turning the page to another picture. 'Dog!' she said, pointing.

'That's brilliant,' Gemma said. 'You might see a red area come up around the injection site later this morning, Fenella, but that'll go in a couple of days. And sometimes after the meningitis vaccine babies get a bit of a temperature, but I'm going to give Laura some liquid paracetamol now to help stop that happening. Make sure you give her plenty to drink, and if she feels a bit hot take off a layer or two. You can give her more paracetamol if you need to in four hours, and if you're worried give us a call.'

'All right. Thank you, Gemma.'

Gemma weighed and measured the baby, recording the figures as well as the vaccination details in the red book. 'Laura's following the same trend line she's been on since birth, a shade under the middle, so I'm very happy. Is there anything you're concerned about, or anything you'd like to chat over?'

'No.' Fenella smiled. 'But I think I'm going to make my husband bring her for the next injections.'

Gemma laughed. 'That sounds like a good plan.'

Her next patient was a little older, so she distracted him from the 'sharp scratch' by getting him to sing 'Old Macdonald Had a Zoo' with her.

'Zoo?' his mum asked, laughing.

'Absolutely,' Gemma said with a grin. 'It makes a change from a farm with cows and sheep. With a zoo, we can have elephants, tigers, lions, crocodiles...'

'Crocodiles!' the little boy said, his eyes going round with excitement.

'A snap-snap here,' Gemma sang.

In all the excitement of the song, the little boy forgot to be upset about the needle.

This was one of the bits of the job Gemma loved: the interaction with her younger patients. If she hadn't decided to go into general practice, she would definitely have worked in paediatrics.

She dispensed a sticker announcing 'I was THIS brave' at the end of the appointment, did the necessary cleaning in the treatment room, and called in her next patient. As it was the school holidays, she also had a couple of teenagers at the clinic who'd missed their meningitis vaccine and needed to catch up.

'So you're off to uni in a couple of months?' she asked the first one.

'*If* I get my grades.' Millie bit her lip. 'I'm dreading results day.'

'You have my sympathy. I still remember mine.' The second time round had given Gemma the grades she'd needed, but the first time had been a disaster. Her year of going off the rails had meant she'd failed her exams spectacularly and she'd had to repeat the second year of her A levels and resit her exams. 'Just remember that there's always a plan B,' Gemma said. 'Even if you don't get your first choice, you're still going to have a good time because you'll be doing the subject you love.'

'I guess.' Millie grimaced. 'Mum's worrying.'

'That's what mums do,' Gemma said. 'But this is one worry you can tick off her list.' She smiled. 'My mum was the same.' Well. Almost. After Sarah's death, her mum had seemed to close off. But her best friend Claire's mum Yvonne had worried about her. And Yvonne had been the one to sit down with Gemma and finally make her get her act together after she'd failed her exams. 'She got me to make a list of what I was worrying about. Then we talked about it and made a plan together. My mum—' well, Claire's mum '—worried about me eating properly, so I got her to teach me how to make some meals that were quick, easy and cheap.'

'That's a really good idea. Thank you,' Millie said.

'Good luck, and I hope you have a wonderful time at uni,' Gemma said when Millie left.

Her clinic finished on time; she sorted out her paperwork, checked on the practice app that Oliver's last appointment had finished, then went to knock on his door.

'Time for lunch,' she said, giving him her warmest smile in the hope that it might thaw him out a bit.

He looked up from his desk. 'Really, there's no need.'

He was going to be stubborn about it? Well, maybe he needed to learn that he wasn't the only one who could be stubborn. He might only be here temporarily, but for those three months he was going to be part of the team. Being snooty and refusing to mix with everyone wasn't an option. 'There's every need,' she said. 'You're new to the village and it's your first day at the practice. We're a team and we look after each other. I thought we could have lunch by the cliffs—the local bakery does the best sandwiches ever. And, as it's your first day, it's my shout.'

When he opened his mouth, she guessed he was about to refuse, and added swiftly, 'No protests allowed.' He looked wary, and she sighed. 'Look, it's just a sandwich and some coffee. A welcome-to-the-practice sort of thing. You're not under any obligation to me whatsoever if you accept.'

He looked awkward, then. 'Thank you,' he muttered.

She'd get a proper smile out of him if it killed her. 'I'm glad that's settled. It's a five-minute walk from here to the bakery, and five minutes from there to the cliffs.'

He followed her out of the door. Still silent, she noticed. OK. She'd start the conversation. Something easy. Food was always a safe subject. 'For the purposes of transparency, the bakery happens to be owned by my best friend, but I stand by what I said. Claire makes amazingly good sourdough and her brownies have to be tasted to be believed.'

'Right.'

Oh, for pity's sake. Could he not meet her halfway and at least make an *effort* at small talk? She tried again. 'Are you not a cake person?'

He wrinkled his nose. 'Not really.'

So he wouldn't be buying cake from her on her regular Friday morning bake sale. 'Looks as if we're opposites, then,' she said lightly, 'because I think cake makes the world go round.'

Was she being paranoid, or was he looking at her as if she had two heads? If she hadn't promised Caroline she'd look after him, she would've walked away and left him to his own grouchy company.

At the bakery, once they'd chosen their sandwiches and he'd ordered an espresso, she added a lemon and raspberry cake to their order along with one of Claire's savoury muffins.

Oliver carried the brown paper bag with their lunch, but he didn't make conversation on the steep path up to the cliffs.

Was he shy, perhaps? He might find it easier to be professional with his patients than with his coworkers, but somehow she was going to have to persuade him to thaw a little. They really didn't need any tension at work.

Finally they made it to the clifftop. Gemma took the picnic blanket from her backpack and spread it on the grass with a flourish. 'Have a seat,' she said with a smile.

'Do you always carry a picnic blanket?' he asked, looking surprised.

She nodded. 'If it's not raining, I usually come up here for lunch. The view's amazing.'

'It is,' he agreed, looking out at the sand and the sea.

'It's the best place I know to clear your head and set you up for the rest of the day.'

He sat down next to her, opened the paper bag,

checked the labels written on the contents and handed her a coffee and a sandwich. 'Thank you for lunch.'

'You're welcome. How was your first morning?'

'Fine.'

He was still being cool. So much for hoping that lunch might win him round.

'Win me round?' The coolness was verging on arctic, now.

She grimaced. 'I said that aloud, didn't I? I'm sorry.' She took a deep breath. 'We don't seem to be getting on very well. I was trying to be nice and look out for a new colleague. If I've come across as in your face or patronising, I apologise.'

He was still looking at her as if she had two heads. She sighed inwardly. What would it take to get a decent working relationship going with her new colleague?

Then again, she hadn't managed to fix her relationship with her parents. She was the common factor in both situations, so maybe *she* was the problem. Maybe she should just give up—on both counts. 'Now I know you're not a cake person, I won't try to sell you a Friday Fundraiser cake.'

'What's a Friday Fundraiser cake?'

'Before Covid, I used to have a cake stall in the waiting room on Friday mornings to raise money for the local cardiac unit. I'd sell cake and cookies to patients, staff, anyone who happened to be around.' She sighed. 'Caroline's given me the go-ahead to do it again now, but it's on a much smaller scale because we don't have as many face-to-face appointments as we used to.' She shrugged.

'But it's better than nothing. All the little bits add up. I do a big fundraiser every three or four months;

my skydive in the spring had to be postponed because of bad weather, so I'm doing it next month. There's no obligation to sponsor me, but if you'd like to then I'd be very grateful, even if it's only a pound.' She gave him a wry smile. 'I've been fundraising for about ten years, so I think everyone else in the practice has got donation fatigue, by now—if I'm honest, probably everyone in the village.'

Donation fatigue?

Ollie thought about it, and then the penny dropped.

'That's why you told Maddie I was fresh meat?'

She looked horrified. 'Oh, no! I mean—yes, I did say that, but the way you just said it makes it sound *terrible*. I'm so sorry. And I'm not...' She shook her head, her eyes widening as a thought clearly struck her. 'Oh, no. Did you think I was some kind of man-eater planning to hit on you?'

It had rather crossed his mind.

And he was pretty sure it showed on his face, because she said quickly, 'That's not who I am.' She bit her lip. 'I barely know you. You could be married with children, or at least involved with someone. Of course I wasn't sizing you up as a potential partner. No wonder you've been so reserved with me, thinking I was about to pounce on you. I'm really sorry.' She grimaced. 'What a horrible way to welcome you to the practice.'

Ollie looked at her. The dismay on her face seemed genuine.

'Look, forget what I just said about asking you to sponsor me,' she said. 'I know they say there's no such thing as a free lunch, but this really *is* one. I just wanted to do what Caroline asked of me and welcome you to the practice. To show you where the best place is to grab a sandwich, even if I am a tiny bit biased, and somewhere nice to sit and eat or even just walk for a bit if you need to clear your head, because when you're new to the area it's always good to have someone showing you these things.'

Even though Ollie didn't quite trust his own judgement any more—not after he'd got it so wrong with Tabby, thinking that she'd loved him as much as he'd loved her—the look in Gemma's eyes seemed genuine. And she seemed to be trying very hard to hold out an olive branch. Maybe he should do the same.

'I think we got off on completely the wrong foot,' he said. 'Let's start again. I'm Oliver Langley and I'm the locum for Aadya Devi, for the next three months.' He held out his hand.

'Gemma Baxter, nurse practitioner,' she said, taking his hand and shaking it. 'Welcome to Ashermouth Bay Surgery, Dr Langley.'

Shaking her hand was a mistake, Ollie realised quickly. His fingers tingled at her touch and adrenalin pumped through him, making his heart start to pound. He couldn't remember the last time he'd been this aware of anyone, even Tabby, and he couldn't quite let himself meet Gemma's eyes. 'Thank you,' he muttered, dropping her hand again.

'Caroline said you were from London. What made you decide to come to Northumberland?'

To escape the fallout of his bad decisions. To hide and lick his wounds. To be a living donor for his twin's kidney transplant. Not that he planned to explain any of that. Even though he knew it wasn't the real reason why, he said, 'My parents moved up here ten years ago. Dad developed angina, and Mum wanted him to retire early and take things a bit easier. So they spend their days pottering around in the garden and going out for lunch.'

'Sounds nice,' she said. 'And they must be so pleased that you'll be closer to them now than you were in London.'

And his twin, but Ollie wasn't quite ready to share that yet. 'What about you?' he asked. 'Are you from round here?'

'Yes. I grew up in Ashermouth Bay. I did my training in Liverpool, but I knew I wanted to work back here,' she said. 'Luckily, when I qualified, one of the nurses at the practice was thinking about retiring, so I had the chance to work here and do my nurse practitioner training part-time.'

'So your family lives here?'

A shadow seemed to pass across her face, or maybe he was imagining it, but then she said, 'Not far from here.'

'And you always wanted to work in general practice rather than at the hospital?'

She nodded. 'I like the idea of really knowing my patients, watching them grow up and looking after their whole families. Being part of a community—in a hospital, you might look after someone for a few days or a few weeks, but it isn't the same.' She looked at him. 'Did you always plan to be a GP?'

'I nearly went into obstetrics,' he said. 'I trained in London. I enjoyed all my rotations, and delivering babies was amazing. But then my dad was diagnosed with angina, and it made me have a rethink.'

'You weren't tempted to specialise in cardiology?'

He shook his head. 'Partly because it was a little bit

too close to the bone. But I realised I wanted to be the kind of doctor who'd be able to pick up a problem before his patient really started to suffer from it. Which meant being a GP.'

'Good plan,' she said.

He finished his sandwich. 'You were right. This bread's as good as any I've eaten in a posh café in London.'

'Wait until you try the muffin,' she said. 'I know you're not a cake person, but this is savoury.' She rummaged in the brown paper bag and brought out a wrapped muffin. 'Your challenge, should you accept it, is to tell me what's in the muffin.'

He liked the slightly teasing look in her eyes. And he was shocked to realise that, actually, he liked *her*.

'So what's in it?' she tested.

'Spices and cheese,' he said.

She gave him a mock-sorrowful look. 'That's much too general.'

'Remember what the G in GP stands for,' he retorted.

She laughed, and it made her light up from the inside. Her dark eyes sparkled and there was an almost irresistible curve to her mouth. And Ollie found himself staring at Gemma Baxter, spellbound, for a moment.

He really hadn't expected this.

It was nearly four months since he'd split up with Tabby. Although he knew he had to move on, he hadn't really noticed any other women since then. Until today: and he really wasn't sure he was ready for this right now.

He needed to backtrack, fast, before he said something stupid. He didn't want to let Gemma close; yet, at the same time, he didn't want to freeze her out. He'd thought Gemma was the careless type when he'd first met her, but he was beginning to realise that there was more to her than that. Someone careless wouldn't be doing a skydive for charity.

The best compromise would be to stick to a safe subject. 'So tell me about Ashermouth Bay.'

'What do you want to know?' she asked. 'About the sort of things that are popular with tourists, or a potted history of the town?'

'A bit of both,' he said.

'OK. Ashermouth Bay used to be a fishing village,' she said. 'Obviously times change, and now the town's more reliant on tourism than on fishing. Though you can still take a boat trip out to see the puffins on the islands offshore, and if you're lucky you might see dolphins and porpoises on the way. There's a colony of seals nearby, too, and they tend to come into the bay when the pups are born—which is basically about now. If walking's your thing, you can walk right along the bay at low tide and go up to the castle; and you can see a bit of an old shipwreck along the way.'

'That's just the sort of thing I would've loved as a kid,' he said.

'The local history group does a ghost walk once a month in the village,' she said, 'with tales of smugglers and pirates. If castles are your thing, there are loads of them nearby—though I'm guessing, as you said your parents live near here, you already know all about them.'

'My mum loves visiting stately homes for the gardens,' he said. 'And I've driven her and Dad to a few when I've come to visit.'

'If you like sport, the village has a cricket team and a football team,' she said. 'And there's an adventure centre based in the harbour if you want to do surfing, paddle-boarding, kite-surfing and the like.'

All things Ollie knew his brother would adore; out of the two of them, Rob was the adrenalin junkie. It was why his twin worked in a fast-paced emergency department in Manchester, was a member of the local mountain rescue team as well as enjoying climbing on his days off, and spent his holidays working for a humanitarian aid organisation. Ollie adored his brother, but he was happy being grounded rather than pushing himself to take extra risks, the way Rob did. The family joke was that Ollie had Rob's share of being sensible and Rob had Ollie's share of being adventurous. 'The cliffs and the beach sound just fine to me,' he said.

She glanced at her watch. 'We need to be heading back.'

'Admin and phone calls before afternoon surgery?' he asked.

'Absolutely.' She smiled at him.

'Thank you for lunch,' he said.

'You're very welcome.'

'Let me help you fold the blanket.' Though when his fingers accidentally brushed against hers, again he felt the prickle of adrenalin down his spine.

Ridiculous.

They were colleagues. He wasn't looking for a relationship. There were a dozen reasons why he shouldn't even think about what it might be like to kiss Gemma Baxter.

But he'd noticed the curve of her mouth, the fullness of her lower lip. And he couldn't help wondering.

He shook himself. They were colleagues, and nothing more. And he needed to make some kind of small talk on the way back to the practice, to make sure she didn't have a clue about the thoughts running through his head.

Once he'd thawed out a little, Oliver Langley had turned out to be surprisingly nice, Gemma thought. Maybe he was right and they'd just got off on the wrong foot. And Caroline had said she'd thought he'd fit in well with the team.

The one thing that shocked her, though, was when Oliver had finally given her a genuine smile. It had completely transformed his face, turning him from that cool, austere stranger into someone absolutely gorgeous. His smile had made her heart beat a little bit too quickly for her liking.

She couldn't afford to let herself be attracted to their new locum. Quite apart from the fact that he might already be involved with someone else, she didn't have a great track record. Even if you ignored that year of disastrous relationships and the following two years of not dating anyone at all while she concentrated on getting through her exams and putting herself back together, her love life ever since had been hopeless. All her relationships had fizzled out within a few weeks. She'd never met anyone that she'd felt really connected to, someone she really wanted to share her life with.

Claire, her best friend, had a theory that it was because Gemma was so terrified of being needy and clingy, she went too far the other way and wouldn't actually let anyone in.

But it wasn't about being needy or clingy. It was about trust. She'd loved her little sister and her parents. But her parents had shut off from her after Sarah's death, lost in their grief, and Gemma had never been able to connect with them since. And maybe that was what was still holding her back, even after she'd had counselling: if she really loved someone and let them close, what if it all went wrong, the way it had with her parents, and they left her?

So it was easier to keep her relationships short and sweet and avoid that risk completely. Make sure she was the one to leave, not them.

Gemma's afternoon was a busy mixture of triage calls and surgery; after she'd finished writing up the notes from her last patient, she changed out of her uniform and drove to her parents' house for her monthly duty visit. She wasn't giving up on them, the way they'd given up on her. One day, she'd manage to get her family back. She just had to find the right key to unlock their hearts.

'Aadya's locum started at the surgery today,' she said brightly.

'Oh,' her mum said.

'He seems nice.'

'That's good,' her dad said.

The silence stretched out painfully until Gemma couldn't take any more. 'Shall I make us a cup of tea?' she suggested.

'If you like, love,' her mum said.

Putting the kettle on and sorting out mugs gave her five minutes of respite to think up some new topics of conversation. What her parents had been doing in the garden; the puppy Maddie was getting in a couple of weeks; how much sponsorship money she'd raised so far for the skydive. But it was such a struggle, when they gave anodyne responses every time. Her parents were the only people she knew who always gave a closed answer to an open question.

How very different it was when she dropped in to see Claire's mum. There was never any awkwardness or not knowing what to say next. Yvonne always greeted her with a hug, asked her how her day was, and chatted to her about the classes she ran in the craft shop next to Claire's bakery. Gemma had tried to persuade her own mum to go along to a class, thinking that she might enjoy the embroidery class or knitting, but she'd always been gently but firmly rebuffed. Her parents simply couldn't bear to come back to the village they'd lived in when Sarah died; they visited once a month to put flowers on their daughter's grave, but that was as much as they could manage.

And they'd never, ever visited Gemma's flat. She knew it was because they found it hard to face all the might-have-beens, but it still felt like another layer of rejection.

After another hour of struggling to get her parents to talk to her, she did the washing up, kissed both parents' cheeks, and drove home. Feeling too miserable to eat dinner, and knowing that a walk and the sound of the sea swishing against the shore would lift her mood, she headed to the beach to watch the changing colours in the sky.

One day she'd break through to her parents again. And then she'd have the confidence to find someone to share her life with—someone who wouldn't abandon her when things got tough—and it would ease the loneliness.

But for now she'd focus on how lucky she was. She

had good friends, a job she loved, and she lived in one of the nicest bits of the world. Maybe wanting more— wanting love—was just too greedy.

Ollie arrived home to find a note through his front door saying that a parcel had been delivered to his neighbour.

When he'd collected it, he didn't need to look at the card that came with it; only one person would send him a mini-hamper with seriously good cheese, olives, oatmeal crackers, and a bottle of good red wine. But he opened the card anyway.

> *Hope your first day was great. If it wasn't, you have my permission to scoff all the cheese. Otherwise, you'd better save me some for Thursday night or there will be Big Trouble.*
> *R*

He rang his twin. 'Thank you for the parcel.'

'My pleasure. It always made my day when I had a parcel in hospital, and I think a first day anywhere deserves a parcel.' The smile in Rob's voice was obvious. 'So how did it go?'

'OK,' Ollie said.

'Your colleagues are all nice?'

'Yeah. Though I got off on the wrong foot with the nurse practitioner, to start with.' Ollie explained his clash with Gemma.

'Olls, I know Tabby hurt you—but don't let that change the way you respond to anyone with two X chromosomes,' Rob said softly.

'I'm not responding at all. I'm not looking to get

involved with anyone. It's only been three and a half months since Tabby cancelled the wedding.'

'I'm not telling you to rush in and sweep the next woman you meet off her feet. Just don't close yourself off from potential happiness, that's all,' Rob advised.

'Mmm,' Ollie said, not wanting to fight with his twin. But thinking about Gemma Baxter unsettled him. That spark of attraction between them on the cliffs, when their hands had touched—he really hadn't expected that. This three-month locum job was meant to give himself the space to get his head straight again. Starting a new relationship really wasn't a good idea.

'Be kind to yourself, Olls,' Rob said. 'And I'll see you on Thursday.'

CHAPTER THREE

THE NEXT MORNING, when Gemma walked into the staff kitchen at the surgery, Oliver was already there.

'Good morning. The kettle's hot,' he said, indicating his mug. 'Can I make you a drink?'

'Thank you. Coffee, with milk and no sugar, please,' she said, smiling back.

He gave her another of those smiles that made her pulse rocket, and she had to remind herself sharply that Oliver was her new colleague and off limits. Yes, he was attractive; but that didn't mean he was available.

After her triage calls that morning, Gemma was booked in for her weekly visit to the nursing home, where she was able to assess any particular resident the manager was concerned about, and carried on with their rolling programme of six-monthly wellbeing reviews to check every resident's care plan and medication needs. Her path didn't cross with Oliver's again that day, and she was cross with herself for being disappointed. 'He's your colleague. No more, no less,' she reminded herself yet again.

At least she had her Tuesday dance aerobics class with Claire to take her mind off it. Or so she'd thought.

'Your lunch date, yesterday,' Claire said. 'He looked nice.'

'He's my colleague—Aadya's locum,' Gemma said. 'And it wasn't a lunch date. Caroline asked me to help him settle in, that's all.'

'You went very pink when he said something to you in the bakery,' Claire said. 'And he looks like your type.'

Gemma gave her a wry smile. 'For all I know, he's already involved with someone. We're just colleagues.'

'Hmm. Talking of colleagues, Andy's got a new colleague. He's single, and our age,' Claire said. 'Maybe you could both come over to dinner at the weekend.'

Gemma hugged her. 'Love you, Claire-bear, but I really don't need you to find me a partner. I'm fine just as I am.'

Though they both knew she wasn't quite telling the truth.

On Wednesday morning, Gemma had an asthma clinic, and her first patient was booked in for a series of spirometry tests. Samantha was forty years old and a smoker, and had persistent breathlessness and a cough. Although at the last appointment Sam had said that she thought her cough was just a smoker's cough, she'd also admitted that she seemed to get more and more chest infections over the winter and had started wheezing when she walked up the hill, so Gemma wanted to check if there was another lung condition such as asthma or COPD that was making Sam's breathlessness worse.

'This is going to help us get to the bottom of your breathlessness and your cough, Sam,' she said, 'so we can get you the right treatment to help you. Just to remind you what I said at the last appointment, I'm going to test your breathing through a spirometer to get a baseline, then give you some asthma medication, get you to sit in the waiting room while the medication takes effect, and run the test again to see if the medication makes a difference.'

'I remembered to wear loose, comfortable clothing, like you said,' Sam said. 'I didn't have even a single glass of wine last night, and I haven't smoked for twenty-four hours. It was murder, last night—I really wanted just a quick cigarette—but Marty wouldn't let me.'

'Good,' Gemma said with a smile. 'How are your headaches?'

'Not great,' Sam admitted. 'Do you think they're something to do with my breathlessness?'

'Very possibly,' Gemma said. 'Now, I just want to run through a checklist to make sure there isn't anything else that might affect the results.' She ran through the list with Sam, and to her relief there was nothing else.

'Great. We're ready to start. Are you sitting comfortably?'

Sam nodded.

'This is how I want you to breathe into the spirometer,' Gemma said, and demonstrated. 'I want you to breathe in and completely fill your lungs with air, close your lips tightly round the mouthpiece, and then blow very hard and fast. We'll do that three times, and then a test where I want you to keep blowing until your lungs are completely empty. I'll put a very soft clip on your nose to make sure all the air goes into the mouthpiece when you breathe out. Is that OK?'

Sam nodded, and Gemma encouraged her through the tests.

'Well done, that's brilliant,' she said. 'Now I'm going to get you to take some asthma medication, and I'd like you to sit in the waiting room for about twenty minutes so it has a chance to open up your airways; then we'll repeat the test and compare the results to each other.'

'My mouth's a bit dry,' Sam said.

'It's fine to have a drink of water while you're waiting,' Gemma said.

'Just not a cigarette?' Sam asked wryly.

'Exactly.'

Gemma helped Sam to take the asthma medication, then saw her next patient for an asthma review while Sam's medication took effect.

'How are you feeling?' she asked when Sam came back into the room. 'Has the medication made it easier to breathe?'

'A bit,' Sam said.

'That's good.'

Once Gemma had done the second set of tests, she compared the two sets of graphs. 'I'd just like to run these past one of the doctors first, if you don't mind?' she said.

'Sure. Do you want me to go back to the waiting room?' Sam asked.

'No, it's fine to wait here. He'll be here in a minute.' According to the roster, Oliver was the duty doctor this morning and was doing phone triage right now. Gemma sent him a note over the practice messaging system.

Before your next call, please can we have a quick word about one of my patients? Did spirometry, but patient not responded as well as I hoped to bronchodilator meds—think we're looking at COPD but would appreciate a second opinion.

Within seconds, a message flashed back.

Good timing—just finished call. Coming now.

Gemma opened the door at his knock.

'Sam, this is Dr Langley, who's working here while Dr Devi's on maternity leave,' she said. 'Dr Langley, this is Sam.' She gave him a potted version of Sam's patient history.

'Nice to meet you, Sam,' Oliver said. 'So may I look at the graphs?'

Gemma handed them over, and he checked them swiftly. 'I agree with you,' he said quietly.

'Sam, this is what a normal pattern of breathing looks like for someone of your height, age, sex and ethnic group,' Gemma said, showing Sam the graph on her computer. 'And this is your pattern.'

'So I'm not breathing out enough air,' Sam said.

'Instead of you blowing most of the air out of your lungs in the first second, there's a shallower curve,' Oliver said. 'It's what we call an obstructive pattern, meaning that you've got a lung condition which narrows your airways, so the air is flowing out more slowly than it should.'

'I was hoping that the medication would open up your airways a lot more, so your pattern would match that of someone who doesn't have a lung condition, and that would've meant I'd diagnose you with asthma,' Gemma said, 'but unfortunately it hasn't. There are some other conditions that can cause breathlessness, so I'm going to send you for a chest X-ray and do some blood tests to check if you're anaemic, or if there's a higher than average concentration of red blood cells in your blood.'

'Chest X-ray?' Sam went white. 'Oh, no. Are you telling me you think I've got lung cancer?'

'I'm just being thorough and ruling things out,' Gemma said. 'From the look of this graph, I think you have something called chronic obstructive pulmonary disease—COPD for short.'

'I agree with Nurse Practitioner Baxter. Chronic means it's long-term and won't go away, obstructive means your airways are narrowed so it's harder for you to breathe out quickly and air gets trapped in your chest, and pulmonary means it affects your lungs,' Oliver added.

Sam grimaced. 'And I've got it because I'm a smoker?'

'We're not judging you, but yes. Nine out of ten cases of COPD are caused by smoking,' Gemma said.

'Though COPD can also run in families,' Oliver said. 'And if you work in a place where you're exposed to a lot of dust, fumes or chemicals, that can contribute.'

'Nobody else in my family gets breathless, and I work in a garden centre. So it has to be the smoking,' Sam said with a sigh. 'I know I shouldn't do it. But I started smoking when I was fifteen, because all my friends were doing it and I didn't want to be left out. And then it got to be a habit. It calms me down when things get tough.

'I've tried to give up a couple of times, and I managed it when I was pregnant because I didn't want it to affect the baby, but Louisa's toddler tantrums sent me right back to having a quick cigarette in the garden to help calm me down, and I never managed to stop again.' She shook her head and grimaced. 'It's just too hard.'

'COPD isn't a condition we can cure, or even reverse,' Gemma said. 'But the best way to stop it getting any worse is for you to stop smoking.'

'We can support you,' Oliver said. 'There are lots of things that can help you—patches and gums and sprays. And you're three times more likely to be able to give up with our support than if you're struggling on your own.'

'We can also refer you for a pulmonary rehabilitation programme,' Gemma said. 'It's a six-week course with other people who have the same condition as you do. Some of the sessions will teach you exercises to help your breathing, but the trainer will also be able to teach you breathing techniques, how to manage stress, and how to manage your condition better.'

'That sounds good,' Sam said.

'We ask all our patients who have asthma or COPD to have a flu jab every year,' Gemma said, 'because when you have a lung condition you're more vulnerable to catching the flu in the first place, and developing complications.'

'And there's a one-off pneumococcal vaccine, which will help protect you against pneumonia,' Oliver added. 'I know it's a lot to take in, and it sounds scary, but we can help you.'

'You'll get a letter so you can book onto the pulmonary rehab course at a time that works for you,' Gemma said, 'and I'll refer you to a counsellor who can help you stop smoking. Plus you'll have regular appointments with me to see how you're doing, and to check that your symptoms are under control and you're not getting any side effects from the medication.'

'Thank you,' Sam said. 'And I'll try really hard to stop smoking. Really, I will.'

'You're not on your own,' Oliver said. 'That's the main thing. We're here to help.'

Once Sam and Oliver had left her consulting room, Gemma took a sip of water. Now she'd seen Oliver Langley with a patient, she could see exactly why the head of the practice had offered him the job. He was kind, supportive and clear without being patronising; he hadn't judged Sam for smoking; and he was a world away from the cold, slightly haughty man she'd first met on Monday morning. The way he'd worked with Gemma, backing her up, had made her feel as if she'd worked with him for years, rather than today being only his third day on the team.

But Oliver was still practically a stranger. And she needed to be sensible instead of noticing how her heart skipped a beat every time he smiled.

She sent him a note across the practice messaging system after she'd written up the notes and before seeing her next patient.

Thanks for your help with Sam's COPD. Appreciated.

You're welcome, he replied.

Gemma liked the fact that he had nice manners. The more she got to know Oliver Langley, the more she liked him.

Strictly as a colleague, she reminded herself, and saw her next patient.

Just when she'd seen her last appointment of morning surgery, her computer pinged with a message.

Are you busy for lunch, or can I buy you a sandwich and we can maybe sit on the cliffs again?

Which sounded as if they were about to start becoming friends.

She messaged back.

A sandwich would be nice. Thank you. Just writing up my last set of notes and I'll be with you.

Crazy.

Ollie knew he shouldn't be looking forward to lunch with Gemma.

But he was. He'd liked the way she'd been with her patient this morning, all calm and kind and reassuring. And the fact that she'd checked with him on a case she wasn't sure about: her patients' welfare came before her professional pride, which was exactly how it should be.

Gemma Baxter was nothing like the man-eater he'd assumed she was when he'd first set foot in the reception area on Monday morning and overheard that comment.

She was *nice*. Genuine.

And if Rob was here right now he'd grin and say that Gemma was just Ollie's type, with those huge eyes and all that fair hair.

He didn't need a type. This was a burgeoning friendship, that was all—and that was fine by him.

Once they'd chosen sandwiches and headed up to the cliffs, he helped her spread out the picnic blanket.

Again, his fingers accidentally touched hers and it felt as if lightning zinged through him. His lower lip tingled, and he couldn't help moistening it with the tip of his tongue.

Oh, for pity's sake. He really needed to get a grip. Work, he thought. That was a safe subject. 'How was your morning?' he asked.

'Pretty good. Thanks for your help with Sam—I've only just taken over the practice asthma clinic, so I'm still finding my feet a bit.'

'No problem. That's what I'm here for,' he said.

'How was your morning?' she asked.

'Pretty good.' He smiled at her. 'I've been thinking. I'd like to sponsor you for your skydive. You said it was next month?'

'Two weeks on Friday,' she said. 'I have to admit, I'm feeling a bit nervous about it now. It's a tandem skydive, so I know I'm going to be perfectly safe with an instructor, but even the idea of stepping out of that plane makes my palms go sweaty.'

'You're clearly not scared of heights, though, or you wouldn't be here on the cliff.'

'No, but I wouldn't choose to go rock-climbing.' She looked at him. 'Though, actually, I guess that could be a potential challenge for the future. Maybe next year.'

He frowned. 'So why are you doing the skydive? I know you said it was for charity, but is it because you're challenging yourself to overcome your fears as well?'

'No, but people get bored of sponsoring the same thing. A skydive's good for raising the profile of the cause, too. There's a good chance it'll go on the local newspaper's website, along with my fundraising page details, so maybe people who don't know me but want to support the cause will donate something.'

'You said you were raising funds for the local hospital's cardiac unit. Is that because you did some of your training there?' he asked.

'No.' She took a deep breath, as if psyching herself up to say something. 'My little sister spent a while there. I'm fundraising in her memory.'

In her memory... Gemma's little sister had *died*?

Before he could process that, she said, 'It was a long time ago now. I caught a bug at school, and Sarah caught it from me. I got better, but she didn't—she was still breathless and struggling. The next thing we knew, she was in the cardiac unit, being diagnosed with myocarditis.'

He'd noticed exactly what she'd said. 'It wasn't your fault. If the bug was going round at school, she could've caught it from one of her friends, not just from you.'

'Uh-huh.'

It sounded as if she still blamed herself, even though as a medic she'd know that wasn't fair. 'Was she on the list for a transplant?' he asked.

'Yes, but we were waiting for months. The right donor just didn't come along.' She looked away. 'Sarah died when I was seventeen and she was thirteen.'

He reached over and squeezed her hand. 'I'm sorry. That must have been devastating for you and your family.'

'It was,' she admitted. 'I've had twelve years to get used to it, but I still miss my little sister. And I really didn't cope very well at the time.' She shrugged. 'This is why I do the fundraising. It won't bring my little sister back and it won't do anything for the donor lists, but the hospital is doing research into permanent artificial hearts. And if that works out, it means another family might not have to lose someone they love dearly.'

'I'm sorry I've brought back bad memories for you.'

'I have a lot of good memories of Sarah.' She smiled, though her eyes were suspiciously shiny and he rather thought she was holding back tears. 'Doing her hair and make-up for a school disco, painting her nails, making cakes with her, playing in the garden.'

Obviously her memories were what carried her through the tough times. 'I'll definitely sponsor you,' he said.

She shook her head. 'I don't want you to feel obliged. It's fine.'

He knew the way to persuade her to accept his offer. 'It's not that I feel obliged,' he said. 'I was very nearly in your shoes, earlier this year.'

Apart from the people in the support group she'd gone to—and that hadn't lasted for long—Gemma had never met anyone else who'd had someone close who needed a heart transplant. 'Someone in your family needed a heart transplant?'

'No. My brother needed a kidney transplant.'

She winced. 'That must've been hard for you all.'

He nodded. 'Rob's a bit of a thrill-seeker. He's an A and E doctor in Manchester. He spends all his free time climbing, and he's on the local mountain rescue team. He took a six-month sabbatical to work with a humanitarian aid agency; he'd gone out to help with a region that had just been hit by an earthquake. He had stomach pains when he'd been there for a couple of days, but he just assumed it was an ordinary tummy upset because he wasn't used to the food and water. And then, when he collapsed, they realised he had acute appendicitis.'

'Poor man—that's really tough.'

'It was. He was airlifted to a hospital, but his appendix burst on the way and he ended up with severe blood poisoning.' Oliver looked grim. 'It wiped out his kidneys, and he was on dialysis for a while.'

'But you got a donor?'

Oliver inclined his head. 'That's the main reason why I came back to Northumbria. We've been recuperating at our parents' house since the transplant.'

She blinked. '*We*—you mean, you were a living donor?'

'It was the obvious solution,' Oliver said. 'Rob's my twin.'

She hadn't expected that. 'Identical?'

'Apparently you can look identical but not actually be identical, so we had to do gene sequencing to check,' Oliver said. 'We're not quite identical. But, even so, getting a kidney from me meant his body was much less likely to reject it, and he's on a lower dose of immunosuppressant drugs than he'd need if anyone else had donated the kidney.'

'So that's why you're working up here now?'

'I was getting a bit stir-crazy,' he said. 'Mum's overdoing the cotton wool treatment.'

Gemma's parents had been too hurt to wrap her in cotton wool. Instead, they'd let their grief build a wall between them and never let her back in. She pushed the thought away.

'I'm the sensible one and it's been driving *me* crazy, so poor Rob is really having to learn to be patient.' He grinned. 'Which will probably do him good.'

'You're both so lucky,' she said. 'Your twin, because he has you; and you, because you could actually do something practical to help.'

'Yes. If it had been a different organ that failed, we would've had to wait for one to become available.' He wrinkled his nose. 'You know yourself, it's not very nice, waiting for someone else to die.'

'No. It'd feel horrible, knowing your loved one's only still with you because someone else lost someone they loved,' Gemma said. 'Though Sarah thought about that, even when we knew it was too late and she was too ill for a transplant to work. She said she'd rather help someone else, even though she couldn't be helped, so she made our parents sign to donate everything that she could.'

'Brave kid,' Oliver said.

'She was. I wish…' Her breath hitched, and he could guess what she was thinking. She wished her sister hadn't died. Wished she'd been the one to be ill, to save her sibling. All the thoughts that had scrambled through his own brain in the early hours of the morning, when he couldn't sleep for thinking of what might have been.

'I often wonder what she would've been doing now,' Gemma said. 'She would've been twenty-five. I think she would've done something with art—she was really good.'

Oliver reached over and squeezed her hand. 'I'm sorry. I know how bad I felt when I thought I was going to lose Rob, earlier this year. It must've been so hard for you.'

'It was,' she agreed. 'And my parents have never recovered from it. They moved from the village, the year after Sarah died, because they couldn't handle all the memories.'

'You said you were seventeen at the time, so I assume they waited for you to finish your A levels before they moved?' he asked.

She shook her head. 'I made a complete mess of my exams and ended up having to resit them. But I didn't have to change schools; my best friend's mum let me stay with them and redo the year.' Yvonne had got her back on the straight and narrow. She'd *cared*. Been the stand-in mum Gemma had desperately needed.

'That's an amazing thing to do for someone,' he said.

'It is, and I'll always be grateful to her. Actually, I've been thinking lately that maybe I could offer a place for a teenager needing support—kind of pay forward what Claire's parents did for me. I live alone, but my working hours are regular so I could be there for someone who needed it.'

Gemma lived alone, and it sounded as if she didn't have a partner.

That really shouldn't make Ollie feel as pleased as it did. He wasn't looking for a relationship and, since Tabby had broken their engagement, he wasn't sure he'd be enough for anyone in any case.

But there was something about Gemma Baxter that drew him. A brightness, a warmth.

She'd come through the kind of nightmare that he'd dreaded happening to Rob and had kept him awake at night for months, and she was doing her best to try to stop other people having to go through it.

No partner.

He really needed to stop this. Yes, he liked Gemma

and he was drawn to her. But he wasn't ready to move on with his life. He needed to be fair to her; all he could offer her right now was friendship.

'It'd be a good thing to do,' he agreed. 'Rewarding. You'd know you were really making a difference to someone's life.'

'So how's your brother doing now?' she asked.

'He's recovering well, but it's driving him a bit crazy not being at work. He knows there's no way he can go back out to do the humanitarian aid stuff or the mountain rescue—with only one working kidney, he's too much of a risk to be on a team. And he's not fit enough to go climbing again, either. He needs to be patient for a bit longer. And, for Rob, "rest" is most definitely a four-letter word.'

'So when did it all happen?' she asked.

'He collapsed at the beginning of March. We did the transplant at the beginning of June, and I got the green light from the surgical team a couple of weeks ago to go back to work.'

'So you're still healing from donating the kidney, really.'

'I'm fine. It means no heavy lifting,' Ollie said, 'but that's about all. Luckily there weren't any complications for either of us, though Rob's not pleased that they've told him to wait a few more weeks before he goes back.'

'That's such an amazing thing to do, being a live donor and giving your brother a kidney.'

'I'm guessing you would've done the same for your sister.'

'Of course I would,' she said. 'Any live donation— a whole kidney, a piece of liver or a bit of pancreas. If I could've saved her...' Her eyes were suspiciously glittery.

'I know how lucky we were,' he said quietly. 'I had the chance to make a difference. And Rob's doing OK.'

'I'm glad.'

Ollie almost asked her to join them both for dinner, the following evening, but he didn't want his twin getting the wrong idea. 'Me, too.' He glanced at his watch. 'I guess we need to be getting back.'

'We do. I meant to mention this earlier, but are you busy on Friday evening?'

No, but he wasn't going to commit himself to anything until he knew what she had in mind. 'Why?'

'There's a pub quiz at The Anchor,' she explained. 'We normally field a team from the surgery. It starts at eight, but we've got a table booked to eat beforehand, if you'd like to join us.'

He really appreciated the fact she was trying to include him. 'Thank you. I'd love to.' He'd planned to spend Sunday with his family, but on Friday evening and Saturday he hadn't really been sure what to do with himself. It would be good to get to know his team a bit better.

'Great. Our table's booked for half-past six. The menu's small but I'd recommend absolutely everything on it. Everything's sourced as locally as possible.'

'Sounds good,' Ollie said. 'Count me in.' He took his phone from his pocket. 'What's your number? I'll text you so you'll have mine. And then you can text me back with the link to your fundraising page.'

'Thanks.' She recited her number, and he tapped it into his phone and sent her a text; a few seconds later, he heard a 'ping'.

'Got it,' she said.

And funny how her smile made the bright, sunny day feel even more sparkly.

CHAPTER FOUR

ON THURSDAY, OLLIE didn't see Gemma at the practice; according to Maddie, Gemma usually had Thursdays off. But he enjoyed showing his twin round the village that evening after dinner.

'What a view,' Rob said from the cliffs. 'I can see why you moved here, Olls. And you said they do kite-surfing in the bay? Fantastic. When can I book a session?'

Ollie cuffed his arm. 'No adventure stuff until your consultant says it's OK.'

'Just one tiny little session?' Rob wheedled. 'Half an hour—thirty teeny, tiny minutes?'

Ollie shook his head. 'Nope. And if you won't listen to me, I might have to casually mention to Mum that Rob the Risk-Taker is back.'

Rob groaned. 'Please don't. You know I love Mum dearly, and I know that she and Dad were worried sick about me when I was ill, but I really can't take much more of the cotton wool treatment. Neither could you,' he pointed out, 'or you wouldn't have escaped here.'

'True,' Ollie admitted.

'I want to escape, too. I've got an interview next week.'

Ollie stared at his twin in surprise. 'You're going back to Manchester already?'

'No. It's local—the hospital down the road. You know I'd taken that six months off to join the humanitarian aid team; as I've spent most of that time stuck in hospital or recovering, my boss has agreed to extend my sabbatical.'

Ollie felt his eyes widen. 'Please tell me you're not going back to an earthquake zone or what have you.'

'No. Apart from the fact that I have a gazillion hospital appointments, even I'm not that stupid,' Rob said. 'I'm hoping to get a part-time post at the hospital here for the next few months, until my consultant's happy with my recovery.'

'And then you'll go back to Manchester?'

'Yes. I'm desperate to go climbing again,' Rob said, 'but I promise I'm not going to do anything that will set my recovery back.'

'I'm glad to hear it,' Ollie said dryly. 'Though I'm not entirely convinced.'

'Seriously, Olls. If I have a setback, I'll be stuck sitting around recovering for even longer. That's not going to help my itchy feet. I don't want to give Mum more excuses to smother me. And, most importantly, I don't want to worry Dad to the point where his angina flares up,' Rob said. 'I couldn't live with myself if he got ill again because of me.'

'Now *that*,' Ollie said, 'convinces me.'

'Good.' Rob smiled. 'So how are you getting on with your nurse practitioner?'

'I'm getting on fine with all my colleagues,' Ollie said.

'Meaning you like her and you don't want to admit it.'

'She's my colleague, Rob. My *temporary* colleague.

It's not a great idea. If we get together and it goes wrong, it'll be awkward at work. We're just going to be friends.'

'You wouldn't let it be awkward because you're a total professional and you put your patients first,' Rob said. 'And there's also no reason why it should go wrong. And, as you said, it's temporary—so why not let yourself be happy while you're here?'

'It's too soon.'

'It's nearly four months. To me, you're on the verge of wallowing—and I can be that harsh because you're my brother and I love you too much to let you carry on being miserable.' Rob shook his head. 'Tabby really hurt you, I know, but the best way to get over a break-up is to meet someone else.'

'That's cynical, Rob.'

'It's a fact, little brother,' Rob said lightly. 'Maybe your nurse practitioner would be good for you.'

'I'm not a user, Rob.'

Rob frowned, 'Of course you're not. What I'm trying to say, in my very clumsy way, is that you've had a rough few months. And you're here for the next three months. Spending a little time with someone you like, getting to know each other and having a bit of fun—it might help you move on. Don't let what happened with Tabby put you off dating anyone else.'

'You're not dating anyone, either,' Ollie pointed out.

'Because I'm still recovering from major surgery.'

Ollie just looked at his brother.

'All right. I like the thrill of the chase and I haven't met anyone who's made me want to settle down. Even though we're practically identical, I'm wired differently from you, Ollie. You can settle. I have itchy feet. And I admit, I get bored easily.' Rob sighed. 'Perhaps it's true about there being a good twin and a bad twin. You're the good one.'

'You're not the "bad twin" at all, Rob. We just want different things.'

'I'm sorry that I caused your break-up with Tabby...'

'You didn't cause the break-up,' Ollie said.

'Look at it logically. It was my fault. If my kidneys hadn't failed, you wouldn't have suggested moving your wedding day and it wouldn't have escalated into—well, cancelling it. Though I still think the reason she gave you for calling it off was seriously weak.'

'She grew up seeing her mum put her life on hold for her dad, and she didn't want that kind of future for herself. I can understand that,' Ollie said, 'even if I don't think I would've given her that kind of future.'

'Maybe you had a lucky escape,' Rob said. 'Because if the going got tough she wouldn't have stuck it out.'

Or maybe he just wasn't *enough* for anyone, Ollie thought.

'You've got your brooding face on. Stop,' Rob said.

'Sorry. I really thought she was the right one. Which makes me pretty hopeless at judging people,' Ollie said.

Rob clapped his shoulder. 'Actually, it makes you human. Everyone makes mistakes. Just don't close yourself off.'

'Be more Rob, and take a risk?' Ollie asked wryly.

'Just as I'm going to try to be more Ollie, and be sensible,' Rob said. 'So, between us, we can be the best we can be. Deal?'

Ollie thought about it. Be more like his twin. Take risks. The idea put him into a cold sweat; over the years, Rob had taken more than enough risks for both of them.

'Olls,' Rob said softly. 'It'll do both of us good.'

Put like that, how could he refuse? 'Deal.'

On Friday morning, Ollie arrived at the surgery to discover a tray of individually wrapped brownies, lemon cake and oatmeal cookies on one of the low tables, with a plastic jar labelled 'Donations' beside them and a folded card announcing 'Gemma's Friday Fundraisers are back!'

Clearly this was what his colleague had spent her day off doing. Baking.

There was another card on the tray, listing the ingredients in each recipe with the potential allergens highlighted in bold.

Smiling, he picked up a cookie and some lemon cake, and dropped some money into her box.

'What's this—buying cake?' Gemma teased, walking into the reception area. 'I thought you weren't a cake person?'

'I'm not. I'm buying this for my next-door neighbours,' he said. 'I thought they might like a Friday treat.'

'That's kind of you.'

'They've kept an eye out for me since I moved in. It's the least I can do,' he said.

'Are you still OK for the quiz team tonight?' she asked.

'Yes.'

'Good. See you there. Triage awaits,' she said with a smile.

Midway through the morning, Ollie was just writing up his notes when Maddie, the receptionist, burst into his room. 'Dr Langley, help! One of our patients has just collapsed in the waiting room.'

'I'm coming,' Ollie said, grabbing his stethoscope. 'Did you see what happened?'

'No. I was helping a patient when someone else in the waiting room screamed and I saw Mrs Henderson on the floor. Apparently she just fell off her chair.'

There were three main causes of collapse: fainting, seizures and heart problems. Given that Maddie hadn't mentioned Mrs Henderson's shaking limbs, it was likely to be fainting or a cardiac issue. 'Get the defibrillator,' he said, 'find out if anyone saw her hit her head, and I might need you to call an ambulance—and manage the patients in the waiting room, please, so we can give her a bit of privacy.'

'Got it,' Maddie said.

The middle-aged woman was still lying on the floor when they went into the reception area.

'Can you hear me, Mrs Henderson?' Ollie asked loudly, shaking her shoulder as he knelt beside her.

There was no response.

He tilted her head back to clear her airway.

'I've got the defib and she didn't hit her head,' Gemma said, joining him. 'The patient next to her said she just collapsed.'

'Do you by any chance know her medical history?'

'Yes. Nicole Henderson has high blood pressure—she's actually due for a check with me, this morning, because the last two medications I've tried with her haven't worked, and she had a bad reaction to beta blockers.'

This was sounding more and more like a cardiac

event. 'Her airway's clear but she's not breathing,' he said. 'I'll start CPR. Can you turn the defib—'

'Already done,' she cut in. 'I'll do the sticky pads. Maddie's got everyone outside so we're good to go. I'll call the ambulance, too.'

She placed the pads on each side of Mrs Henderson's chest. He stopped doing CPR so the machine could analyse Mrs Henderson's heart rhythm. The recorded voice on the defibrillator informed them it was administering a shock, then told him, when it had no effect, to continue CPR.

Gemma had got through to the emergency services. 'The ambulance is on its way,' she said.

Between them, they kept going with chest compressions and breathing, stopping only when the defibrillator's recorded voice told them it needed to check the patient's heart rhythm.

By the time the paramedics arrived and loaded her into the ambulance, Nicole Henderson still hadn't regained consciousness.

'This isn't looking great,' Ollie said wearily. 'Poor woman. Hopefully they'll get her heart restarted on the way in to hospital.'

They both knew that the longer it took to restart the heart, the worse the prognosis. And, given that Gemma's sister had died from a heart condition, Ollie knew this must be tough for her. 'Are you OK?' he asked.

She nodded. 'I just feel I've let my patient down.'

'You couldn't have predicted this,' he said. 'And we did our best here. In some ways, this is the best place she could've collapsed, because we have a defib and enough knowledge between us to give her the right help.'

'I know. It's just...' She grimaced.

He reached out and squeezed her hand. 'You had the defib switched on and the pads ready almost before I could ask. Nobody could've done more. And she might be fine.'

Except the hospital called later that afternoon to say that Nicole Henderson hadn't made it.

He typed Got a minute? on the practice messaging system and sent it to Gemma.

Yes.

Ollie made her a mug of coffee and rapped on her door. 'Sorry, it's not good news. She didn't make it.'

Gemma sighed. 'Poor woman. She was the head of the local junior school. She wasn't popular—let's just say her predecessor was very different and everyone was upset when she retired, because she always fought for the kids and she was great with the parents and teachers—but even so I don't think anyone would actually wish her dead.'

'Don't blame yourself,' he said. 'I reviewed her notes when I wrote up what happened, and I would've treated her the way you did.'

'If only she hadn't rescheduled her appointment from last week.'

'It might still have happened, and it might've been somewhere that didn't have a defib.'

'I suppose so. Thank you for being kind.' She took a deep breath. 'I have referrals to write up and I'm guessing you have paperwork, too. So I won't hold you up. But I appreciate the coffee.'

'You're welcome.' He paused. 'I don't mean this to

sound as tactless as it does, but will the quiz tonight be cancelled?'

She shook her head. 'I think, if anything, we need a reminder that there's a bright side to life. And that's not meant to sound callous.'

Gemma Baxter wasn't anything remotely approaching callous, he thought. 'OK. I'll see you later.'

The pub where Ollie had arranged to meet Gemma and the team was only a few minutes' walk from his cottage; when he arrived, the rest of his team was already there, and Gemma stood up to wave to him.

He hadn't seen her out of her uniform before; her faded jeans hugged her curves, and her hair was loose rather than tied back as she wore it for work. Yet again, he was struck by how pretty she was, and it almost made him tongue-tied. Which was crazy. He wasn't looking to get involved with anyone. Yet his twin's words echoed in his head.

'Spending a little time with someone you like, getting to know each other and having a bit of fun—it might help you move on.'

He made his way over to their table.

'Time for introductions,' Gemma said. 'Everyone, this is Oliver—he's Aadya's locum for the next three months.' She swiftly introduced him to the people round the table he hadn't yet met.

'Hello, everyone.' He smiled. 'Can I get anyone a drink?'

'No, we're all sorted,' Kyle, one of the other practice doctors, said, smiling back. 'I heard about Nicole Henderson. You've had a bit of a rough start to your time with us.'

'I'm just sorry I couldn't do more,' Ollie said. 'I hope it's not going to worry Aadya Devi's patients, the idea of having to see me when I've already lost a patient.'

'You and Gemma did everything you could,' Kyle said. 'Nobody's going to blame you.'

Ollie nodded his thanks. But the time he'd sorted out a pint and ordered his food, he was chatting with the others as if he'd always known them.

The quiz turned out to be great fun; although he was woefully inadequate on the local history round, he managed to get a couple of the musical intros that the others couldn't remember, as well as a really obscure geography question.

'How on earth did you know that?' Maddie asked.

'My twin's a climber,' Ollie said. 'He's the adventurous one; I'm the one with common sense.'

'There's nothing wrong with having two feet on the ground,' Kyle said. 'As I would dearly love to tell every single holidaymaker here who tries one of the water activities for the first time and tries to keep up with people who do it all the time, and ends up with a sprain or a strains or a fracture,' he added ruefully.

'Rob—my twin—got a bit excited about the idea of kite-surfing,' Oliver said. 'But he's having to be more me at the moment. He's recovering from a kidney transplant.'

'Ouch. That sounds nasty,' Fayola, their midwife, said. 'What happened?'

'Burst appendix followed by blood poisoning, and it wiped out his kidneys. He was helping with the aftermath of an earthquake at the time,' Ollie explained.

'Oh, now that's unfair,' Lakshmi, their pharmacist, said, sounding sympathetic. 'Poor guy.'

'He's doing well now,' Ollie said. 'But that's why I moved up here from London for a while, to support him and our parents.'

He caught Gemma's raised eyebrow; but he wasn't comfortable putting himself in the role of hero. Anyone would've done the same, in his shoes. Nobody else needed to know that he'd been the living kidney donor.

In the end, their team came second.

'And if anyone hasn't sponsored our Gemma for the skydive,' the quizmaster said, 'come and see us at the bar, because we've got a sponsorship form right here. And there's a collecting tin if you've got any spare change.'

Ollie really liked the fact that the whole village seemed to be so supportive of Gemma's efforts. It felt good to be part of a community like this. In London, he'd found that people kept themselves to themselves a lot more.

They stayed on for another drink after the quiz was over, and then the others all had to be back for their babysitters. Ollie looked at Gemma. 'Do you need to be anywhere right now?'

'No. Why?'

'I was going for a walk on the beach, to see the first stars coming out—something I couldn't really do in London. Do you want to join me?'

'That'd be nice,' she said.

They walked down to the beach together. The sea looked almost navy in the late summer evening light, and the first stars were peeking through. The moon was low and shone a silvery path across the sea. The waves were swishing gently across the shore, the rhythm soft and almost hypnotic, and Ollie felt the day's tensions starting to melt.

'That's the thing about living by the sea. If the day's been tough you can go for a walk and let the swoosh of the water wash the misery away,' she said.

'There were good bits to the day, too,' he said. 'But, yeah, losing a patient in my first week here is a bit of a shaky start.'

'It wasn't your fault,' she said. 'If it's anyone's fault, it's mine, but you argued me out of that earlier. We did our best, and that's all anyone can ask.'

'I guess.'

She stopped. 'Oliver.'

He stopped, too, and turned to face her. 'What?'

'Right now,' she said, 'I think you need a hug.' To his surprise, she took a step towards him and wrapped her arms round him.

Being this close to her meant he could smell the floral scent of her perfume. Light, sweet and summery, it made him think of sunshine. Being hugged by her was like being bathed in sunshine, too, and he couldn't resist wrapping his arms round her.

The waves swished onto the shore, and all Ollie was aware of was the beating of her heart, in the same strong, fierce rhythm as his own. The connection was irresistible, and he found his face pressed against hers. And then it was, oh, so easy to tilt his face just a fraction more, so the corner of his mouth was brushing against hers. His mouth tingled, and he couldn't help holding her closer, moving his face just a fraction further so he was really kissing her, and she was kissing him back.

His head was spinning and it felt as if fireworks were going off overhead, bright starbursts. Even though he knew he shouldn't be doing this—it was too soon after Tabby, and Gemma was his new colleague and he didn't want to complicate things—he couldn't help himself. This felt so *right*. Kissing Gemma, the sea singing a lullaby in the background, her arms wrapped as tightly round him as his were round her...

The moment seemed to last for ever, a moment of sweetness that was like balm to his aching heart.

And then it ended, and he found himself taking a step back and staring at Gemma.

'I'm sorry,' he said. 'That wasn't meant to happen.' A momentary—and major—lapse of reason.

'I think we've both had a tough day and we got caught up in the moonlight,' Gemma said. 'Let's pretend it didn't happen.'

The problem was, Ollie knew he'd rather like it to happen again. But she clearly didn't, so he'd have to ignore his feelings. 'OK. Can I at least walk you home? I know you're local and you're perfectly capable of looking after yourself, but it's dark and...well, it's the way I was brought up.'

'Gallant. I like that.'

And there was no edge to her tone, no mockery; Ollie had the strongest feeling that Gemma understood him and appreciated him.

They walked back to her flat in a companionable silence. At the entrance to the flats, she said, 'Would you like to come in for coffee?'

Part of him did; yet, at the same time, he knew it wasn't a good idea. He could still remember the touch of her mouth against his and the scent of her hair; it would be more sensible to put a little distance between them so he could get his common sense back. 'Maybe another time?'

She nodded. 'Sure. Goodnight, Oliver.'

'Goodnight, Gemma. See you at work on Monday.'

Ollie spent Sunday with his family, as planned; and the influx of summer visitors and extra people needing medical help meant that he didn't actually have a proper lunch break until Wednesday. He'd just stepped into the bakery when he realised that Gemma was there.

'Great minds think alike,' he said with a smile. 'Are you heading up to the cliffs?'

'I certainly am,' she said. 'You're welcome to join me.'

'Thanks. I'd like that.'

Once they were settled on her picnic blanket, he said, 'So do you have much planned for the week?'

'I'm babysitting my goddaughter Scarlett—Claire's three-year-old—on Friday night, so she and Andy can have a proper date night. Which means I get Claire's amazing macaroni cheese for dinner; then Scarlett and I will sing our way through all the songs from *The Little Mermaid* during her bath; and then I get cuddles and tell her stories until she falls asleep.'

She grinned. 'And then I have a hot date with a classic rom-com, a mug of tea, and some of Claire's ginger cake. Friday night doesn't get better than this.'

His idea of a perfect Friday night sounded a lot like Gemma's. Cuddling up on the sofa with a good film, winding down after a busy week...

'How about you?' she asked.

'Nothing in particular,' he said. 'I might go for a

walk on the beach on Saturday. Didn't you say something about a shipwreck being visible?'

'There is, at low tide.' She took her phone from her bag and looked something up. 'Low tide is at four o'clock on Saturday afternoon. If you don't mind a friend tagging along, maybe I could join you for that walk and tell you all the touristy stuff about the wreck.'

'I'd like that,' he said. 'And maybe we can grab fish and chips afterwards, and eat it sitting on the harbour wall.'

'Great idea,' she said with a smile. 'I haven't had fish and chips for ages. Which is a terrible admission, given that we live in a seaside village.'

Funny how her smile made him feel so warm inside. 'Fish and chips is mandatory,' he said, smiling back. 'I like mine with lots of salt and vinegar, but shhh, don't tell our patients that because I nag everyone about their salt intake...'

She laughed. 'Me, too. For both!'

Gemma spent most of Thursday cleaning her flat and baking for her charity cake stall; on Friday, she didn't see Oliver more than once in passing, though he did text her at lunchtime to check that she was still available for their walk on Saturday afternoon.

On Friday afternoon, Mrs Brown, the history teacher she remembered from school, came in. 'I'm so sorry, wasting your time coming in with something as minor as a rash,' she said. 'I did go to the pharmacy on Monday, but the hydrocortisone cream they gave me hasn't helped. The rash is spreading.' She grimaced. 'The itchiness is *unbelievable*. And it's keeping me awake at night.'

'Let me have a look, Mrs Brown,' Gemma said.

Mrs Brown rolled up her cotton trousers to her knees, and Gemma examined the rash. There were pinpricks of deep red on the edges, and the middle sections were raised with a flat surface.

'It looks like an allergic reaction, so we'll start with the obvious stuff. Have you made any changes to your detergents or toiletries over the last couple of weeks?'

'No, and it's not a change in formulation because they're the same batch I've used for a couple of weeks. I'm paranoid about ticks since Harvey—my spaniel—got one last year, so I always wear long trousers on dog-walks, and I haven't brushed against any plants or knelt on anything with bare legs.' Mrs Brown shook her head, seeming puzzled. 'I haven't eaten anything out of the usual, and my blood-pressure tablets are the same ones I've been on for years and years.'

'So that rules out all the usual suspects,' Gemma said.

Mrs Brown grimaced. 'I did wonder if it was shingles—I've heard that's horribly itchy.'

'Usually a shingles rash is only on one side of the body and doesn't cross the midline. This is on both shins, so I'm pretty sure it's not that,' Gemma said. 'Have you ever had eczema or psoriasis?'

'No, and the only things I'm allergic to are penicillin and fabric plasters—neither of which I've been in contact with for years.'

'OK. It's possible to develop allergies at any time of life,' Gemma said, 'so what I'm going to prescribe is something generic that should help. Colloidal oats to wash with, an emollient to keep your legs moisturised, a slightly stronger steroid cream to use twice a day to try and calm the rash down, and an antihistamine which should stop the itching. Until that kicks in, cold compresses are your best friend. And obviously you're sensible enough to know not to scratch.'

'So you've no idea what's causing it?'

'There are about three thousand different rashes,' Gemma said with a smile, 'so, at the moment, all I can say is it's a red, itchy rash and we don't currently know the cause. Or, if you want it in medical-speak, it's erythematous idiopathic pruritic macules.'

'Which sounds a bit more impressive,' Mrs Brown said with a wry smile.

'If it doesn't improve in the next three or four days, come back and I'll do a swab test and refer you to the dermatologist.' Gemma printed out the prescriptions and handed them over. 'Cold compresses will definitely help to stop the itching.'

She changed at work and went straight to Claire's, where she enjoyed a catch-up with her best friend before Claire and Andy went out for the evening.

Spending time with Scarlett was always fun. They drew pictures and played games until dinner, and then it was bath time.

'Just one more, Aunty Gemma!' Scarlett pleaded.

'Nope. We've done *all* the songs,' Gemma said, and lifted her goddaughter from the bath to wrap her in a towel. 'Time to dry off before you get all wrinkly. And then it's a glass of milk, brush your teeth, and a story.'

'Two stories? Please, please, *please*?' Scarlett wheedled.

Gemma laughed. 'All right. Two stories. Let's get you dry and put your PJs on.'

Given the disaster of her love life—since she'd grad-uated, all her relationships had ended really quickly—Gemma thought that her goddaughter was probably the nearest she'd ever get to having a little one of her own. And she knew she was lucky. Some people didn't even have that.

After she'd settled Scarlett to sleep, she made herself a mug of tea and switched on the film. It was one of her favourites, and she must have seen it a dozen times over the years, but it still made her smile.

Apart from one thing.

The main actor's colouring was exactly the same as Oliver's. And Oliver's smile—rare, but genuine—made her heart beat just as fast as the actor's did.

She really was going to have to be sensible tomor-row. Even though there was something about him that made her want to forget all about caution. Or maybe especially because he tempted her to stop being care-ful and take a risk, she corrected herself. He was only here temporarily. The most they could offer each other was a summer of fun. Which might be a good thing: but Gemma was scared that if she let him close then she'd start to want more. And what if he didn't want the same? What if he left after three months and didn't ask her to go with him?

So it would be better to stick to being friends. Forget that kiss and the way his had made her blood feel as if it was fizzing through her veins.

Oliver Langley was her colleague.

Full stop.

CHAPTER FIVE

SATURDAY WAS BRIGHT and sunny, and Gemma met Oliver at the harbour.

'Time for your touristy trip,' she said. 'We'll start with the spooky local legend, see the seals, then see the shipwreck,' she said with a smile.

'Bring it on,' Oliver said, smiling back. 'What's the spooky bit? A grey lady or something?'

'No, it's a barghest.'

'I've never heard of that,' he said.

'It's a huge black dog with massive teeth and claws and fiery eyes, which only comes out at night. Apparently if you see him, it's a portent of doom. It's left up to your imagination what that doom might be.' She laughed. 'It's very similar to the "black dog" story told all over the country, though. My theory is that the legend was started by smugglers, who hung lanterns with red covers round their ponies' necks to make it look like fiery eyes. If people were scared of the legend of the giant black dog, it meant they'd stay away from the cliffs—and that would mean they were less likely to discover the smugglers' tunnels and any contraband.'

'So there were smugglers at Ashermouth Bay?' he asked.

'There were in most places along the coast in the eighteenth century,' she said. 'There are tunnels in the cliff which lead to the Manor House and the rectory. They used to smuggle brandy, gin and tea. I remember doing the *Watch the Wall, My Darling* at school, and our teacher told us all about the tunnels. Most of the older houses in the village have little hiding places.'

'That's fascinating,' he said. 'Can you actually go down the tunnels now?'

'Strictly guided tours only, and it depends on the tide,' she said. 'The teacher who told us about the tunnels also said that she went in them when she was our age, with some friends; they had to be rescued by the lifeboat team, and one of her friends nearly drowned. And then she casually mentioned that there are rats everywhere, and huge spiders.'

'Enough to put you all off the idea of being brave and exploring by yourself?'

'Indeed.'

Gemma enjoyed walking with Oliver along the damp sand. A couple of times, his hand accidentally brushed hers and sent a zing of awareness through her skin; yet again, she remembered the way he'd kissed her on the beach a week ago, and it made her knees weak. Not wanting to be needy, she took refuge in the guided tour she was supposed to be giving him. 'Next, we have the seals,' she said. 'There's a big colony of grey seals, a bit further up the coast, but these ones are common seals. Their pups are born in June and July, and everyone comes to see them in the bay.'

Oliver looked entranced by the seals, the babies with their white fur and their parents undulating their way slowly along the sand, while others ducked and dived in the water.

'That's lovely. I can see why people come here,' he said.

They'd just reached the roped-off area when they saw a small boy running on the sand. A woman ducked under the rope—his mother, Gemma guessed—but before she could reach him he fell over, next to one of the seal pups. An older seal lunged at him, and he screamed.

'Jake!' the woman called, and sped over to grab him.

'Hopefully the seal just scared him, rather than bit him,' Gemma said.

But the little boy appeared to be clutching at his hand and crying.

'Can we help?' Oliver asked as the woman, carrying the child, ducked back under the rope next to them. 'I'm a doctor—my name's Oliver—and Gemma here's a nurse practitioner.'

'The seal bit him,' the woman said. 'I told Jake not to go near them. I *told* him we had to look at them from afar, but he ran off and went into the roped-off area before I could stop him.'

'We saw him fall,' Gemma said.

'I know seals are protective of their pups at this time of year—that's why the ropes are there—but I...' She shook her head, looking anguished.

'Let's get you over to the lifeguards' hut. They'll have a first-aid kit,' Oliver said.

Between them, they ushered Jake and his mother to the lifeguards' hut.

'Hey, Gem. What's happened?' the lifeguard asked.

'Hi, Callum.' Gemma explained swiftly and introduced Oliver.

'Could we have some hot water, some antiseptic and a dressing?' Oliver asked.

'Sure. I'll fetch them,' Callum said.

Gemma crouched down by the little boy, who was still crying. 'Jake, will you let me look at your hand?'

He shook his head, guarding his hand, and her heart sank.

'Jake, do you want to see a magic trick?' Oliver asked.

It was the last thing she'd expected but, to her relief, the distraction worked, and the little boy nodded.

'See how my hands are open?' Oliver asked, waggling his fingers. 'I need you to put your hands exactly like that, making a star shape with your fingers—but I want you to hold them *really* still—and then I want you to guess the magic word.'

Genius, Gemma thought as the little boy opened both his hands, the shock and pain of the bite forgotten.

'Please!' Jake said.

She couldn't help smiling. 'That's a good magic word.'

'But not the one I'm looking for,' Oliver said. 'Try again.'

Gemma examined Jake's hand while Oliver encouraged the little boy to guess more magic words.

To her relief, the bite was shallow, more of a graze than anything else; but she also knew that a seal's mouth could contain bacteria that could cause a very nasty complication, and the little boy would need a course of antibiotics.

'It's going to sting a bit,' Gemma warned when Callum brought the hot water and antiseptic over. 'Unfortunately our surgery's closed until Monday morning or I'd say call in and we'd prescribe antibiotics.'

'Antibiotics?' Jake's mum looked shocked.

'Are you local or on holiday?' Gemma asked.

'On holiday from Birmingham—this is our first day.'

'Then you need to go either to the walk-in centre in the next town, or to the emergency department at the hospital,' Gemma said. 'Take a seal letter with you, and they'll sort out some tetracycline to make sure an infection doesn't start.'

'Seal letter?' Oliver asked.

'Tetracycline's the most effective antibiotic against the Mycoplasma organism in a seal's mouth,' Gemma explained. 'It's why we have a seal letter for people to take to whatever medical department they go to. If a seal bite isn't treated properly, and the wrong antibiotic is given, the person could develop a complication called "seal finger".'

'Abracadabra!' Jake shouted.

'That's the right magic word. And look what I've found behind your ear,' Oliver said, plucking a coin from behind Jake's ear.

The little boy's eyes were round with amazement. 'That's real magic!'

'It certainly is,' Oliver said with a smile.

'Jake, I'm going to need to wash your hands with some very special soap and water.'

Callum had got a bowl of warm water ready, along with antiseptic soap, and Gemma encouraged Jake to wash his hands.

It obviously stung and the little boy pulled his hands out of the water and cried, but then Oliver stepped in again.

'I'll wash my hands with you,' he said. 'And we'll

sing a special washing hands song. Do you know "If You're Happy and You Know it?"'

Jake nodded.

'We're going to change the words a bit,' Oliver said, taking his watch off and stuffing it into the pocket of his jeans. 'Instead of "clap your hands", we'll sing "wash your hands". Ready? And we'll get your mummy to sing it, too.'

'Yay!' Jake said, the stinging forgotten.

Oliver got them to sing along. It didn't matter that his voice was flat; he was so good with the little boy that it put a lump in her throat.

When Jake's hands were clean, Oliver gently helped dry them.

The wound was still bleeding a little bit—to Gemma's relief, because it meant she didn't have to hurt Jake by squeezing the wound to make it bleed. She put a pad over it and a dressing.

'Here's the seal letter,' Callum said, handing it to Jake's mum. 'And I've written the phone number and address of the walk-in centre and the hospital's emergency department on the back for you.'

'Thank you. I'll take him now,' Jake's mum said. 'And thank you, both of you, for helping.'

'That's what we're here for,' Oliver said with a smile.

Once Jake and his mum had left, Callum said, 'Thanks for the back-up, guys. Really appreciated.'

'No worries. Give my love to Sadie when you see her next,' Gemma said, and shepherded Oliver out of the lifeguards' hut. 'Sadie's his big sister. She was one of my sister's best friends,' she explained.

'I'm guessing everyone knows everyone in Ashermouth Bay?' Oliver asked.

'Pretty much,' she said with a smile.

'I have to say, I've never heard of "seal finger" before,' he said.

'To be fair, it's probably not that common in London,' she said.

'But it happens a lot here?'

'There have been a few cases, over the years. I didn't like to say, in front of Jake's mum, but it involves inflammation and cellulitis, and it used to mean the finger would have to be amputated.'

'That's pretty major stuff. So how do you know all about seals?'

'I was a seal warden, the summers when I was fifteen and sixteen. It meant I did a two-hour shift on the beach, most days, talking to visitors about the seals, answering their questions, advising them where to get the best views of the seals and also making sure they stayed well clear of the roped-off area where the seals were resting. If you get too close to the pups, you could scare the mum away and there's a risk she'll abandon the baby.'

'A seal warden.' He raised an eyebrow. 'You're full of surprises.'

'I wanted to be a vet, when I was fifteen,' she said. 'Though, after Sarah died, I decided I wanted to help people rather than animals, so I trained to be a nurse instead.'

'You're good with people,' he said. 'So do you have pets?'

'No. I work full-time, it's just me at home and I live in a flat, so it wouldn't be fair to have a dog. But I do walk a couple of dogs down my road, sometimes.' She looked at him. 'I assume you don't have pets, either?'

'No, and for the same reason. It really wouldn't be fair in London.'

Which reminded her. He was here temporarily. 'Do you think you'll go back to London?'

'I'll see how things go with Rob,' he said. 'Probably.'

And it was ridiculous that her stomach swooped in disappointment.

She kept the conversation light, telling him more about the seals and pointing out the shipwreck. They climbed up the path to the castle on the other side of the bay, then walked back along the cliffs and back down to the harbour. Every so often, his hand brushed against hers, and it felt like electricity zinging along her skin.

What if his fingers caught hers?

What if he held her hand?

It made her feel like a teenager again, waiting for the boy she had a crush on to notice her.

But Oliver had clearly had second thoughts since their kiss on the beach, and he was exquisitely polite with her. Gemma was cross with herself for being disappointed; hadn't she learned the hard way not to rely on other people for her happiness? So she pasted a bright, sparkling smile on her face and pretended everything was just fine.

When they reached the harbour and stood in the queue for the fish and chips, Ollie said, 'This is my shout, by the way.'

'We'll go halves,' Gemma countered.

He shook his head. 'You were kind enough to show me round. It's the least I can do.'

She smiled. 'All right. Thank you.'

They sat on the harbour wall, eating their fish and

chips from the recyclable boxes, watching the boats and the gentle swish of the sea. How much slower life was here than it was in London, Ollie thought. And he was really beginning to enjoy living by the sea.

After they'd eaten, he walked her home. A couple of times, his hand brushed against hers, and he was so tempted to hold her hand. But that wasn't the deal they'd agreed. They were friends; and he still didn't trust his judgement. He didn't want to rush this.

They came to a halt outside a small block of flats.

'Would you like to come in for coffee?' she asked.

Ollie knew he ought to make an excuse, but he was curious to know what Gemma's inner sanctum was like. 'That'd be nice,' he said.

'I'm on the ground floor,' she said, and let them into the lobby before unlocking her front door. 'The bathroom's here on the left.'

She said nothing about the closed door on the right, which he assumed was her bedroom.

'Living room,' she said as they walked into the next room. 'And my kitchen-diner's through there. You take your coffee without milk, don't you?'

'And no sugar. Yes, please,' he said.

'Take a seat, and I'll bring the coffee through.'

The whole room was neat and tidy. The walls were neutral, as were the comfortable sofa and armchair with a reading lamp, but there was a throw the colour of sunshine across the back of the sofa, and the material of the cushions was covered in sunflowers. On the mantelpiece there was a vase of sunflowers—clearly Gemma's favourite flowers.

There were framed photographs surrounding the vase; one was of Gemma herself, and a younger girl who looked so much like her that Ollie guessed it was Sarah. There was another of Gemma holding a baby, which he guessed would be the goddaughter she'd mentioned earlier in the week, plus one of her with her fellow students at graduation. There was a photo of Gemma in a bridesmaid's dress, laughing with the bride; he vaguely recognised the other woman, and guessed that was Claire.

There were no photos, he noticed, of Gemma with her parents. Given how family-oriented Gemma seemed, that surprised him.

On the wall was a framed pen-and-ink drawing of seals on the beach.

'That's an amazing picture,' he said when she came back in, carrying two mugs of coffee.

'Sarah drew me that for my sixteenth birthday. It still amazes me to think she was only twelve at the time.'

'She was very talented,' Ollie said, meaning it.

Tears shimmered for a moment in Gemma's dark eyes. 'I loved her so much. But I know she'd be furious with me if I moped around—just as I would've been furious with her if I'd been the one who'd died and she'd been left behind to deal with it.'

If Rob had died from that burst appendix, Ollie thought, he wasn't sure he would've coped well with it. And he was thirty, not a teenager.

'I think she'd be really proud of you,' he said. 'You don't mope at all. Look at what you've achieved. You're a nurse practitioner, and you make a difference to people's lives every single working day. Plus you've raised a lot of money for the cardiac centre where she was treated.'

* * *

His kindness was nearly Gemma's undoing. 'I hope she'd be proud of me,' she said.

'What's not to be proud of? If you were my sister, I'd be boasting about you,' he said.

Sisterly wasn't quite the way she was feeling about him, but she damped that down. If he'd wanted to take things further between them, he would've taken her hand on the beach or said something.

'Thank you,' she said instead.

'So you're a reader?' He gestured to her bookcase.

'I love historicals,' she said. 'Yvonne—Claire's mum—got me reading historical crime when I was in sixth form, to give me a break from studying. I loved *The Cadfael Chronicles* series. And then I discovered historical romance.' She paused. 'So are you a reader?'

'Not as much as my mum would like,' he said with a smile. 'I tend to read non-fiction. Journals and the like. And I have a bad habit of watching documentaries.'

'Nothing wrong with that,' she said. 'Though I love films. Musicals and comedies, mainly.'

'With a bit of skydiving on the side.' He smiled. 'The sort of thing my twin would do.'

'I'm really not that brave,' she said. 'The skydiving's a one-off. Though I'm doing a sixty-mile cycle ride down the coast, next month.' She gave him a sidelong look. 'Are you a cyclist?'

'No. But I'll sponsor you,' he said.

'I wasn't dropping a hint.'

'I know, but it's important to you. And I'm your friend, so I'll support you.'

Friend.

Oliver had just made it very clear how he saw her.

So she'd just have to stop secretly wishing for more.

It was another busy week; and Mrs Brown called Gemma on Tuesday. 'I've been taking photographs of the rash, just so you can see how it's changed.'

Gemma looked at the photographs. 'It's definitely looking angrier. It's spreading, and the spots are coalescing.'

'And it's so, so *itchy*. It's keeping me awake at night.'

'Can you email the pictures to me, please?' She gave Mrs Brown the surgery's email address. 'I'm going to have a word with one of my colleagues,' she said, 'and I'll call you back.'

When the photographs arrived, she sent over a note through the practice messaging system.

How are you with rashes? Could do with another pair of eyes.

Oliver called her. 'Is your patient with you right now?'

'No. She's just sent me some photographs. I've added them to her notes.' She gave Oliver the details.

'Let's have a look.' He paused, and she guessed he was checking the file on his screen. 'Actually, you've treated it as I would've done. If it's not responding to steroid cream, I'd say ask her to do a swab test, to see if there's bacterial or viral involvement.'

'And if it's not that, then a referral to Dermatology?'

'Good call,' he said.

Gemma rang Mrs Brown and asked her to drop into

the surgery later that morning to do a swab test, then called her next patient.

Eileen Townsend was eighty-one, diabetic, and her daughter had brought her in because she was having a lot of falls. Gemma knew that diabetes could cause elderly patients to have more falls than non-diabetics, because hypoglycaemia could cause light-headedness. She always worried about her elderly patients having a fall, with the extra risk of breaking bones; and reduced mobility often went hand in hand with foot care problems, which a diabetic might not notice.

'I help Mum with her medication,' Mrs Townsend's daughter said, 'and she had her six-monthly check with you three months ago.'

Gemma nodded. 'Nothing's changed since then?'

'Not really,' Mrs Townsend said.

Gemma double-checked her notes. There had been no hospital admissions and no suggestion that Mrs Townsend had had a stroke or developed Parkinson's. Maybe postural hypotension? 'Are you feeling light-headed at all before you fall, Mrs Townsend?'

'No. It just happens,' Mrs Townsend said.

'Would you mind me assessing you physically?' she asked.

'No. Just tell me what I need to do.'

'Can you stand up for me, please?'

Mrs Townsend stood up, and Gemma was pleased to see that she didn't sway, raise her arms or move her feet to balance.

'Wonderful. Can you lift one foot off the floor, just a little bit?'

She struggled to balance on her right foot, and Gemma made a note.

'Lovely. Can you walk round the room for me?' Gemma chatted to her as she walked, and was pleased to see that Mrs Townsend didn't stop walking when she answered a question.

'That's great. And, lastly, I'd like to try one more thing. I'd like you to sit down, walk over to the window, turn round, walk back to the chair and sit down again.'

Gemma timed her, and was pleased to note that it took less than twelve seconds.

'That's all really good,' she said. 'The only thing I think you're struggling with is balance. There are some good strength and balance exercises you can do using a chair—I can print some off for you.' She smiled at Mrs Townsend's daughter. 'And if you can help your mum do the exercises, that'd be brilliant. Though I'd like to try and set up some classes locally. I'll run that one by the head of the practice, and if I can make it happen I'll let you know.'

'Of course I can help my mum,' Mrs Townsend's daughter said.

'Brilliant. The other thing I'd like to do is send the occupational health team out to you for a hazards assessment of your home.'

'I've already checked the hazards. There aren't any trailing wires, I make Mum wear slippers with proper soles so she doesn't slip on the floor, and there aren't any rugs she can trip over,' Mrs Townsend's daughter said.

'That's excellent,' Gemma said. 'But it's not just about hazards you can see—it's looking at how you use the space and what they can do to help. So they might suggest putting risers on the bottom of an armchair to make it easier for your mum to stand up, or a grab rail next to a toilet or a bath. Plus they can set you up with an alarm you wear round your neck, Mrs Townsend, so you can get help really quickly if you do have a fall.'

'I don't want to wear something round my neck,' Mrs Townsend said. 'I'm old, not useless.'

'Of course you're not useless,' Gemma said. 'But you've had a few falls, and your daughter's worried about you—just as I'd be worried if my mum had a few falls. I'd be panicking that she'd fall at night and nobody would know—so she'd just have to lie there in the cold, unable to get up again until someone came in the next morning.'

Mrs Townsend's daughter nodded. 'That's my biggest fear. Mum, if you wore something round your neck so I knew you could get help when you needed it, that'd stop me panicking so much.'

'I suppose you're right,' Mrs Townsend said with a sigh. 'I don't want to lose my independence.'

'An alarm would actually give you a bit more independence because it'd stop your daughter worrying so much,' Gemma said gently.

'All right. I'll do it,' Mrs Townsend agreed.

'I'll sort out the referral,' Gemma promised, 'and they'll call you in a few days to organise a visit.' She printed off the exercises. 'These will all help with your balance and core strength, which means you're less likely to fall.'

'Ballet's meant to be good for that,' her daughter said.

'I'm too old to start being a ballerina,' Mrs Townsend said. 'I can't do all that leaping about.'

'Actually, there are special classes for older beginners,' Gemma said. 'My best friend's mum does it. And not only is it good for her balance, it's also meant she's made new friends. She says it's the best thing she's ever done. I can get the details from her, if you like.'

'That would be really good,' her daughter said. She smiled. 'Your social life will be better than mine, at this rate, Mum.'

'All right. I'll give it a go,' Mrs Townsend said.

Once her patient had gone, Gemma sent a note to Oliver over the practice internal email.

Are you busy at lunch, or can I run something for work by you?

The reply came swiftly.

Of course. Let me know when you've seen your last patient this morning.

Thank you, she typed back.

As usual, they bought lunch from Claire's and headed up to the cliffs.

'So what did you want to run by me?' Oliver asked.

'I had an elderly patient this morning—she's diabetic, and she's had a few falls. I'm sending the occupational health team out to her to see if they can tweak a few things and sort out an alarm she can wear round her neck, but I also checked her balance in the surgery, and I've been thinking for a while that maybe we could work with local instructors to set up some balance and light resistance training for our older patients. Say, a six-week course. That way, we're doing some pre-emptive health work instead of waiting for one of them to have a fall and maybe break a hip.'

'That's a good idea. Some of my patients in London went on a course to teach them the basics,' Oliver said, 'and then they could carry on at home.'

'I was thinking chair exercises,' Gemma said. 'A warm-up, some balance work and some resistance training. One of my friends manages the local gym, and she was saying their studio's not used that much during the day—the gym's classes are all just after the morning school run to grab the mums on the way home from school, lunchtime for the office workers, and in the evenings for everyone else. I was thinking, some of those spare spots could be used for a course. Maybe we could join forces with the gym, and between us we could split the cost.'

'And a gym would have light weights and resistance bands available. That's a good idea.' He looked at her. 'If I'm not interfering, would you like me to help you put a proposal together for Caroline, with a cost-benefit analysis?'

'That'd be nice.'

'OK. Are you free this evening?' he asked.

'Sorry. It's Tuesday, so it's my dance aerobics class with Claire.' She paused. 'Though it's actually my friend who manages the gym who instructs the class. I could sound her out after the class and see how practical it'd be.'

'Great idea. Do that, and maybe come over to mine on Thursday evening if you're free. I'll cook,' he offered.

'You'll cook?'

'Don't look so surprised. I've managed to survive my own cooking for the last decade or so,' he said.

'All right. You're on.' It was a combination of business and friendship, she reminded herself, not a date.

'Is there anything you don't eat?'

'I'm not a huge fan of red meat, but other than that I don't have any allergies or major dislikes.'

'Just an addiction to cake,' he teased. 'OK. What time?'

'Seven?' she suggested.

'Seven's fine.'

'How did you get on with the swabs for Mrs Brown?' Oliver asked when he saw Gemma in the staff room, the next day.

'The bacterial one showed just the usual skin flora,' she said, 'but the viral test was positive for HSV1. My poor patient was horrified, even though I explained that it's the Herpes simplex version that causes cold sores, not the sexually transmitted disease,' Gemma said.

'Two-thirds of the population has HSV1,' Oliver said. 'Most of the time it stays dormant, but she might get a flare-up if it's really sunny, or if she's got a cold, or if she's stressed.'

'I've prescribed her a course of antivirals,' Gemma said.

'It's an interesting presentation,' Oliver said. 'You don't often see it on the shins.'

'But imagine how horrible it's been for her—being so itchy in the sticky heat we've had,' Gemma said. 'I've told her to keep up the cold compresses, and I've referred her to Dermatology. How's your morning been?'

'Sprains, strains and hay fever,' he said. 'And an asthma case I want to keep an eye on.'

* * *

Gemma had swapped her usual Thursday off for Friday, that week, so she could do the skydive; she was too busy for a lunch break, but Oliver texted her in the afternoon to check their dinner meeting was still on.

She played safe and took a bottle of white wine and a hunk of local cheese from the deli. 'I thought you'd prefer this to chocolates,' she said. 'It's a local artisan cheese.'

'Perfect. I love cheese,' Oliver said with a smile. 'You didn't have to bring anything, but I'm glad you did. Come through.'

Even though she knew Oliver was only renting the place for a couple of months, his cottage still felt personal rather than being like temporary home; there were photographs on the mantelpiece and a couple of journals on the coffee table.

'Can I be nosey?' she asked, gesturing to the mantelpiece.

'Sure. They're very obviously my twin and my parents,' he said.

He hadn't been kidding about Rob being his identical twin. The only way she could tell them apart in the photographs was that Rob had shorter hair, in an almost military cut. But, weirdly, it was only the photographs of Oliver that caused her heart to skip a beat.

'So did you train together?' she asked, looking at the two graduation photographs.

'No. He went north-west, so he could take advantage of the climbing locally, and I went to London,' Oliver said.

'He looks nice.'

'He is. He's one of the good guys,' Oliver said. 'Anyway. I assume you walked here, as you haven't asked me for a car permit, so can I get you a glass of wine?'

'That'd be lovely, thank you.' She took a last look at the photographs—and oh, how she envied him the graduation photographs with his parents and his brother. They all looked so close, so like the family she longed for. The family she'd once had.

She followed him into the kitchen, where he'd set a little bistro table for two.

'Something smells wonderful,' she said. 'Is there anything I can do to help?'

'Just sit down,' he said with a smile, and took a casserole dish out of the oven. 'It's an oven-baked risotto. Chicken, aubergine and artichoke.'

He'd paired it with a dish of baby plum tomatoes, a green salad and balsamic dressing.

'This is really delicious,' she said after her first taste. 'I might have to beg the recipe.'

'It's a foolproof one from the internet. I'll send you the link,' he said with a smile. 'So how did you get on at the gym?'

'Pretty well. Melanie said that it'd be nice to give something back to the community, and she's got a couple of mornings where we could have a slot for a class. She's prepared to do some training to make sure she's teaching the class properly. She suggested doing it with a nominal charge for the six-week course, and then a discounted rate for anyone who wants to do the follow-up classes.'

'So if the practice paid for the six-week course, our patients would benefit and so would the community,' Oliver said. 'I've put together some figures from my old practice, showing how much strength and balance training reduces the risk of falls, so we can see the cost savings between paying for a course of preventative strength and balance training and treating patients after they've fallen.'

'That,' she said, 'is brilliant. It's Caroline's first week back, this week, so I'll leave it until next week before I talk to her about it—but then perhaps we could see her together and talk her through the project?'

'That works for me,' Oliver said. 'So do you go to the gym a lot?'

'Mainly my dance aerobics class. The rest of the time, I'm training for whatever fundraising I'm doing. The skydive is this month; I'm doing a sixty-mile cycle ride along the coast next month. And then I was thinking about doing a swimming thing. I'll do it in the pool at the gym, but if you add all the lengths together it'll be the equivalent of swimming the English Channel.' She smiled. 'Just without all the grease, choppy seas and having to wait a couple of years to book a slot to do it.'

'And it's a lot safer.'

'There is that.' She took a deep breath. 'I have to admit, I'm a bit scared about tomorrow. I've never jumped from a plane before.'

'You'll be fine,' he said, and his belief in her warmed her all the way through.

CHAPTER SIX

FRIDAY MORNING DAWNED bright and sunny. Gemma, who'd worried about the event being rained off, felt more relaxed; yet, at the same time, adrenalin fizzed through her.

Today she was going to jump from a plane. She was going to jump two miles up from the ground. And, OK, it was a tandem jump and the experienced sky-diver would be in control…but it was still a long, long way down.

She showered, then dressed in loose, comfortable clothing and trainers, following the instructions that had come from the skydiving company. Her phone buzzed almost constantly with texts from people wishing her good luck, including one from Oliver. Though there was nothing, she noticed, from her parents. Not that they ever wished her luck when she was doing a fundraising event. Would they ever soften towards her and be close again? she wondered. If she was honest with herself, probably not. But she wouldn't give up on them. She wouldn't stop trying to get through to them. She owed it to Sarah to get their family back together.

Even though her stomach felt twisted with nerves,

she made herself eat a bowl of porridge, then headed out to her car.

Except the car didn't look right.

A closer examination told her she had a flat tyre. Oh, no. It would take her ages to fix it. She didn't have time; and it looked as if she was going to miss her slot. If she called a taxi, would she get to the airfield in time? She dragged a hand through her hair. Of all the days to get a flat tyre...

'Is everything OK, Gemma?'

She glanced up to see Oliver in his running gear. 'Flat tyre,' she said. 'And I haven't got time to fix it. I was just about to call a taxi and hope it would get me to the airfield in time for my slot.'

'I'll take you,' he said.

'But—'

'It's my day off,' he cut in gently. 'All I planned to do today was go for a run and clean the house. Both of them can wait. Besides, by the time a taxi gets here, we could be halfway to the airfield.'

She knew that was true. 'Thank you,' she said. 'I really appreciate it.'

'No problem. Come with me.'

It wasn't long until they were at his house. 'Give me thirty seconds to change my shorts for jeans,' he said. 'Luckily I was still warming up when I got to yours, so I'm not disgustingly sweaty and in need of a shower.' The cheeky grin he gave her made her heart feel as if it had done a somersault.

He came downstairs a few moments later, having changed his clothes. 'Let's go,' he said. 'Can you put the airfield's postcode into the satnav?'

'Sure.'

Her nerves must've shown in her voice because he asked gently, 'Are you OK?'

'Yes. Well, no,' she admitted. 'I'm trying not to think about the stats of how many parachutes fail.'

'Very few,' he said. 'According to my twin, fewer than one in three thousand people even sprain an ankle when they jump out of a plane.'

'Does he do a lot of that sort of thing?'

'Yes. He likes the adrenalin rush. You'll be fine. Think of the money you're raising.'

Her palms were sweaty and the back of her neck itched. But she couldn't back out now.

'I really appreciate you giving me a lift,' Gemma said when they arrived at the airfield.

'No problem.' Ollie paused. 'I've been thinking about you. I might as well wait for you. By the time I get back to Ashermouth, it'll be time to turn round and come to collect you, so I might as well sit in the sun with a mug of tea and watch the planes.'

'I can't ask you to give up your day off like this.'

'You're not,' he said. 'And it's fine. You're the one actually doing the skydive. I'm surprised Claire didn't come with you.'

'She was going to, but the girl who was covering for her called in sick this morning, and Friday's a busy day at the bakery.' Gemma shrugged. 'It's fine. I'm a grown-up.'

Gemma was a brave and capable woman, from what Ollie had seen of her so far; but for a moment vulnerability showed in her eyes. 'Hey. You're Gemma Baxter, village superstar, and you can do this. You can do anything,' he said. Even though he knew physical contact with her wasn't a sensible idea, he was pretty sure she needed a hug, so he wrapped his arms round her and held her close for a few moments. 'Go and sign in and do your safety briefing,' he said.

Gemma wasn't sure whether the adrenalin bubbling through her was because of what she was about to do or because Oliver had hugged her, or a confused mixture of the two, but she duly went off for the safety briefing, training and fitting of protective equipment.

Oliver was waiting with the supporters of her fellow skydivers, and gave her an encouraging smile. 'Hey. I imagine Claire would've taken a photo of you in your gear, so give us a grin.' He lifted his phone and took a snap. 'Nope. That was more like a grimace. Let's do it again.'

'Say cheese?' she asked wryly.

'No. Say yoga and put both thumbs up.'

'What?' But she did it, and he grinned.

'Perfect. Now go earn that sponsor money. I'll be there to applaud as you land.'

Gemma followed the instructor to board the aircraft. It looked impossibly tiny.

'Let's get you attached to me,' her instructor said. Once he'd put the four clips in place, it felt almost as if she was wearing him like a backpack.

During the fifteen minutes it took to get the plane up to ten thousand feet, the instructor did the equipment check and the final brief.

'Here we go,' he said, and the door opened.

A rush of cold wind filled the plane, and Gemma felt goose-bumps prickle over her skin. She was going to be the fourth and final jumper from their batch, giving her nerves even more time to sizzle.

Finally it was her turn. She sat on the edge of the doorway, ready to go. The fields below looked like a patchwork of gold and green; puffy bits of white clouds billowed here and there.

'One, two, three—go!' the instructor said.

And then they tipped forward. They were head-down, plummeting down to the ground in free-fall.

Even though Gemma knew they were falling at a hundred and twenty miles an hour, she felt weightless, as if they were floating on air. She'd expected it to feel a bit like a roller coaster, with all the swooping; but because there were no twists and turns or sudden changes of direction, it was fine.

The instructor tapped her on the shoulder, and she uncrossed her arms, bringing them up in front of her as she'd been taught down on the ground.

It was incredibly noisy.

And incredibly exhilarating.

And somehow it was peaceful, all at the same time; in her head, she could hear Tom Petty singing 'Free Fallin''.

The cameraman she'd hired to take a video of the skydive reached out to give her a fist bump, and she grinned.

She was really, really doing this.

She brought her hands in momentarily to make a heart symbol, to remind everyone what she was fundraising for, and yelled, 'Sarah, this is for you!' Even if nobody could hear her on the video, they could at least lip read. Then the instructor opened the parachute. Instead of the jolt she'd expected when the canopy opened, it was a gentle, steady rise.

It took them about five minutes to float all the way down. As she'd been told earlier, she lifted her knees and straightened her legs as she was sitting down. The ground rushed up to meet them; but the landing was smooth, the canopy came down behind them, and the ground crew were there to help them out of the parachute and harness.

All of them gave her a high five. 'Well done! Do you know how much you've raised?'

'Unless anyone's donated since I got on the plane...' She told them the amount, smiling broadly. Everyone had been so generous.

Oliver met her with a broad smile. 'How incredible were you?'

'Thank you.' She grinned. 'Sorry, I'm all over the place right now. I'm still full of adrenalin from the skydive.' Which was only half the reason; Oliver's nearness was definitely making her feel all wobbly.

'You were so brave.'

'My palms were sweating, my heart was thumping and I thought I was going to pass out in the plane. Even though I knew it was safe, it was terrifying. The bit where you sit on the edge of the plane, just before you lean forward and fall out...'

'It sounds horrendous. But you did it.'

'All I did was jump out of a plane, strapped to someone else.'

'You're still amazing,' he countered.

She took off the kit, went to the debriefing, collected the website link for her video so she could share it with everyone who'd supported her, then sent a round-robin text to tell everyone she was down safely and she'd done it.

'So what's the plan now?' he asked.

'Home, please. I need to change that flat tyre.'

'Tell you what. Make me a cheese toastie, and I'll fix it for you.'

'But you've already rescued me once today. It feels as if I'm taking advantage of you.' Taking advantage of him. That could have another meaning. And the vision of Oliver all rumpled and lazy—smiling, after making love with her—made the blood rush straight to her face.

'You're not taking advantage of me,' he said.

Was it her imagination or was there extra colour in his cheeks, too? Was he remembering that kiss on the beach and wondering what it would be like if it happened again? For a moment, she couldn't breathe.

'If anything,' he said, 'you're doing me a favour because I can put off doing the chores.'

'Maybe I can do some chores for you in exchange, then,' she said.

'Five ironed shirts for a flat tyre?'

'Bargain,' she said. 'Let's collect your ironing on the way back.'

'Deal,' he said.

By the time he'd finished changing her tyre, she'd ironed five shirts and had the toasted cheese sandwiches ready to go.

'Thank you for saving me from the tyranny of the ironing board,' he said.

'Thank *you* for putting the spare tyre on for me,' she said. 'I'll call in to the tyre place this afternoon and get it sorted out.'

'You're very welcome.'

Once he'd eaten his sandwich, he smiled at her. 'I'll let you get on with the rest of your day. See you at The Anchor tonight for the skydive celebrations.'

'Thanks, Oliver. For everything.'

And his smile made her feel as if the world was full of sunshine.

That evening, when Gemma went to The Anchor to meet up with her friends and colleagues, people seemed to be congratulating her from the moment she walked through the door. She was greeted with hugs, offers of extra sponsorship, and glasses of Prosecco mixed with raspberry liqueur.

The landlord took the website address and password from Gemma and showed the skydive on the pub's large television screen, and everyone cheered at the moment when she jumped out of the plane.

Although the room was busy, she was very aware that Oliver was with the rest of the practice team.

'Hey. You were incredible,' he said.

Did he really think that? The idea made her feel all warm and glowing.

And why had she not noticed before just how blue his eyes were, and how beautiful his mouth was?

'All I did was jump out of a plane. And people have been so generous. If the money helps with the research and it stops another family having to lose their Sarah…' Her throat felt tight.

As if he guessed what was going through her head, he wrapped his arms round her. 'You're making a difference.'

And now her knees really had turned to jelly.

Being held by Oliver Langley made her all in a spin.

She was so aware of him: the warmth of his body, his strength, the citrus scent of his shower gel. She almost—almost—closed her eyes and tipped her head back, inviting a kiss. It was scary how much she wanted him to kiss her.

But then the noise of their surroundings rushed in at her.

They were in the village pub. In front of everyone. And she was in danger of acting very inappropriately.

She took one tiny step back; he released her, but she noticed that he was looking at her mouth. So did he feel this weird pull of attraction, too? She wasn't quite sure how to broach it. Not here, not now; but maybe the next time they spent time together—as friends— she'd be brave and suggest doing something together. A proper date.

Gemma enjoyed the rest of the evening; when she left to go home, as soon as she walked outside she suddenly felt woozy.

'Gemma? Are you all right?' Oliver asked, coming out to join her.

'Just a bit dizzy, that's all.' She winced. 'Probably too much Prosecco. Rookie mistake. People kept refilling my glass, and I didn't even think about it. I don't make a habit of getting drunk.' At that point, she tripped and Oliver caught her.

'Everyone does it at some point,' he said. 'Put your arm round my waist and lean on me. I'll walk you home.'

'Thank you. And sorry for being a burden. I feel like such an idiot.'

'It's fine,' he reassured her.

Just like that moment earlier when he'd hugged her,

it felt lovely to have his arm round her. Gemma leaned her head against his shoulder, again noticing that gorgeous citrus scent. 'You're such a sweetie,' she said.

He laughed. 'That's the bubbles talking.'

'No. You were all starchy and grumpy when I first met you. But that's not who you are. You're warm and lovely. And you smell lovely.' She squeezed him gently. 'Oli-lovely-ver.'

'Come on, Skydive Girl. Let's get you home.'

He was laughing. With her, not at her. And he had a really, really lovely laugh, Gemma thought.

When they got to her flat, he asked for her keys, unlocked the door and ushered her inside. 'Let me make you a cup of tea. You need to rehydrate a bit, or you'll feel terrible in the morning.'

'Oli-lovely-ver,' she said again. 'Thank you.'

'Come and sit down.' He guided her to the sofa. 'One mug of tea. Milk, no sugar, right?'

'Perfect.' She beamed at him.

Gemma Baxter was a very sweet drunk, Ollie thought. She'd made him smile, with that 'Oli-lovely-ver' business. He filled the kettle and switched it on, then hunted in the cupboards for mugs and tea. He'd noted earlier that Gemma was neat and tidy, and things were stored in sensible and obvious places, he discovered.

But when he went back into the living room with two mugs of tea, he realised that she was fast asleep on the sofa. It was probably a combination of a reaction to the adrenalin that had been pumping through her system all day and the drinks that people had bought her that evening.

He put the mugs down on the coffee table. What

now? There was a throw resting on the back of the sofa; he could tuck it over her and leave her on the sofa to sleep off all the Prosecco. Though then she'd probably wake with a sore neck or shoulder as well as a shocking headache.

Or he could carry her to her bed. She'd still have the hangover headache tomorrow, but at least she'd be comfortable.

He lifted her up, and she didn't wake at all. She just curled into him, all warm and soft. And there was a hint of rose and vanilla in her hair that made him want to hold her closer. Not that he'd ever take advantage like that.

He carried her to her room, pushed the duvet aside and laid her down on the bed.

Not wanting to be intrusive, he left her fully clothed, though he did remove her shoes. Then he tucked the duvet round her, and she snuggled against the pillow. He closed the curtains; the noise didn't wake her, so he pulled the door almost closed and went back into her living room.

He could leave her to sleep it off and write her a note; but he didn't really want to leave her on her own. If she was ill in the night and something happened, he'd never forgive himself.

The sofa was way too short for him to lie down on, but he could sort of sprawl on it and wrap the throw round himself. He'd slept on uncomfortable sofas often enough in his student days. OK, so it was years since he'd been a student, but he'd be fine. The most important thing was that Gemma was safe.

He finished his mug of tea, quietly washed up, then settled himself on the sofa with the throw. He dozed fitfully, and checked on Gemma a couple of times during the night; to his relief, she was fine.

The next morning, he washed his face, borrowed Gemma's toothpaste and used his finger as a makeshift brush to stop his mouth feeling quite so revolting, then went into her kitchen to make coffee. He also poured her a large glass of water, and took it through to her.

'Good morning.'

Gemma kept her eyes firmly closed.

Someone was talking to her. But she lived on her own, so that wasn't possible. Was she hallucinating?

A male voice. Not Andy's Northumbrian accent, so she hadn't stayed over at Claire's—anyway, why would she stay over at Claire's when she only lived a few minutes' walk away?

And she could smell coffee. So she couldn't be at home, because she lived on her own and there was nobody to make coffee for her. Yet this felt like her own bed.

What was going on?

She squinted through one eye.

Someone was standing next to her bed, holding a mug—hence the smell of coffee—and a large glass of water.

Not just someone: Oliver Langley.

Horror swept through her. What was Oliver doing here? She couldn't remember a thing about the end of the evening, yesterday. Oh, no. Had she thrown herself at him? Please don't let her have reverted to the way she'd behaved in that awful year after Sarah died, and made a fool of herself...

Hideously embarrassed and ashamed, she mumbled,

'So sorry.' Her face felt as if it was on fire and she couldn't look at him. Still with her eyes closed, she began, 'I, um, whatever I did or said last night—'

'You fell asleep on your sofa while I was making you a cup of tea,' he cut in. 'I carried you in here, put you in bed, took your shoes off and covered you up. And I slept on your sofa.'

She wasn't sure whether to be relieved, grateful or mortified. He'd clearly stayed to keep an eye on her because she'd been that tipsy last night. How shameful was that? 'Thank you for looking after me.'

'Sit up and drink some water,' he said. 'You'll feel better.'

Still cringing inwardly, she did as he suggested. And he was right; the water helped. 'Thank you.'

'I'm going to make us some toast,' he said. 'I hope you don't mind, but I used some of your toothpaste.'

'Of course I don't mind. Help yourself to anything you need. There are towels in the airing cupboard and a spare toothbrush in the bathroom cabinet.'

'Actually, I used my finger.' He grinned. 'Took me right back to being a student.'

'I'm so sorry,' she said again. 'I don't normally drink more than a glass or two of wine. I don't know what happened last night.'

'People were topping up your glass while you were talking,' he said. 'Plus you were still on a high from the skydive.'

She swallowed hard. 'We…um…didn't…?'

'No. I wouldn't take advantage of anyone like that.'

'Of course you wouldn't. You're one of the good guys.' A hot tide of shame swept through her. 'I'm sorry.

I didn't mean to imply you'd…' Oh, help. She was digging herself into a bigger hole here.

'Besides,' he said, a tiny quirk at the corner of his mouth, 'if I had spent the night with you, I rather hope you'd remember it.'

The heat of the shame turned to something else equally hot: a surge of pure desire.

This really wasn't a good idea.

Oliver was in her bedroom. She was in bed. Fully clothed, admittedly, but in bed. And she'd made way too many mistakes of this type before.

'Let's go into the kitchen and have that toast,' she said.

Paracetamol, more water, the mug of coffee and three slices of toast later, Gemma felt human again, and she'd pretty much got her thoughts sorted.

'So let me start again. Thank you for looking after me last night. I apologise if I made a fool of myself. And—' she took a deep breath, cringing inwardly but knowing this had to be done '—I apologise if I threw myself at you.'

'You didn't throw yourself at me,' he said quietly. 'And there's no need to apologise. You were a bit woozy and you fell asleep when I went to make you a mug of tea. I didn't want to leave you on your own. If it had been the other way round, I'm pretty sure you would've looked after me.'

'Of course. That's what friends do.'

'What makes you think you threw yourself at me?'

The question was mild; yet the true answer would shock him, she was sure. She certainly wasn't going to admit that he was absolutely her type and she really liked him. He'd made it clear he only saw her as a friend.

Which meant she'd have to confide in him. Tell him what a mess she'd been.

'It's a bit of a long story. When I was seventeen,' she said, 'I had a bit of a...difficult year.'

The year Gemma's sister had died, Oliver remembered.

'I didn't deal with it very well. I tried lots of ways to escape,' she said. 'I never did drugs or cigarettes, and I've never been a big one for alcohol—but I had sex. Lots of sex. I kind of went through most of the lads in the sixth form and I earned myself a shocking reputation.'

Because she'd been hurting. Because she'd been looking for a way to avoid the pain. Seventeen, and so vulnerable. Ollie's heart went out to her. The boys of her own age wouldn't have thought about why she was throwing herself at them and held back; at that age, the testosterone surge would've taken over and they would've been more than happy to sleep with her. It wouldn't have occurred to any of them that they were taking advantage of someone vulnerable. No wonder this morning Gemma had thought they'd spent the night together: she'd obviously been taken advantage of before.

He reached across the table and took her hand. He squeezed it once, just enough to be sympathetic, but letting her hand go again before the gesture crossed the border into being creepy. 'I'm sorry you had such a rough time.'

She shrugged. 'It was self-inflicted.'

'Didn't your parents...?'

The stricken look on her face stopped him. Clearly, they hadn't. 'I'm sorry,' he said. 'I didn't mean to trample on a sore spot.'

'They were hurting, too. It's pretty difficult to support a teenager who's gone off the rails, and even harder to do that when your heart's broken,' she said softly. 'They just folded in on themselves after Sarah died. I couldn't talk to them about anything. I couldn't tell them how I was feeling, how much I missed my sister, how hard it was to get up in the morning. So I went for the escape route. Or what I thought was one. It was just a mess and I feel bad now because they already had enough to deal with. I just made it worse.'

'What about counselling?' he asked.

'I had counselling in my first year at uni and that really helped me, but when I suggested it to my parents they pretty much blanked me. They're not ones for talking.' She swallowed hard. 'After they moved from Ashermouth Bay, I never lived with them again.'

'You said you stayed with your best friend's family.'

She nodded. 'Claire was worried about me and the way I was behaving. She talked to her mum about it, but even Yvonne couldn't get through to me. Not until results day, when I failed all my exams really badly. Claire dragged me back to her place and made me sit down with her mum. Yvonne said that it was time for plan B, a chance to get my life back into gear. She said she'd been thinking about it and she and Claire's dad had agreed that I could move in with them. I'd resit the second year of my A levels, while Claire would be doing the first year of her catering course at the local college. The deal was, I'd stop the sex.' She shook her head.

'I think the only saving grace of that awful year

was that I'd insisted on using condoms, so I didn't get pregnant or catch an STD. But I got called a lot of fairly nasty names. Yvonne said she understood why I was sleeping around, but that behaviour was only hurting me more instead of making things better. She said from that day onward I was going to be one of her girls, part of her family.' She swallowed hard. 'And it was so good to be part of a family again. To feel that I belonged. That I was loved.'

Ollie was seriously unimpressed by Gemma's parents—however tough life was, however miserable it made you, you didn't just give up on your remaining child, the way it sounded as if they had. But he was glad someone had been there to step in and help. 'Claire's mum sounds really special.'

'She is. And what she did for me... I want to pay that forward,' Gemma said earnestly. 'I'd like to offer a troubled teenager a place to stay. A place to get their Plan B sorted. I want to be someone who won't judge because she's been there and knows what it feels like— someone who offers a second chance to get things right, and the support that teenager needs to get through it.'

'I've only known you for a little while, but that's enough for me to know you'd be amazing in a role like that. The authorities will snap you up.'

'You really think so?'

'I really think so.' He reached over to squeeze her hand again. 'Thank you for being so honest with me. I want to reassure you that I'm not going to gossip about you with anyone.'

'Pretty much everyone in the village knows my history. Though thankfully nobody seems to hold it against me nowadays.' She gave him a rueful smile. 'But thank you.'

'It's fine.' Ollie could almost hear his twin's voice in his head. *You like her, so tell her. Take a risk. Be more Rob.* 'Gemma. I like you, and I think you might like me. We're becoming friends, but...' He took a deep breath. *Be more Rob.* 'I want to be more than that.'

'I don't have a good track record,' she warned. 'I've kind of gone the other way from my teens. Claire says I'm so scared of being needy again, I don't let anyone close. So my relationships tend to fizzle out after only a few weeks.'

'I understand that,' he said.

Gemma had trusted him with her past; maybe he should do the same. 'My track record isn't great, either,' he said. 'I was supposed to get married at the beginning of May.'

'When you gave Rob your kidney?'

'A month before the operation. But he wouldn't have been well enough to be at the wedding.'

'Why didn't you just move the wedding?' she asked.

He appreciated the fact she'd thought of the same solution that he had. 'Tabby—my fiancée—called it off. Her dad had ME, so she grew up seeing her mum having to look after him as well as work and look after the kids. And she didn't want that kind of life for herself.'

'But you donated a kidney. Your brother was the one on dialysis, the one who might have problems if his body rejects the new kidney, not you,' Gemma said.

'Her view was what if something happened to me, too?' he said dryly. 'Though when I look back I'm pretty sure it was an excuse.'

'Do you think she fell for someone else and just didn't want to hurt you by telling you?'

He shook his head. 'I think she was having cold feet. She didn't want to marry me because she didn't love me enough. You're right in that Rob's kidney was an excuse. But the real reason—and I know it's real because she told me—is that I wasn't enough for her.' He wrinkled his nose. 'And that's messed with my head a bit.'

'It would mess with anyone's head,' Gemma said. 'I'm sorry you got hurt. But the problem was with her, not you.'

He wasn't so sure. 'With me not being enough, and you not letting anyone close, we might be setting ourselves up for trouble,' he said. 'Maybe we can just see how things go.'

'I'd like that,' she said.

For the first time since Tabby had broken their engagement, he actually felt positive about the idea of dating someone. Dating *Gemma*.

'I'm going to give you the rest of the day to get over your hangover. And I'm not going to kiss you right now, because neither of us is particularly fragrant.' He held her gaze. 'But, just so you know, I'm planning to kiss you tonight. I'd like to take you out to dinner.'

'Actually,' she said, 'I'd rather like to take *you* out to dinner. And I'll drive. I'll book a table and let you know what time I'll pick you up.'

'That's bossy,' he said, but the fact she was asserting herself appealed to him. 'OK. But I'll meet you here. The walk will do me good. Let me know what time.'

'You're on,' she said, and her smile made his heart skip a beat. He couldn't remember the last time he'd felt this enthused about an evening out.

Maybe, just maybe, he and Gemma could help each other heal from the unhappiness of their pasts. And maybe they could go forward together. Tonight would be that first step.

CHAPTER SEVEN

ONCE OLIVER HAD LEFT, Gemma showered and washed her hair; being clean again made her feel much more human and sorted out most of her hangover.

And it also gave her time to think about what had happened this morning. Now Oliver knew the very worst of her: but it hadn't made a difference to him.

He liked her.

Really liked her.

He'd told her he was planning to kiss her, tonight, and it made her feel like a teenager again—but in a good way, light-hearted and carefree, rather than in an angsty, world-on-her-shoulders kind of way.

He'd suggested going out to dinner. The place where she really wanted to take him tended to be booked up weeks in advance. But it was always worth a try, so she rang them to ask if they could possibly squeeze in a table for two.

'You're in luck,' the manager told her. 'I've just had a cancellation. I can fit you in at eight.'

'That's perfect,' Gemma said. And it was a very good sign.

She texted Oliver.

Managed to get table for eight. Pick you up at seven thirty? Dress code smart-casual.

Should she add a kiss at the end, or not? Then again, they were officially dating. She took a risk and added a kiss.

He replied immediately.

Seven-thirty's perfect. I'll walk over to your place. x

Excitement bubbled through Gemma's veins. He'd sent her a kiss back by text. And he was going to kiss her properly tonight...

She caught up with the chores, then took some flowers down to the churchyard. 'Hey, Sarah. I've met someone. You'd like him,' she said, arranging the flowers in the vase on her sister's grave. 'His ex was pretty unfair to him and broke his heart. It's early days, but we're going to see how things go between us.' She finished arranging the flowers. 'I miss you, Sarah. I wish you were here so I could chat to you while I was getting ready tonight.' But her little sister would always be with her in her heart. 'Love you,' she said softly, and headed back home.

Gemma took care with her make-up that evening, and wore her favourite little black dress. At seven thirty precisely, her doorbell buzzed. She pressed the button on the intercom.

'Hi, Gemma. It's Oliver.'

'Right on time,' she said.

'Can I come up?'

'Sure.'

Her heart skipped a beat when she opened her front door. She'd seen him in a suit for work, and wearing jeans outside the surgery, but Oliver Langley dressed up for a night out was something else. Tonight he wore dark trousers, highly polished shoes, and a blue linen shirt that really brought out the colour of his eyes.

'You scrub up very nicely, Dr Langley,' she said, feeling the colour slide into her face.

He looked her up and down. 'Thank you. You look beautiful, Gemma,' he said. 'Your hair is amazing.'

She'd straightened it so it was smooth and shiny and fell to her shoulders. 'Thank you.'

To her surprise, he handed her a bunch of sunflowers. 'For you.'

'Thank you. They're gorgeous. Was that a lucky guess, or did you know they were my favourites?' she asked.

'You had sunflowers in a vase the first time I came round,' he said.

He was that observant? She was impressed. The men she'd dated in the past had never really noticed that sort of thing. The few dates who had actually bought her flowers had chosen red roses or something pink—a safe choice, and she'd appreciated it because she loved flowers, but these ones felt more special.

'Plus,' he added, 'they make me think of you because you're like sunshine.'

'What a lovely thing to say.' The more so because it felt like a genuine compliment. 'Come in while I put them in water.'

'So where are we going tonight?' he asked, following her into the kitchen.

'The Lighthouse. It's a pub in the next village down

the coast—it used to be a lighthouse, hence the name, but after it was decommissioned it was turned into a bar and restaurant.' She smiled at him. 'It's foodie heaven, so I think you'll enjoy it. Plus the views are pretty amazing.'

'Sounds lovely,' he said.

She put the sunflowers in a vase. 'You're OK about me driving you?'

He laughed. 'I might be starchy sometimes, but I'm not sexist. I'm absolutely fine with you driving.'

Gemma was a careful, competent driver. Not that Ollie had expected anything less. She drove them to the next village and parked outside what looked at first like a lighthouse, and then when they walked through the front door he realised that the whole of the wall overlooking the sea was made of glass.

'Does this mean we get to see the sunset while we eat?'

'Sort of. We're on the east coast, so we get more of the sunrise than the sunset,' she said, 'but the sky and the sea will still look very pretty.'

Once they were seated, he asked, 'What do you recommend?'

She glanced up at the chalk board and smiled. 'Crab cakes are on the specials today. Definitely them for a starter,' she said. 'For the mains, just about anything; everything's as local as possible, so the fish is particularly good.' She paused. 'Is it just cake you're not a fan of, or sweet stuff in general?'

'I'm not really a pudding or cake person,' he said. 'Which is another difference between me and my twin. Rob will do almost anything for chocolate.'

'That's a pity, because the salted caramel cheesecake here is amazing. But, since you don't like puddings, I'd recommend the cheese plate,' she said. 'They're all local artisan cheeses, and the team here makes their own oatcakes. Actually, it's really hard to choose between pudding and cheese. I might have to toss a coin.'

He ordered the same starter, main and sides as Gemma. The portions were generous and the food was excellent, but the company was even better. He felt more relaxed with Gemma than he'd felt in years. How weird was that? He hadn't been looking to start dating anyone. And yet here he was, on a first date with a woman he liked very much. A woman he wanted to kiss. A woman who made him feel as if the sun was shining through the middle of a rainstorm.

And now was his chance to get to know her better.

'So when you're not chucking yourself out of a plane or whatever for fundraising,' he said, 'what do you do for fun?'

'Play with my goddaughter,' she said promptly. 'I have my dance aerobics class on Tuesday nights; if Yvonne is hosting a crafting workshop on an evening or a Saturday afternoon, I go to support her and I'm in charge of making coffee. Sometimes I have a girly night in with my friends; that usually involves cake, watching a film, a glass of wine and a mug of hot chocolate. Oh, and a big bowl of home-made sweet popcorn.' She smiled. 'What about you?'

'I run in the morning before work. In London, I used to run along the Regent's Canal, and here I get to run along the harbour and the beach.' That was something Ollie still found a sheer delight; the sound of the sea really calmed him and pushed any worries away. 'When

Rob was in Manchester and I was in London, we used to play virtual chess, though as we live nearer each other right now we can do that in person. None of my close friends in London have children yet, so most weekends I'd go with a group of them to watch the rugby or cricket.'

'I get the running, but cricket?' she teased. 'A game that takes days to play rather than a few minutes. Not my thing at all.'

'Rugby?'

She wrinkled her nose. 'Sorry. I'm not into watching any contact sports. I keep thinking of all the medical complications—the torn rotator cuffs, the sprains, the fractures and the cases of herpes gladiatorum. I'll stick to my dance aerobics.'

He loved the teasing glint in her eyes. 'OK. So we've established that you like sweet and I like savoury; I like cricket and rugby and you don't. How about music?'

'Anything I can sing and dance to,' she said promptly, 'and I reserve the right to sing off key. You?'

'Rock,' he said. 'Rob dabbled with the idea of being a rock star. He thought we could be the next Kaiser Chiefs. We started a band when we were thirteen. He was the singer and lead guitarist, one of our friends was the drummer, and he made me learn the bass guitar and do the harmonies. I can't hold a tune, so I was absolutely pants.' He grinned. 'And so was he.'

'Oh, that's cruel,' she said.

'No, it's honest,' he said, laughing. 'Our drummer was out of time, too. It was fun, but we were awful. Our parents were so relieved when we gave it up. Then Rob discovered a climbing wall and found out that not only did he love climbing, he was really good at it.'

'What about you? Are you a climber?'

'Slogging your way up a sheer rock face, when it's chucking it down with rain and there's only a tiny little rope between you and disaster? Nope. That's really not my idea of fun,' he said. 'I'd much rather sit in the dry, watching rugby. Or playing chess.'

'I don't play chess,' she said. 'But Claire's family is really into board games. We used to have game nights every Friday—anything from board games to charades or cards. We'd have build-your-own fajitas for dinner first, which was Yvonne's way of sneaking extra veg into our diet without us noticing. It was a lot of fun.'

'It sounds it,' he said.

'So where did you learn to do that magic trick, making a coin appear behind that little boy's ear?'

'My rotation in paediatrics. The consultant taught me that a magic trick is the best way to distract a child and get them to relax. There's the coin one, and for the older ones there's the one with the magic envelope.'

'Magic envelope?' Gemma asked. 'Tell me more.'

He ran through the rules. 'You write a number on a piece of paper, and put it in a sealed envelope. Then you ask them the year they were born, the year they started school, how many years it's been since they started school, and how old they'll be at the end of this year. Get them to add the four numbers together and tell you what it is. Then you ask them to open the envelope. They'll discover that it contains the number they just told you—which is basically double whatever this year is.'

'That's clever,' she said.

'It's a simple maths tricks but it's handy for distracting an older child when you need to get a blood

sample, or you're going to do something that's going
to be a bit uncomfortable.'

'I'll remember that one,' she said. 'So today the G
in GP stands for "genius".'

He laughed. 'I can't take the credit. It was my consultant who taught me.'

'Ah, but *you've* just taught *me*,' she pointed out.

Once they'd finished their meal; Gemma excused herself to go to the toilet and paid the bill on the way so
Oliver wouldn't have the chance to argue.

'Thank you for dinner,' he said as they left the restaur-
rant. 'Next time we do something together, it's my treat.'

So there was definitely going to be a next time?
Maybe this time her relationship wouldn't all be over
almost as soon as it had begun; the hope made her feel
warm all over. 'That'd be nice,' she said with a smile.
'Shall we go and have a last look at the sky and the sea?'

They walked over to the edge of the cliffs, hand in
hand. Such a tiny contact, but so sweet. She could really get used to holding hands with Oliver Langley. And
she wanted more. A lot more.

The bright colours of the sunset had faded to a rosy
afterglow, and the moon was a tiny sliver of a crescent
in the darkening sky. 'There's Jupiter,' Gemma said,
pointing out the bright planet, 'and Mars. If you look
out to the east in the early morning, you'll see Venus.'

'In London, I never really got to see the sky properly,' he said. 'Out here, it's magical.' He turned her to
face him. 'You make me feel magical, too, Gemma,' he
said softly. 'And, right now, I really want to kiss you.'

'I want to kiss you, too,' she said.

He dipped his head and brushed his mouth against hers, and her lips tingled at the touch.

'Sweet, sweet Gemma,' he said softly, and kissed her again.

It felt as if fireworks were going off in her head. She'd never experienced anything like this before, and she wasn't sure if it made her feel more amazed or terrified.

When Oliver broke the kiss and pulled away slightly, she held his gaze. His pupils were huge, making his eyes seem almost black in the twilight.

She reached up to touch his mouth, and ran her forefinger along his bottom lip,

He nipped gently at her finger.

Suddenly, Gemma found breathing difficult.

'Gemma,' he said, his voice husky. 'I wasn't expecting this to happen.'

'Me neither,' she whispered. And this was crazy. She knew he was only here temporarily, and he'd probably go back to his life in London once his locum job here had finished and his twin had recovered from the transplant. Was she dating him purely because being a temporary colleague made him safe—she wouldn't be reckless enough to lose her heart to someone who wouldn't stick around? Or would it be like the misery of all those years ago when her parents had moved and left her behind?

'We ought to be heading back,' she said. Even though both of them knew there was no reason why they couldn't stand on the cliffs all evening, just kissing, the unexpected intensity of her feelings scared her.

'Uh-huh,' he said—but he held her hand all the way

back to the car. And he kissed her again before she unlocked the door.

Gemma drove them back to Ashermouth Bay and parked outside his cottage.

'Would you like to come in for a cup of coffee?' Ollie asked.

Was he being polite, or did he really want to spend more time with her? Or did he mean something other than coffee? It was hard to judge. She wanted to spend more time with him, yet at the same time she thought it would be a mistake. What was the point of getting closer to him if he wasn't going to stick around?

Should she stay or should she go?

'Gemma? I'm asking you in for coffee,' he said quietly. 'I'm not going to rip your clothes off the second you walk in the front door.'

She felt the colour fizz through her face. 'Like the boyfriends in my past, you mean.'

'I wasn't being snippy. Back then, you were seventeen and hurting and maybe not in the place to make the right choices for you. It's different now. I just wanted to let you know that I appreciate you've been honest with me about your past and I'm not going to make assumptions or pressure you to do anything you're not comfortable with.'

So coffee meant just coffee. It meant spending a bit more time with her. Funny how that made her heart feel as if it had just flipped over and eased the tightness in her chest.

'Then thank you. Coffee would be nice.'

'Good.' He took her hand, lifted it to his mouth, pressed a kiss against her palm and folded her fingers over it.

The gesture was unexpectedly sweet, and melted away the last vestiges of her misgivings.

Inside the house, he connected his phone to a speaker. 'Would you like to choose some music while I make you a cappuccino?'

'Cappuccino? As in a *proper* cappuccino?' she checked.

He nodded.

'So are you telling me you have a proper coffee maker in your kitchen? A bean-to-cup one?'

'With a frothing arm. Yup.' He grinned. 'Busted. I didn't tell you that gadgets are my bad habit. Rob gives me quite a hard time about it.'

She groaned. 'And to think I've been giving you instant coffee, when you make the posh stuff.'

He smiled. 'It's OK. I didn't judge you.'

'Didn't you?' She raised an eyebrow at him.

'Only a little bit.' He gave her a little-boy-lost look. 'So I guess I owe you a kiss for being judgmental, then.'

'Yes,' she said. 'I rather think you do. Because there's nothing wrong with instant coffee.'

'Would you choose instant coffee over a proper cappuccino?' he asked.

'No,' she admitted. 'But bean-to-cup machines are a bit—well, fancy.'

'They're a brilliant invention,' he said, laughing. 'As I'll prove to you.' He closed the curtains, put the table lamp on and switched off the overhead light; then he came back over to her. 'One apology kiss coming right up.'

His mouth was soft and warm and sweet, teasing her lips until she opened her mouth and let him deepen the kiss.

'Hold that thought,' he said, 'and choose some music.' He unlocked his phone and went into the streaming app. 'Pick something you like, then come and supervise, if you like.'

'My expertise is in drinking cappuccinos, not making them,' she said. But she picked a mellow playlist, then followed him into the kitchen.

His movements were deft and sure, and the cappuccino was perfect.

'If you ever get bored with being a doctor, you could make a decent barista,' she teased.

He inclined his head. 'Thank you.'

She enjoyed sitting with him on his sofa, his arm around her while she rested her head on his shoulder, just listening to music. Every so often, Oliver kissed her, and each kiss made her head spin.

'Much as I've enjoyed this evening,' Gemma said, 'I'm not going to overstay my welcome. Thank you for the coffee. I'll wash up before I go.'

'No need. Everything will go in the dishwasher,' he said. 'So what are your plans for the rest of the weekend?'

'Tomorrow morning, I'm training for the sponsored cycle ride—seeing how far I can get in two and a half hours,' she said. 'But I'm free in the afternoon, if you'd like to do something.'

'Maybe we can go for a walk,' he suggested.

'That'd be nice. Round the next bay, there's a ruined castle. It's really pretty on the beach there.'

'Great. What time works for you?' he asked.

'About three?' she suggested.

'I'll pick you up,' he said. He kissed her again, his

mouth teasing hers. 'Thank you for this evening. I've really enjoyed it.'

'Me, too,' she said, feeling suddenly shy.

'Sweet dreams. See you tomorrow,' he said, and stole a last kiss.

On Sunday morning, Gemma did a long cycle ride, setting an alarm on her watch so she knew when to turn round at the halfway point. Back home, she was pleased to discover that she'd managed thirty-five miles, which meant she was more than halfway to her goal. If she kept doing the short rides during the week and the longer rides at the weekend, she should be fine for the sixty-mile sponsored ride.

In the afternoon, Oliver picked her up at three and drove her to the next bay. It was a pretty walk by the ruined castle and down the cliff path to the sands.

'This is perfect,' he said. 'A proper sandy beach.'

The beach was quiet; there were a couple of families sitting on picnic blankets with small children painstakingly building sandcastles next to them with the aid of a bucket and spade. There were three or four dogs running along the wet sand further down, retrieving tennis balls to drop at their owners' feet; and some couples walking along the edge of the shore, ankle-deep as the waves swooshed in.

Gemma slipped off her shoes and dropped them in her tote bag. 'There's enough room in my bag for your shoes, too,' she told Oliver. 'Let's go for a paddle. There's nothing nicer than walking on flat, wet sand.'

'Agreed—but I'll carry the bag,' he said, and put his shoes in her bag.

They both rolled their jeans up to the knee, then

strolled along the shoreline. The sea was deliciously cool against their skin in the heat of the afternoon.

'This is my idea of the perfect afternoon,' he said.

She smiled at him. 'Mine, too.'

They didn't need to chatter; just walking together, hand in hand, was enough. Oliver felt so familiar that it was as if she'd known him for years, not just a few short weeks. Gemma couldn't remember ever feeling so relaxed with someone she was dating. It took her a while to work out just what it was about Oliver: but then she realised.

She trusted him.

He'd seen her at her worst, and he hadn't rejected her. He hadn't taken advantage of her, either; instead, he'd looked after her. Cherished her. Made her feel special.

But then Gemma glanced out to sea and noticed something. 'Oliver, do you see those two boys swimming a bit further out? They look as if they're in trouble.'

He followed her gaze. 'I agree. Do you get rip tides here?'

'Thankfully, not in this bay,' she said. 'But there aren't any lifeguards on this beach, just the public rescue equipment. Do you mind hanging onto my bag and I'll go and see what I can do?' When she could see him about to protest, she reminded him gently, 'It's not that long since the transplant. If you overexert yourself or get an infection, you'll regret it.'

'I know you have a point,' he said, 'but I feel useless.'

'You won't be useless at all,' she said. 'You can call the ambulance, because it's pretty obvious at least one of them is going to need treatment. Don't worry, I'm not going to do anything stupid and I won't put myself in danger—because that just means another person will need rescuing.'

'You two out there! If you're OK,' she yelled to the boys, 'wave to me!'

One of the boys was clearly struggling to stay afloat, submerging completely from time to time; the other looked panicky, and neither of them waved back at her.

'I'm going in,' she said to Oliver. 'Call the ambulance.'

She ran up to the bright orange housing containing the lifebuoy ring, then went back to the sea. Although she and Oliver been walking at the edge of the sea, with the waves swishing round their ankles, the water felt colder than she'd expected. She swam out to them, knowing that Oliver was calling for back-up medical help. But, in the short time it took her to reach them, the struggling boy had gone under again, and this time he hadn't bobbed back up.

She dived under the waves and managed to find him and get him to the surface.

'I'm not sure whether you can hear me or not,' she said, 'but you're safe. Don't struggle. I'm taking you back to shore.' She trod water for a moment, holding him up, and turned to the other boy. 'I know you're scared and tired, but grab this ring and try to follow me back to shore. Don't worry about being fast. Just keep going and focus on one stroke at a time. I'll come back for you and help you, but I need to get your friend to shore first.'

'My brother,' the other boy said, his voice quavery and full of fear. 'His name's Gary.'

'OK. I've got him and I'll get him back to shore,' she reassured him. 'You're not on your own. Try and get to a place where you can get both feet on the ground and your head's above water, and I'll come back for you.'

She focused on getting Gary back to the shore. Ollie was there to meet her, and a couple of other people had clearly noticed what was going on and had gathered beside him.

'The ambulance is on its way here,' he said.

'Good. This is Gary. His brother's still out there, trying to make his way in,' she said. 'He's got a lifebuoy but I said I'd go back to help him.'

'I'll go,' one of the men said. 'I'm a strong swimmer. Oliver said you were both medics, so you'll be needed more here.'

'Thanks,' she said.

'People are bringing towels and blankets,' Oliver said, and helped her to carry Gary to a towel that someone had spread out.

'Brilliant,' she said gratefully. 'He went under a few times, and I'm not sure whether he's still breathing. I just wanted to get him back here so we could do something.'

Oliver knelt next to the boy and gently shook his shoulder. 'Gary? Can you hear me? Open your eyes for me.'

The boy didn't respond.

He and Gemma exchanged a glance. This wasn't a good sign.

'Checking his airway,' Oliver said, tilting the boy's head back and lifting his chin. 'Clear,' he said. But he frowned as he checked the boy's breathing. 'I can't feel any breath on my cheek, I can't hear breathing sounds, and his chest isn't moving, so I'm going to start CPR. Is the other boy OK?'

Gemma looked over to the sea. 'Looks it. The guy who went in to help him—they're close enough to be walking in, now,' she said.

'Good.' Oliver started giving chest compressions, keeping to the beat of the song 'Stayin' Alive'.

Gemma knew that chest compressions were their best chance of keeping him alive. But she also knew that giving chest compressions meant a lot of exertion, and it really hadn't been that long since Oliver had donated a kidney to his brother.

'Come on, Gary, you're not going to die on me,' Oliver said.

'Let me take over for a couple of minutes,' Gemma said. 'We'll split it between us so neither of us gets too tired.'

The other boy ran over and threw himself down next to them. 'Is my brother all right? He's not going to die, is he?'

'Not on our watch, I hope,' Oliver said. 'Can you tell us what happened?'

'We were swimming. Not far out, because we're not that stupid. And we haven't been drinking or anything. We just wanted to have a bit of fun. But then Gary went under. He said he was getting cramp in his foot and he couldn't swim any more. I tried to get him but I couldn't.' The boy's face was pale with fear. 'He can't die. He can't. Our parents will never forgive me.'

Gemma knew how that felt. 'We're not going to let him die,' she said, and kept doing the compressions.

The man who'd helped with the rescue came over, carrying the lifebuoy. 'I'll put this back,' he said.

At that point, to Gemma's relief, Gary started to cough. Oliver helped her roll the boy onto his side. As she'd expected, his stomach contents gushed out of his mouth; there seemed to be a huge amount of salty water. But at least he was breathing,

'What's your name?' Oliver asked the older boy.

'Ethan.'

'Ethan, we've got an ambulance on the way. You might want to find your parents and grab your stuff.'

'There's just me and Gary here. Our parents wanted to go and see some garden or other. We said we wanted to stay here, because gardens are boring. We just wanted to have a sw—' Ethan broke off, almost sobbing.

'It's OK,' Oliver said. 'Gary's going to be OK. Go and find your stuff and come back to us.'

Other people had brought towels and blankets, and between them Gemma and Oliver put Gary into the recovery position and covered him with towels to keep him warm.

By the time Ethan got back with their things, the paramedics had arrived. They took over sorting out Gary's breathing and Ollie helped them get Gary onto a scoop so they could take him back to the ambulance.

'Looks as if you could do with checking over, too, lad,' one of the paramedics said to Ethan. 'Come on. We'll get you sorted out.'

'Can we call your mum and dad for you?' Gemma asked.

'No, I'll call my mum.' Ethan swallowed hard. 'Thank you, everyone. But especially you,' he said to Gemma. 'You saved my brother's life.'

'Next time you swim in the sea, make sure you warm up your muscles properly before you go in, because then you're less likely to get cramp,' she said, clapping his shoulder. 'Take care.'

* * *

'He has a point,' Ollie said when the paramedics had gone. 'Without you bringing Gary in he'd have drowned, and Ethan was struggling as well—if you hadn't given him that lifebuoy, he could've drowned, too.'

She shrugged. 'Anyone else would've done the same as me.'

Why wouldn't she accept a genuine compliment? Why did she do herself down? he wondered. 'Impressive swimming, Nurse Practitioner Baxter.'

'Not really.' She shrugged again. 'Growing up in a seaside town means you do all your swimming safety training actually in the sea, with the coastguard trainers.'

'I did mine in the pool round the corner from school,' he said. 'The whole thing with the pyjamas as a float.'

'A pool's good. But I'm glad I did my training in the sea. Open water's a bit different—if nothing else, it's colder and there's the tide to think about. Are you OK?' she asked.

'Doing CPR didn't overexert me, if that's what you were worrying about. But right now I think I need to get you home so you can get out of those wet clothes. Sorry, I don't have a towel or spare clothes in the car I can offer you.'

'That's not a problem, but I don't want to ruin your car seat. Do you have a plastic bag I can sit on?' she asked.

'No, but I have a foil blanket.'

She blinked. 'Seriously?'

'Seriously.' When they got back to the car, Ollie fished the foil blanket out of the glove compartment.

'So how come you keep a foil blanket in your car?' she asked.

'It's a mix of my mum and my brother. Because Rob does the mountain rescue stuff, he always has a foil blanket with him. When our parents moved here, he made them keep one in the car in case they ever get stuck somewhere; and then Mum made me put one in my car.'

'It feels a bit of a waste, using it to sit on, but I guess at least it'll keep your seat dry. I'll buy you a replacement,' she said.

Ollie smiled at her. 'It's fine—you look like a mermaid with wet hair.'

'It's going to be impossible by the time I get home.' She plaited it roughly.

'Let's get you home,' he said, and drove them back to her flat.

'You're welcome to come in for a cup of horrible instant coffee, given that I don't have a posh coffee machine like you do,' she said with a smile.

He laughed. 'I might go for tea, in that case, but only if you're sure.'

'I'm sure. Put the kettle on and make yourself whatever you want to drink. Everything's in a logical place. I'll be as quick as I can.'

By the time she'd showered and washed her hair, dressed in dry clothes again and put her wet things in the washing machine, Ollie had made himself a mug of tea and her a mug of coffee.

'Thank you,' she said gratefully. 'I could do with this.'

He raised his mug to her. 'To you. Without you, there could be a family in mourning right now.'

'To us,' she corrected. 'Without you giving him CPR, Gary wouldn't have stood a chance.'

He grimaced. 'It still feels weird, the post-Covid "don't give rescue breaths" protocol.'

'Circulation's the really important thing, though,' Gemma pointed out. 'If your heart stops, you die; if you collapse, you need chest compressions getting your circulation going more than you need breaths inflating your lungs.'

'I know, but it still feels a bit off,' he said.

'I'm going to ring the hospital and see how Gary is,' she said. When she put the phone down, she looked relieved. 'They said he's comfortable—but, then, that's the usual hospital comment to anyone who isn't family—and his parents are with him. I've given them my number if Gary and Ethan's parents want to get in touch.'

'This wasn't quite what I had in mind for a romantic afternoon stroll,' he said ruefully.

'No, but we've made a difference to someone, and that's a good thing,' she said.

He kissed her. 'Yes. It's a very good thing.'

CHAPTER EIGHT

OVER THE NEXT couple of weeks, Gemma and Oliver grew closer. It was fast becoming the happiest summer she could ever remember. On the evenings and weekends when she wasn't at a gym class or helping Yvonne with an event or already had arrangements with friends, she spent her time with Oliver—everything from dinner to walking on the beach, to watching the sunset on the cliffs and watching the stars come out over the sea. No pressure, no regrets or baggage: just enjoying each other's company.

Walking hand in hand in the famous rose garden at Alnwick with Oliver was the most romantic Saturday afternoon Gemma had ever spent. The sun was bright but not fiercely hot; the scent of the flowers was incredibly strong and made her feel as if they were strolling through an enchanted storybook garden. And when Oliver pulled her into a secluded arbour and stole a kiss, it made her feel as if the air around them was sparkling with happiness.

Even the monthly visit to her parents, the next day, was bearable this time.

'I went to the rose garden at Alnwick yesterday,' she

said. 'It's really amazing. I've never seen so many roses in one place before.'

'That's nice,' her mum said. The usual shutdown. Except this time it didn't hurt as much. Being with Oliver had taught Gemma to look at things a little differently. He appreciated her for who she was—and maybe she didn't need to change her parents. Maybe it was time for her to face the fact that this was the best she was going to get. So instead of feeling miserable that they wouldn't—or couldn't—respond, she should see not having a fight with them as a win.

'I took some photos to show you,' she said brightly, and opened up the app in her phone. 'I nearly bought you a rose bush in the shop, but then I thought it might be nice to choose one together.'

'We'll see,' her father said.

Meaning no.

'OK. We'll put a date in the diary, have a nice afternoon together—with tea and scones—and then I'll buy you a rose bush. Or another plant, if you don't want to be bothered with roses,' she said.

Even though she didn't manage to pin them down to an actual date, they hadn't rejected her out of hand. This was progress, of sorts.

Better still, she had Oliver to go back to at the end of the day. Instead of feeling lonely and hopeless, the way she usually did after seeing her parents, she'd be spending the evening with someone who *did* want to spend time with her.

'How was your visit?' he asked.

'They actually looked at the photographs of Alnwick,' she said. 'And I got a smile.'

* * *

Ollie's heart ached for her. If he'd been in her shoes, he knew his parents would've wanted to spend as much time as they could with him, rather than push him away. 'A smile is good,' he said. But he rather thought she needed a hug, and held her close.

Taking her out for dinner would be the easy option; he wanted to make her feel special and cherished. So he'd do something for her instead of paying someone else to do it. 'How about I make us dinner? We could sit in the garden in the sun, with a glass of wine, and just chill.'

'That would be lovely. Can I help make dinner?'

He was about to say no, he wanted to spoil her, but then he realised: she'd said before that her parents stone-walled her. Right now, she needed to feel included. 'Sure. But I'll fine you a kiss for every time you get under my feet in my little galley kitchen,' he said, keeping it light.

'Challenge accepted. And I'll fine you two kisses for getting under my feet.' Her smile reached her eyes, this time, and he knew he'd said the right thing.

On Monday, they had a meeting with Caroline, the head of the practice, about the strength and balance classes for the elderly.

'It was Gemma's idea,' Oliver said. 'But I have friends whose practices have trialled something like this and they shared their stats with me. The cost-benefit analysis shows it'd be a good investment; the amount spent on the classes will be more than offset by the amount saved by not having to treat so many falls.'

'Plus there's the soft side of things: the effect it'll have on the community. I've spoken to Melanie at the gym,' Gemma said. 'She thinks it's a great idea and she's prepared to do the training to make sure she gets the right balance of exercises—um, I didn't actually intend that pun,' she said, when Oliver pulled a face at her. 'She has morning weekday slots available. She suggested a nominal fee for the first six weeks; and then reduced-price classes for people who wanted to continue.'

'You've really worked it out between you, haven't you?' Caroline asked. 'Much as I'd like to go with my heart rather than my head, we do need to look at it in the context of all our patients, because we have to allocate costs fairly. Let me read what you've put together, and I'll come back to you by Friday.'

On Friday, Caroline agreed to the plan.

Celebratory dinner tonight? Oliver suggested by text.

Gemma had been going to Claire's. She texted her best friend, asking if she could invite Oliver.

So I get to meet him properly? YES!

That was the immediate reply.

She texted Oliver.

I'm at Claire's for dinner. Come with me?

Would he think this was taking things too fast, meeting her best friend so soon?

Fortunately she had work to distract her—including a call with Mrs Brown, whose itchy rash had disappeared before the dermatology department could do a biopsy.

And then Oliver texted her back.

I'd love to. What are C's favourite flowers?

She almost sagged in relief.

You really don't have to take flowers, but gerberas.

Good. Let me know what time.

Meeting Gemma's best friend. That was a sign she was letting him a lot closer, Ollie thought. Which was a good thing.

At the same time, he felt faintly intimidated. He knew that Claire would assess him—just as Rob would assess Gemma, if Ollie let them meet each other. And he was pretty sure that the uppermost question in Claire's mind would be whether he'd be good for Gemma or if he'd hurt her.

He hoped he knew the answer, but all he could do was be himself.

After work, he bought a large bunch of zingy orange gerberas and a bottle of good red wine. He didn't have a clue what kind of gift to take a three-year-old, but Gemma had mentioned reading stories to her goddaughter, so he asked for a recommendation in the village bookshop and came out with a book he hoped Scarlett didn't already have.

From what Gemma had said, they'd arrive at just about bedtime for Scarlett, so she'd get a cuddle and a story.

Claire greeted them both with a hug. 'Nice to meet you properly, Oliver,' she said.

'And you,' he replied. 'Thank you for inviting me.' He handed over the gifts he'd brought.

'That's so sweet of you.' She beamed at him. 'And to think of Scarlett, too? Thank you so much. Come through and I'll get you a drink.'

In the living room, Gemma scooped up her god-daughter, who flung her arms round Gemma's neck, squealing, 'Aunty Gemma!'

'Oliver, this is Andy and Scarlett,' Gemma introduced him quickly. 'This is my friend Oliver.'

Andy nodded and smiled.

'Hello,' Scarlett said shyly.

'Oliver brought you something nice,' Claire said, and gave Scarlett the book.

'It's a story about a mermaid!' Scarlett said with a gasp of delight, looking at the front cover. 'Can we read it now, Aunty Gemma?'

Claire coughed. 'Words missing, Scarlett. What do you say to Oliver?'

'Thank you, Oliver,' the little girl said solemnly.

'My pleasure,' Oliver said.

'Come and read it with us,' Gemma said.

And somehow he found himself doing the voice of the shark, who became best friends with the mermaid.

It gave Ollie a jolt.

Sitting here with Gemma, a little girl cuddled between them, reading a story… It was lovely. Sweet, domesticated, and exactly what he'd hoped for when he'd been engaged to Tabby. He wanted to settle down. Have a family. Read stories, build sandcastles, maybe have a cat or dog.

Except he didn't know what Gemma wanted. Did she want to settle down and have a family? She'd spoken about offering a home for a troubled teen; what about babies?

It was too soon to discuss that. He'd known Gemma for a few weeks, and they'd barely started dating. What did she want from a partner? Would he be enough for her? He'd always thought of himself as grounded and sensible, but since Tabby had told him he wasn't enough for her it had made him doubt himself, wonder if instead he was staid and boring. And Gemma herself had said that her relationships tended to fizzle out. They'd agreed to see how things went between them. He really should stop thinking about the future and concentrate on the here and now.

But Ollie still felt as if he fitted here. Once Scarlett was in bed, asleep, and Claire had served the best lasagne he'd ever eaten, he found it easy to chat to Gemma's best friend and her husband, as if he'd known them for years.

Even when he insisted on helping clear up in the kitchen and Claire grilled him, he still felt comfortable.

'Just be careful with her,' Claire said quietly. 'She's not had a great time, the last few years.'

'You and your family made a difference, though,' he said, equally quietly.

'She told you?' Claire looked surprised.

He nodded. 'About Sarah, about her difficult year and about moving in with your family. I'm glad she had you all looking out for her.'

'I don't want to see her hurt again,' Claire said.

'I won't hurt her,' Ollie promised. 'I know she's special.'

Claire gave him a long, assessing gaze. 'I believe you. The question is, will she?'

It gave Ollie pause for thought, but he still found himself becoming closer to Gemma as the next week ticked past. And closer to Ashermouth Bay, too; in London, neighbours could pass you in the street without having a clue that you lived next door. Here, everyone knew everyone. When he went for his morning run, people would wave or call a greeting across the street. If he popped out to the shops, he'd bump into patients who'd stop for a chat, and not just about their health.

Ollie really liked being part of the community here. Being on the surgery's pub quiz team, joining in with all the jokes and good-natured teasing, being right in the middle of things. He was beginning to think that this was exactly where he belonged. And maybe he should think about staying here instead of going back to London.

On Tuesday morning, Ollie had a nervous patient. 'How can I help, Mrs Parker?' he asked.

'It's my little boy,' she said. 'Yesterday, nursery said James was a bit grumpy. This morning, he's covered in spots. I think he's got chickenpox.'

'I had heard there was an outbreak,' Oliver said. 'How old is James?'

'Three.'

'Chickenpox is usually pretty mild, at that age,' Oliver said, clearly trying to reassure her. 'Were they red spots, practically coming out as you looked at him?'

'Yes,' Penny said.

'In a day or so, they might start to blister and be itchy. He'll have a bit of a temperature, he might tell you he has a tummy ache, and he might be off his food,' Oliver said. 'Keep him at home until five days after the last spots have crusted over. Give him some paracetamol to bring his temperature down, try not to let him scratch the spots, and use calamine lotion to stop the itching.'

Penny bit her lip. 'It's not just James, though.' She smoothed a hand over her bump. 'It's this little one.'

'Would I be right in guessing that you didn't have chickenpox when you were young?' Oliver asked.

'When I was in primary school, there was an outbreak and Mum sent me to play with every single kid who had it,' Penny said. 'But I never got it. And the baby's due in a month. And I read...' Her voice sounded choked. 'If I get it, and the baby's early...'

'First of all, don't panic,' Oliver said. 'We can check your booking-in bloods and see if you've got any antibodies for chickenpox. If you have, panic over; if not, then we can give you some antiviral medicine. It might not stop you getting chickenpox, but it'll be much less severe and it will help to protect the baby as well.'

'Thank you.' Penny's smile was less wobbly now. 'I was so worried.'

'Of course you were,' Oliver said. 'But we can do a lot to help. Try not to look on the scary side. And definitely don't search things on the Internet, because that's where people like to outdo each other on the horror stories.'

'It's a bit late for that,' Penny said wryly. 'But thank you.'

When she'd gone, he rang the hospital and got them to run a test on Penny's booking-in bloods, explaining the situation and that he had a very anxious mum waiting for the results.

'You're looking twitchy,' Gemma said later that afternoon in the staff rest room. 'Too much coffee?' she teased.

'No. Waiting for test results. I had a worried mum in this morning; her baby's due in a month and her little one has gone down with chickenpox—which she hasn't had.'

'Penny Parker?' Gemma asked.

'Do you know her?'

'We were at school together. She's an absolute sweetheart,' Gemma said. 'So James has chickenpox? Scarlett is in his nursery class, so no doubt she'll be bringing a letter home to warn parents to look out for spots and a temperature.'

Thankfully, the results came in half an hour later, and Ollie was able to ring Penny and tell her that she was immune and didn't need to worry.

On Wednesday evening, Ollie was playing a board game with Gemma when his doorbell rang.

'Are you expecting visitors?' Gemma asked.

'No,' Ollie said, and frowned. 'I hope next door are OK. Jim was saying his knee was giving him a lot of trouble. I've been trying to persuade him to come in so I can examine him properly and maybe refer him for an X-ray.'

When he opened the door, he was surprised to see his twin on the doorstep. 'Rob! I didn't know you were coming over this evening.'

'I'm bored,' Rob said. 'Bored, bored, bored. And, just in case you didn't get the message, first time round, I'm—'

'Bored,' Ollie finished, smiling. 'Got it. Come in.'

'If Mum wraps any more cotton wool round me,

I'm going to start looking like a very out-of-season snowm— Oh. Hello.' Rob looked at Gemma, then at his twin. 'Sorry, Olls. I didn't realise you had company.'

'Rob, this is Gemma. My girlfriend.'

Gemma's eyes widened for a moment; but then she smiled, and it felt as if the world was full of sunshine.

'Gemma, this is my—'

'Older, and infinitely more charming twin brother,' Rob said with a smile. 'Robert Langley—Rob, to my friends. Lovely to meet you, Gemma.' He shook her hand, then glanced at the table. 'So who's winning?'

'Gemma is,' Ollie said. 'Go and make coffee, Rob.'

'I've got a better idea. *You* make the coffee, and I'll take your turn for you on the game,' Rob said.

Which clearly signalled his intention to grill her, Gemma thought. No doubt this was how Oliver had felt at Claire's. Well, all she could do was be herself and hope that Rob would like her.

'Olls showed me your skydive video,' Rob said when Oliver had gone into the kitchen. 'I'm impressed.'

'Coming from someone who does stuff for humanitarian organisations and is on a mountain rescue team, you shouldn't be,' Gemma said. 'What I did was only for a few minutes. You do it all the time.'

'Sadly, I won't be able to do the aid stuff in future, because of the kidney—I'm too much of a risk,' Rob said. 'So do you do a lot of this sort of thing for fundraising?'

'I'm sure Oliver's already told you—my little sister had myocarditis and she didn't get a transplant in time. I've been fundraising for the local hospital ever since

I qualified and came back here to work. They're doing research into permanent artificial hearts.'

'Which would be a huge game-changer,' Rob said. 'Is it too late to sponsor you for your skydive?'

'Yes, but I do a cake stall at the surgery on Fridays.'

'Cake? Excellent. Make Olls buy some for me. He hates cake, but I don't,' Rob said.

She smiled. 'I will. Let me know your favourite sort, and I'll make it for this Friday.'

'Anything with chocolate,' Rob said. 'So what else are you planning?'

'I do two big events a year. The skydive had to be postponed so the next one's a bit close—I'm doing a sixty-mile cycle ride down the coast next month,' she said, 'and then after that I'm considering doing a swimming challenge, though I'm planning to swim in the pool at the gym rather than the actual English Channel.'

'Good idea, because then you don't have to wait a couple of years for a slot and then hope that the weather conditions will work out,' Rob said. 'Given the cliffs I've seen along here, I assume you've done climbing or abseiling?'

She shook her head. 'Not for me. Too scary. I'd rather walk along the top of the cliffs and enjoy the view in safety.'

'Or along the beach and rescue a drowning teenager,' Rob said.

Oliver had told his brother about that? She flapped a dismissive hand. 'Everyone around here does their school lifesaving stuff in the sea. Anyone else would've done the same thing.'

'But you're the one who actually went in to get him,' Rob said softly.

'Oliver wanted to, but I didn't want him overexerting himself. I know technically he's allowed to swim in the sea again, but there's a big difference between casual swimming and towing someone in. Plus we needed someone to get in touch with the emergency services. It was a team effort.'

'Uh-huh.' But Rob's smile held approval. 'Olls says there are all kinds of things here. Kite-surfing—'

'No, no and no. Be more me,' Oliver said, coming back into the room. 'Your consultant would have kittens if he could hear you.'

'I know,' Rob said mildly. 'He's given me the green light to go back to work part time. Mum's panicking. But I'm going to be sensible. I told her about that bargain we made: I'm going to be more Ollie and you're going to be more Rob.'

'Me being the sensible one, and Rob being the—'

'Almost sensible one,' Rob cut in with a grin.

The bickering, Gemma could see, was purely for show; the way Oliver and Rob looked at each other told her how much they loved each other.

She thoroughly enjoyed playing the board game with Oliver and his brother; despite the physical distance between them over the last few years, they were clearly very close and talked to each other a lot. The same kind of relationship she would've had with Sarah, she thought wistfully. Love and acceptance of each other, flaws and all.

'I like her, Olls,' Rob said when Gemma left at the end of the evening. 'A lot. She's the complete opposite of Tabby. And she's perfect for you.'

'It's early days,' Ollie said. 'And I'm only here temporarily.'

'Don't overthink things,' Rob advised. 'You still haven't decided whether you're going back to London or somewhere else. Stick around for a bit. See how it goes.'

Ollie wanted to. But he still couldn't quite shake himself of the fear. Would he be enough for Gemma, the way he hadn't been for Tabby? Or was he setting himself up for heartache again?

Two days later, Penny rang Gemma. 'Gem, I'm so sorry to do this—Mum's away or I'd call her. I don't know what else to do. It's Gran.'

Gemma knew that Penny's grandmother was staying for a few days while her bathroom was being refitted. 'What's happened?'

'She's got a really high temperature.' Penny dragged in a breath. 'I don't know if it's flu, or something else.'

The spectre of Covid, Gemma thought, which could be deadly in older patients.

'I'm so sorry. I just don't know what to do. I can't leave James, and—'

'I'm on my way,' Gemma said. 'I'm your friend. And friends help each other. See you in a minute.'

She filled Oliver in.

'The pizza's not coming to any harm in the fridge,' Oliver said. 'I'll turn the oven off now. Let's go. We'll take my bag with us. And my car,' he added.

Penny greeted them with relief at her front door.

'Run us through your gran's symptoms,' Oliver said.

'Her temperature's thirty-nine, she's got a headache, she's been coughing and says it's hard to breathe, and she's tired and she doesn't want to eat.' Penny bit her lip.

'There are plenty of viruses that do exactly the same thing, including summer flu,' Oliver said. 'Try not to worry.'

'Has she mentioned any loss of smell or taste?' Gemma asked.

Penny shook her head.

'That's a good thing,' Oliver said. 'Let's go and see her.'

Penny introduced Oliver and Gemma to her grandmother, and Oliver listened to the elderly woman's chest while Gemma checked her pulse. Mrs Bailey was coughing, and admitted that it hurt more when she breathed in.

'Crackles,' Oliver said to Gemma quietly. 'How's her pulse?'

'Fast. I'm thinking pneumonia,' Gemma said.

'I agree,' Oliver said. 'Mrs Bailey, we think you have pneumonia. You need antibiotics, but the surgery isn't open at this time of night so I can't prescribe them. We need to get you to hospital.'

'But how did Gran get pneumonia?' Penny asked, looking distraught.

'Lots of things cause pneumonia. Have you ever had chickenpox, Mrs Bailey?' Oliver asked gently.

'Not that I remember. Anyway, I don't have any spots.'

'Chickenpox doesn't always cover you completely with spots; sometimes there might only be one or two little ones,' Gemma said.

'And James has chickenpox. I'll drive you to hospital, Gran,' Penny said.

'You're eight months pregnant and you're worried

sick. I'll drive,' Oliver said. 'I'll call the emergency department to let them know we're coming.'

Penny shook her head. 'I can't ask you to do that—and, if Gran's got chickenpox, what if you get it from her?'

'I won't. My brother and I both had it when we were six,' Oliver said. 'And I remember because it was Christmas and it snowed, and we couldn't go out to make a snowman.'

'If you want to go with Oliver and your gran, Penny,' Gemma said, 'I'll stay here and keep an eye on James.'

Penny's bottom lip wobbled. 'Gem. I don't know how to thank you.'

'Hey. You were there for me when I needed a friend. James will be fine with me,' Gemma said, giving her a hug.

'He's asleep right now,' Penny said.

'If he wakes up, I'll give him a cuddle and read him a story until he goes back to sleep,' Gemma promised.

'You're one of the best,' Penny said. 'Both of you are.'

'Let's get your gran comfortable in my car,' Oliver said.

At the hospital, Florence Jacobs, the registrar on duty, examined Penny's gran and admitted her to a ward. 'It's a precaution,' she said to Penny. 'Pneumonia can be a bit nasty. I'd rather have your gran here so we can monitor her for a couple of days and make sure the antibiotics are working. You can come back in and see her tomorrow, and bring anything you want to make her a bit more comfortable.'

'But—what about her nightie, and her things?'

'Call Gemma and ask her to pack a bag,' Oliver said. 'I'll bring it back here when I drop you home.'

'I can't ask—'

'You're not asking. I'm offering,' he said gently.

'I've ruined your evening with Gemma.'

'It's fine,' he said with a smile. 'Everyone needs a friend to lean on from time to time. Call Gemma.'

'You're so lovely,' she said.

Oli-lovely-ver. He could hear Gemma's voice in his head, and it made him smile. 'My pleasure.' It was good to feel part of a community. Part of Gemma's community. And Oliver found himself wondering what the chances were of Aadya deciding to take a little more maternity leave so he could stay a bit longer. He liked working in Ashermouth Bay, and he liked being with Gemma. More than liked.

And, even though Ollie still didn't trust his own judgement, after Tabby, Rob liked her.

Maybe he and Gemma could be good for each other.

Maybe she was the one he ought to let close.

And maybe, just maybe, he'd be the one that she finally let close, too...

CHAPTER NINE

THE FOLLOWING SATURDAY AFTERNOON, Yvonne was running a workshop and Gemma was helping out. But Ollie had managed to get tickets to see a band he really liked and had talked Gemma into going with him. They grabbed some burritos before the show, and were in the queue early enough to be at the front.

'Are you sure about this?' she asked. 'What if someone knocks into you?'

He could guess what she was worried about: his scar. 'I'm fine,' he said. 'Really.' He stole a kiss. 'But I appreciate the concern.'

During the show, he stood behind Gemma with his arms wrapped round her. It was good to hold her close. And on an evening like this: it was perfect, with the buzz of the crowd and the sheer joy of being there seeing a band he'd liked for years. Gemma knew some of their hits and sang along with everyone else, and Ollie didn't care that neither of them was singing in tune. This was just great. Especially as she was leaning back against him to be even closer.

'That was fantastic,' she said, as they walked back to his car with their arms wrapped round each other.

'It's been a while since I've been to a show,' he said.

'I guess in London you have a lot more choice,' she said.

'There's a lot of good music here, too,' he said.

When he'd driven her home, she asked him in for coffee.

And he spent so long kissing her in her kitchen that they completely forgot about the kettle.

'Um. Sorry,' he said, when he finally broke the kiss.

'I'm not.' She stroked his face. 'Stay tonight?'

His heart skipped a beat. 'Are you asking…?'

She blushed, making her look even prettier. 'Yes.'

He stole another kiss. 'Then yes. Please.'

'Mind you, I've got to be up early to do the cycling training,' she warned.

'I would offer to do it with you,' he said, 'except I don't have a bike and, even if I borrowed one, I'm not used to cycling long-distance so I'd hold you back.'

'Fair comment,' she said.

'But is there something else I could do to support you?'

'We could do with another race medic,' she said. 'But that's a bit of an ask.'

'The event's important to you,' he said, 'so I'll support you. Sign me up and let me know the details.'

'Really?'

'Really.' He held her gaze. 'And tomorrow maybe I could meet you at the end of your ride and take you for lunch.'

'I'm going to be hideously sweaty,' she said. 'Not fit to go out.'

'In that case, how about I cook you a late Sunday lunch here, with proper crispy roast potatoes?' he suggested.

'That,' she said, 'would be perfect.' She kissed him.

Then she took his hand. 'It's been a while since I've done this.'

'Me, too,' he said.

'There's a bit of me that's…well, scared,' she admitted.

He stroked her face. 'I won't hurt you,' he promised. 'We don't have to do anything. I can just sleep with you in my arms, if you want. Or I can go home on my own, if you decide you're not ready for this.'

'Oli-lovely-ver,' she said. 'I trust you. And I—I want to make love with you.'

'Good,' he said.

'Do you—' she blushed even harder '—have any condoms?'

'Yes,' he said.

'Then come to bed with me, Oliver,' she said.

He kissed her, and let her lead him to her bedroom.

Gemma woke in the middle of the night, her head cradled on Oliver's shoulder and her arm wrapped round his waist. Closing her eyes, she listened to his deep, regular breathing.

Oliver had been a generous lover. Even though the first time they'd made love should've been awkward and a bit rubbish, it hadn't been. It had felt like—like coming home, she thought. The first time it had ever felt this good, this right.

Maybe this time she'd made the right choice. Maybe this time she'd found someone worth being close to.

Finally, she drifted off to sleep.

When her alarm shrilled the next morning, she leaned over to the bedside table to switch it off. Oliver nuzzled the back of her neck. 'Good morning.'

She turned back to face him and smiled. 'Good morning.' The morning after the night before, she'd half expected to feel shy with him; but instead she just felt happy. As if everything was in its right place.

'I'll get up and head for home so you can get ready for your training,' he said. 'See you for lunch.'

'I look forward to it,' she said. 'What can I bring?'

'Just yourself.' He kissed her again. 'Enjoy your training. Come over whenever you're ready. I plan to do lunch for two o'clock, but let me know if you need it to be later.'

'It sounds perfect. Thank you.'

Once he was back home, Ollie downed a protein shake, changed into his running gear, and went for a run along the sea.

The sun was shining, the sky was the perfect shimmery blue of summer, and life felt good. He couldn't remember the last time he'd felt this happy; and he knew it was all because of Gemma.

He'd finished setting the bistro table in the garden when his phone pinged.

See you in ten minutes.

She was as good as her word, too, not keeping him waiting; and when he opened the door she greeted him with a kiss and handed him a brown paper bag.

'What's this?'

'Host gift. I did consider flowers,' she said, 'but I don't get gardener vibes from you. So I thought you might like these.'

He looked in the bag to discover locally roasted

coffee—beans, rather than ground, in deference to his coffee machine—and locally made chutney. 'Thank you. That's lovely. Lunch will be another twenty minutes, so shall I make us coffee and we can sit in the garden?'

She kissed him again. 'That'd be lovely. And something smells gorgeous.'

Gemma, he thought, appreciated him. She paid attention and she'd noticed what he liked.

So maybe this time he'd got it right. And it filled him with joy.

It was a busy week at the practice; Penny's grandmother recovered from her pneumonia, quite a few more of the children in the village came down with chickenpox, and Ollie found himself treating sprains and strains from tourists who'd overdone sporting activities on holiday as well as gardeners who'd wanted to make the most of the good weather. Every day he felt that he was getting to know the people in the village a little more, and really making a difference at the practice. And every night, he and Gemma made love, and it made him feel as if the barriers he'd put round his heart were melting away.

Until Thursday evening, when Gemma was doing something with Claire and he was catching up with some journals, and his phone rang.

He glanced at the screen and felt a flush of guilt as he saw the name of one of his colleagues at the practice in London. 'Hey, Mandy,' he said. 'Sorry, I've been a bit hopeless about staying in touch.'

'It's fine. We know you've had a lot on your plate, with Rob and the transplant.'

'So what can I do for you? Did you and Tristan fancy

coming up for a weekend? You'd love the beaches here. You can walk for miles.'

'It's not that,' she said. She took a deep breath. 'I just thought it might be better if you heard the news from someone you know, rather than come across it on social media and what have you.'

Ollie had pretty much ignored social media since he'd been in Northumbria. 'What news?'

'Tabby. She's, um, engaged.'

Tabby. Engaged. To someone else.

He blew out a breath. 'Right.'

'I'm sorry, Ollie. I know you loved her.'

But she hadn't loved him. At least, not enough to marry him. And it had hurt so much when she'd told him. It had taken him months to get over the misery of knowing that he wasn't what she wanted: that he'd got it so wrong. 'I hope she's found someone who can make her happy,' he said, meaning it.

'Are you OK, Ollie?' Mandy asked.

'I'm fine,' he reassured her, even though he was still processing the news. 'And Rob's doing well. He's got a part-time post in the Emergency Department at the hospital near here, to keep him out of mischief for a while.'

'That's good.'

He managed to keep the conversation going for a bit, and extracted a promise that she and Tristan would try to find a spare weekend to come up and visit.

But when he put the phone down, he had time to think about it. Time to brood.

Tabby was engaged to someone else.

It was a good thing that she'd moved on; but the news brought back all his insecurities. Engaged. To be engaged again this soon, Tabby must've started dating the guy within days of calling off the wedding. Which just went to prove that he really, really hadn't been enough for her.

So was he kidding himself that he was enough for Gemma?

Yes, she'd let Ollie close to her; but was he setting himself up for another failure?

The more he thought about it, the more he convinced himself that he was making a huge mistake. His job here was temporary and his contract ended in a couple of weeks' time—as did his sabbatical from his practice in London. He was perfectly fit again after donating a kidney. Which meant that he really ought to think about going back to London.

But that wasn't fair to Gemma, either. He knew how much she loved it here. He couldn't expect her to leave the place where she'd grown up and go back to London with him.

So he was going to have to find a way of letting her down gently.

The question was—how?

Something was wrong, Gemma was sure.

Oliver had suddenly gone distant on her. Too busy for lunch on Friday, she could accept, because she knew how busy they were at work. Suggesting that she have a girly night with Claire and little Scarlett on Friday evening was Oliver being nice. But when he was too busy to see her on Saturday, and went to see his family on Sunday—without asking her to join him and meet his parents as well as seeing his brother again—she started to wonder if she was missing something.

Had Oliver changed his mind about being with her?

His contract at the surgery was due to end in a couple of weeks, when Aadya was coming back from maternity leave. What then? Would he go back to London? Move elsewhere?

She had no idea. But the one thing she was pretty sure about was that, whatever Oliver decided to do, he wouldn't ask her to go with him.

She texted him on Sunday evening.

Everything OK?

It took a while for him to text her back, but it was cool and polite and told her nothing.

Yes, thanks.

What now?

She could be pathetic and wait for him to dump her, the way she'd been at seventeen.

Or she could take control. Be the one who ended it.

When Oliver made excuses not to see her on Monday, that decided her.

She texted him.

Can I call in for a quick word on the way back from the gym tomorrow?

He took so long replying that she thought he was going to say no. But finally she got the answer she wanted.

Sure.

No suggestion of dinner or a drink.

OK. She'd take the hint. And no way was she going to let him do the 'it's not you, it's me' line. She'd been there and done that way too often.

She showered and changed at the gym after her class, then cycled over to Oliver's cottage and rang the bell.

When he opened the door, he didn't smile or kiss her, the way he had last week.

It was as if they'd stepped into some parallel universe. One where they'd never made love, never kissed, weren't even friends.

And this really felt like the rejections from her teens. The boys who'd ghosted her or who'd ignored her, once they'd got what they wanted.

Clearly she hadn't learned from her mistakes.

And how stupid she'd been to think that they were getting closer. Obviously for Oliver it had been just sex.

'Would you like some coffee?' he asked.

But she could see from his face that he was being polite.

She wasn't going to let herself be needy enough to accept. 'No, thanks,' she said. 'This won't take long. I've been thinking...we took things a bit too fast.'

His expression was completely inscrutable. He merely inclined his head.

And this was excruciating, making her realise how stupid she'd been.

'I think,' she said carefully, 'we should go back to being just colleagues.' She couldn't quite stretch it to friendship. Not when he was going to be leaving anyway.

'You're right,' he said.

'Good.' Though there was one last little thing. 'I understand if you've changed your mind about helping at the cycle race.'

He shook his head. 'I promised I'd help. It isn't fair to let you down at the last minute.'

It wasn't fair to let her down, full stop. To let her close and then freeze her out. Then again, she was as much to blame. She'd obviously tried so hard not to freeze him out that she'd been too needy. No wonder he'd backed away. 'As you wish,' she said. 'Though I think we should travel separately.'

'Of course,' he said.

'Right. Well, see you at the surgery,' she said brightly, and wheeled her bicycle round so he wouldn't see even the tiniest trace of hurt in her face.

We should go back to being just colleagues.

Not even friends. Just two people who worked together.

The words echoed in Ollie's head. Although part of him knew he was being unfair—he'd pushed her away ever since he'd heard the news about Tabby's engagement—part of him felt as if she'd stomped on a bruise. He hadn't been enough for Tabby, and he clearly hadn't been enough for Gemma, either, otherwise she would've fought for him. Or maybe it was his fault for messing it up in the first place. Backing away from her instead of telling her what was going on in his head. No wonder she'd dumped him.

But he was only here for another couple of weeks, so it shouldn't matter. He could keep up the facade until his contract ended.

Though lunch without her felt lonely; and he was

really aware now of how echoey the little cottage was. How quiet, without Gemma chattering and laughing and teasing him.

Somehow he got through the weekend.

And then, the following Wednesday, Caroline asked to see him.

Was she going to ask him to leave the practice early, to get rid of any tension in the staff room?

To his shock, it was the opposite. 'Aadya wants to come back part-time,' she said. 'And I think we have enough work to justify another full-time GP. You've fitted into the practice really well.'

If only she knew.

'So I'd like to give you first refusal of the new post,' Caroline said.

The answer was obvious. For Gemma's sake, he'd have to say no.

As if she'd anticipated his refusal, Caroline said, 'I know you'd need to sort things out with your practice in London, and I'd be happy to accommodate that. So don't give me an answer now. Think it over for a week.'

'Thank you. I will,' he said, giving her his best and brightest smile.

Stay at Ashermouth Bay.

If Caroline had asked him this a week or so ago, Ollie knew he would've jumped at the chance.

But that was before he'd learned that Tabby was engaged again. Before he'd realised that he was fooling himself if he thought he'd be enough for anyone. Before he'd pushed Gemma away.

The answer would be no. It couldn't be anything else. But he'd be courteous about it and do what Caroline asked, waiting until next week to give her an answer.

And then he'd leave.
Go back to London.
And pretend he'd never met Gemma Baxter.

CHAPTER TEN

THE DAY BEFORE Gemma was due to do the sponsored cycle ride, Ollie had just bought a pint of milk from the village shop when he bumped into her.

'Oliver,' she said, and gave him a cool nod.

But her face was blotchy and he thought she'd been crying. Even though he knew it was none of his business and he should leave it, he couldn't help asking, 'Are you all right?'

'Fine, thank you.'

Cool, calm—and a complete fib. 'You're not all right,' he said softly. 'What's happened?'

She swallowed hard. 'It's Sarah's birthday. I'm trying to celebrate the day. But...'

'It's hard,' he finished. And, even though he knew he wasn't enough for her, he couldn't just leave her like this, clearly heartbroken and trying to be brave. 'Do you want me to come with you to the churchyard, for company?'

She shook her head. 'I can't go today.'

He frowned. 'Why not?'

'Because... Never mind.'

That didn't sound good. At all. 'In that case, I'm making you coffee. No arguments. It's what any—'

he chose his words carefully '—colleague would do for another.'

He shepherded her back to his cottage; she sat at the kitchen table in total silence while he made coffee. This really wasn't like Gemma; she was usually bright and bubbly and chatty.

'So why can't you visit your sister today?' he asked.

'Because our parents are visiting her.'

What? 'Surely they'd want to be with you, too?'

Gemma wouldn't meet his eyes. 'It's difficult. Her birthday, her anniversary—those days seem to bring all the misery of her dying back to them, and they can't handle seeing me as well. It kind of feels as if they still blame me for having the virus in the first place, though I'm probably being paranoid. And then they remember how I went off the rails and made everything worse for them, and…' She shook her head. 'It's just easier to give them space today.'

Oliver went to put his arms round her, but she leaned away. 'Don't. I can't… Not now.'

He wasn't entirely sure whether she was rejecting him or rejecting everyone. Hadn't she said to him that she was hopeless at relationships? And he'd frozen her out because his self-doubts had got in the way.

'Sorry. I'm not good company. I'd rather be on my own right now. Thanks for trying. Sorry to waste your coffee.'

And she left before he could find the right words to stop her.

Oliver thought about it for the rest of the morning.

He might not be able to offer Gemma a future, but he could do something to make her life a bit better. Maybe.

He headed for the bakery to see Claire.

'I'm a bit busy,' she said coolly, and he knew he deserved the brush-off.

'It's about Gemma,' he said. 'It's Sarah's birthday today.'

'Yes. She's coming over tonight for fajitas and board games, to take her mind off it.' Claire frowned. 'Is that why you're here? You want to come, too? But I thought you and Gemma had…'

'Split up? Yes. It's my fault. You can yell at me some other time, but right now is all about Gemma and her parents.'

Claire rolled her eyes. 'Don't talk to me about *them*. I mean, I'm a mum myself now, so I kind of get how hard it must've been for them when Sarah died, but I hate the way…' She stopped. 'Never mind.'

'You hate the way they just abandoned Gemma after Sarah died. And you don't get why they're not wrapping her in cotton wool because she's the only child they have left,' he guessed.

'She told you?' Claire looked shocked. 'Well, that's a good thing. I'm glad she's talking about it. But you're right. I wish her parents…' She grimaced. 'Mum's tried. I've tried. They're just cocooned in their grief and they can't see what they still have.'

'Maybe they need someone who didn't know Sarah to make them see things differently,' Ollie said. 'Like me.'

Claire frowned. 'Why would you do that?'

'Because I care about Gemma.'

'Even though you broke up with her?'

'Claire, as I said, you can yell at me about this another time,' he said, 'but I really need to know where Gemma's parents live.'

Her eyes widened. 'You're going to tackle them *today*?'

'It's probably too much, on Sarah's birthday. I was thinking tomorrow morning,' he said.

'But you can't. It's the race tomorrow. You promised Gem you'd be a race medic.'

'Exactly.' Oliver enlightened Claire about his plan.

'If this goes wrong,' Claire warned, 'Gemma's going to get hurt.'

'She's already hurt. If her parents refuse to listen to me and continue to stay away, what's changed?'

'I guess.' She sighed. 'I have huge reservations about this, and I really don't think you're going to get anywhere with them. But I suppose at least you're trying, for Gemma's sake.' She gave him the address.

'Thank you,' he said.

For the next part of his plan, Ollie rang Rob. 'I need to call in a favour for tomorrow,' he said.

'What kind of favour?' Rob asked.

'I need you to pretend to be me, and be a medic for a sixty-mile sponsored cycle race.'

Rob sounded puzzled. 'Why aren't you going to be there?'

'There's something that needs fixing,' Ollie said. 'I need to do it tomorrow, but I also need to be a race medic. The only way you can be in two places at the same time—or at least seem to be—is if you have an identical twin. Which is why I need your help.'

'Does Gemma know about this?'

'No.'

'Olls, I can't pretend to be her partner.'

'You don't have to. I'm not her partner any more.'

'What? But she's *lovely*, Olls. Why? What happened?'

'I'm not enough for her, just as I wasn't enough for Tabby.' Though Ollie knew he had to be honest. 'I pushed her away. Yes, I'm an idiot and I regret it, but it's too late.'

'Olls—'

'No, it's OK,' he said. 'This isn't about me. It's about her.'

'So what's this fixing you have to do?' Rob asked. Ollie explained.

'And you're doing this why, exactly?'

'Because it's something I think I can fix for Gemma.'

'You're in love with her, aren't you?'

'I'm not answering that.'

'You don't have to. I *know*,' Rob said. 'All right. I'll help you. But only on condition you actually talk to her and tell her how you really feel about her.'

'There's no point. I'm not enough for her.'

'Did she actually say that?' Rob asked. 'You said yourself, you pushed her away. Stop being an idiot and talk to her. She can't guess what's in your head.'

'I need your help, Rob.'

'Of course I'm going to help you. I owe you everything,' Rob said softly. 'Without you I'd still be on dialysis, waiting for a kidney that might not come in time. But it's precisely because I owe you that I don't want you to mess this up. Promise me you'll talk to her.'

Ollie sighed. 'All right. I promise.'

CHAPTER ELEVEN

ON THE MORNING of the cycle ride, Gemma felt drained, but she'd be letting people down if she didn't do the race. She drove to the village where the starting point was and got her bike out of the back. She couldn't see Oliver's car anywhere, but when she went to register she saw him by the race marshals' tent.

Except it wasn't Oliver.

Even though Rob had let his hair grow out so they really did look identical, Gemma could tell the difference between them. Seeing him didn't feel the same as when she saw Oliver.

So it seemed as if Oliver had sent his twin to be here in his place.

Which just proved he didn't want to be with her and he was going back to London. Why had he even bothered talking to her and being sympathetic yesterday?

It wasn't Rob's fault, so she wasn't going to take it out on him. She went over to him and smiled. 'Thank you for the support, Rob,' she said.

His eyes widened. 'But I'm Oliver.'

She just looked at him, and he sighed. 'We're identical. I even did my hair like Olls does, and I'm wearing his clothes, not mine. How did you know?'

'I just do. Thank you for—well, doing what he clearly didn't want to do.'

'Gemma, we need to—'

'No, we don't need to talk,' she cut in softly. 'But I appreciate you turning up. And I have a race to cycle.'

'Good luck,' he said.

Ollie's doubts grew as he drove to the village where Gemma's parents lived.

What if they weren't there?

What if they were, but refused to talk to him?

Well, he'd just have to persuade them to listen.

When he rang the doorbell, her mum answered. 'Sorry, I don't buy things at the door.'

'I'm not selling anything, Mrs Baxter.'

She frowned. 'How do you know my name? I've never seen you before in my life.'

'My name's Oliver Langley. I work with Gemma,' he said. 'May I come in? Please? All I'm asking is for ten minutes of your time.'

'Ten minutes?' She looked confused.

'For Sarah's sake,' he said softly.

She flinched, but then she nodded. 'Come in.'

She didn't offer him a drink, but she did at least invite him to sit down.

'Firstly,' he said, 'I'd like to say how sorry I am about Sarah. I didn't know her—but my brother had a burst appendix and severe blood poisoning earlier this year, which wiped out his kidneys. So I know how it feels to worry about my brother being on dialysis, and whether my kidney would be suitable for him. Whether it might go wrong and we'd lose him.'

'Twelve years.' A tear trickled down Mrs Baxter's

cheek. 'Twelve birthdays we haven't spent with our little girl.'

'And that's hard,' Ollie said. 'I know how desperately
I would've missed Rob.' And now was his chance to tell
them. 'I'm a doctor. I work with Gemma at Ashermouth
Bay surgery. I know how much she misses her sister.
How much she misses *you*.'

Neither of Gemma's parents responded.

'I know it's difficult,' he said gently. 'Every time
you look at Gemma, you see Sarah in her. Of course
you do. They're sisters. If we'd lost Rob, my parents
would've found it really hard seeing me, because Rob's
my identical twin.'

That made her parents look at him.

'I would've found it hard to see them, too, because I'd
see him in their smiles and little mannerisms. But,' he
said, 'it would've been a lot harder *not* to see them. Cut-
ting myself off from them might've worked in the short
term, but in the long term we'd all have missed out on
so much.' He paused. 'You're missing out on Gemma.'

'I don't think there's anything more to say, Dr Langley,' Mr Baxter said.

'You said you'd give me ten minutes,' Oliver reminded them.

'Gemma doesn't need us,' Mrs Baxter said.

'Oh, but she does,' he said. 'She might look as if she's
moved on with her life and she's completely together,
but she's not. She went off the rails, the year Sarah died.'

Both her parents flinched.

'I'm not judging you,' he said. 'We nearly lost Rob,
and I know how bad that felt. How much worse it must
have been to lose your thirteen-year-old daughter—way,
way too young. But Gemma still needs you. Both of

you. She's a qualified nurse practitioner and she looks as if she's totally together and getting on with her life. But she's not. She spends nearly all her spare time raising money for the local cardiac ward, the one that treated Sarah. She pushes herself outside her comfort zone, trying to help so another family won't have to go through what you all went through. And she's amazing. She did a skydive last month. Next month, she's going to start swimming the equivalent of the English Channel.

'Right now, she's doing a sixty-mile cycle ride.' He paused. 'And you know what would make the difference to her? If you were there to meet her at the end of the race.'

'We can't,' Gemma's mother said. 'It's too late. We don't...' She shook her head.

'She's never going to give up on you,' he said. 'I know she comes to see you once a month and she'll keep doing that. Even though you reject her over and over and over again, she'll still keep trying. You lost Sarah, but you still have one daughter left. She's not giving up on you. Don't give up on her.'

'She was—difficult, after Sarah died. We couldn't cope with her behaviour,' Mrs Baxter said.

'She told me. But she's past that, now. She's a daughter you can be proud of,' Oliver said. 'She works so hard. And she's amazing.'

'Why are you here?' Mr Baxter asked.

'Because I care about Gemma. I can't bring Sarah back, but I can at least try to help Gemma mend the rift with you.'

'Does she know you're here?' Mrs Baxter asked.

'No,' Oliver said. 'I'm actually supposed to be supporting the race, being one of the medics.'

'Then why are you here?' Mrs Baxter asked.

'Because I wanted to talk to you. My twin brother agreed to pretend to be me,' Oliver said. 'So I haven't totally let her down. She's still got a race medic. Though I am going to have to apologise later for not telling her the entire truth.'

'What do you want from us?' Mr Baxter asked.

Had he really not been clear enough? 'I want,' Oliver said, 'you to see Gemma as she really is. I want you to be there when she cycles past the finish line. I want her to see you clapping.'

'You want us to go there for the end of the race,' Mrs Baxter said.

'I know it won't be easy for you,' he said. 'That it'll take time to mend things properly. But, if you take this first step, she'll come to meet you with open arms. And I'm happy to drive you there myself.'

'I don't know if we can. It's too hard,' Mr Baxter said.

Oliver wanted to bang their heads together and yell at them to stop being so selfish, but he knew it would be pointless. And now he really understood why Gemma had spent that year desperately searching for love—and why she hadn't let people close since, not wanting to be let down again.

And he was just as bad, he realised with a flush of guilt. He'd hurt her as much as her parents had, doing exactly the same thing: pushing her away.

'OK. Thank you for your time,' he said. 'If you change your mind, I think she'll be over the line at about two o'clock.' He took a notepad from his jacket pocket and scribbled down the address. 'This is where the finish line is. This is my phone number, if you want to talk to me. And this—if you want to go on the internet and see her jumping out of a plane for Sarah.

'Your brave, brilliant daughter. The one who's still here and needs her family. The whole village is proud of her—but that's not enough. She needs *you*.' He checked his phone and copied down the link to the video of her skydive, then handed over the paper to Mrs Baxter. 'I'll see myself out,' he said quietly.

He didn't think they'd turn up today. But maybe, just maybe, they'd think about what he'd said. And maybe they'd thaw towards Gemma in the future.

He could only hope.

A mile before the end of the race, Gemma saw the cyclist in front of her wobble precariously, and then almost as if it was in slow motion the bike lurched to the side and the rider hit the ground.

Gemma stopped immediately.

The cyclist was still on the ground.

Another cyclist stopped, too.

'Are you all right?' Gemma asked.

'I can't get up,' the woman said. 'My arm hurts.'

Between them, Gemma and the other cyclist who'd stopped to help lifted the bike off her.

Gemma really wished Oliver was there with her; but he'd sent his brother in his stead, because he didn't even want to be with her today.

She pushed the thought away. Right now, this wasn't about her; it was about helping this poor woman.

They helped her get to her feet; her left shoulder looked slumped and slightly forward, sending up a red flag for Gemma.

'I'm a nurse practitioner,' Gemma said. 'Can I have a look at your shoulder while we call the race medic?'

'I don't want the race medics. If they come, they won't let me finish and I have to do this.' There were tears in the woman's eyes. 'I lost my husband to leukaemia six months ago. I need to finish this for him. I have loads of sponsorship.'

'OK,' Gemma said. 'But at least let me make you comfortable. You look in pain.'

'It hurts,' the woman admitted, 'but I'm not giving in.'

'Shall I call…?' the other cyclist asked.

'No. Because if I'm right and she's broken her collarbone, we'll walk this last mile and I'll wheel both cycles,' Gemma said.

'I can't ask you to do that,' the woman said.

'You're not asking, I'm offering,' Gemma said, 'because it's important to you to finish and this is the only way it's going to happen. I'm Gemma, by the way.'

'I'm Heather.'

They both looked at the cyclist who'd stopped.

'I'm Paul,' he said.

'Paul, thank you for stopping to help,' Gemma said. 'Can I get you to tell the medics we're on our way, when you've finished the race? But make it clear that Heather's going nowhere in an ambulance until she's gone over the finishing line.'

'Of course I'll tell them. But I'm not leaving you both to walk in on your own—you're too vulnerable. I'll walk behind you with my rear light flashing,' he said, 'to make sure nobody crashes into you. And I'll call the race organisers to tell them what we're doing.'

'That's so kind,' Heather said, tears filming her eyes.

'You're one in a million,' Gemma said. 'Let's have a look at you, Heather.' She gently lowered the neck of Heather's cycling top and examined her clavicle, noting that swelling had already started. 'Is it tender here?'

'Yes,' Heather said through gritted teeth.

'I've got a bandage and some painkillers in my bag,' Gemma said. 'I think you've broken your collarbone. It's going to get more painful—and you definitely need to go to hospital for an X-ray to check how bad the break is and whether you're going to need pins—but for now I can make you a sling to support your arm and give you some painkillers. Are you on any medication, or is there any reason why you can't have paracetamol?'

'No and no,' Heather said.

'Good. Paul, can you let them know we'll need an ambulance? Tell them it's a fractured left clavicle and she'll need an X-ray,' Gemma said.

Paul quickly phoned the race organisers to let them know what was happening, and Gemma took the medicine kit from her bike, gave Heather painkillers and strapped up Heather's arm to stabilise it. 'Now, you need to move that arm as little as possible or you could risk doing serious damage,' she warned. 'The deal is, you walk beside me and I'll wheel our bikes. It's only about another mile. Fifteen to twenty minutes and we'll be there.'

'Thank you both so much,' Heather said.

The three of them started to walk along the road, with other cyclists sailing past them.

'So why are you doing the cycle ride, Gemma?' Heather asked.

'For my little sister. She needed a heart transplant but a suitable heart couldn't be found in time,' Gemma said.

'That's hard,' Heather said. 'Was she very young?'

'Thirteen, and I was seventeen,' Gemma said. 'I'm nearly thirty now; but I still miss her.' She swallowed hard. 'It was her birthday yesterday.'

'She'll know. Just as Mike knows I'm doing this. I'm such a klutz. Trust me to fall off and break my collarbone. If anyone had said I would be able to even stay upright on a bike, let alone ride one for sixty miles...' Heather gave a rueful smile. 'Mike was the one for sport, not me.' She swallowed hard. 'I turned him down so many times when he asked me out. I didn't think it could work between us because we're so different.'

Like Gemma and Oliver.

'But I'm glad I gave in,' Heather continued. 'Because those three years we had together were the best of my life. Even the bad bits, when we got the diagnosis and when he had chemo—at least we had each other. And I know he's up there right now, looking down, proud of me doing this.' She looked at Gemma. 'What about your partner? Is he here?'

'No. He was meant to be the race medic, but his brother's doing it instead.' She shrugged. 'It wouldn't have worked out between us anyway. He's going back to London.'

'You sound like me,' Heather said. 'Don't make the same mistakes I did. I'm glad of the time Mike and I had together—but it could've been so much more if I hadn't been so stubborn. We might've had time to have kids.'

'I have no idea if Oliver wants kids,' Gemma admitted. And she found herself telling Heather the whole story, how she'd accidentally fallen in love with her new colleague but she was pretty sure he was going to leave her and go back to London. She wasn't good at letting people close; she was so terrified she was going to be needy and clingy and stupid again, like she'd been after her little sister's death, that she went too far the other way and backed off when they were getting too close. 'And then he went distant on me, too—and it just escalated. I didn't want to be the one who was left behind, so I suggested being just colleagues. And he didn't try to argue me out of it.'

'Do you know for definite he's going back to London?'

'What is there to make him stay here?'

'You?' Heather suggested. 'Talk to him. Be honest about how you really feel.'

'He's not even here today,' Gemma said. 'He sent his brother.'

'But he didn't have to send anyone at all,' Heather pointed out. 'Maybe he thought you didn't want him there—but he hasn't let you down, has he? He sent someone else to take his place.'

'I guess.'

'What have you got to lose? If you let him go without telling him how you feel, he might be being just as stubborn as you and you're both missing out.'

'And if he doesn't want me?'

'Then at least you'll know the truth. You won't spend your time full of regrets and wondering if things would've been different if you'd been brave enough to talk to him.'

Ollie brooded all the way to village where the race was due to finish. He was pretty sure Gemma's parents wouldn't turn up; he just hoped he hadn't made things worse for her. Maybe Claire and Rob had been right and he shouldn't have interfered.

He went over to the marshals' tent to see his brother.

'How's it going?' he asked.

'Fine—I've treated two cases of dehydration, one of saddle sores and one poor guy who skidded across some tarmac and made a bit of a mess of his arm. Apparently we've got someone coming in shortly with a broken collarbone.' Rob looked at him. 'How did it go?'

'Awful.' Ollie grimaced. 'Have you seen Gemma?'

'Yes, and you're in trouble. She knew I wasn't you before I even opened my mouth.'

'What did she say?'

'She didn't give me a chance to explain. She said she had a race to ride.'

'I'll face the music later,' Ollie said. 'Thanks for helping. I'll take over from you now.'

'I'm fine. Actually, I'm enjoying having something to do. Go and wait for Gemma by the finish line. And make sure you've got a seriously, seriously good apology ready, because you're going to need it,' Rob warned.

Oliver made his way through to the finish line, knowing he'd messed things up. He felt as if the world was sitting on his shoulders. He had no idea where to start fixing this.

Why hadn't he just left things alone?

And then his phone rang.

It was a number he didn't recognise. He thought about ignoring it; but right now he had nothing better to do and it would waste some time while he waited.

'Dr Langley?' a voice he didn't recognise said on the other end.

'Yes?'

'It's Stephanie Baxter. Um, we thought about what you said. We've been talking. We...um...wondered if we could wait with you.'

Hope bloomed in his heart. Gemma's parents were coming to watch her finish the race? 'Of course you can.' He told her exactly where he was. 'See you soon. And thank you.'

'No. Thank *you*,' she said. 'Because you've just given us a second chance with our daughter.'

Ollie really, really hoped she was right.

People were lining the streets of the village where the race ended, cheering and clapping.

Gemma forced herself to smile, even though she felt like crying. Everything had gone so wrong with Oliver. Was Heather right? Should she be brave and tell him how she felt? But what if he still went back to London without her? She didn't want to face rejection yet again.

She plodded on, one foot in front of the other, and kept Heather going with words of encouragement that weirdly kept her going, too.

'I think,' Paul said, 'Heather needs to ride over that finish line.'

'She can't ride with a broken clavicle,' Gemma said.

'She won't be holding the handlebars,' Paul said. 'If I lift her onto the bike, we can be either side of her to keep the bike stable and we'll steady it while she pedals for the last ten metres.'

So Heather would get to fulfil her dream. 'You're on,' Gemma said.

Between them, they got Heather onto the bike. They co-opted a couple of people lining the route to hold their bikes for them while they helped Heather, who was smiling and crying at the same time as they supported her over the finish line.

The medics were there, waiting to help Heather to the ambulance; for a moment, Gemma thought Oliver was standing there, but her heart didn't have that funny little skip and she realised that it was Rob.

Stupid.

Of course Oliver wouldn't be there.

'Well done,' Rob said, clapping her shoulder. 'That was an amazing thing to do.'

'It wasn't my time that mattered,' she said. 'It was Heather finishing that was important.' She couldn't bring herself to ask where Oliver was. 'I'd better collect my bike and finish officially.'

Paul was waiting for her, and they rode over the finish line together, with people cheering and clapping all around them.

She dismounted and hugged him. 'Thank you. What you did...'

'The same as you did,' he said, 'for a complete stranger. Because we're all in this together. And we want to make a difference.'

'Yeah.'

'I'll look after Heather's bike,' Paul said, 'because I think you've got some people wanting to see you.'

Gemma looked up and saw Oliver standing there. But what really shocked her was that her parents were next to him. Her mum and dad had tears running down their faces, and they held out their arms to her.

She couldn't quite process this.

Why were her parents here? She hadn't even told them where the race was, just that she was doing it.

Oliver took her bike. 'Go to them,' he said softly. 'I'll be waiting when you've talked.'

She stared at him—'But…' She couldn't even begin to frame the questions buzzing through her head.

'I interfered,' he said. 'I'll apologise later, but I think you and your parents need to talk. Don't worry about your bike. I'll go and put it in my car. Give me your race number and I'll sort out any paperwork for you.'

'I…'

'Swap you the paperwork for a recovery drink and a recovery bar,' he said, pushing them into her hands. 'I'll feed you properly later, but you need to replenish your glycogen stores.'

'Spoken like a doctor,' she said wryly, and handed over her race number.

'And like the brother of someone who does this sort of thing himself, so I kind of know the drill. Go with your parents,' he said. 'When you're ready, I'll be in the marshals' tent, where I was supposed to be.'

'Mum. Dad.'

'Our girl. Sixty miles you cycled. And you helped that lass who'd fallen off her bike—you didn't just leave it to the medics to sort her out,' her dad said.

'Well—you *are* a medic. Nurse practitioner,' her mum said.

'How…? Why…?' Gemma cleared her throat and tried again. 'I didn't expect to see you here.'

'Your young man came to see us,' her mum explained.

Gemma frowned. Oliver wasn't hers any more.

'He told us about his brother. How he nearly died.'

There was a catch in her dad's voice. 'And he said how much you missed our Sarah. How much you missed *us*.'

'We haven't been proper parents to you,' her mum said. 'Not since Sarah died. We just couldn't get past losing her. And then, when it wasn't quite so raw any more, you...'

Gemma looked at them. She could let them off lightly, brush it under the carpet. Or she could be honest: and that might be a better way. Because at least then any relationship they managed to build would be on a solid foundation, with no areas where they were scared to tread. 'I was difficult to handle,' she said. 'I went off the rails. Because I couldn't cope with losing my little sister *and* losing my parents. Sleeping with all those boys—it made me feel loved again, just for a little while.'

Her dad flinched. 'It wouldn't have happened if we'd been there for you.'

'I'm not blaming you—either of you,' Gemma said. 'What happened, happened. I'm acknowledging it and I've moved past it.'

'Yvonne was the one who saved you. She was the mum I should've been to you. And I was grateful to her for stepping in, because I couldn't do it.' Colour flooded Stephanie's cheeks. 'At the same time, I was so jealous of her. You moved in with her and it felt as if you preferred someone else's family to your own. As if I'd lost both my girls.'

'You never lost me, Mum,' Gemma said. 'I needed to live with Claire's family to get through my exams. You weren't in a place where you could help me—and I couldn't deal with all that extra travelling to get to school. Things were hard enough. And I never gave up on you. I come and see you every month—even though you never come to see me, and getting either of you to talk to me is like pulling teeth. But I promised Sarah I'd never give up, and I've always hoped that one day I'd get some of my family back.'

'He's right about you, your young man,' her dad said. 'He said you'd never give up on us. And you're a daughter we can be proud of. All that money you raise for charity.'

'For the ward where Sarah died. Where they're doing research into permanent artificial hearts,' Gemma said. 'So maybe one day soon no other family will have to wait for a donor heart and risk losing their Sarah.'

'He showed us your video. You, jumping out of a plane,' her mum said. 'And he told us where we could find you today. We watched you help that woman. And we're—' her voice cracked '—we're so proud of you. Can you ever forgive us?'

Gemma had no words. She just opened her arms.

And, for the first time in too many years, her parents wrapped her in a hug. A real, proper hug. The hug she'd been so desperate to have.

'We love you so much, Gemma,' her dad said.

'It probably doesn't feel like it,' her mum said. 'But we do. And we're so sorry we let you down.'

'It's hard for us, going back to Ashermouth. But if that's where you want to be, then we'll come there to see you,' her dad said. 'Your young man's right—it's time we remembered we had another daughter. We want you in our lives. Properly. The way it should've been all along. It's been so...' His mouth moved but no words came out.

She wasn't going to push them into talking more.

Not right now. 'I know,' she said softly. 'I want that, too. And I know it's not going to be magically fixed overnight. We've got a lot of talking to do. But, now we've started, it'll get easier. And if we work at it, we'll make it. Together.'

'We do love you, Gem,' her mum said.

Words she'd wanted to hear for far too long. And both her parents had said it now. 'I love you, too,' she said shakily.

'You'd better go and see your young man,' her dad said. 'But we'll call you tomorrow.'

'And we're so proud of you.' Gemma's mum hugged her again.

'I'll talk to you tomorrow,' Gemma said. Tears blurred her vision as she made her way to the marshals' tent. Oliver had seen the chasm between her and her parents, and he'd laid a huge foundation plank across it.

Your young man.

Did she dare to hope that what he'd done—taught her parents to see her for who she was—meant he really cared about her? Was this his way of saying that maybe they had a future together? Or was this a goodbye present, a way of telling her that he couldn't be there for her but he hoped her parents would be?

Heather had advised her to talk to him. Tell him how she really felt.

And there was only one way to find out the answers to her questions…

Ollie sorted out the race admin for Gemma, then went back to the marshals' tent to help Rob. Various cyclists had come to the medics for help as they'd finished, with sprains, strains and saddle sores.

To his relief, his twin didn't ask him any awkward questions, just let him help treat their patients.

Finally Rob nudged him. 'I'll finish up here. You have a visitor.'

Ollie looked up; when he saw Gemma standing by the table, his heart skipped a beat.

'Hi,' she said.

He couldn't tell if everything was all right or not, but he wanted to let her set the pace. 'Hi.'

'Is Heather all right?' she asked Rob.

'The ambulance took her to hospital. Paul's looking after her bike and he's going to take it back to his place for now, then drop it over to hers,' Rob said. 'Obviously I didn't have your number, but I've taken theirs and texted them to Olls so you can get in touch with them.'

'Thank you,' she said. She looked at Ollie. 'Can we go somewhere quiet and talk?'

'Sure.' Ollie nodded to his twin, then followed Gemma out of the tent. They headed towards the sea, and found a quiet spot away from the crowds.

'That was a really kind thing you did, helping Heather over the finish line like that.'

'It wasn't just me. Paul helped, too. She had a broken clavicle. No way could she have wheeled that bike herself without jolting her arm.' Gemma shrugged.

'You could've waited with her until the marshals came.'

'No, I couldn't. It was important to Heather to finish the race and they would've stopped her. She was doing it in memory of her husband, who died from leukaemia, and we were so close to the end. It's just what anyone else would've done in an event like this when they saw someone was struggling.'

Ollie wasn't quite so sure, but Gemma clearly didn't believe she was special. 'I sorted out the race admin stuff for you,' he said.

'Thank you.' She took a deep breath. 'I didn't expect to see you today. When I saw Rob and realised you'd sent him in your place, I assumed...' Her voice tailed off.

'The worst? That I'd abandoned you?' The way her parents had when she was seventeen, and the way they'd stonewalled her over the last few years?

'Yes,' she admitted.

'I saw how upset you were yesterday and I wanted to do something about it. I know I was interfering. But I didn't want to let you down with this, either—which is why I talked Rob into taking my place,' Ollie explained.

'How did you even find my parents?'

'I asked— Never mind,' he said, not wanting to make things awkward between Gemma and her best friend. 'And I was warned not to interfere.'

'But you went to see them anyway.' Her eyes were red, as if she'd been crying.

He'd been so hopeful when her parents had called him and asked to stand with him at the end—so sure that he'd helped them start to reconnect with Gemma. Maybe he'd got it wrong. Maybe this had been the last straw, and instead they'd told Gemma never to see them again. Guilt flooded through him. 'I'm sorry if I've made things worse.'

'No, you made them...' She swallowed hard. 'Today was the first time in more than a decade that my parents told me they loved me.'

Ollie didn't know what to say. It was a good thing; yet, at the same time, his heart broke a little for her.

She'd tried so hard for all those years, had refused to give up: yet all that time she'd been hurting. Lonely. Wanting to be loved.

'They told me they were proud of me.'

'Good. And so they should be,' he said. 'You're an amazing woman.'

'But not,' she said, 'amazing enough for you.'

'Oh, you are,' he said.

'Then I don't get why you backed away from me. I don't understand you, Oliver. Not at all.'

Because he'd panicked. 'I just wanted to help.'

'You did. You've built a massive bridge between me and my parents—it's early days and there's still a lot to work through, but we're finally starting to see things the same way.' She looked at him. 'What I don't understand is why you did that. You and I…we agreed just to be colleagues.'

'Yes.' He knew he should tell her that wasn't what he wanted—but what if she rejected him?

When he didn't explain further, Gemma said, 'Heather told me she thought her husband was her complete opposite and it'd never work out between them. She held out for a long time before she agreed to date him—and then he was diagnosed with leukaemia. He died last year. And she said she'll always regret she wasn't brave enough to let them have more time together.'

His heart skipped a beat. Was Gemma saying that was how she saw their situation, too? Was this her way of telling him she wanted to try to make a go of things?

'She said it's important to be honest, to tell someone how you feel about them and not waste time.' Gemma took a deep breath. 'It scares me to death, saying this—

but at the same time I know I'll always regret it if I don't. So I'm going to say it. I know you want to go back to London, and I'm not going to trap you or ask you to stay; but I also don't want you to go without knowing the truth. That I love you.'

She loved him.

The words echoed through his head.

She loved him.

But then his insecurities snapped back in. 'How can I be enough for you?'

It was the last thing Gemma had expected him to say.

But then she remembered what he'd told her. How his ex had called off the wedding. 'Is this about Tabby? Are you still in love with her?'

'It's sort of about her,' Oliver said. 'But, no, I'm not still in love with her. One of my old colleagues told me that Tabby had got engaged again. And it made me think. I wasn't enough to make her love me, so why should I think I'd be enough for someone else?'

'Oliver Langley, do you really have no idea how amazing you are?' she asked. 'Look at the way you work with us in the practice. You fitted right in. You're part of the team. You've helped me make some innovations that will make our older patients' lives better. And you've just managed to do something that my best friend's family has tried and failed for do for over a decade—you talked to my parents, you got them to listen to you, and you changed their view of me. You've done what I thought was impossible: you've actually got us talking and starting to heal that rift.

'And, apart from all that, I love you. You make me feel like a teenager again—not full of angst and worry, but seeing all the possibilities in life.' She bit her lip. 'I thought you might have feelings for me, too. Until you backed away.'

'I do have feelings for you. I love you,' he said, 'and I know it's the real thing, because I feel different when I'm with you. The world feels a better place, full of sunshine and hope.' He paused. 'But how do I know I'm not fooling myself? How do I know I'll be enough for you?'

'Do you trust me?' she asked.

He was silent for so long that she thought he was going to tell her he didn't. But then he nodded. 'I trust you.'

'Then believe me. I think you're enough for me. You're the first man I've let close in years and years. You're everything I want in a partner. You're kind, you're funny, you notice the little details, and you make my heart feel as if it's doing cartwheels when you smile at me.' She took a deep breath. 'I know you're meant to be leaving in a few days, but—'

'Actually,' he cut in, 'I don't have to leave. Caroline says that Aadya wants to come back part-time, and the practice has expanded enough that she could do with another full-time doctor. She's given me first choice of the post.'

'So you could stay here?'

'Yes.'

'And is that what you want?'

'I want,' he said, 'to be with you. I've learned that I like being part of a small community—*this* community. I like living in a village where I know everyone and everyone knows me. Where people support each other. I want to live and work in a community where people really connect with each other.' He looked at her.

'But most of all I want to live with you. I want to make a family with you—whether we have children of our own, whether we support a teen in trouble, or whether it's a mixture of the two.'

So he'd remembered what she'd said to him about paying it forward.

'I saw you with your goddaughter,' he said, 'cuddling her and reading a story. When we read that story to her together. And it made me realise that was what I wanted. You, and our family.' His blue eyes were full of warmth and love. 'This probably isn't the right time to say this, when you've just done a sixty-mile bike ride.'

'Strictly speaking, that's fifty-nine miles cycling and about a mile's walk,' she pointed out.

'A mile's walk pushing two bikes and supporting someone with a broken collarbone,' he said. 'Which is a lot more effort than cycling. Gemma, when I came to Ashermouth Bay, I was miserable and lonely and in a lot of denial. And then I met you. And I found out how the world really ought to be—full of love and sunshine. You make the day sparkle. And I want to spend the rest of my life with you.' He dropped to one knee. 'I probably ought to wait and do this somewhere really romantic. But I can virtually hear my twin yelling in my ear, "Be more Rob!"—and your friend Heather was right. It's important to be honest, to tell someone how you feel about them and not waste time. So I'm going to take the risk and tell you. I've learned that it's not the showy stuff that matters: it's what's in your heart. And I love you, Gemma Baxter. I really, really love you. Will you marry me and make a family with me?'

Marry him.

Make a family with him.

He was offering her everything she wanted. More than that: he'd actually got her parents to make the first move, to start to heal the rift between them.

She leaned down and kissed him. 'Yes.'

* * * * *

BABY MIRACLE
FOR THE ER DOC

KATE HARDY

MILLS & BOON

For my readers.
Because writing for you got me through lockdown.

CHAPTER ONE

ROBERT LANGLEY WALKED through the doors of Asherwick General Hospital.

How good it felt to be back on the side of the hospital where he *belonged*. To be the fixer again, not the fixee.

Not in a helicopter, being evacuated after a burst appendix. Not developing severe blood poisoning that went on to wipe out his kidneys. Not lying in a hospital bed, on dialysis. Not on the operating table, while his twin Oliver was in the operating theatre next door—a living donor, having a kidney cut out for Rob. Not stuck at home after the transplant, with his mother wrapping him in so much cotton wool that he was beginning to resemble a snowman.

The last six months had been tough. Rob had had to come to terms with the fact he'd never again be able to work for the humanitarian aid organisation where he'd volunteered; with only one working kidney, and a transplanted one at that, he was too much of a potential liability. The mountain rescue team where he volunteered had offered him a support role when he was well enough to come back, but they'd made it clear that he couldn't do the rescue work he'd been used to doing for them. Desk job only.

It had been months since he'd climbed anywhere. Months since he'd done anything riskier than playing chess with his twin. Months since he'd worked—apart from the day the previous weekend when he'd taken Ollie's place among the medics for a sixty-mile fund-raising cycle race.

And right now Rob was desperate for a bit of normality. He wanted his life back. His lovely, *busy* life.

He'd taken the first step at the weekend. While he'd been recuperating, he'd let his hair grow out so it was more like his twin's, with his fringe flopping over his eyes, and he'd shaved every day because it was another way of filling the endless seconds until his life went back to normal. But on Saturday morning he'd walked into the barber's and asked them to shave it back to his normal crop, just shy of military barbering. He hadn't shaved for a couple of days. And this morning, when he'd looked in the mirror, he'd seen himself again. Not the patient who could barely do a thing for himself that he'd been forced to be for so long.

His consultant had agreed that Rob wasn't quite ready to go back to climbing, but could go back to work part-time, and now he had a temporary post working three days a week as a registrar in the Emergency Department at Asherwick.

It was so, so good to be back. The fact that nobody knew him here made it all the better, because nobody would fuss that he was overdoing things, or treat him as anyone other than normal.

Rob knew better than to overdo things. The last thing he wanted was to be stuck recuperating again. But it would feel so good to be seen as a doctor first, not as someone recovering from a kidney transplant. To help someone instead of being the one who needed help. To do the job he'd spent years training to do and knew he did well.

'Hello! I wasn't expecting to see you here.'

Rob stared at the woman who'd just spoken to him. He'd never seen this woman in his life before. And he would definitely have remembered her: slight, with dark hair in a pixie cut and huge brown eyes, a heart-shaped face and a generous mouth. She reminded him of a young Audrey Hepburn. All she needed was the little black dress instead of a white coat, the enormous hat and a pair of dark glasses, and she'd be a ringer for Holiday Golightly.

According to her lanyard, she was Dr Florence Jacobs; given they were both in the Emergency Department, it was a fair assumption that she was one of his new colleagues.

Before Rob could apologise for having no idea who she was, she asked, 'How's your patient with chicken-pox pneumonia doing?'

'Patient?' What patient? He hadn't treated anyone for months, let alone anyone with chickenpox. Or pneumonia.

She looked disappointed, as if he'd just outed himself as the sort of doctor who couldn't be bothered to remember his patients. Which wasn't who he was at all. 'The elderly woman you brought in, a couple of weeks ago.'

'I'm sorry. I think you must have the wrong person.'

She frowned. 'I'm sure it was you. Just your hair was different.'

His hair was different?

Then the penny dropped.

'Ah. You must mean Oliver. My twin,' he explained. GPs didn't usually bring their patients to the Emergency Department, but Oliver Langley was the kind of doctor who went above and beyond. And Oliver was the sort of person people remembered; he exuded warmth and kindness and made friends in the blink of an eye. 'I can ask him for you, if you like.'

'It's OK. I just…' She flapped a dismissive hand, and a tide of colour swept through her face. 'Never mind.'

Clearly she was embarrassed at making a mistake, and Rob didn't want things to feel awkward between himself and his new colleague. 'Let's rewind that and start again. Good morning. I'm Robert Langley,' he said. 'I'm the new part-time registrar. Rob, to my friends.'

'Florence Jacobs. Senior Reg. Good to meet you.'

Though she didn't offer a shortened version of her a name, he noticed. Did that mean she was the sort who kept a distance between herself and her colleagues? Or did she not like shortening her name?

He shook her hand and his palm tingled.

Uh-oh. That wasn't good.

He was supposed to be concentrating on his new job, not getting side-tracked by attraction. Even if Florence Jacobs was a) single and b) interested in him, he was only here for a few months before he went back to his old job in Manchester. Although Rob was happy for all his relationships to stay short and sweet, he knew from experience that his girlfriends didn't necessarily see things the same way; there was no guarantee that Florence would be interested in a fling. So it was better to keep things strictly professional rather than act on that pull of attraction he felt towards her. His life had been complicated enough for the last few months. He wanted things kept nice and simple. Just him and his job. No expectations he couldn't fulfil and no girlfriends to be let down when his low boredom threshold kicked in.

'I see they've already given you a lanyard. That's good. Come with me and I'll show you where the staff kitchen is,' she said. 'And you're rostered in Resus with me today, so if there's anything you need just let me know.'

He gave her his best smile. 'Thanks. That'd be great.'

'Welcome to Asherwick General,' she said.

Robert Langley was gorgeous.

Absolutely gorgeous.

Like a young Hugh Grant, without the floppy hair and smooth skin. Though, actually, Florence rather liked the stubble. And those startling blue eyes, the brighter because there was no fringe getting in their way. Part of her was seriously tempted to reach out and touch his face, find out whether the stubble was spiky or soft.

But she'd learned the hard way: getting close to someone netted you a broken heart, broken dreams and a divorce. So she wasn't going to act on that flare of attraction to their new registrar. Besides, looking like that, he must have women queuing a mile deep to date him—if he hadn't already been married for years.

So she switched her head to friendly and professional mode, smiled and led him through to the kitchen. 'We have a kitty system here. Everyone gives their subs to Shobu on Reception once a month and she keeps us stocked with tea, coffee and stuff. Any special dietary requirements, just let her know.' She gestured to the cupboards. 'Mugs and plates are there, cutlery in the drawer, and if we're lucky it's someone's birthday and they bring in cake.'

'Or if someone starts in the department and wants to say hello to his new colleagues,' Rob said, and placed the carrier bag he'd been holding on the worktop. 'Cake, cheese straws and fruit.'

'That,' Florence said with a smile, 'is definitely a good way to say hello.' He'd been thoughtful about it, including things for people who didn't like cake or had other dietary requirements. It was such a nice thing to do, and it made her warm to him.

He took everything out of the bag, including a note.

Please help yourself!
All the best from your new colleague,
Rob Langley

He placed it on the worktop. Then he glanced at his watch. 'We haven't got time for coffee. Not if we want to get a decent handover rather than making people stay on after their shift.'

She liked that, too. He was thinking of their colleagues who were already busy. A team player. Good. That was exactly what they needed. Their last three temps hadn't been team players at all. 'Agreed. Let's go through,' she said.

She introduced him to everyone they passed; and they'd just got to Resus when the red phone shrilled.

Florence answered it, made a few notes, and blew out a breath.

'ETA ten minutes. Elderly patient, fallen and banged his head. He's lost a lot of blood; he collapsed in the ambulance but they've stabilised him,' she said. 'Though he's also a bit confused.'

'So we're looking at an urgent cross-match of blood, getting fluids into him, possibly a transfusion, and then a CT scan from his head to his hip to check for other injuries,' Rob said.

She liked the way his thoughts chimed with hers. 'Exactly.'

Everything was ready by the time their patient arrived.

As the paramedics talked her through what they'd done, she could see that his blood pressure was low, thanks to the blood he'd lost.

'Mr Walker, do you know where you are?' Rob asked.

'I'm not at home, am I?' the elderly man asked, sounding confused.

'No, you're at Asherwick General.'

'My cup of tea…' He looked anxious.

'Do you remember anything that happened?' Florence asked.

'No.' Mr Walker began to shake his head, and stopped, wincing. 'My neck hurts.'

'We think you had a fall and hit your head,' Rob said. 'Your wife's on her way in, with your daughter. I'm Dr Langley, and this is Dr Jacobs. We're going to look after you. I'm just going to take a tiny sample of blood, if that's all right.'

'Yes.' Mr Walker's face crumpled. 'I want Lizzie.'

'She'll be here soon,' Florence reassured him, assuming he meant his wife or his daughter. She glanced at the monitor, deeply unhappy with his blood pressure reading; he'd clearly lost a lot of blood, meaning that not enough was going to his vital organs. 'We're going to get some fluids into you,' she said.

Rob was already on top of it. And he'd done the blood sample without a fuss while they'd been talking to their patient. He might be new and he might only be a temporary colleague, but he was already acting as if he'd been part of the team for years. Unlike their last couple of temps, who'd seemed to wait to be told what to do.

Once Mr Walker was stabilised and they'd stemmed the bleeding, she sent him for an urgent CT scan; then she and Rob went to see his wife and daughter.

'I'm Dr Jacobs and this is Dr Langley,' she introduced them swiftly.

'Lizzie Walker,' his wife said, 'and Jeannette.'

'He was asking for you earlier,' Rob said. 'We told him you were both on your way.'

'Your husband's having a scan at the moment so we can check him over properly and see if he's got any other injuries. He's lost a bit more blood than we'd like, so we're going to give him a transfusion,' Florence said. 'Can you tell us what happened?'

'I'm not sure. He'd gone downstairs to let the dog out and make us both a cup of tea,' Mrs Walker said. 'He must've slipped on the stairs, though I didn't hear him fall. I was in the shower. It was only when I was getting dressed that I heard the dog barking. I thought it was a bit odd, and when I went out I saw Pete lying at the foot of the stairs and there was blood everywhere. I called the ambulance, and I put a blanket over him to keep him warm because I didn't want to risk moving him. He couldn't remember falling, so whether he blacked out or something happened...' She shook her head. 'I don't know. I'm sorry.'

'You did the best thing, keeping him warm and calling the ambulance and not moving him,' Florence reassured her.

'There was so much blood.' Mrs Walker's face was pinched.

'Scalp wounds always seem scary and bleed a lot,' Rob said, 'because the skin's thicker and there are more veins and arteries. But we've stopped the bleeding now.'

'Is Dad going to be all right?' Jeanette asked.

Florence didn't have enough information to be able to answer that. 'We're looking after him,' she said instead. 'He did seem a little bit confused.' Had he just missed his footing, or had he had a stroke, or was it something else—had he banged his head hard enough to cause an internal bleed? 'Can I ask about his general health before the fall? Any medical conditions?'

'He was fine,' Mrs Walker said.

Jeanette sighed. 'Oh, Mum. That's not quite true. Dad's memory is starting to go a bit.'

'We manage,' Mrs Walker said defensively.

'Nobody's assigning any kind of blame,' Florence said gently. 'We're just trying to put the clues together to work out what happened and what caused it, to help us decide on the best treatment to give him.'

Mrs Walker grimaced. 'We're just getting old. Jeanette's right, Pete's a bit forgetful. He's got high blood pressure, but he takes his medication every day—I bought him one of those weekly pill box things to make sure.' She bit her lip. 'Do you think he had a stroke and that's why he fell? Is that why he can't remember anything?'

'We'll know more when we've seen the scan,' Florence said.

'But if you can give us a full run-down of his medical history, that would really help us work things out,' Rob said, giving her a warm smile.

Mrs Walker and her daughter both seemed to react well to his charm; Florence left him to do the talking and noted down everything they said.

'Thank you—that was very helpful,' she said when they'd finished. 'We'll come and get you as soon as he's back in the department, so you can see him.'

'Stroke?' Rob asked when they'd left the relatives' room.

'Or a bleed on the brain from his fall,' she said. 'I'll be happier when we've seen the scan.'

Mr Walker had just been brought back to the department, and the initial blood tests—pending the full cross-match—meant they were able to start the blood transfusion.

But he was agitated and wouldn't settle.

'Mr Walker, I need you to lie on your back for me and keep your arm still so I can treat you,' Florence said gently. If he kept moving, they wouldn't be able to get the blood into him and the risk of organ failure was growing by the minute.

'My neck hurts,' he said again.

Rob sat next to him and held his hand. 'I know, and we're going to do something about that. But for now we need you to lie still, just for a little while, so we can help you. Florence is going to get you some pain relief, and then we'll bring your wife and your daughter to see you.'

'I can't let them see me covered in blood.' Mr Walker twisted on the bed. 'Not like this.'

'Lie still for us,' she said gently, 'and I'll wash your face so they won't be worried when they see you.'

'Neither of us is going anywhere,' Rob said. 'You're safe. I'm hanging onto you, and Florence will clean you up. So you're perfectly safe to lie still and let us help you. Deal?'

For a moment, Florence thought Mr Walker was going to refuse, but then the fight went out of him. 'All right.'

She and Rob exchanged a glance. Agitation and sudden changes in mood could suggest a stroke or something affecting the patient's ability to process information. Or maybe he was just horribly scared. Until they'd seen the results of that scan, she couldn't be sure.

Florence gently washed Mr Walker's face, getting rid of all the blood, talking to him all the while. Rob thought how nice she was, how gentle and kind. And he'd noticed that she was calm under pressure; he liked that, too.

He liked his new colleague a lot.

Though he needed to be sensible about it and not act on that attraction. He wasn't great at relationships; plus he was only here for the next three months. As soon as he was fit enough to climb again, he'd be back in his old job in Manchester—the other side of the country. So it'd be better not to start anything in the first place.

Once the scans were back, Florence reviewed them with him. 'I'm glad to see there's no sign of a bleed on the brain or a fracture to the skull,' she said.

They'd done a scan from the top of his head to his hip, to check for other injuries. 'No sign of internal damage or any other fractures either,' Rob said. 'With luck, he'll just have some bruising and that wound on the back of his head.'

'I'm still admitting him so we keep him in overnight for observation,' Florence said. 'I've got a funny feeling. Yes, that confusion could be from the shock of the fall and hitting his head; but, given that his daughter was concerned about memory loss, we need to keep an eye on him.'

'I agree,' Rob said.

Once they'd settled Mr Walker with his family and organised admitting him, they were called to deal with a patient who'd collapsed with a suspected heart attack. He arrested in the middle of Resus, but thankfully they were able to save him and send him up to the cardiac ward.

'I think we're both overdue a break,' Florence said to Rob. 'Would you like to come with me and I'll show you where the canteen is?'

'That'd be nice. Thank you. Coffee is on me,' he added.

'It's your first day, so it's my shout,' she corrected.

'Tell you what—you buy the coffee, I'll buy the cake,' he said.

She smiled. 'That's a deal.'

'Any particular cake you prefer?'

'Cake is cake,' she said.

'Got you.'

In the cafeteria, she bought them both a cappuccino, and he bought two slices of a rich-looking chocolate brownie. 'Ollie—my brother—is a cheese fiend. He doesn't understand what a joy chocolate cake is,' Rob said as they sat down.

'You're right: it *is* a joy—and not just because of the sugar rush,' she said with a smile.

All of a sudden Rob's chest felt too tight. It was nothing to do with his kidney transplant and everything to do with the way that smile transformed her face, changing her from the quiet, capable and serious doctor into someone who was lit up from the inside.

He hadn't expected to be knocked sideways by her smile. And he didn't have the faintest clue what to do about this. Stick to being sensible—being more like his twin, in accordance with the pact they'd made—or follow his impulses?

Of course he should hold back. He and Florence barely knew each other. But being aware of that didn't stop the longing.

'You were good with Mr Walker's wife and daughter,' she said.

He shrugged off the compliment. 'Families worry, and that makes a patient even more anxious. I've always thought one of the best things you can do for a patient is to keep their families calm.'

'Good point,' she said.

'When he started getting agitated, I was beginning to think we'd have to sedate him—which would have been horrible for him and his family.'

'Luckily it didn't come to that. And you were really good with him,' she said. She looked at him over the rim of her mug. 'So where were you before you came here?'

This was where Rob knew he needed to be careful about how much information he gave. He didn't want his past getting in the way. Didn't want to seem weak. 'Manchester,' he said. Which was true, up to a point.

Just he'd been in the middle of taking a sabbatical to work abroad. 'You?'

'I trained in Leeds, then moved here just over a year ago,' she said, 'to be near my family.'

'Me, too. My parents retired near here,' he said. It was the truth; just not the whole truth, because if the appendicitis and blood poisoning hadn't happened he would still have been working for the humanitarian organisation, or by now he would've been back in Manchester and spending his spare time with the local mountain rescue team, really making a difference and using his skills. But he was glad Florence had mentioned her family. He needed to head her off. Since she'd moved back here to be close to them, it followed that she was likely to be happy to talk about them. It would be the perfect distraction. 'So your family's local?'

'My parents live in the next village—I grew up here,' she said. 'My older sister moved back here two years ago when she retired.'

Hang on. Florence looked as if she was around the same age as he was, thirty. Even if there was a ten-year gap between her and her sister, that didn't quite stack up. 'Retired?'

'Lexy's a ballerina,' Florence explained. 'She's thirty-six—a lot of ballerinas retire in their thirties, because dancing takes such a toll on their hips and knees—and anyway she doesn't want to tour with the company any more now her oldest has started school. So she's done her teaching qualification, and she's set up her own ballet school. All three of her daughters dance with her—even Darcey, the two-year-old.'

Rob noticed a hint of wistfulness along with the pride in her face when she spoke about her nieces, and wondered what was behind that.

And he noticed that Florence hadn't said anything about a husband. He couldn't help a swift glance at her left hand. There was no ring, though that didn't mean anything; she could still be in a committed relationship.

He needed to damp down that zing of attraction towards her, fast. Those huge brown eyes. The generous curve of her mouth. The way everything suddenly felt a little bit brighter when she was in the room.

'Darcey? It's an unusual name.'

'After Darcey Bussell. Lexy called her girls after famous ballerinas. Margot—the oldest—is named after Margot Fonteyn, and Anna, who's four, is named after Anna Pavlova.'

Even Rob had heard of the ballerinas. 'Got you.'

He managed to keep the conversation work-based for the rest of their break, then walked with Florence back to the department.

It was a busy afternoon and, although he hated to admit it, he was tired by the time he got home. There was a note in his letterbox saying that a parcel had been delivered next door; even before he picked it up, he had a pretty good idea who'd sent it. The person he'd done exactly the same thing for, a couple of months back; the person whose thoughts so often chimed with his.

There was a note attached:

You are only allowed to open this if you DIDN'T overdo things on your first day.

'Yeah, yeah, Olls,' he said with a grin, and opened it. The parcel contained a bottle of good red wine and some seriously good chocolate.

Perfect for his first evening after work.

Rob texted his twin. Thank you for the parcel. I so deserve this.

His phone rang seconds later. 'So how was your first day?' Oliver asked.

'Wonderful. It was so good to be back, Olls. To save lives—we had an arrest and we got him back. And even if it's only three days a week, it's so much better to know I'm making a difference again instead of being stuck at home.' Stuck feeling too ill even to pace about. It had been Rob's worst nightmare.

'Glad you enjoyed it. Are your colleagues nice?'

Rob thought of Florence Jacobs. 'Very.' Though he wasn't going to admit to his twin that he'd been drawn to one new colleague in particular.

'And you paced yourself?' Oliver checked.

'Stop nagging. Of course I did. I'm a bit tired, now,' Rob admitted, 'but I've got tomorrow off to recover. Working every other day is going to ease me back into things. I know it'll be a while yet before I'm ready to go full time again, but working part time is way, way better than doing nothing.'

'That all sounds a bit sensible for *you*. So you actually meant it about being more Ollie?' his twin teased.

'Yes.' Mostly. He wasn't sure if he was actually capable of putting down roots.

Though he was very aware of how impersonal his rented flat was. The one thing that Rob did envy Ollie was the way his twin always seemed able to make a place feel like a home, even on the same day he moved in. Rob was never in a place for long enough to make it feel properly like home; he was too busy chasing the next adventure, making the next difference. And even his flat in Manchester—currently rented out to a colleague—was just a place to stay between the emergency department, climbing and his overseas work.

Maybe he should try taking a few more leaves out of Ollie's book.

Tomorrow, he decided, he'd print out some of the photos on his phone and stick them in frames on the mantelpiece. That might make his flat feel less anonymous and soulless.

'I'm starving, so I'm going to say goodbye now and cook dinner,' he said.

'You mean, you're going to stick something in the microwave,' Oliver teased.

'It's perfectly nutritious. There are two portions of my five a day, and I'm having an apple afterwards.' Unlike his twin, Rob never had been big on cooking. It always felt like a waste of time where he could be doing something more active and more interesting. His rule was that if it took more than five minutes, it was off the menu. 'I'll call you tomorrow,' he said. 'Give Gemma my love. And thank you for the care package.'

'You're welcome. And you can always come here for dinner after work, if you're tired. I don't mind cooking for you.'

'That's kind,' Rob said. Though Ollie was newly loved up; given that the kidney transplant had been the thing to break his brother's engagement, the last thing Rob wanted now was to put pressure on Ollie's new relationship. Even though Rob liked Gemma very much and thought she was a million times better for Ollie than Tabby had been, and also wasn't likely to behave in the same way, he still didn't want to make things difficult. 'Oh, by the way. How's your patient with chickenpox pneumonia doing?'

'She's completely recovered,' Oliver said. 'But I don't remember telling you about that. Why do you ask?'

'One of my new colleagues remembered you bringing her in. She thought I was you.'

'Oh?' Oliver sounded intrigued.

'And I'm hungry,' Rob said, 'so I'm going.' Before he said anything about Florence Jacobs that his twin might misinterpret.

Florence walked into the kitchen, her footsteps echoing.

It was more than a year now since she'd moved back to Northumbria. More than a year since her divorce. More than two years since her world had collapsed.

And, although she'd grown up only a few miles away in the next village, this place still didn't feel like home. A single person's flat. Empty. This wasn't the life she'd planned for herself; she'd thought by now she'd have children at preschool—children who'd grow up close to their cousins, the way Florence had been close to her sister.

Instead, she was on her own. And she just didn't have the strength to try again.

She didn't regret moving back from Leeds. Being close to the family she loved, being able to see her nieces grow up—that meant the world to her. And it was nice not having anyone at work pitying her, or the whispered conversations that stopped abruptly when she walked into the staff kitchen.

She knew her colleagues in Leeds had speculated about the break-up of her marriage, and it was obvious they'd all guessed Dan's affair had been at the root of it because Florence had adored her husband. But telling them the whole truth would've been so much harder.

That she and Dan had tried for a baby for three years, the tests had shown that he was the one with the fertility problem, and he'd refused flatly to adopt, foster or to go through IVF with a sperm donor. He'd refused to go to counselling, too, and he'd given her an ultimatum of a baby or him.

How ironic that now she had neither. And Dan had ended up marrying a single mum who'd given him the children he hadn't been able to have himself but had refused to give Florence: the woman he'd had an affair with. The more she thought about it, the more she realised that maybe Dan's issues hadn't been with having children; it had been having children with *her*. And just what was so wrong with her that the love of her life hadn't wanted to make a family with her?

She shook herself. 'Enough of the pity party,' she told herself crossly. Time to look on the bright side. Focus on what she did have, not what she didn't. She loved her family and lived close enough to see a lot of them; she had a job she adored; and she had good friends who looked out for her. She was lucky.

Though she knew exactly what had unsettled her today.

Robert Langley.

Her new colleague was charming, great with patients, and he treated all staff as equally important—whatever their position on the ward. He thought on his feet, so he was good to work with. He was more than easy on the eye.

And maybe that was the problem.

Because in some ways he reminded her of Dan, when they'd first got together. Dan, who was urbane and charming and got on well with everyone. Dan, who she'd thought she'd be with for ever: until he'd changed the goalposts and broken her heart in the process.

Rob hadn't mentioned having a partner or children, and she'd got the impression that there was something a little remote about him. As if that charm was a barrier to stop people seeing who he really was, behind it.

'Or maybe you're overthinking things and being incredibly unfair to your new colleague, Florence Jacobs,' she said out loud.

To get her balance back, she needed to go for a run and get the endorphins flowing, and have dinner. And until then she wasn't going to allow herself to think about Robert Langley.

CHAPTER TWO

Two days later, Rob was in Minors. In the middle of the morning, a man came in after a car accident where he'd been rear-ended while waiting in a queue of traffic. He rolled his eyes at his wife. 'I'm sorry we're wasting your time, Doctor. I'm only here because my wife won't stop fussing.'

'Actually,' Rob said, 'your wife has a point. Even though modern cars have good crumple zones, the impact might have affected you more than you think.'

'And he was slurring his words earlier,' his wife said. 'When he rang me I couldn't understand a word he said.'

'Because I was standing on the side of the road waiting for the tow truck and I was *cold*,' her husband said crossly, 'not because I had an undiagnosed bleed to my brain or something. You watch too many hospital dramas, Mags. They're not going to need to airlift me somewhere.'

Rob had to hide a smile. 'OK. Did the airbag go off?'

'No. I was sitting in a queue of traffic waiting to turn right when the guy rammed into me. I had my lights on and my indicator going, but he said he didn't see me. Idiot. He wasn't looking where he was going.'

'The car's likely to be written off,' his wife said, 'so it was quite an impact.'

'Let me check you over,' Rob said. He checked his patient's neck and head, got him to follow a moving finger with his eye, then checked his back. 'Your muscles are pretty tight from the impact, so you're going to be sore for a week or so. You need good painkillers and rest—and I *mean* rest. Plus it'll help you to do some gentle stretching.'

'See? You made a fuss about nothing,' the man said to his wife.

'No, it was a good call,' Rob said. 'Until the beginning of this year, I would've been on your side. Now I know better.'

The man looked curious. 'What made you change your mind?'

'A burst appendix,' Rob said. 'I was working abroad and I assumed my stomach pains were just because I wasn't used to the food or water. And me a doctor. You'd think I'd know better.' He gave a rueful smile. 'So I've learned not to ignore things any more. The quicker you get something checked out, the easier it is to pick up a problem and get it sorted before it turns into something serious.'

'Got you,' the man said.

'You might find your back feels more painful over the next couple of days. If it feels worse in a week's time, come back or see your GP to get checked over—and none of the stiff upper lip stuff, OK? Because all that'll do is mean your recovery will be longer.'

'OK,' the patient said.

Rob gave his patient a prescription for painkillers—stronger ones than were available to buy over the counter at a pharmacy or supermarket. 'There's a week's worth. Take two with food, maximum eight in twenty-four hours, and if they're not touching the pain then come back.'

When it was time for his break, he headed for the staff kitchen. Florence was there, and his heart did a weird little flip. Rob had to remind himself that it wasn't a good idea to act on the attraction he felt towards her.

'Kettle's hot,' she said.

'Cheers.' He put a couple of spoons of instant coffee into a mug and added boiling water to dissolve it, then enough cold water so he could start drinking it. 'How was your morning?'

'I had a whole run of Colles' fractures—and it's not even icy this morning,' she said.

'Yeah, it goes like that sometimes.'

She paused. 'So you had a burst appendix at the beginning of the year?'

He looked at her, surprised. 'Hospital gossip travels fast here.'

'No. I was in the cubicle next door to your patient who'd been rear-ended, so I heard what you said. Though I haven't repeated it to anyone else.'

'Thank you.' He gave her what he hoped was a casual smile. 'It wasn't my finest moment. Helping with the aftermath of an earthquake and ending up needing treatment myself.' He wasn't quite ready to admit how serious it had got after the burst appendix. The blood poisoning. The dialysis. The horror of being *stuck* when he was desperate to be on the move again.

'Good advice you gave your patient, though.'

'It's not so easy to follow advice if you have a Y chromosome,' he deadpanned.

She laughed. 'At least you're honest about it.' She smiled at him, and again his heart did that little flip. Her mouth was beautiful. He had difficulty stopping himself reaching out to trace the lower curve with his forefinger. Which was crazy. He hadn't felt this kind of unstoppable attraction towards someone in years—not since he was twenty-four, in his first job after graduating, and fallen for a fellow medic.

Except Janine had had a five-year plan that included marriage, a mortgage and children; and that was completely incompatible with Rob's own plans to travel the world. It had ended in tears, and Rob had never really forgiven himself for not being what she needed and for hurting her. It was why he made sure all his girlfriends knew he didn't do serious: so he'd never hurt anyone again.

This pull he felt towards Florence unnerved him. Why now? Why her? What the hell was going on in his head? Equally pretty women had crossed his path in the last few months, so it wasn't that he'd been starved of female company—even though he hadn't been well enough to take things further.

What was so special about Florence Jacobs?

Before he could analyse it further, she said, 'Has anyone mentioned the department Christmas dinner to you? It's Friday next week, but we've still got a day or two to finalise numbers, so I'm pretty sure we can squeeze you in if you want.'

'Christmas dinner?' Right now it was the last week of September. He stared at her in surprise. 'In October?'

'Which is the closest to Christmas we'd dare to organise it. You know what it's like in November and December. The department's so busy that nobody would be actually able to go,' she pointed out.

'True,' he said. And he knew Ollie would nag him to accept the invitation. Going for the meal would be a good way of getting to know his new team, even though he was only going to be here for three months. Gone just after Christmas. 'Thanks. I'm not on duty next Friday, so I'd like to go. Do you need a deposit or the full payment?'

'I'm guessing that it's the whole lot, as Shobu collected the rest of the money and the menu choices from everyone last week,' she said. 'Oh—and partners are welcome, too.'

'No partner. Just me,' he said.

He was single?

There was absolutely no reason for her pulse to kick up a notch.

Robert Langley was simply her new colleague, and anyway Florence wasn't interested in another relationship—not after the way her marriage had collapsed. She wasn't risking her heart again. And there was no reason to think that Rob was attracted to her, either. 'OK. Have a word with Shobu,' she said.

'I will. Oh, and I meant to tell you—your chicken-pox pneumonia lady is doing just fine.' He smiled. 'I asked my brother when I spoke to him, the other night.'

'That's good to know.' And it warmed her that he'd bothered to ask. That he'd remembered.

Florence spent the next week and a half telling herself that Robert Langley was just one of her colleagues

and kept him at a friendly but professional distance...
until she walked into the hotel where the department's
Christmas meal was being held.

Shobu had obviously told him that they all dressed
up: the dress code for their Christmas party was dinner jackets and cocktail dresses. Florence hadn't been
prepared for just how amazing Rob looked in a tux-
edo and bow tie instead of his white coat. Not a black
tie, though; when she got closer, she discovered it was
black with a dark grey paisley pattern. Incredibly styl-
ish. Incredibly sexy. He still had that designer stubble
that made her want to touch him.

And she needed to get a grip.

'Didn't fancy a polka dot red tie, then?' she said,
aiming for teasing and hoping he wouldn't guess how
attractive she found him.

'I thought red might be a tiny bit too showy-offy,'
he said. 'You look amazing, by the way.'

'Thank you.' She'd borrowed a dress from Lexy: a
simple black shift dress that came down to just above
her knee and had a boat neck. She wore a single strand
of pearls and matching earrings—also Lexy's—and
her sister had insisted on doing her make-up, while her
nieces all told her she looked like a princess. 'Though
it's borrowed finery. I'm more one for scrubs or a white
coat.'

'Still lovely,' he said.

He was being polite, she told herself. There was no
reason to feel that flush of pleasure. No reason to feel
a little tingle at the ends of her fingers. No reason for
her breath to catch.

The breath-catching feeling got worse during the
meal, because she was sitting next to Rob. And some-

how they ended up brushing hands; every time it happened, her pulse rate went up another notch.

She needed to get things back on an even keel. Find a safe subject.

But, as she turned to him to say something innocuous about how lovely the food was, she caught his eye.

Oh, help.

Up this close, she could see how gorgeous his eyes were. How long his lashes were. How beautiful the shape of his mouth was.

Thinking about his mouth was a bad idea. Because the next step from that was thinking about how that beautiful mouth might feel against her skin. And her kissing days were over. She wasn't going to let herself be vulnerable again.

'Lovely food, isn't it?' she asked brightly, hoping nobody could hear the note of panic in her voice—and hoping even more that nobody would guess what was behind it. Especially Rob.

'Very nice,' he agreed.

He shuffled slightly in his seat, and the chairs were close enough together that his leg pressed briefly against hers. Even through the material of his trousers, she could feel the warmth of his skin, and it made her want to press against him.

'So there's dancing after this?' he asked.

Dancing. Up close and personal...

No.

Her scrambled brain needed to find an answer before he wondered why she wasn't saying a word.

'They'll play all the Christmas hits, and everyone will be jumping about and singing their heads off,' she said. Which was safe dancing. Enjoying yourself with your friends and colleagues. Not dangerous dancing, one on one.

'With your sister being a ballerina, does that mean you like dancing?'

She'd loved it. And Dan had been an excellent dancer. It was one of the reasons she'd fallen for him in the first place: dancing with Dan had been like floating on air.

They hadn't danced together for a good year before he'd left her. And she hadn't had a clue that he'd been dancing with someone else.

Not wanting to let the old hurts spoil tonight—or let herself wonder what it would be like to dance with Rob—she deliberately misinterpreted his question so he wouldn't take it as an invitation to ask her to dance. 'Follow in her footsteps? No. I went to ballet lessons when I was five, for about a term, but it wasn't for me. I loved the music, I loved watching Lexy dance at home—and dancing with her—but I wasn't like her. I didn't want to put in the hours and hours of practice, the way she did.'

For a second, there was a glint in his eyes, as if he recognised the subterfuge: stick to a safe, neutral topic.

And then how ridiculous was it that she felt almost disappointed when he did precisely that and asked, 'What made you decide to be a doctor?'

'I wanted to do something where I'd help people,' she said, 'and when I did my rotation in the Emergency Department it made me realise that was where I wanted to be.' Since he'd opted for the safe topic, it would only be polite to ask him the same. 'What about you?'

He grinned. 'Ah, now. When I was thirteen, I flirted with the idea of being a rock star.'

Florence could just imagine it; and she could all too

clearly imagine Rob on stage. Whatever role he'd taken in the band, even if he'd been stuck at the back behind a drum kit, he would've drawn all the attention. Just as he was holding her attention now. Her mouth felt as if it was glued to the roof of her mouth. Rob as a rock star... She shook herself mentally and strove for a note of friendly teasing. 'So how much of a flirtation was it? You thought about doing it and mimed a bit, or do you actually play something?'

'Oh, I had a proper band—me, my brother and a friend.' He laughed. 'I was going to be the lead guitarist and singer, Ollie did the bass and harmonies, and our mate Micky was the drummer. We used to practise in our garage.' He laughed even more. 'Weirdly, the whole street seemed to go out within five minutes of us turning our amps on.'

'You were that good?' she teased.

'We were terrible. And I mean *really* terrible. I'm not sure who was most relieved when we stopped, our parents or our neighbours.'

His eyes crinkled at the corners when he laughed. That gorgeous, gorgeous blue. It made her stomach swoop just to look at him.

He must know the effect he had on women. Yet he hadn't claimed that his band was brilliant and he could've been a pop star if he'd wanted to. He'd laughed about his own hopelessness. There was no posturing, no side to him. She liked that. She liked *him*. And that was enough to tip her into confessing, 'I never wanted to be in a band, but Lexy and I used to sing into hairbrushes in the kitchen on a Sunday morning.'

'So you can sing?' He looked interested.

'I can just about hold a tune,' she said, 'but it's more

the sort of thing I do in the car with Mum, or with Lexy and the girls. There's no way you'd ever get me up at the mic at a karaoke night.'

'Got you.'

'So, when you gave up the idea of being a rock star, what made you decide on medicine?' she asked.

'I fell in love with climbing,' he said, 'and I joined the local mountain rescue team. And it was a fairly easy step from learning first aid for mountain rescue to wanting to do full-on emergency medicine.' He smiled. 'I always found it a bit hard to sit still, as a kid, so I like the pace in the department. It suits me.'

And she found herself wondering what else would suit him. What else he liked. What made him tick.

Which was crazy. She didn't want to get involved with anyone, outside friendship. So why did Robert Langley snag her attention like this? Why couldn't she take her eyes off him? Why was she aware of every tiny shift in his body and every time his hand accidentally brushed against hers?

Thankfully the Head of Department saved her from blurting out something stupid by tapping a spoon against his glass and then doing the usual speech before giving out the 'secret Santa' presents. She wondered whose name Rob been given; this late on, she guessed that Shobu had probably swapped names with him.

The gifts were the usual mix of novelty socks, Christmas tree decorations for beards, good chocolate, mugs with rude slogans and silly games. Florence ended up with a gorgeous scented candle; Rob was given socks sporting polar bears wearing Santa hats.

And then the dancing started.

* * *

Rob had been very aware of Florence all through dinner. Every time his hand had brushed against hers, every time one of them had shifted in their chairs and accidentally pressed a leg against the other's, it had increased his awareness of her. The dress she was wearing made him think even more of Audrey Hepburn. And he really wanted to dance with her. Hold her close. Sway with her to sweet, soft music.

The sensible side of him knew that he should jam a lid on that attraction before it spilled over. Even though he knew from general chat in the staff kitchen that Florence was single, it didn't mean that she was looking for a relationship; though, from the way her gorgeous brown eyes had widened at him, he was pretty sure that she'd felt that same simmering awareness of him during dinner.

He ought to keep his distance. Dance with her in a group. Keep it all light and friendly and totally above board.

Except he was finding her irresistible.

He danced with two of the nurses, one of the other doctors and two of the support staff; all the while, he knew exactly where Florence was on the dance floor, even when his back was to her. For pity's sake. He wasn't looking for a partner. He wanted to concentrate on getting fully fit again so he could go back to his old life—or, at least, as much of it as possible. Climbing. Things that his past girlfriends had lost patience with—which was another of the reasons why his relationships never lasted. And why was he thinking about relationships now? This was ridiculous.

But he couldn't take his eyes off Florence. *The way she moved.*

* * *

Florence had been dancing all evening. Exactly the fun, safe dancing she'd intended to enjoy. But all the while she'd been very aware of exactly where Rob was on the dance floor. He'd admitted to being a terrible singer, but he was a good dancer. He paid attention to the way his partner moved. And she noticed that he danced with every single woman in their group, smiling and charming them: though in a nice way, not a sleazy way. He was inclusive, making sure that everyone had a good time.

Rob Langley was good with people.

And he was more than easy on the eye.

And he was single...

She shook herself. Not happening. Temporary colleagues only, she reminded herself. No complications, no disappointments, no heartbreak. She was done with having her heart broken and her dreams trampled into dust.

She smiled. Chatted to her colleagues. Danced. Smiled a bit more.

And then, at the end of the song, she felt as if she was tingling all over.

Rob was there.

Right next to her.

'Dr Jacobs. Would you care to dance?' he asked.

How could she possible resist? Though she made an attempt at a casual, 'Sure.'

Except this *would* have to be the song where the lights dimmed and everything slowed right down. The song where they ended up swaying close.

Before, she'd been chatting and laughing during a dance with a group of people.

Now, she was in his arms. Holding him close. Close enough to feel the warmth of his skin through his shirt, the warmth of his hand against her back.

Florence could hardly breathe.

Despite her high heels, she wasn't quite tall enough to dance cheek to cheek with him, but his nearness made her feel almost dizzy. How long had it been since she'd danced with someone like this? Even Dan…they hadn't danced together for years. They'd been too busy fighting about making babies—or, rather, *not* making them.

And this time Rob wasn't chatting about his teenage years and asking her about her family. He was holding her close enough for her to be able to feel the warmth of his body, the beat of his heart.

She pulled back slightly and risked glancing up at him. The intensity of his gaze practically seared her.

So did this mean he felt the same way that she did? As if the whole of the dance floor had just melted away, all the people and the music vanished into space, and there was just the two of them in the room? Did he, too, feel this sweet, crazy longing?

Maybe the questions showed in her eyes, because he drew her closer. Stooped a little more, so they were actually dancing cheek to cheek. And then she felt the touch of his lips at the corner of her mouth. Like gossamer. No pressure, no demands: just light and sweet and so very tempting.

Only a kiss. One little, tiny kiss.

What would be the harm in following his lead and kissing him back?

Not giving her common sense the chance to talk her out of it, she turned her face slightly so her lips brushed against his, and it sent a tingle through her whole body: as if every vein, every nerve-ending, had suddenly lit up. It almost knocked her off balance; except his arms were round her, holding her safely so she didn't fall, guiding her round the dance floor.

This wasn't meant to be happening.

For pity's sake. They were in a public place. Among lots of people they both worked with. It wasn't appropriate to start snogging his face off, as if they were teenagers.

Except then he kissed her. Still light, still gentle. And Florence couldn't think straight any more after that.

She was aware that the song had changed but the tempo hadn't. If she had any sense, she'd make herself take a step backwards and suggest he dance with someone else. Except she couldn't. She wanted his arms wrapped round her and hers round him, cocooning them both. She wanted to feel his heart beating in time with her own.

Even when the music changed tempo again and she managed to back away enough so that they both danced with other people, she was still so aware of Rob and how it had felt to kiss him. It set little tingles running all the way through her, and she was shocked to realise that it was desire.

It had been so long since she'd felt like that about anyone. Since she'd allowed herself to feel like that about anyone, because memories of the bitterness with Dan had held her back. And it threw her, to the point where she had no idea what to do about it.

Rob hadn't set out intentionally to kiss Florence. It had just happened. But it had shaken him. He couldn't remember the last time he'd felt like this: like a teenager who finally summoned up the courage to risk being knocked back by the girl he'd liked for ages and kissing her.

Florence hadn't knocked him back.

And he hadn't known her for ages, just for a couple of weeks.

He needed to be sensible. Like his twin. He remembered the deal they'd made. *Be more Ollie.* What would Oliver do now? He'd dance with his colleagues and his colleagues' partners, he'd make small talk, and he'd smile a lot. OK. It was a plan. A good plan. Rob followed it to the letter.

But, all the while, he was so aware of exactly where Florence was in the room. Moth to a flame, magnet, any cliché you wanted to pick: it was a mash-up of all of them. The end result was the same. There was a definite connection between them, and he wanted to explore it and find out what it meant. At the same time, he wanted to back off. And he wasn't used to being confused like this. He worked in emergency medicine, and all his favourite pastimes needed the same ability he needed at work: to be able to assess a situation and make a fast, informed decision. No dithering.

So why was he dithering now? Why was he such a mess?

Rob had planned to be sensible and say a cheerful goodnight to Florence at the end of the evening, just as he had with his other colleagues, but what came out of his mouth was something different. 'Do you have to rush off, or could you stay and have a drink with me?'

'The hotel's closing,' she said, her gorgeous brown eyes looking huge in the low light.

'Not for residents.'

She looked surprised. 'You're staying here tonight?'

'Yes.' It had been his back-up plan so, if the bone-deep tiredness that still occasionally hit him kicked in, he wouldn't have to worry about getting back to his rented flat. Not that he was going to tell her about any of that. 'Come and have a drink with me at the bar,' he said.

'A nightcap?'

Would she stay? Or would she back off? He wanted her to stay; but at the same time he wasn't used to re-acting to someone like this. And his mouth felt so dry he couldn't speak. He just nodded.

'All right. I'll have a glass of wine with you, on con-dition I buy the drinks.'

Funny how that made him feel like punching the air. Not that he'd be stupid enough to do that in front of her. Relief loosened his tongue again. 'I don't think they'll let you pay. The bar is for residents only,' he said with a smile. 'Though you can buy me a coffee some time next week instead, if it makes you feel better.'

What?

Why had he said that, as if he was setting up a date?

But she didn't run a mile. She just nodded. 'It's a deal.'

He found them a table in a quiet corner of the bar, checked what she wanted to drink, and bought them both a glass of dry white wine. And, while they chat-ted, he found himself watching her while she sipped her wine. Remembering how that mouth had felt against his, the warmth and the pressure and the sweetness. He wanted it to happen all over again. Wanted to kiss her back. Wanted to feel her melt into him.

When he caught her eye, she blushed. So was she thinking the same? Was she remembering how it had felt to kiss him? Did she want more?

She put her glass down. 'I should go.'

That would be sensible. But before he could stop himself, he said, 'Though there's another option.' His pulse kicked up a notch at the very thought of it, making him catch his breath and knocking all his common sense out of his head. 'You could stay.'

'Stay.'

She'd clearly just remembered that he had a room. Somewhere they could be private. Somewhere they could explore what was happening between them.

He could see the argument warring in her expression—should she stay, or should she go? What was holding her back? Did she think it would be difficult between them at work?

'If it makes a difference,' he said, 'this would be just between you and me, until we're both sure where this is going.'

There was a long, long pause.

Finally, she asked, 'And if I decide to stay?' There was the tiniest, tiniest crack in her voice.

Did she feel as nervous as he did?

He wanted to reassure her, yet at the same time he needed to let her know that he wanted her. 'I don't know,' he said. 'I wasn't planning this.' It was crazy. He was used to making fast decisions—*good* decisions—but they were judgements based on past experience.

This felt new. Like a step into the unknown. And it made him catch his breath.

Or maybe the admission was the reassurance she

needed: that he felt as much at sixes and sevens as she did. Because then she smiled. 'Yes.'

One little word.

And it made all the difference.

He stood up in silence and stretched his hand out to her. She stood up, took his hand, and walked to the lift with him.

The lift was surprisingly small, only just big enough for both of them to fit. Once the doors had closed behind them, Rob cupped her face gently in his hands and brushed his mouth lightly against hers.

She shivered when he broke the kiss.

'It wasn't supposed to happen like this,' he said softly, 'but life throws curveballs as well as good things. And nowadays I'm minded to catch the good things.'

'Me, too,' she said, and the look on her face told him she'd had some hard curveballs in the past.

He took her hand as they left the lift and kept holding it all the way down the corridor.

Please don't let the card key fail him and break the understanding between them. Please let them stay in this glorious, shiny bubble. Just the two of them and this shimmery feeling.

To his relief, his card key worked first time. He opened the door, stood aside to let her go into the room first, then slid the card into the slot by the light.

The lamp in the corner of the room was the only one lit, and she looked suddenly nervous as she perched on the edge of the chair. Yeah. He knew how that felt.

'You can change your mind,' he reassured her quietly. 'I can call you a taxi. There's no pressure to do anything you don't want to do, Florence.'

Giving her the choice seemed to decide her. 'Or there's another option,' she said, her voice husky.

His heart skipped another beat. 'What might that be?'

She stood up, closed the gap between them and kissed him.

It felt as if fireworks were going off in his head, splinters of gold and silver and starlight. As if he'd come back to life again after all these months of being stuck. She didn't see him as a patient; she saw him as a man. She wanted him as much as he wanted her. And this was going to happen.

When he broke the kiss, he turned her round and undid the zip of her dress, kissing his way down her spine as he did so.

She gave a little wriggle. He wasn't sure if it was pleasure or awkwardness, so he erred on the side of caution and turned her back round to face him. 'Everything all right?' he checked.

'Yes.'

'Good.' He kissed her lightly, then eased the dress over her shoulders and let it pool on the floor.

'You're beautiful,' he whispered, and traced the lacy edge of her bra with one finger.

She moistened her lower lip with the tip of her tongue, and his pulse speeded up.

'You're fully dressed. I think we need to even up the balance,' she said.

'I'm in your hands,' he said.

She struggled a bit with his bow tie, but finally managed it. His shirt was next, and he found breathing difficult as she undid each button, her fingers brushing against his skin and sending little shocks of pleasure across his nerve-ends.

Waiting wasn't something he was good at; but if he rushed her now he knew she'd back away and he'd never have another chance. So he let her set the pace, let her fingers explore the breadth of his shoulders, the muscles of his back. Every stroke, every touch drove him crazy with need. He was practically quivering when she stopped. 'Florence?'

Please don't let her call a halt. He took her hand, lifted it to his mouth, and kissed each fingertip in turn. 'I'm trying to let you set the pace,' he said. 'But my self-control is shredding by the second. I'm not sure how much longer I can hold out.'

Oh, the things that rueful smile did to her insides.

Rob Langley was charming, and he knew it.

But he was also sexy as hell, and Florence wanted him. The way she'd felt when he'd danced with her—it had been a long, long time since she'd felt like that. For a couple of years before her marriage had turned bad, if she was honest about it. And she wanted to feel like that again. Come back out of the cold loneliness of her life. Let him heat her blood to boiling point.

He'd given her the control.

Time to make it snap.

She stood on tiptoe and kissed him.

Things went a bit fuzzy after that. The next thing Florence knew, they were lying on the bed together, both naked. She had absolutely no idea who had removed whose clothes and when. And it wasn't because she'd drunk too much wine: it was Rob's touch that made everything else feel irrelevant. Rob was kneeling between her thighs and kissing his way down her body, nuzzling the hollows of her collar bones, working his way downwards to tease each nipple in turn, then kissing his way down over her abdomen.

All Florence could think of was the way he made her feel. The warmth spreading through her as he stroked her skin, teased her with his mouth and his hands until she was quivering and nearly hyperventilating with need. She wanted him so much, it made her head spin.

Her climax shimmered through her unexpectedly. She'd almost forgotten what it felt like, that rush of pleasure bubbling through her.

'OK?' he asked.

'Very OK.' She couldn't help grinning.

He grinned back. 'Good. I wanted the first time to be for you.'

An unselfish lover. Something Dan hadn't been when their marriage had been exploding. Sex had been more like fighting. The memory made her catch her breath; but it wouldn't be fair to dump this on Rob now. So she made herself smile as if nothing was wrong.

The brittleness must've shown, though, because he kissed her very gently—reassuring, not demanding. 'You can still change your mind.'

'No, it's…complicated,' she said.

'There's someone else?'

She shook her head. 'I wouldn't do that. Just…a bit of baggage. Unwanted baggage. Ignore it.'

'Better than that. I'll try to make you forget it,' he said softly. He kissed her again, and aroused her with his hands and his mouth until she was quivering with need; it shocked her how desperately she wanted this. He ripped open the foil packet, slid on the condom, knelt between her thighs and eased into her. He waited for her to adjust to the feel of him inside her, and then he began to move.

The waves of pleasure built again and she wrapped her legs round him, drawing him deeper.

This time, they hit the peak at the same time, and they held each other tightly until the little aftershocks had died away.

'Better deal with the condom,' he said, gently disentangling himself, and headed for the en suite bathroom.

Was this her cue to leave?

It had been so long since she'd done anything like this. She couldn't remember what the etiquette was. Did she get dressed and leave? Or did she stay?

She was still trying to work her way through the dilemma when he came back from the bathroom. And that was when she noticed the scar on his lower abdomen. It was in the same place as she'd expect to see a scar from an appendectomy, but the colour of the skin made the scar look newer than he'd said it was.

Clearly he realised what she was seeing, because he grimaced. 'Sorry. I should've put a towel round me or something.'

She shook her head. 'It's not that. It looks…new.'

He could trust her—or he could back away.

He took a deep breath while he thought about it, then decided. 'OK. Short version: I had a kidney transplant back in June. My consultant cleared me to go back to work part time, so I'm easing myself back into things. That's why I'm only doing three days a week on the ward.'

Her eyes narrowed. 'A kidney transplant is a pretty major thing.'

He sighed. 'I know. The head of department knows about it but we agreed to keep it between us. I don't want people thinking I'm weak or I can't do my job.'

'Why would they think that?'

'Because…' He sighed. 'Because that's how I've felt for months, being unable to do anything I'd normally do. I've hated people treating me as if I'm fragile. That's not who I am.'

'Definitely not a delicate little flower,' she agreed.

'Are you…?' She was. That little glimmer in her eyes. She was *teasing* him. All the fight went out of him. He gave her a rueful smile. 'No. Though I'm kind of behaving like one. It's just…you've seen me as *me*. I don't want that to change.'

'I'm not going to judge you,' she said. 'It sounds to as me as if you're already doing quite enough of that for yourself.'

'Maybe,' he admitted. 'It's messed with my head, not being able to do what I've always done. Feeling as if I've been stuffed into a box that gets smaller every day.'

'Tell me,' she said softly. 'It isn't going any further than me.'

'I've already worked out for myself that you're not a gossip.'

'Thank you,' she said. 'Just for the record, I didn't tell anyone what I heard you say about your appendix.'

'Thank you.' He blew out a breath. 'I was volunteering for a humanitarian aid organisation, helping out after an earthquake. I have skills that can be useful and I like working in challenging situations. I'd been feeling a bit rough, but I put that down to a change in water and food.' He shrugged. 'It turned out it was my appendix, which then ruptured. I ended up with severe blood poisoning and it wiped out my kidneys. I was on dialysis for a while.' And he'd felt every second dragging by, slower than a glacier scraping across a valley. 'I needed a transplant. Ollie—my brother—was a live donor and gave me one of his kidneys.'

'That's an amazing thing to do for someone,' she said.

'I know. He's an amazing man.' He looked at her. 'And I appreciate you listening.'

'No problem.' She looked at him. 'So what now?'

'Now I've completely ruined the mood?'

'I was the one who brought up the subject,' she said. 'So you can't take the entire blame.'

'I guess,' he said wryly. 'I can call you a taxi, if you'd like. Or...' He took a deep breath. 'Or you can stay. Fall asleep with me. Let go and forget the world, just for a little while. Just you and me. No baggage.'

It was tempting.

So very, very tempting.

After all, what did she have to go back to? An empty flat that still didn't feel like home. Or she could stay here, curl up in the arms of the man who'd just made her feel so amazing. Forget everything that had made her miserable in the last few years. Enjoy this warmth and closeness, just for a while. No promises, no complications.

The decision was easy.

'I'll stay,' she said.

He smiled, and helped her tidy up their clothes, before taking her hand and drawing her back to bed. He lay on his back, and she curled into him, resting her head on his shoulder and letting her fingers entwine loosely with his.

She'd worry about tomorrow later.

Tonight, she'd just *be*.

CHAPTER THREE

THE NEXT MORNING, Florence woke, feeling warm and comfortable. It took a moment for her to realise she wasn't in her own bed. And another to realise that a body was cuddled round hers, an arm wrapped round her and keeping her against him. And another to remember the night before: dancing with Rob, kissing him, making love...

Which meant she'd just made her life complicated.

They hadn't actually made any promises to each other.

But how was she going to face him this morning?

She didn't want another relationship. After the misery of the way her marriage had ended, she didn't want to risk her heart ever again. Last night, she'd given in to temptation—and the possibilities filled her with panic.

Would Rob see this as the start of something? Last night, he'd said about forgetting the world for a while. No baggage. They'd agreed on one night: but how would he see things this morning?

Even though she knew they really needed to talk about this, the whole thing scared her stupid. If he did want it to be the start of something, she wasn't sure she could face the risk of it all going wrong, just as it had with Dan. She'd be setting herself up for rejection—and she'd already faced enough of that with Dan. She didn't want to be the one who wasn't good enough, all over again.

Plus there was the fact he'd made it clear he was only here temporarily. What was the point of starting something, letting herself fall for him, only for him to leave?

Whatever way she looked at this, it was going to end up with her being the one left. Again. She couldn't see any alternatives.

And even if her fears were all baseless—even if Rob did want a relationship, even if he changed his mind and stayed here, even if she could be brave enough to take the chance—what he'd told her last night made it clear that he was the last person she should let herself fall for. He'd had a kidney transplant. Which meant that, even though his brother was the donor of the kidney, he'd need to take immunosuppressant drugs to stop his body rejecting the new kidney. As a doctor, Florence knew that immunosuppressant drugs affected fertility. So being with Rob would put her back in exactly the same position as she'd been with Dan: with her partner unable to have children without medical intervention. And who was to say he wanted children anyway?

She couldn't handle the infertility issue again.

So it would be better to leave right now. Call a halt to this, before either of them could get any more deeply involved. She'd have to regard last night as nothing more than a fling—a fling that had made her feel amazing, but it wasn't to be repeated so she needed to stuff her emotions and all the longing back in the box where they belonged. And she'd have to keep things strictly professional between them for the rest of his temporary stay in their department.

His breathing appeared to be deep and even. What were the chances of her being able to move his arm away from her, wriggle out of bed, get dressed and leave without him waking? she wondered.

Probably slender, but she was going to try. Even though she knew it was cowardly and a bit mean. At least it might save them both a bit of embarrassment. She'd text him later to apologise.

Carefully, she slid her fingers under his arm and moved it upwards.

He responded by murmuring and drawing her closer.

Oh, help. So there was no way out of this.

OK. She'd try another approach. Be brisk and efficient. Wake him, tell him she needed to leave—without making any excuses—and ask him to look away while she dressed at the speed of light.

She took a deep breath, moved his arm away and slid to the side of the bed. 'Rob. *Rob*.'

He was awake instantly. 'Florence?'

'Sorry. I need to go.'

She climbed out of bed. Then she made the mistake of looking at him. Those gorgeous blue eyes. The stubble that had made her want to touch his face. The sensual curve of his mouth.

It made her remember how he'd made her feel last night. He'd been generous, focusing on her pleasure. Even the first time had been way better than a first time should've been: no awkwardness or embarrassment, just exploring and delighting in their discoveries. They'd made love twice more in the night, and their bodies had been so in tune...

She needed to go. Now. Before she compounded her mistake, lost herself in Rob's arms again, and started to want things she couldn't have.

'Sorry,' she mumbled.

His hair was too short to be rumpled, but somehow he still managed to look all rumpled and sexy. And she was so tempted to forget all the worries spiralling in her head and climb back into bed with him.

'Why don't you stay for breakfast?' he said. 'We can order room service. Then I'll give you a lift home.'

For a second Florence could imagine it: sharing coffee with him, stealing bits of croissant from each other's plates, poring over the weekend papers and doing the crossword together...

Domestic and lovely—everything she missed from the best part of her marriage, and everything she couldn't let herself wish for again.

'Sorry. I can't. I'll get a taxi. Would you mind... um...?' Her face heated. Considering how intimate they'd been last night, asking him to avert his gaze while she dressed would make her sound like a teenager, not a sensible thirty-two-year-old.

To her relief, he didn't make her ask out loud. He just said, 'Sure,' and closed his eyes.

'Thank you.' She retrieved her clothing and dressed swiftly. As soon as she got home, she'd shower and brush her teeth and change her clothes, but for now she was going to have to brazen it out. 'I...um—I guess I'll see you at work.'

'Yeah.' His eyes were still closed, and his expression was completely unreadable.

This was one of the most awkward and embarrassing mornings she could ever remember. She didn't have a clue what to say to him—and telling him about Dan would make her feel pathetic and whiny. She was an adult who should've got over the betrayal by now. And none of this was Rob's fault. But she just couldn't explain how she felt. The words stuck in her throat.

Wanting to get out of the situation as fast as possible, she headed for the door. 'Thanks for...' Her manners deserted her: how could she possibly thank him for sex? Squirming, knowing she was behaving badly but unable to stop herself, she fled.

Thankfully she managed to get a taxi almost immediately.

Home, she thought. Home, for a hot shower, and wash some common sense back into her head.

Because she and Rob were going to have to work together for the next couple of months, and their patients had to come first. There wasn't room for embarrassment and awkwardness. She'd have to find a way of fixing this.

But she needed a shower and mug of disgustingly strong coffee before she could even start to think how to do that.

It was the worst 'morning after' Rob could ever remember.

Last night, Florence Jacobs had been soft and warm and gorgeous. He thought the sex had been good for both of them. She'd stayed; she'd slept in his arms; and while he'd been sliding into sleep he'd planned to ask her to stay for breakfast in the morning, and then suggest that maybe they could do something together—either today if she wasn't busy, or the next time they both had a day off if she already had other plans. Maybe a walk on the beach or a pub lunch: time to get to know each other without any pressure. She was the first woman in a long while he'd wanted to get to know better.

This morning, if she'd been able to get out of bed without waking him, he was pretty sure he would've woken to find she'd vanished without even a note. As it was, she hadn't been able to get dressed and leave quickly enough.

What had gone wrong?

The more he thought about it, the more mystified he was. He was pretty sure he hadn't done anything to hurt her or upset her, but she'd made it very clear she didn't want to get to know him better. That, for her, last night was a one-off.

Maybe it was something to do with the baggage she'd mentioned last night rather than something he'd done.

But now he was beginning to realise how quite a few of his girlfriends had felt—because he was usually the one who left. The one who didn't commit. And he'd probably been fooling himself when he'd thought they'd stayed friends: because being the one who was rejected really wasn't a nice feeling. It was the first time Rob had ever felt that way, and he didn't like it. The whole thing made him feel cross with himself for wanting something he couldn't have, and ashamed of the way he'd treated his exes.

Somehow he and Florence were going to have to find a way to rewind to their professional relationship, leave the embarrassment behind and focus on their patients.

Except now he knew what it was like to kiss her. How it felt to have her skin sliding against his. The expression in her eyes when she climaxed.

He wanted more.

But she clearly didn't.

'Get a grip,' he told himself, and headed for the bathroom. A cold shower would sort his head out. And then he'd work out a plan to repair the mess he'd made.

A shower and a mug of coffee didn't make things better. Florence was completely out of sorts. Even sewing, her favourite hobby, didn't absorb her the way it usually did; instead of losing herself and her worries in the rhythm, she found herself stopping and unpicking her work. In the end, she gave up and texted her sister.

Can I come over for coffee? Xx

The reply was instant:

Course you can. xx

Lexy greeted her at the door with a big hug, then took a step back and frowned before ushering Florence into the kitchen. 'What's happened? I expected you to be buzzing after last night. You love departmental nights out. Especially when there's dancing.'

'It was fine,' Florence fibbed.

'Just "fine"?' Lexy gave her a sidelong look, then put a mug of coffee and a chocolate muffin in front of her. 'Max has taken the girls to get some bread for lunch, so they'll probably feed the ducks on the way home. We have half an hour. Talk.'

'There's nothing to say.'

Lexy folded her arms and stared at Florence.

'Don't give me your scary ballet teacher look,' Florence said, but she caved anyway. 'I did something stupid.'

Lexy waited.

Florence blew out a breath. 'I...um...had a one-night stand.'

'With?'

Florence didn't want to answer that, so she mumbled and looked away.

'And you used protection?'

'Yes. Of course.'

'Not *completely* stupid, then.' Lexy raised an eyebrow. 'Assuming you were both consenting adults, what's the problem?'

Florence groaned. Time to confess all. 'He's my new colleague. My new *temporary* colleague.'

'And?'

Why didn't her sister get it? Florence covered her face with her hands. 'I just can't believe I did that. Spent the night with someone I hardly know.'

'It probably did you good. It's more than past time you let yourself get over Dan,' Lexy said gently.

'But he's not going to be around for long. This thing—it doesn't have any kind of future.'

'Also not a problem. You could just think of him as your transition man. The fling who helped you move on from Dan,' Lexy said. She frowned. 'Unless you really like him.'

That was the scary thing. Florence rather thought she did. She'd enjoyed talking to him at the departmental Christmas dinner. She'd enjoyed teasing him and flirting. She'd enjoyed kissing him. Making love with him.

And he was the first man she'd actually noticed since Dan.

'I don't know what I think,' she said. Which wasn't

a *complete* fib; right then, she was more confused than she ever remembered being.

'Floss, these things happen. Where you work, it's intense. Like a pressure cooker. Everyone needs to let off steam from time to time.'

'I guess. But I don't do this sort of thing. I don't have flings.'

'Maybe it's time you did.' Lexy look fascinated. 'Have you got any pictures from last night? Is he cute?'

'No pictures—and very cute,' Florence admitted. He was like every movie star or pop star crush she'd had as a teen: tall, dark hair, amazing eyes, amazing cheekbones. A beautiful mouth. And the way he moved...

'He's going to be working at the hospital for a few more weeks, at least. So, if you like each other, you could make it a longer fling instead of a single night,' Lexy suggested.

'I can't do that.' Florence bit her lip. 'And I have to work with him.'

'Plenty of people have relationships with their colleagues, Floss. You're professional enough not to let it get in the way at work.'

'It's not just that. I...um...pretty much bolted this morning. Goodbye and—' She groaned, covering her face with her hands. 'Oh, this is bad. I almost said thank you for...' She choked on the words, embarrassed beyond belief. Her sister was just about the only person in the world she'd admit this to.

'Thank you for the shag?' Lexy burst out laughing. 'Oh, sweetheart.' She hugged Florence. 'And now you're feeling like a teenager and you don't know what to do about it.'

'Pretty much. I didn't behave well. He offered to order us room service breakfast.'

'That's nice. Thoughtful.'

'And I just bolted.'

'Look on the bright side. It means he'll know you're not used to one-night stands.'

'I feel so stupid.'

'You're human, Floss. We all do things we regret. It's fine.' Lexy smiled at her. 'So tell me about him.'

'There's not much to tell. He's an emergency doctor, he works with me, and apparently he climbs.'

'Why's he temporary?'

'He had a burst appendix when he was out helping in an earthquake zone. It wiped out his kidneys and he needed a transplant. His family's round this way, so he's here for a while to be near them.'

'It sounds as if he's had a rough time.'

Which made Florence feel even worse about running out on him like that. She couldn't even text him to apologise, because now she thought about it she didn't actually have his number.

'What aren't you telling me?' Lexy asked.

Trust her sister to get straight to the point. 'When you have a transplant, you have to take medication to stop your body rejecting the new organ. And it affects your fertility.'

Lexy made the connection immediately. 'So, if you date him and you let yourself fall for him big-time, you're risking another Dan situation.'

At last she got it. 'Yes.'

'Except not everyone reacts like Dan did. This guy might not be a total arse who wouldn't consider IVF or adoption because it threatens his sense of masculinity,'

Lexy said. 'You're overthinking this, Floss. If you like the guy, date him. See where it goes.'

'I can't face putting myself in another Dan situation,' Florence said. 'But, on the other hand, I can hardly say to him, hey, we can extend our one-night stand if you like, but first I need to know if you want children—and if you'd be up for IVF with donor sperm, if you didn't freeze your own sperm before the transplant and the immunosuppressants make you infertile.'

'That'd be a teensy bit full-on,' Lexy agreed. 'Does he know about Dan?'

'No. Nobody at the hospital knows what happened in Leeds. Just that I was married before, it didn't work out, and I'm focused on my work.' And, if she told herself that often enough, Florence was sure she'd be able to do it. Focus on her work and not think about the missing bits of her life.

Lexy hugged her again. 'Honey, I know you're scared. But you can't keep a barrier round yourself for ever. You're the one who's missing out. It's like learning to dance or sewing. You can't do the new step or stitch at first, because it keeps going wrong. But you try again and again. You break it down into little chunks. You practise. And eventually it clicks.'

'Dating isn't anything like learning to dance or sewing,' Florence protested.

'It so is,' Lexy said, and ruffled her hair. 'It's about facing the fear. What's the worst that can happen? You start dating him, you find out that you don't really like each other, and you agree to be just friends.'

No. The worst thing that could happen would be falling in love with him, and finding out that he didn't want children. Which Florence knew was being contrary, because not having a partner in the first place was the quickest way of making sure she didn't have children. 'Uh-huh,' she said.

'Talk to him,' Lexy advised.

'I will,' Florence fibbed.

'Of course it's going to be a bit awkward when you see him next. But smile, ask him if you can go for coffee in your break, and explain you had a bit of a tough time at the end of your marriage and you've forgotten every bit of dating etiquette you ever knew, and can you please start again with a clean slate and maybe go out for a drink one evening after work?'

It sounded so easy when her sister put it like that. So simple. One step after another.

So why did it feel so daunting?

Once Florence had left, Rob had a shower, changed and went to the restaurant for breakfast. He knew he needed to refuel, but he couldn't face the idea of room service on his own. Not after the way Florence had rejected him. He just wanted to get out of that room and away from these uncomfortable feelings.

Coffee and a bacon sandwich restored some of his equilibrium, but not by that much. He packed his overnight bag, tidied the room and went to Reception to settle his bill.

Part of him was tempted to drive to Ashermouth Bay and see Oliver, but he was pretty sure that his twin would have plans with Gemma. He knew they'd both be generous and kind enough to ask him to join them, but he didn't want to play gooseberry—and he also didn't want to ruin their day with his bad mood.

His parents? No, because his mother would notice he was antsy and she'd fuss.

Friends—apart from the fact that it was several hours' drive to Manchester and there wouldn't be much daylight left when he got there, they'd all be busy either working at the hospital or already out in the peaks.

Climbing.

The thing he missed more than anything. The one thing that could make him feel better. Feeling the wind in his hair, pushing his body to the limits, being at one with the earth. But he also knew he wasn't fit enough to do it, and he wasn't going to be selfish enough to put a rescue team at risk just because he was out of sorts.

Instead, he spent most of Saturday cleaning his flat and hating every minute of it.

The place still didn't feel like home, even after he'd followed through on the ideas of putting family photographs on the mantelpiece. How did his twin manage to make somewhere feel like home within ten minutes, while everything Rob did felt temporary?

'For pity's sake, stop whining and snap out of it,' he told himself crossly. 'You're so, so lucky. You've got a family who loves you as much as you love them—including a brother who loves you enough to give you a kidney so can you function again instead of being stuck in a hospital bed. You're doing the job that gives your life meaning. You've got a roof over your head. You have friends, even if most of them happen to be on the opposite side of the country right now. You have absolutely *nothing* to be miserable about.'

Though the thought wouldn't go.

What was so wrong with him that Florence had backed away from him so fast?

Was it because he'd suggested it being just a one-night thing and she thought it had been a mistake?

And maybe she was right. He didn't have a great track record, How many relationships had he let fizzle out because he hadn't been prepared to put enough effort in? How many women had he hurt—without meaning to—because he hadn't thought about anything but the next challenge, the next adventure?

He still didn't have an answer by the time he saw her again in the department on Monday.

His skin suddenly felt too tight. Awkward didn't even begin to cover it.

'Good morning!' she said, all bright and breezy and smiley—just as she was with all their other colleagues.

But he noticed that she didn't meet his eyes. Clearly this was awkward for her, too.

No way could he discuss the situation with her, especially here. The last thing he wanted was gossip running like wildfire around the hospital; he might be here only temporarily, but she wasn't, and it wouldn't be fair to make her the centre of gossip.

He was just going to have to make the best of it. Treat her as if she was just any other team member, and not the woman who'd made him feel as if he'd come back properly to life.

He switched into polite professional mode, too. 'Morning.' Hopefully they wouldn't be rostered in Resus together today, where they'd have to work closely together—and, even worse, risk accidentally touching. He was relieved to discover that they were both on Minors, which would mean they were unlikely to see each other unless one of them needed a second opinion, and he could focus on his patients.

All went according to plan until mid-afternoon, when he could hear someone literally bellowing with pain.

'Please excuse me a second,' he said to the patient whose sprained ankle he'd been examining, and headed for the bay where the ambulance had brought in a man whose arm was in a sling but who was clearly in terrific pain because he yelled and swore every time the movement of the trolley affected his arm.

Florence was a few moments in front of him. 'What's happened?' she asked.

'This is Joe, aged forty-five. He's a builder, fell backwards into a hole, and he's hurt his shoulder,' the paramedic said. 'I'm guessing it's a dislocation. We've given some pain relief but it hasn't touched the pain, and we've put his arm in a sling and a blanket between his arm and chest to support it.'

'I've dislocated a shoulder before, playing rugby, and it didn't hurt anything like this,' Joe said, then roared with pain and swore again. 'For pity's sake, please don't move my shoulder! You're killing me!'

'I need to check whether it's a dislocation or a fracture before I can give you any real pain relief,' Florence said. 'So I'm sending you for an X-ray—I'm sorry, you're clearly in a lot of pain, but if you can grit your teeth and put up with it for a few more minutes we'll know what we're dealing with and can treat you properly. If it's a dislocation, we can fix it here—we'll give you a sedative to relax you and pull it back into place. If it's a fracture, you might need surgery. Either way, it's going to take a couple of months to heal because there will be soft tissue damage.'

'OK. Thanks for being honest,' Joe said. 'And I'm sorry for swearing. It just— Argh!'

'Let's get you to X-Ray,' Florence said. 'Is there anyone we can call for you?'

'It's OK. They called my wife from the ambulance and she's on her way in.'

'If it's a dislocation,' Rob said, 'I'll help with the traction.'

She didn't look at him, but nodded. 'Thanks.'

The X-ray files came through on the computer a few minutes later, showing that Joe had indeed dislocated his shoulder—but it was like no dislocation Rob had ever seen before. 'It's wedged,' he said in disbelief. 'No wonder he's in so much pain.'

'I've never seen anything like that in fourteen years of medicine,' she said.

Fourteen years. Assuming that included her years as a student, that made her two years older than him. And, strictly speaking, Florence was his senior, so he'd better listen to her. 'What's the plan?' he asked.

'More pain relief, sedation to relax him, and traction,' she said. This time, she looked at Rob. 'You're sure you're OK to help?'

Oh, for pity's sake. If she hadn't slept with him, she wouldn't have seen the scar and he wouldn't have told her about the transplant. She'd promised not to treat him any differently—and yet that was exactly what she was doing. Last week, she wouldn't even have questioned whether he was OK to help. He wouldn't be here in the first place if he wasn't OK to work.

So much for thinking that he'd come to a place where they'd see him for himself, not as someone who needed special treatment. Annoyance made him sharp. 'Yes,' he said tightly. 'The information I gave you about my kidney was privileged. I've already told you I would never put a patient at risk, so I'd prefer you not to mention it again. Fortunately nobody else is here to overhear you. I really don't want that information spreading.'

She flinched slightly at the rebuke, and there was a slash of colour across her cheeks. 'I was out of order. Sorry.'

'Apology accepted. We'll draw a line under it and move on,' he said.

And he didn't mean just her comment about his operation. They needed to move on from the weekend. From the mistake they'd both made. The one that loomed between them and made everything awkward and scratchy. He held her gaze for long enough that he hoped she'd worked out what he wasn't saying.

She nodded. 'Agreed.'

'Good.'

She gave Joe a mild sedative and painkiller. 'I think this is going to need three of us.'

Because she still thought he was under par?

Either he'd said it aloud or it was written all over his face, because she said, 'Because it's wedged, and it's going to need more than two people to sort it.'

It was a good call, and he knew he was being oversensitive. 'I'll go and grab someone,' he said.

The first person he found was Ranj, one of the junior doctors. 'Ranj, have you got a minute?' he asked. 'We've got a patient with a dislocated shoulder—it's wedged—and Florence thinks it'll take three of us for the traction.'

'Wedged?' Ranj whistled. 'That sounds horrific.'

'He's in a lot of pain,' Rob said.

'Poor guy. I'll help,' Ranj said, and followed him back to the patient.

Florence was sitting next to Joe, holding his hand and talking him through what they were about to do. 'We'll try to be as fast as we can, Joe, and the sedative should take most of the edge off it,' she said, 'but if you need to swear your head off to get through the traction, do it because none of us will be offended. We've all heard worse. Or tell us the most terrible dad jokes you know. You've got a captive audience and we'll be forced to laugh.'

Rob liked the way she'd assessed Joe's character so quickly and put him at ease; Joe was still clearly in a great deal of pain, but thanks to Florence he was much more relaxed than when he'd first come into the department.

'I can't think of any jokes,' Joe said.

'Right. Then tell us about the best Christmas dinner you've ever had,' she suggested.

'My mum's,' Joe said. 'She does everything you can think of. Loads of veg, all the trimmings, and she does the best roast potatoes in the world. They're fluffy in the middle and crispy on the outside. But don't tell my wife—she's competitive about roast potatoes, and she and Mum fight over the best way to do it.'

'Choose your potato wisely, make sure you have edges when you cut them, shake them after you parboil them and use very hot fat,' she said promptly. 'None of that covering in semolina malarkey.'

So she was a cook? Rob wouldn't have a clue how to do roast potatoes. Not unless you could get them for the microwave.

'I dunno about semolina,' Ranj said, 'but my mum

covers her roast potatoes with a spice mix before she puts them in the oven and they're awesome.'

Between them, they got Joe talking and distracted—and did the traction to unwedge his dislocated shoulder.

'All right. You're done,' Florence said. 'Don't go rolling your shoulder for a few days, but I'd like you to try lifting your arm for me now.'

Joe looked unsure, as if remembering the severe pain last time he'd tried lifting his arm, but he did as she'd asked. 'Oh, my God. I can actually move my arm again and it doesn't hurt!' His grimace turned to a beaming smile. 'That's amazing. Thank you so much.'

'It's still going to hurt a bit when those painkillers and sedative wear off,' Florence warned. 'You're going to need painkillers for a few days. I'm also going to put you in a sling, and you need to rest that arm for the next five days.'

Horror flashed across Joe's face. 'I can't do that! I've got loads to do at work.'

Yeah. Rob knew how that felt: wanting to get on with your job and being told to rest instead. The unbearable frustration. Ranj had gone again, so he felt safe admitting to his past. 'For what it's worth, mate, I've learned the hard way that it's better to do as you're told and rest,' he said quietly. 'Otherwise you end up having to rest even longer to fix the damage you did by doing things too early.'

'You dislocated your shoulder?' Joe asked.

'Burst appendix,' Rob said. 'And there's nothing worse than having to sit about and rest for even longer than you were originally told, and realising it's your own fault for being stubborn and not listening to someone who does actually know better. Trust me.'

'Trust you, you're a doctor?' Joe asked with a grin.

'Something like that.' Rob exchanged a glance with Florence, and felt as if he'd been seared. Her brown eyes were almost sparking with anger. Though it wasn't surprising that she was annoyed. He'd bitten her head off for alluding to his transplant, and here he was shooting his mouth off about precisely the same thing just a few minutes later. What a hypocrite.

'No heavy lifting for at least six weeks,' Florence said. 'It looks as if there's a bit of tissue damage, but hopefully we can manage it with physio—otherwise you'll need surgery.'

'Which means even more time off work?' Joe asked.

'Got it in one,' Florence said. 'I know it's not what you want to hear, but I'm afraid Dr Langley's right. Healing takes time. I can give you some exercises to do over the next few days to help with stiffness, and I'll refer you to physio.'

'I'll leave you to it and go back to my patient,' Rob said. 'All the best, Joe. And listen to Dr Jacobs. She knows her stuff.' Even if things weren't great between them personally, right now, he respected her professionally.

He went back to his patient with the sprained ankle, strapped it up and gave advice for ongoing care. He tried not to be disappointed that Florence still seemed to be avoiding him. And he lied to Oliver that evening on the phone, saying that he was absolutely fine. He wasn't fine. At all. But he also didn't know how to even start fixing this.

CHAPTER FOUR

THERE WAS NO thaw between Rob and Florence during the next week.

Maybe he'd been a bit *too* sharp, he thought, snapping at her when she'd asked if he was really OK to help with traction. She clearly hadn't meant it as a dig at him. She'd been concerned about both her patient and her colleague. If he was completely honest with himself, in her shoes he would've asked the same question.

He would've apologised to her, except he was still smarting from the way she'd walked out on him the morning after the Christmas party. Previously, he'd always stayed on friendly terms with anyone he'd dated—well, OK, he hadn't actually *dated* Florence, he'd done it the wrong way round and slept with her before dating her—and it rankled that she'd been so desperate to leave that she hadn't even had breakfast with him the next morning. She'd made it very clear that she didn't want to date him.

Suck it up and move on, he told himself.

He needed to treat her the same as he treated all his other colleagues, or someone would notice and rumours would start flying, which would make things even worse.

He just about managed it.

But on Friday he felt distinctly rough in the middle of his shift. Hot, and shivery, and there was a pain in his lower back.

If a patient with his own medical history had walked into the department with those symptoms, Rob would have sent him straight to the renal department for an urgent consultation.

Was this a sign of the transplant failing? He knew the stats. Twenty per cent of transplants failed in the first year, despite the patient taking medication to stop their body rejecting the new organ.

Intellectually, he knew that it was more likely he'd come down with some other kind of infection; the immunosuppressants he was taking to avoid his body rejecting the transplant meant he was more susceptible to viruses and urinary tract infections. But the fear still rippled through him. What if his body was rejecting Oliver's kidney? Would he end up back on dialysis, stuck in bed and resting for months and months until another kidney was available, resenting every second he was stuck inside?

He didn't want to walk out of his shift, but he wasn't going to be stubborn and leave it too long. He was on an early shift, so he'd finish work mid-afternoon. He'd go and have a chat with the renal team then. In the meantime, he needed to keep going. The best way to get his temperature down a bit and take some of the edge off the pain would be paracetamol. He headed to the staff kitchen, and had just grabbed some water and taken two tablets out of a foil pack when Florence walked in.

'Are you all right?' she asked.

'Fine, thank you.' He winced inwardly as he heard how snippy he sounded. He hadn't meant to be mean.

'You look like crap,' she said.

Right. So she wasn't pulling punches, either.

She gave him a very pointed look. 'So I'll ask you again. Are you all right?'

'I'm not sure,' he admitted. 'I was fine when I came to work.'

'And now?'

He might as well tell her. Then she could tell him that he probably had a bug or a UTI. Confirm his self-diagnosis. And he could go back to work. 'Hot, shivery and there's a bit of a pain in my lower back.'

She took the temperature gun from its box in the first-aid drawer and aimed it at his forehead. 'Thirty-eight point five,' she said, showing him the red screen.

Officially a fever. No wonder he felt hot and shivery.

'Go to the renal department,' she said. 'Now.'

He'd already thought this through. 'I'll go in a couple of hours' time, at the end of my shift.'

'No, you'll go *now*.' She raised her eyebrows. 'I'm in charge of Minors today, and you're on my team, so you'll do as I tell you.'

She was pulling rank on him? For a second, he stared at her in shock. Then he dropped his gaze. 'Bossy,' he muttered.

'It's most likely to be a bug or a UTI, but there's also the chance it's what you fear it is, and you need to get it checked out,' she said. 'I've heard you telling our patients not to be stubborn and do what they're told. So I suggest, *Dr* Langley, that you take your own advice.' She folded her arms. 'Actually—to make sure you do, I'm coming with you.'

'You don't need to do that.'

'Yes, I do. I'm responsible for my team's well-being.'

He shook his head. 'I'm in the middle of my shift. I can't just walk out and leave everyone to pick up the slack.'

'You're on an early.' She glanced at her watch. 'That means we've got three hours until you were done anyway. If they sign you off, we can manage until the end of the shift. And I haven't had my break yet, so I'm taking it now. We're going to the renal department.'

He was feeling rough enough to give in gracefully and let her usher him to the renal department.

'Let me know when he's done,' she said to the secretary, 'and I'll sort out transport.'

'I can dr—' he began, then stopped as she gave him a very pointed look. Since when could brown eyes freeze you like that?

Florence Jacobs could be seriously scary.

Though she was absolutely right. Of course he couldn't drive. He was way too distracted with pain and worry, and he'd be a danger to other road users.

'Thank you,' he said instead.

'You're welcome. I'd better get back to the department.'

And she still hadn't had a rest from work. She'd spent her break looking after him. 'I'm sorry,' he said.

'There's nothing to apologise for. When you're feeling rough at work, you need a colleague to look out for you,' she said.

Which put him in his place. She'd just made it clear that she saw him as a colleague, and a temporary one at that.

Though he knew she could've just left him to struggle on. Instead, she'd helped him. Bossily, but she'd helped him.

'I'll see you later,' she said, and left him to the ministrations of the renal department.

Rob Langley must feel absolutely dreadful if he was actually listening to her and doing what she suggested, Florence thought.

What she'd said to him was true enough. She would've done the same for any of her colleagues who were feeling ill on shift: made sure they were OK, and arranged cover if there were more than a couple of hours of their shift left.

But she still felt guilty about the way she'd behaved towards Rob almost a fortnight ago. She'd bolted from his hotel room, the morning after they'd spent the night together, without any explanation. He'd done nothing wrong, and she'd treated him badly. And she'd been starchy with him ever since, thanks to a mixture of awkwardness and shame. He'd snapped at her for nearly breaking his confidence, and that had stung enough for her to avoid him as much as possible.

Perhaps now was their chance to get back on an even keel.

She took the head of their department to one side to let him know that Rob was in the renal department, getting checked over, then got on with her shift.

The renal team called literally two minutes after the end of her shift. Perfect timing. She did the handover, then headed to the renal department to find Rob. He was sitting in the waiting area, looking terrible.

Did that mean he'd had bad news? Was his body rejecting his brother's kidney?

'How are you doing?' she asked.

'Fairly rubbish,' he admitted. 'They've run all the tests. The good news is that it's just an infection and they can give me something to clear it up.'

Not that his transplant was failing. He must be so relieved. 'Glad to hear it.'

'But the bad news,' he said with a grimace, 'is that they're signing me off for a week to recuperate.'

'Which is probably sensible,' she said.

'Rest is a four-letter word. Literally and metaphorically,' he said. 'Remember the guy with the dislocated shoulder who hated the idea of being off work for a few days? I know exactly how he felt.'

'You don't have any choice. Suck it up, Dr Langley,' she said.

Which told him.

'And I'll give you a lift,' she added. 'Lucky for you I'm on an early as well, and I've done my handover, so you don't have to go and wait for me in the cafeteria or anything until my shift is done.'

'Thank you,' he said. 'I owe you.'

She shook her head. 'It's what any colleague would do for another. You'd do the same for me. Where do you want me to take you? You said your parents live near here. Shall I drop you there?'

He rubbed a hand across his face. 'Don't take this the wrong way. I love my mum and dad dearly. I'd do anything for them. But my mum practically cocooned me after the transplant and I couldn't stand it. It's why I found myself a short-term flat lease when I started the job here. I really can't face going home to my parents. Mum'll go into panic mode and drive me crazy, and the last thing I want to do is snap at her and hurt her when I know she loves me and she's got my best interests at heart.'

She liked the fact he clearly knew himself well, and was thinking of his mother's feelings. 'Your brother's, then?'

'He's busy at work. Anyway, he's already done more than enough, giving me a kidney.' He lifted one shoulder in a casual shrug. 'I admit that I appreciate the lift, but I'll be fine on my own in my flat.'

She disagreed. 'Rob, you're feeling rough now and you're brewing an infection, so you've probably got a couple of days of feeling even worse before the meds kick in. If you feel anywhere near as terrible as you look, you need someone else around.' But Rob was stubborn. Telling him would put his back up, or make him do the equivalent of sticking his fingers in his ears and singing 'La, la, I can't hear you'. She'd appeal to the clinician in him, so it would be his own idea. 'If you had a patient in this position, what would you recommend? Would you be happy for your patient to be on their own?'

'No.'

Before she realised it, the words were out. 'Then that leaves us with just one solution. Come and stay with me.'

Had his consultant just given him something that had a side-effect of hallucinations? Rob wondered. Had Florence Jacobs just invited him to stay with her?

But they weren't even friends. They were temporary colleagues. And they'd had a one-night stand almost a fortnight ago that had made her back away from him so fast, there had practically been scorch marks under her feet. Why on earth would she invite him to stay with her?

'I'm sorry. Did you just…?'

Colour flooded through her face. 'I haven't been very fair to you. Very nice to you. So it's…' She blew out a breath. 'Look, there aren't any strings. It's what I'd do for any other colleague in your situation.'

Including one she'd slept with?

But she'd just specifically said no strings.

Maybe it was because he was feeling rough that his head wasn't working properly and he couldn't quite understand what she meant.

He'd probably said it out loud, because she clarified, 'It means if you feel really rough, you won't be on your own—you'll be staying with someone who's a medic and will know when to panic and when to back off.'

Which was a good point, he knew. It was why he ought to ring his brother. But he didn't want to risk getting in the way of Oliver's happiness, the way he had before—even though Gemma was very different from Tabby, Rob still didn't want to put a burden on Oliver.

And staying with Florence meant he'd get the chance to know her better.

He knew it wasn't sensible—but it was too much of a temptation to resist.

'No cotton wool?' he checked.

'I'm not a fan of the stuff outside work,' she said. 'It's not eco-friendly. The bleaching and mixing means it doesn't biodegrade. Bamboo cloths or muslin are better.'

He couldn't help smiling. 'Good point. OK. Thank you. That'd be nice. As long as you let me contribute. I'm not a great cook, but I can do the basics. I'll do my share.'

'Apart from the fact you're not well enough, you're my guest,' she said.

'Guests always bring something nice for their host.' He shrugged. 'Perhaps I can pay for some takeaways to be delivered, then.'

'We'll argue about that later. Let's go while you can still stand up.'

He liked the fact that she was brisk with him.

He liked *her*.

But he still wanted to know why she'd been so desperate to escape that Saturday morning.

Maybe spending time at her place and getting to know each other meant she'd feel comfortable telling him whatever had spooked her—and then they could move on. Maybe take things forward. Because the more time he spent with her, the more he realised he liked her. And Florence was the first woman in years who'd intrigued him enough to want more from a relationship.

'Would it be OK to stop at my flat and pick up some clean clothes and my medication?' he asked.

'Yes, of course.'

They didn't chat on the way to his place, once he'd given her the postcode for her satnav, but it was a comfortable silence rather than an awkward one. And he noted that Florence was as competent and confident when driving as she was in an emergency room, saving a life.

At his flat, she refused his offer of a mug of coffee. He packed an overnight bag quickly with a couple of changes of clothing, his medication, his laptop and a couple of books.

'You pack light, I see,' she said with a smile.

He shrugged. 'I learned that from climbing; keep it

light and keep it simple, so you have room for the important stuff.'

'That's a good life lesson,' she said.

What did that mean? She'd said that night that she had unwanted baggage...

He shot her a sidelong glance, but her expression was unreadable. And now wasn't the time to probe—not when he was feeling like death warmed up and he was likely to misread all the signals. Better to keep his mouth shut.

By the time she parked the car, all he wanted to do was to curl up in a ball and sleep for a month.

'You look all in,' Florence said gently. 'Come and sit down. I'll get you a hot drink and something to eat.'

'Thank you, but I'm not really hungry,' he said.

'You need to eat, and so do I, so you might as well eat with me,' she said firmly. 'Is there anything you don't eat?'

'Grapefruit,' he said, 'because of the medication I'm on, and for the same reasons I'm keeping my salt intake low. Other than that I eat anything.' As far as he was concerned, apart from good chocolate and cake, food was merely fuel. There was a world out there to conquer, and Rob wasn't going to waste time selecting herbs, chopping them finely, and decorating the top of every dish. Any more than five minutes in a microwave or a stir-fry pan, and the recipe wasn't for him.

'Let's go.' She took his bag and ushered him inside, and he didn't have the energy to protest that he could carry his own bag—especially because he knew that right at that moment it would sap his already diminishing energy.

'The guest room is here on the left,' she said, setting

his bag down and indicating the door. 'Mine's next to it, the bathroom's opposite, and the kitchen and living room are at the end of the hallway. Take your time to freshen up, then come and sit down when you're ready. I'll be in the kitchen.'

'Thanks.' He opened the door and smiled. He had a feeling her guest room was geared to her nieces, as the double bed had a bright pink duvet and there were three teddies wearing leotards, tutus and ballet shoes sitting on the pillows; each teddy had an initial embroidered on the leotard. He had a sudden vision of three little girls all cuddled up in that big wide bed with their teddies, and Florence sitting on the end of the bed, reading them a story.

And then his head morphed that into something even weirder. Three little girls with his own blue eyes…

No, no and absolutely no.

Clearly the infection had addled his brain as well as threatening his kidney. Since when did he ever fantasise about settling down and having kids? He spent his time working and climbing. There wasn't time for a family in the middle. He'd never met anyone who'd tempted him to want to settle down and have kids. And, if he ever did, he'd expected it to be someone who was a fellow adventure junkie, not someone who was domesticated and settled.

Yet the woman in his fantasies had been Florence.

Slightly spooked, he concentrated on hanging up his clothes and putting his wash bag in Florence's bathroom, then splashed his face with water. He still felt terrible, but he could hardly just crawl under the covers and sink into oblivion. The very least he should do was tell Florence that he was heading for bed. He went to the kitchen, and discovered her busy doing something on the stove.

'Something smells nice,' he said.

'It's a quick dish: pasta with lemon and asparagus. I'm adding some sautéed chicken to give it a bit more protein, so it'll still be light on your digestion but nutritious,' she said. 'Three more minutes and it'll be done.'

From his mum, this would've felt like fussing and made him feel smothered; from Florence, it felt thoughtful and made him feel cosseted. It was a weird sensation, and he wasn't sure whether it worried him or settled him. His head was all over the place. That momentary vision of three little girls—their daughters—was definite proof that he was ill.

'Is there anything I can do to help?' he asked.

'Just sit down at the table,' she said. 'This pretty much looks after itself. Do you want tea or coffee?'

'I…' He blew out a breath. 'Sorry, right now I'm too tired even to think, let alone make a decision.'

'Water, then,' she said, and added a slice of lemon to the glass.

He went over to the table—which she'd already laid—and sat down, grateful.

She'd given him space, with no pressure.

If there hadn't been the awkwardness between them, he would've hugged her. But he didn't want to risk making it even more awkward. 'Thank you,' he said. 'I appreciate this so much.'

'You're welcome.'

'I like the bears with tutus.'

She winced. 'Sorry. I'll move them and change the duvet cover to something more masculine.'

He laughed, then winced as it hurt. 'It's not going to

kill me to sleep under a pink duvet cover. I take it your nieces sometimes come and stay?'

'Yes.' She gestured to the fridge. 'And they're the ones who've drawn me those lovely pictures.'

He glanced over and did a double-take. 'Is that a dinosaur in a tutu?'

'Oh, yes. That's one you might not have come across before—a ballet-saurus.' She grinned. 'Margot loves dinosaurs even more than she loves ballet. Lexy and I took the girls to see the animatronic dinosaurs at the Natural History Museum in London over the summer, and Margot was in seventh heaven.'

He could imagine it. Florence, making a fuss of her nieces, taking them on days out and reading them stories. Domestic. The kind of things that usually made him want to run a mile because he liked to be in the big wide world, untrammelled, pushing himself to the limit.

But his life was going to have to change. And he was going to have to come to terms with being boxed in, at least for the next week.

'Margot's the oldest, isn't she?' he said. 'Then Anna and Darcey.'

She looked pleased that he'd remembered. 'That's right.'

And then he found himself wondering: if Florence had a daughter, would she name her after a ballerina?

Oh, for pity's sake. It was none of his business. And he didn't want to think about Florence having babies. Particularly as he was still spooked by that vision of his own three small daughters…

The pasta was amazing. Rob didn't usually pay much attention to food, other than good chocolate, but this was something else. 'This is fabulous,' he said.

'It's a very easy recipe.' Florence looked at him. 'You're not a cook, then?'

'I'm too busy to spend time in the kitchen. Ollie's the cook, not me, and he loves his gadgets. I'm very good at sticking TV dinners in the microwave, though,' he said. 'Or I can do stir-fry. Anything that takes less than five minutes.'

'Got you.' She looked at him. 'So is that because you'd rather spend your time climbing than skivvying in the kitchen?'

'Yes. Though climbing is still off the cards for a while.' He grimaced. 'I'd never be stupid enough to climb on my own and put the rescue team at risk, but I also know I'm not fit enough to manage the kind of routes I enjoy most—so I'd slow any climbing partners down to the point where none of us would enjoy it. And I'm sensible enough to know that if I push myself too hard, too fast, I'm going to end up in an even worse state than I am right now and have to wait even longer before I get my life back. But...' He grimaced again. 'It's still frustrating.'

'You miss it?'

'More than anything. Climbing, for me, is like breathing,' he said.

'I've never climbed,' she said. 'The most I've ever done is walk up and down the steep cliff paths at Ashermouth Bay.'

Which was nothing like climbing: cliff paths were simply a difficult walk without any of the fun. How could he explain it to her? 'It's the most amazing feeling. Pushing your body to its limits, getting to the top of a climb, and knowing you've earned that spectacular view,' he said.

'So kind of like a runner's high?'

'Better than that. The only thing like it is sex.'

Oh, no.

How could he have just said that?

'I—um—' He didn't dare look at her.

'A climb is as good as a climax?'

She sounded amused, so he risked a look. 'Yes.' And then he wished he'd kept his mouth shut when she met his gaze. Because it looked as if she was remembering that night. And he could remember every second of pleasure they given each other. It shocked him to realise just how much he wanted to experience it all again.

Did *she*?

Was that faint hint of colour in her cheeks telling him that she, too, had been thrown by what had happened between them?

But he couldn't ask. Not now, when he was barely capable of standing up, let along carrying her to her bed. He needed this conversation to be back to a neutral subject. Fast. Before he said something that caused an unholy mess. 'Can I do the washing-up?'

'No. Not just because you're a guest, but because you look absolutely exhausted. Go and sit on the sofa,' she directed. 'Feel free to put whatever you want on the TV.'

'I would normally argue,' he said, 'but I admit this bug has knocked me for six.' And he hated it. He hated feeling so weak. The words burst out of him. 'It feels like it did when my kidneys first packed up. I can't bear to think of having to rest for ages again. This just isn't me. I'm really not this weak, *pathetic* individual.'

'Go and sit down. It's fine,' she said gently. 'And, just for the record, resting doesn't make you weak or pathetic. It means you're being sensible and giving your body a chance to heal.'

'I guess,' he lied. He still hated feeling weak and vulnerable and having to rely on other people. He was strong and capable; he was the fixer, not the fixee.

'Rob, do you think your patients are weak and pathetic?' she asked.

He frowned. 'No. Of *course* not. They're ill or they've been in an accident and they need my help.'

'And the difference between them and your situation is…?'

He didn't have an answer for that, so he huffed out a breath.

'Don't be so hard on yourself,' she said gently. 'Go and sit down.'

'OK,' he muttered, and went into the living room. It was comfortable and cosy; the mantelpiece was crammed with framed photographs that he guessed were of her family and the people closest to her, but he didn't have the energy to be nosey and have a proper look.

Resting doesn't make you weak. It means you're being sensible and giving your body a chance to heal.

She'd been kind. She'd tried to settle some of his restlessness.

And she was right. He wouldn't judge his patients in the same way that he judged himself.

He needed to apologise to her for being snippy and difficult. And he intended to fill her house with flowers to make up for being a rubbish house guest.

He switched on the TV and flicked through the channels until he found a nature documentary, then settled back on the sofa to wait for her to join him. Although he tried to keep his eyelids open, they seemed to have a mind of their own and kept closing. He blinked hard, but they simply refused to stay open...

Florence finished washing up, drying the crockery and cutlery and putting it away.

From the sounds in the room next door, Rob was watching the kind of documentary she liked, too. Finding something in common with her temporary house guest would be a good idea.

But, when she went to join him, she discovered he was sound asleep on the sofa.

She tucked a throw round him; he murmured in his sleep, but he didn't wake.

He looked absolutely exhausted. She'd let him rest for a while, then wake him so he could go to bed, she decided. She curled up in the chair and watched the documentary, though she couldn't concentrate on it properly; she was way too aware of the man sleeping on her sofa.

A man who hated resting and said that he was happiest when he was busy.

A man who had craved adventure, given that he'd worked for a humanitarian aid organisation and loved climbing.

The man she'd made love with, two short weeks ago. The man who'd be sleeping in the room opposite hers, only few steps away...

No. She wasn't going to let herself think about bed and Robert Langley in the same sentence. She'd invited him to stay purely because he was ill, he was her colleague and he needed a bit of support. She wasn't attracted to him. Her heart didn't skitter every time she looked at him. The way his mouth had felt against her was totally irrelevant.

And if she told herself that often enough, she'd start to believe it.

Perhaps.

An hour later, she shook his shoulder gently until he woke.

'Wh…?' He blinked at her, his eyes fuzzy with sleep.

'Go to bed,' she said gently. 'Or you'll get a crick in your neck that'll annoy you all day tomorrow.'

'I…' He blinked again, as if trying to focus. 'Sorry. I didn't mean to crash out on you.'

'No need to apologise. I let you sleep for a bit because you looked too exhausted to move, but I wouldn't leave you on the sofa all night.'

He stared at the throw she'd placed round him. 'You put a blanket over me.'

'So you didn't get cold. I don't want my house guest complaining about the lack of services,' she quipped, trying to keep it light.

He followed her lead. 'Don't worry. I'll leave you a review on all the hospitality websites saying that you're a hostess who goes above and beyond.'

His smile was the sweetest, loveliest thing she'd ever seen. So much for keeping this light and teasing. If she wasn't careful, she'd fall for him. Which would be a very bad move.

'I'll see you tomorrow. And thank you, Florence. For looking after me without making me feel miserable and mollycoddled. I can't begin to tell you how much I appreciate that.' This time, there was an intensity in his gaze that made her stomach swoop.

'No problem,' she said. And she really hoped he

didn't hear the slight squeak in her voice. 'See you to-morrow. I'll let you have the bathroom first. Feel free to use anything you like, and the towels are all clean.'

'Cheers.' He still looked terrible, but not quite as bone-deep tired as he had earlier. 'See you tomorrow.'

CHAPTER FIVE

ROB WOKE THE next MORNING, his head all woozy. He was still hot and shivery, but he felt slightly better than he had the day before. Until he glanced at his watch and realised that it was half-past ten. Apart from the fact that he never slept this late, he was Florence's guest. Lying in bed all day and keeping her waiting around to dance attendance on him was incredibly selfish.

Really, he ought to get up and go home.

He dragged himself out of bed and into the bathroom, showered and cleaned his teeth, then dressed swiftly and went to find Florence. She was sitting in a chair by the window in the living room, holding a wooden hoop in her left hand and concentrating on something; he watched her for a moment and realised that she was stitching. Rob had never met anyone who sewed before.

'Morning,' she said, smiling at him.

That smile did weird things to his insides. Weird things he wasn't comfortable thinking about. He didn't react to people like this. 'Morning,' he muttered. 'Sorry I slept in.'

'It's fine. You're ill. It probably did you a lot of good, getting some rest. How are you feeling?'

'A lot better,' he said.

She raised an eyebrow. 'Want to let your common sense answer, rather than your pride?'

In other words, he still looked as bad as he felt. Busted. 'Better than yesterday,' he said, 'but, OK, I admit it: not that much.'

'These things take time,' she said.

Yes. And resting made him feel so boxed in and miserable. He hated being still. Always had, always would. Oh, to be halfway up a mountain somewhere…

'What would you like for breakfast?' she asked.

'I don't expect you to wait on me,' he said. 'It's more than enough that you offered to let me stay with you for a few days. I'll sort myself out.' Then he thought about it. She was at home at this time on a Saturday. She hadn't said anything yesterday about being on a late shift today. 'Are you off duty today?'

'Yes.'

Oh, no. 'So does that mean you've had to cancel your plans because of me?'

'They were movable,' she said.

So she *had* had to cancel her plans. He groaned. 'I'm so sorry. I didn't mean to ruin your day off.'

'You haven't ruined it. I'd tell you if there was a problem.'

He wasn't so sure. She hadn't told him what the problem was when she'd bolted, the weekend before last; and the subject had remained off limits between them ever since. But he felt too rough right now to deal with emotional stuff, so he decided to take what she'd said at face value. 'OK. Thanks.'

'Help yourself to whatever you want in the kitchen.'

'Thanks. Can I make you a coffee?'

'That would be lovely,' she said. 'A splash of milk, no sugar, please.'

'Toast?'

'Apart from the fact I've had breakfast,' she said, nodding at her sewing, 'I need to keep my hands clean for this.'

'What are you making?'

'A ballet-saurus for Margo.' She lifted the hoop to show him a blob of stitches in various shades of green and pink.

Was that meant to be a dinosaur wearing a tutu, like the drawing he'd seen on her fridge last night? 'I'm glad you told me what it was,' he said, 'because I'm afraid I wouldn't have guessed.'

Florence chuckled, and Rob realised just how pretty she was. She sparkled, and that smile made the whole room feel as if it had just lit up. It made him want to walk over to her and kiss her—which was the last thing he should do. The last time they'd kissed, it had all been wonderful—and then it all gone badly wrong. Staying here would give him a chance to find out what the problem was, and he couldn't afford to blow it by giving in to his impulses. He made them both a mug of coffee and took hers in to her.

'Thanks. That's perfect,' she said, giving him another of the smiles that made him feel all quivery.

He tried not to think about that and watched her sew. Though that too was a mistake, because her fingers were so clever, so deft—and it made him think about how those fingers had felt against his skin. How she'd touched him, heated his blood. How much he wanted to repeat that.

She glanced up and noticed him watching her. 'What?'

He definitely wasn't going to tell her what was in his head. 'I've never seen anyone sit and sew before,' he said instead.

'Not your mum or any of your girlfriends?'

He shook his head. 'One of my exes used to knit things, but she got very offended when I didn't wear a sweater she'd made for me to climb in. I explained that wicking material was much more efficient at regulating my temperature and a lot lighter than the sweater she'd knitted, and I didn't mean to offend her...but she was still hugely upset with me. She dumped me, two days later.'

'I can see both points of view—she'd tried to do something nice for you and of course she'd be upset that you didn't like it, but maybe she should've checked with you before doing all that work.' Florence raised an eyebrow. 'Remind me never to cross-stitch anything for you.'

'You mean, make me a blob I won't appreciate?'

She laughed and indicated her sewing. 'I know this looks like a blob. It's the back stitching—the little bits of detail—that'll bring it to life. When it's done, Margot will love it.' She put the hoop down, picked up her phone and scrolled through it. 'Here. I did this one for my best friend's birthday. This is before and after adding the detail.'

He looked at the blocks of colour, then at the peacock with all the iridescent colours and the delicate fronds on its tail feathers. 'That's impressive. It must've taken you a long time.'

'It got me through my divorce, last year.' And then she looked shocked, as if she hadn't meant to say that.

Was that what she'd meant about baggage?

He needed to tread carefully: acknowledge what she'd said, but not say anything that could be considered in the slightest bit judgemental. Give her an opening, if she wanted to talk—and he would most definitely listen, but not make her feel under any obligation. 'Uh-huh.'

When she didn't elaborate—and it was none of his business anyway, he reminded himself—he said, 'So have you done sewing like that for very long?'

'Years,' she said. 'Mum taught Lexy and me when we were teenagers, as a stress-reliever. It got us through our exams. It's like counting dance steps, or counting reps in the gym. You have to concentrate on counting the stitches and there isn't any room left in your head for your worries. It gives you a proper mental break.'

'That's what climbing's like, too,' Rob said. 'I concentrate on where I'm going to put my hands and my feet; I guess it's like you have to concentrate on where you put your needle.'

She gave him a wry smile. 'Except if I go wrong I can just unpick a few stitches, whereas if you go wrong there's going to be pain and possibly broken bones.'

'Not if you belay properly—fixing your rope, so if you slip you won't fall far,' he added in explanation, seeing the confusion flit across her expression when he mentioned belaying. 'But, yes, it's the same thing. You have to concentrate on what you're doing.'

'And at the end of it you've got something to show for it, and you don't feel guilty about wasting your time, the way you might feel guilty if you'd just spent a couple of hours playing games on your phone,' she said.

That was exactly how he felt about climbing. 'It's the buzz of achieving something,' he said. 'Pushing yourself further—though does that happen in sewing?'

'It can. You start by making something simple in one or two colours, and you work up to stitching something more complex with maybe lots of very similar colours,' she said. 'Or create your own patterns rather than just following someone else's. It's the same feeling.' She paused. 'Since you're here for a few days, I could teach you how to sew.'

'I can't stay here for a few days,' Rob said, aghast. 'That's way too big an imposition.'

'OK,' she said. 'If you want to be stubborn about it—not to mention stupid—you can always call a taxi and leave this morning. And then, when you've collapsed and someone has to ring your brother from the hospital to tell him where you are, you can explain to him that not only were you ill in the first place and didn't tell him, you also refused a colleague's help. My guess is he'll go for the big guns and call your mum.' She shrugged. 'Maybe that's what you actually want in the first place, despite all your protests.'

He shuddered. 'No. *Really* no.' He looked at her. 'Sorry. I don't mean to sound ungrateful. I feel guilty about being a burden on you. You had to change your plans today because of me.'

'You're not a burden. If I was the one who was ill and could do with someone just to be there for a few days in case I needed help, you'd offer to do it, wouldn't you?'

How could she be so sure that he was that nice? Though he thought about it. Of course he'd offer to help. He was a bit single-minded, but he was a team player too and he wasn't completely selfish. 'I guess.'

She looked at him. 'You're not well enough right now even to walk to the park, but I think you need something physical to do, to distract you. That's why I suggested teaching you to sew.'

Sewing. He couldn't quite get his head round the idea. 'Forgive me for being rude, Florence, but men don't sew.'

'I'll remember that next time you're suturing someone's forehead,' she said dryly.

He laughed. 'I don't mean *that* kind of stitching. That's more like tying knots and doing it neatly so your patient has minimal scarring. I can do that, no problem.'

'OK—but you're still wrong,' she said. 'There was the guy in the POW camp in the Second World War who made samplers and he stitched rude messages about Hitler in Morse code in the borders.'

'Seriously?'

'Seriously. And it was my grandfather who taught my mum how to sew. His doctor was way ahead of her time and recommended it to help him relax. So don't genderise sewing.'

'Got it.'

'And right now you're stuck resting. You're bored.'

That didn't even begin to describe how he felt. Fidgety. Unable to settle. Filled with fear that it was all going wrong and he'd end up back on dialysis again, and he'd be stuck waiting for months for another replacement kidney and feeling the walls close more and more tightly round him when he was desperate to be outside in the mountains. And underneath it all something else that he wasn't used to dealing with: his growing feelings towards Florence. That made him twitchy, too.

'Why not give this a try?'

He thought about the needlework he'd seen on the

walls in stately homes while accompanying his parents. 'But isn't it all alphabets and flowers?'

'Grandad liked stitching birds and dogs. But, if you're going to be stereotypical about it, you can stitch a motorbike, or a car, or...' She gave him a pointed look. 'A tiger.'

That was how he felt. Like a caged tiger. Had she realised that? If so, she was maybe the first person ever to see what made him tick. And he wasn't sure whether that excited him or unnerved him more.

'Start with something simple to get the hang of the technique. A bookmark would give you a quick result, so you get the hit of finishing.'

'Are you saying I'm impatient?'

She lifted an eyebrow. 'Aren't you?'

Not at work; but, in his private life, he supposed he was. Though he'd never understood why. 'OK. If you've got the time, then thank you. It'd be lovely if you taught me.'

'You're on.' Leaving her stitching on the table by her side, she went to the sideboard and took out some material, a box filled with threads, and a file. 'What do you want to stitch?'

'I'll be guided by you,' he said.

She opened the file and took out a pattern. Her huge brown eyes glittered with mischief as she met his gaze. 'Something simple, then. A stylised rose.' She opened the box of threads so he could see the colours better. 'Pick two colours.'

He noticed now how much pink there was in her living room. Cushions. The rug. The curtains.

And he knew she was expecting him to choose a traditionally masculine colour.

Given her comment about not genderising things, he wondered if her ex had done that. He'd heed her warning and not make the same mistake.

'Pink or red for a rose, right?' he asked.

'There's no reason why you can't stitch a blue rose if you want to. Or yellow. Or orange. And the leaves don't have to be green, either.'

'Hey. You told me not to genderise.' He smiled. 'Anyway, my mum's favourite flowers are pink roses. Maybe I can make something for her.'

'A motif like this—if you repeat it three times, it'd make a nice bookmark,' she said. 'I can give you a demo first, if you like, or you can just go straight in and I'll talk you through.'

Talking it through. He had a feeling they weren't just talking about sewing. Well, they were on the surface—but Rob knew it went deeper than that. And, if this was the key to understanding her more, he was all for it. 'Straight in,' he said.

She talked him through setting up the strip of material in a hoop and where to start working on the pattern. Putting a needle through holes that were already there in the material sounded simple. It *was* simple. And he picked it up quickly enough that Florence didn't need to talk him through more than two rows.

He started to find a rhythm: and then it ground to a halt. The stitching didn't look how hers did, all neat and flat and shiny. And he didn't understand where he'd gone wrong. The more he looked at it, the less he could work it out.

She glanced over at him. 'Problem?'

'Yes. But I don't know what,' he admitted.

'Let's have a look.' She peered at it. 'OK. You've

done a couple of stitches the wrong way round, which is why it looks a bit uneven, and you haven't been entirely accurate with your needle placement—my guess is you're trying to stitch as fast as you can. It's not a race, Rob. It's about finding a rhythm and filling your head. Unpick this back to where you went wrong, and try again.'

He did.

And he had to unpick things several times.

But then he started to get what she meant. There was a rhythm to this, like climbing. He had to concentrate on what he was doing, so there wasn't enough room in his head for the frustration and impatience that had been overwhelming him. And he could see the simple shape of a stylised rose taking shape on the fabric as he worked, all pink and perfect.

Part of him would've loved to send a selfie of him sewing to his twin. But then he would have to admit both to the infection and to the fact that he was staying with Florence; and he wasn't ready to pick his way through all the complicated explanations that would entail. So he concentrated on the sewing. Stitch by stitch by stitch.

This was surreal, Florence thought. If anyone had told her a month ago that she'd be giving needlework lessons to a man like Robert Langley—and in her own living room, to boot—she would've laughed.

But here they were.

She could tell how frustrated he was by the constraints of his health, and this was the second-best distraction she could think of. Her first choice of distraction was completely inappropriate; though it hadn't helped when Rob had compared the rush of climbing to the feel of an orgasm. She could remember exactly what it had felt like when Rob had touched her or brushed his mouth against her skin, and the memories made her ache.

Right now, she was so aware of Rob. The warmth of his body. The scent of his skin. His height. Those stunning blue eyes.

And when she'd touched his hand earlier to guide him with the needle, it had felt as if she'd been galvanised.

Had he felt it, too? That tingle starting on the skin and running the whole length of each nerve? Did he want to touch her as much as she wanted to touch him?

Oh, for pity's sake. The man was *ill*. The last thing he needed was for her to hit on him. She ought to treat him as a patient. Even if her body was urging her to treat him like a lover. Not to mention that he was the last person she should let herself fall for. If she was going to risk her heart again, it would be with someone who wanted the same things that she did: to settle down and have a family.

She supposed that was academic, because she didn't actually want to trust someone with her heart again. She'd felt so worthless and unlovable after Dan's betrayal; not only hadn't she been enough for him, he hadn't wanted to have children with her. She hadn't been able to work out just what was so wrong with her that he hadn't wanted her, and she'd closed in on herself over the last couple of years. To trust someone with herself again was akin to climbing a mountain. She didn't want to take that risk.

Though she still wanted Rob.

It wasn't possible. She couldn't have Rob without the risk. And there was no guarantee he wanted a relationship with her. He was here on a temporary contract; but she was pretty sure that he'd go back to his old life in Manchester rather than renewing his contract or looking for a permanent job here. He'd move on. And she'd be left behind.

Better to suppress the longings.

'So is it helping?' she asked, when she'd had to unpick a row for the third time because she couldn't concentrate with him next to her.

'Surprisingly, yes,' he said. 'If anyone had told me that sewing would be fun, I wouldn't have believed them.' He shook his head. 'If Ollie could see me now...'

Even though he didn't finish the sentence, she could guess what he meant. 'Your brother wouldn't laugh at you,' she said.

'No. He's one of the good guys. And much nicer than I am,' Rob said.

'You're hardly a bad guy, Rob,' she said.

'No? I'm the reason my brother's wedding got cancelled.'

She stared at him, surprised. 'Why?' She was pretty sure it wasn't because Rob had had a fling with the bride-to-be. Apart from the fact he was clearly close to his brother, he wasn't the sort to lie and cheat. What you saw was what you got.

He sighed. 'Because Ollie gave me a kidney. And Tabby—his fiancée—panicked that he'd become ill and she'd have to look after him.'

Florence frowned. 'That's a bit shallow, as well as very misinformed. The donee rather than the donor is the one who's more likely to have problems after a transplant.'

'Ollie says he can understand why she panicked. Her dad has chronic fatigue syndrome and her mum has had to give him an awful lot of support over the years. Tabby didn't want that sort of life for herself. But I agree with you. I think Tabby was shallow and a bit on the selfish side, and she definitely wasn't right for my brother.' He sighed. 'I just hate that Ollie got hurt when she called everything off. And that wouldn't have happened if I hadn't needed a kidney.'

Guilt mingled with pain glittered in his eyes. But it wasn't Rob's fault that his brother's fiancée had got cold feet. 'Maybe,' Florence said carefully, 'your brother had a lucky escape. Because surely it would've been worse if they'd got married and he'd thought everything was fine, and then life threw a curveball and she walked away?'

'I guess,' Rob said. 'Thankfully he's met someone else now. Someone who loves him for who he is. Who understands him. Who cherishes him.'

Was it her imagination, or did Rob sound wistful? And, if she was right, was that wistfulness because he wanted someone to feel that way about him, too? Was that why he'd never settled down before—because nobody had made him feel like that?

Not that it was any of her business.

'It's good to have someone who always has your back,' she said. 'Someone who won't let you down.'

That sounded heartfelt.

And Florence had said this morning that she was divorced.

Had her husband let her down? There wasn't a nice

way of asking, and the last thing Rob wanted to do was to make her feel awkward or bring back any bad memories.

Then, to his surprise, she said, 'I owe you an apology.'

He frowned. 'For what?'

'For...' She squirmed slightly, and her cheeks went very pink. 'That Saturday morning. I...um...bolted.'

'Yes, you did,' he said, trying to make his voice sound as neutral as possible.

'It wasn't a nice thing to do. And I'm sorry.'

'You don't need to apologise—' though he was really gratified that she had '—and I'm sure you had your reasons.'

'I...' She dragged in a breath. 'Baggage, I guess. You're the first person I've slept with since I split up with Dan.'

Dan, he presumed, was her ex-husband. And Rob was the first man she'd slept with since the split?

That changed things.

Significantly.

Florence clearly wasn't the sort of person who followed her impulses, the way he did. Spending the night with him had been out of character for her. What had made her do it? Had the attraction between them been strong enough to overcome her common sense? Did she regret it? Well, of course she'd regretted it, because she'd bolted the morning after. But she'd had time to think about it now. So what did she want? A fling to help her get past whatever had gone wrong with her ex? Or did she want something more—something Rob wasn't sure he was capable of giving her?

Not that this was about him. It was about her.

'Was the split very long ago?' he asked. If it was re-
cent, still raw, he needed to tread very carefully indeed.
The last thing he wanted to do was to hurt someone
who'd been so kind and lovely to him.

'Nearly two years since he moved out, and it took a
while for the divorce to come through,' she said. 'We
wanted different things. It didn't work out.'

Rob was pretty sure there was a lot more to it than
that, but he wasn't going to pry. If Florence wanted
him to know, she'd tell him. In the meantime, he'd re-
spect her privacy. 'I'm sorry. I've never been engaged,
let alone married or divorced, but I know from friends
that it can be rough.'

'Yeah. It was,' she said. 'But it's past. I'm over it.
Over him. And I like my life as it is. No complications.'

Which told him exactly where he stood. And it was
pretty clear to him that she'd offered to let him stay
because she'd felt guilty about the way she'd behaved
after their night together. She didn't want more. This
was her way of making it up to him.

'I agree. No complications is a good thing,' he said.
'But?'

He could bluff it.

Or he could tell her.

Because he was beginning to realise that Florence
Jacobs was very clear-sighted. She'd see a problem the
way she saw a bit of cross-stitch gone wrong; she'd
understand the big picture, she'd untangle things and
unpick them, and help him see the way forward. Was
she the one who could help him adjust to this new life,
the one without most of the things he loved? Could
she teach him how to put down roots and not long to
be elsewhere?

But he didn't have the words. Not yet. 'No buts,' he said. And, even if she was prepared to help him, she needed to be clear about what she was letting herself in for. 'I was born with itchy feet—and probably my brother's share, too. So complications…aren't helpful.'

'I understand.'

The shutters went right back up in her eyes. Though that was probably a good thing. Rob didn't trust himself to be able to stay away from Florence; he needed her to want to stay away from him, too. Keep herself safe.

'Don't stitch for too long,' she said, moving back to her own seat. 'Apart from the fact that sitting for a long while in one position isn't good for you, stitching for hours will make your hand ache.'

'Got you,' he said. But he wanted to finish the bookmark. Prove to himself that he could do this.

Florence Jacobs was the domesticated sort. And that meant she was the last person he should let himself fall for. Rob wasn't domesticated. He'd never been able to settle. He wouldn't fit into her world. But the more he was getting to know Florence, the more he liked her.

Could he domesticate himself for her?

Though that was assuming that she wanted to be with him, when she'd already made it pretty clear she saw him purely as a colleague. It was an arrogant assumption: and Rob wasn't arrogant. He was impulsive and fidgety, but he didn't think that the world revolved around him.

But all the same, he thought about it.

Particularly during the evening, when he sat and watched a film with her. Unless it was a fast-moving action film, usually he didn't manage to last through a whole film without getting bored and fiddling with his phone. But this time, even though it was the kind of costume drama that would normally bore him rigid within minutes, he discovered that he could actually sit still and pay attention.

What was it about Florence that made him able to do that?

And was it something that could last?

Was Florence Jacobs the person he'd never thought he'd needed by his side—but who actually made his world a much, much better place? Was she someone he actually wanted to commit to, the way Oliver was committed to Gemma? How did you even know when you met that someone? He'd never met anyone he'd wanted to commit to before. Not even Janine.

Was Florence the one?

The questions spun round his head, and he couldn't work out the answer.

'You look all in,' she said quietly.

'I...' Yes. It was probably why he wasn't thinking straight: he still had a fever. His brain was scrambled by the infection. And so was his common sense. 'Sorry.'

'Don't apologise. Go and get some rest. I'll see you tomorrow.'

Rest wasn't something he was good at. But he'd try. 'OK. See you tomorrow.'

CHAPTER SIX

WHEN ROB WOKE, the next day, he felt a lot more human. And it was a reasonable time for a Sunday morning, he was relieved to note when he looked at his watch: eight o'clock. He went into the kitchen, intending to make coffee, and saw a note propped against the kettle, with a door key sitting next to it.

On early shift. Hope you're feeling better. Text me if you need anything. Help yourself to anything you want for breakfast and lunch, and I'll cook dinner when I get home. Have left you spare door key in case you need to go out. F

She'd been so thoughtful. He wasn't quite up to going out, but it was good to feel that he had the option and he wasn't trapped.

But then there was dinner.

He didn't want Florence to come home after a busy shift and feel obliged to cook for him. He wasn't going to offer to cook a roast dinner or anything like that himself, because even when he was fully fit he knew his limitations; but he could arrange a delivery. A couple of minutes looking on the internet netted him the information he needed: the local pub did a delivery service, and the menu was excellent.

He texted her.

Thanks for note. Am feeling better. No need for you to cook tonight—it's my turn to provide dinner. Not going to cook something, but could get dinner delivered from The Golden Lion, unless you know somewhere better?

He added a link to the menu.

Let me know what you want and what time, and I'll organise. R

Should he add a kiss?

No. It'd make her uncomfortable, he decided, and sent the text as it was.

After he'd eaten some toast and had a shower, he tried doing some stitching, but it didn't feel the same as it had when Florence had been there beside him. He flicked through the TV channels, but nothing caught his eye.

Sit and read a book, perhaps? He browsed through her shelves. There were a few medical texts and a scattering of classics, mixed in with some modern novels. He knew from the film last night that she liked costume dramas, and when it came to reading she clearly liked historical romances set in Jane Austen's era. But there was nothing that grabbed his interest.

He looked at the photographs on her mantelpiece. He knew she was close to her family, so he wasn't surprised to see framed photographs of Florence holding three different babies—he'd guess they were her nieces, and from the way she was dressed up it was fairly obvious that it was their christening days—and as bridesmaid to a woman who looked so like her that she could only be Lexy, Florence's older sister. There was a graduation photo with Florence's parents and her sister surrounding her, looking thrilled and proud; an amazingly graceful photo of her sister on stage, wearing a tutu and doing some kind of leap, which he guessed must've been taken by the theatre's official photographer; and a picture of what looked like Florence and Lexy as teenagers in a garden somewhere, laughing and clearly loving being together. It made him smile; he had photos of himself and Oliver like that, too.

He took a closer look at her fridge. It was covered with children's drawings, held to the door by cutesy magnets—everything from acerbic Jane Austen quotes through to pictures of cupcakes. There was the 'ballet-saurus' from her oldest niece that he'd seen the other night, a cat with 'Anna' printed laboriously across the top which was clearly the middle niece's drawing, and a scribble from the baby with 'Darcey' obviously written by an adult on the top. There were also a few group photographs, too; he recognised some of the people as their colleagues in the emergency department, so the snaps had clearly been taken on a team night out.

Others showed Florence posing with a woman he guessed was probably her best friend. Florence clearly liked stately homes and costume museums as much as his mother did. Rob thought for a moment how well she'd get on with his mum; Ollie would approve of her, and his dad would be charmed by her...

And what then?

They'd liked Janine, too. But Janine had wanted

commitment he hadn't been able to give. Rob hadn't wanted to settle down with her—and he knew he'd hurt her. Just as he had the potential to hurt Florence. These photographs were proof of exactly who Florence was: someone with roots, someone who had sticking power.

Rob didn't have that. He liked the buzz of new things, of exploring. Which made him the complete opposite of what Florence needed.

OK, so his failed kidneys meant his exploring would be very much limited in the future. Technically, there was no reason why he couldn't try to stay in one place. No reason why he couldn't offer Florence more than just a fling. But he'd never managed to make his relationships last before. What was to say he could do it now? The last thing he wanted to do was start something where she'd end up hurt when he walked away. So, even though part of him thought that Florence might be different—she held his interest, the way nobody had before, and he could be *still*, with her—it wasn't fair to her to take that risk and let her down.

Which meant he'd just have to suppress all of these wayward feelings towards her.

And, much as he hated it, he knew he needed to rest. The more he rested now, the quicker he'd be better, and the quicker he could be on the move again. The quicker he could move out of Florence's flat again. The safer they'd both be.

Still feeling a bit out of sorts, he started up a game of virtual chess with Ollie.

His brother texted back.

Rob, it's Sunday. If you're off duty today, want to come over and play this properly instead of virtually?

Yes. And no. He texted back.

Sorry, Olls, can't do today.

He knew that Ollie would assume he was working and had simply made the chess move during a break.

Maybe next week?

He definitely didn't want to see his twin until he was looking a lot more normal, because he didn't want Oliver worrying about him.

He messaged his mum next.

Just checking in. You and Dad OK? All fine here. Love you. x

His mother replied straight away.

Are you ill?

He lied.

No. Why would you think that?

Had his mother developed some weird sort of sixth sense?

You're sounding soppy.

That made him smile. Of course he did. How well she knew him. He texted back.

Sometimes my job makes me appreciate my family.

Which was true. He wasn't actually at work right now; though he rather hoped she'd take the implication that he was. It wasn't an outright barefaced lie; more of an insinuation.

Having a rubbish shift? Come for dinner tonight. Roast chicken and extra-crispy roast potatoes. Apple crumble and custard.

Things she knew would always tempt him. But if she saw him like this she'd be horrified and worried sick. Not that he felt like driving—and if he got a taxi she'd worry that he obviously wasn't well enough to drive. He could ask Florence to go with him, but that would lead to such a knot of complications he wouldn't be able even to begin to untangle it. So it was better to stick to bare bones and offer an alternative, just as he had to Oliver.

Sorry. Maybe next weekend?

All right. See you then. Talk to you in the week. Love you. x

I'd better be back to normal by then, he thought.

Love you, too, Mum. Say hi to Dad for me. x

So Rob was organising dinner? Florence was impressed.

Thank you. Food at Golden Lion great. Gnocchi for

me, please. About seven? Am calling in at Lexy's on my way home.

The reply came almost immediately.

Perfect. Will arrange. Pudding?

No, but thanks for the offer.

What, you're saying no to salted caramel profiteroles??? Shocking!

She could just imagine him smiling as he typed. Those stunning blue eyes, flickering with mischief as he tried to tempt her. That beautiful mouth... Instead of repeating a polite refusal, she found herself typing back.

Go halves on the profiteroles?

Works for me. *Yum*. See you later. x

This was ridiculous. They weren't actually dating, even though they'd slept together. And yet this felt light-hearted and sweet, like an exchange between people who'd just started dating each other. Exciting. Full of potential. He'd even typed a kiss; or maybe that was just Rob being his exuberant self and she was overthinking this. Though, for a second, Florence could imagine sitting across an intimate bistro table from him, reaching across to offer him a taste of something from her plate...

Oh, help. She really needed to be careful. She liked the man she was getting to know and it would be all too easy to fall for him. How could she let herself fall for someone who'd made it clear he wasn't going to be around for long? That was the quickest way to risk having her heart broken again. Stupid. She needed to keep him firmly in the friend zone and resist the temptation to make it anything more. Though the more time she spent with Rob, the more she was starting to think that he'd be worth taking the chance on.

On her way home from her shift, Florence called in at her sister's house for a mug of tea and cuddles with her nieces.

'Aunty Floss, Aunty Floss, look at me doing a pirouette!' Anna said.

'And me!' said Darcey, not to be outdone.

'I'm a ballet-saurus doing a bourrée,' Margot announced, and ran after her sisters on tiptoe, pretending to roar.

'Girls, you're exhausting,' Lexy said. But she was smiling. 'Go and show Daddy your new routines, so I can have five minutes with Aunty Floss.'

'OK. Get the grilling over with,' Florence said when her nieces had scampered away.

'So why did you call off going to the park with us yesterday? Were you on a date with Transition Man?' Lexy asked.

Florence sighed. 'Don't call him that.'

'So you *were* seeing him.'

'Not in the way you think. He's my temporary house guest.'

'Oh? How come?' Lexy looked intrigued.

'Don't get ideas. It's *platonic*,' Florence insisted. 'He was taken ill at work. He thought it might be his body rejecting the donor kidney, but thankfully it turned out to be an infection. So he's staying in my spare room for a few days until he's better.'

Lexy grinned. 'So you're playing doctors and nurses with him? I love it.'

'No, I am not. And also not in the sense *you* mean.' Florence folded her arms and glared at her sister. 'I would've done the same for anyone else on my team, if they'd been in his shoes.'

'But,' Lexy said, 'that doesn't alter the fact that you spent the night with him after your department's Christmas dinner. Or the fact that you really like him.'

'Lexy, that's irrelevant. I'm fine as I am,' Florence fibbed.

'Florence Emily Jacobs, remember what happened to Pinocchio,' Lexy warned. 'I know a fib when I hear it. You're lonely. And you're still letting Dan and his behaviour control you. Otherwise you'd be dating again and finding someone you want to spend time with, instead of locking yourself away to protect your heart.'

'I'm not locking myself away,' Florence protested, even though she knew her sister had a point.

'Transition Man is staying with you, so it's a good chance to get to know him better.' Lexy paused, her eyes narrowing. 'One thing. I get that he's ill, but you've done a full shift today. I hope you're not planning to cook dinner and wait on him hand and foot when you get home?'

'No. He texted me with a menu this morning and he's ordering dinner for us both from The Golden Lion.'

'That's an improvement on Dan—who would definitely be a contender for the World's Most Selfish Man Award,' Lexy said. 'The more I hear about Transition Man, the more I like the sound of him.'

'Don't get ideas,' Florence warned. 'We're colleagues. We might become friends. But he's not going to be around for more than a couple of months, so there's no point in starting anything.'

Lexy sighed. 'I won't nag. Well, not much. But, y'know, if the sex was good…what's the harm in having a mad fling with him?'

'Alexandra! You have *children* about!' Florence said in a scandalised stage whisper.

'They're busy showing Max their latest dance routine. We'll hear the second they're on their way back here and need to watch what we say in front of them,' Lexy said, completely unabashed. 'I know you hate me calling him "Transition Man", but I do think you should consider making him that. It might be good for both of you.'

'No, it wouldn't.' Florence groaned. 'I love you, Lexy, but please can we just change the subject?'

The girls came running back in, then, and of course Florence had to cuddle all three of them, listen to Margot reading a story, praise Anna's drawing and handwriting, and sing nursery rhymes and clap along to songs with Darcey.

She adored every second she spent with her nieces, and was grateful to Lexy for being so generous with her children. But, on the way home, Florence thought again how much she would've loved children of her own. Dan had said he only wanted children that were his own flesh and blood; but had that been an excuse? Considering how quickly he'd accepted being a dad to the children of his new partner, did that mean he thought Florence wouldn't be any good as a mum? And, if so, just what had been so wrong with her?

She shook herself. 'Stop the pity party,' she told her-self out loud. 'You're lucky. You're close to Lexy and the girls, you have good friends, and you love your job.'

That was enough.

It would have to be enough.

She walked into her flat to find the table laid ready for dinner, and everything was neat and tidy.

Rob greeted her with a smile. 'Hey. How was your shift?'

Dan hadn't asked her that for years before their split. And she ought to stop comparing Rob with her ex. They were very, very different. 'Fine, thanks. You're looking better today,' she said.

'I feel a lot more human,' he said. 'Did you have a nice time with your sister and the girls?'

'I did. And I have more drawings for the fridge.' She produced them from her bag and swapped them over from the last three. 'I'll put these in a file,' she said, scooping up the ones she'd taken from the display. 'Something for the girls to look back on when they're older—and they'll know that I valued them enough to keep them.'

'That's nice,' he said. 'It's good for kids to know they're valued. I'm pretty sure our parents have still got every drawing Ollie and I ever did, even the scribbles.'

Rob clearly had a good relationship with his parents and his brother, so he was capable of being a family man. 'Do you want kids of your own, one day?' The words spilled out before she could stop them.

But he didn't look in the least bit offended by her nosiness; and he didn't seem at all thrown by her ques-tion. 'I've never really thought about it,' he said. 'I'm looking forward to being an uncle when Oliver and

Gemma get round to starting a family—but, given that I'm not great at sticking around, I don't think I'd be a very good dad.'

Which didn't quite answer her question. She hadn't asked if he thought he'd be a good dad; she'd asked if he wanted to be a dad at all. But pressing him for clarification would make things awkward. She shouldn't have asked the question in the first place. Instead, she changed the subject. Their meal arrived, ten minutes later, and she managed to keep the small talk going for the rest of the evening.

One thing she was clear on, though, by the time Rob admitted he was shattered and needed to head for bed: whatever Lexy had suggested, and however tempting she found him, Robert Langley couldn't be her transition man. If Florence let him that close again, she wouldn't want to let him go—and he'd made it plain that he wasn't the sort to stay. And, even if he did stay, how did she know she'd be enough for him? How did she know he wouldn't see the same flaws in her that Dan had seen and leave her for someone else?

She didn't think Rob was the type to cheat—he had more integrity than Dan—but surely he needed someone who shared his wanderlust? Florence didn't want to travel the world or sleep under the stars in the middle of a desert. She wanted a home and a family, a garden and a dog and blissful domesticity: everything that Rob had hinted he didn't want. So it'd be sensible to avoid the heartbreak by keeping him at a professional distance.

On Monday, Florence had a case that made her think about Rob. The way the boy's mother described him was exactly the way Rob had described himself as a child: and the patient had been diagnosed with ADHD. It made her wonder. During her break, she did a bit of research on her phone. The more she read about ADHD, the more she thought it sounded like Rob. And he was bright; if he hadn't struggled academically at school, nobody would've picked it up then.

She'd seen for herself how frustrated he got when he couldn't be up and about, doing things. Maybe this was the root of it. And, if it was, maybe knowing that would help him.

She was still mulling it over when she walked into her kitchen that evening and something smelled gorgeous.

'Perfect timing. Chicken stir-fry, as promised,' Rob said.

How nice it was to have someone actually cook for her. To share: something she and Dan hadn't done for months before he'd walked out. 'Thank you. I feel very spoiled,' she said.

'That was the idea.' He dished up, and sat opposite her.

'This is pretty impressive, from someone who claims he can't cook,' she said after her first taste.

'I didn't say I *can't* cook. I said I don't cook anything that takes more than five minutes,' he reminded her. 'So how was your day?'

'Fine. I was in Minors.' She looked at him. 'Actually, there was a case I think you might find interesting. I had a boy in this afternoon who'd fiddled with his pen when he got bored in class, taken it to pieces and ended up with the spring jammed in his palm. I had to send him to X-Ray to make sure I wasn't going to damage anything when I removed it.'

Rob grinned. 'That sounds exactly like the sort of thing I would've done as a kid.'

Just what she'd thought, too.

'Mum always brings up my first day at school. Apparently, I was at the bottom of the playing field and climbing a tree before the teachers realised what I was doing—and then I fell out of the tree.'

She stared at him in shock. 'That's terrible! Were you badly hurt?'

'Nope. I didn't even have a bruise. Though I did break my arm twice during my time at infant school. Running on ice isn't the most sensible thing to do, and I'm afraid I didn't learn my lesson well enough the first time round,' he admitted.

'So you were the adventurous child in the class?' she asked.

'I was the fidget with a low boredom threshold,' he said. 'For everyone else, the highlight of the day was story time. For me, it was torture. There was nothing worse than having to sit still and listen for what felt like years. I'd far rather have been running round the field.'

'You didn't think about becoming an athlete rather than a rock star, then?'

He looked surprised, then pleased, that she'd remembered what he'd told her about his teenage band. 'No. One of the teachers thought I needed something to challenge myself, and he suggested I try climbing. I loved it. It was an obvious next step from climbing to joining the mountain rescue team, then think about a career in medicine.'

'I was thinking,' she said. 'You say you've always had itchy feet.'

He wrinkled his nose. 'More than that. I think I got Ollie's share, too.'

'Have you ever thought there might be a reason for that?'

'Such as?'

She looked awkwardly at him. 'This is going to sound a bit rude, so I apologise in advance. The lad I told you about with the spring stuck in his hand, today—you said it sounded like you.'

He frowned, as if wondering where she was going with this. 'Yes.'

'His mum said he has a very low boredom threshold. He's always fidgeting. Very bright.' She looked him straight in the eye. 'He was diagnosed with ADHD, a couple of years back.'

Rob stared at her. 'Are you saying you think *I* have ADHD?'

'I can't really make a clinical judgement because it's not my field. But I was thinking,' she said, 'it might be an explanation for the way you feel. Why you get frustrated quickly. Why you need to move.'

'Nobody's ever suggested...' He thought about it. 'No. I can't be on the spectrum. Otherwise Oliver would have ADHD, too.'

'The siblings of someone with ADHD are more likely to have it, too,' she said, 'but that's not always the case.'

'But Ollie's my twin.'

'I know, but are you actually identical?' She grimaced. 'Sorry. That's a stupid question. But my best friend's brothers look very like each other, enough for people to confuse them, and they're not twins.'

'Actually, that's a fair question. We always thought

we were identical, until the transplant. Obviously they had to check, as part of the work-ups, and it seems we have some differences between us in DNA.'

'That's possible?' she asked, surprised.

'There's something called a copy number variant,' he said. 'Normally you get two copies of every gene, one inherited from each parent. But some areas in the genome have up to fourteen copies of a gene, and that's where you can have variations. Plus, as you get older, your DNA changes due to environmental factors. So even if you start off as identical—monozygotic—twins, you're not actually going to be identical by the time you get to later life.'

'I had no idea that was even possible.'

'Neither did we,' he said. 'I don't know enough about the genetic side of ADHD but, if it involves a copy number variant, that might explain why Ollie and I are so different, given we were brought up the same way.' He gave her a rueful smile. 'At one point, I thought there might be something in the whole "good twin, bad twin" thing.'

'There's nothing bad about you,' she said.

It warmed Rob that she'd gone straight to his defence. 'I wasn't fishing, but thank you for having faith in me.' Her theory made sense. A lot of sense. But at the same time it made him feel as if someone had taken the ground from under his feet.

'I can't believe none of us has picked it up before. I mean, OK, it's not the sort of thing we diagnose in the Emergency Department, but Ollie's a GP. And none of our teachers ever mentioned it.'

'If you weren't falling behind in classes, they probably assumed you were…' She stopped.

'A lively child. That's what every single teacher put in every single report. Every single year.'

'It's not a bad thing, Rob. Just a possible explanation.'

Florence was the first person ever to have suggested it. She'd seen something in him that nobody else had ever seen. It made him feel as if she saw him more clearly than anyone had before—and she wasn't judging him. She wasn't pitying him, either. Her brown eyes were full of sympathy and understanding.

'It would explain a lot. Why Mum had to put me on reins as a toddler because she knew otherwise I'd abscond, but Oliver didn't need them because he'd walk nicely. Why I need to climb or just *move*, even as an adult. Why I fidget all the time. Why I can just about sit through an action film, but anything slow doesn't stand a chance.'

'Low boredom threshold, bright, fidgety: it fits,' she said. 'Though I apologise for being—well, intrusive. It wasn't my place to…' She grimaced.

'I don't think you're being intrusive,' he said. 'You've just given me an explanation for a puzzle I'd never been able to solve. Something that never even occurred to me or anyone else.' He looked at her. 'What made you think of it?'

'It's just that everything the boy's mum said sounded so much like the way you talk about yourself. And it made me wonder.'

'Now you've said it, I can see it.' He shook his head. 'We always assumed it was just me just "being Rob". But there's a reason. Something that isn't a f—' He stopped.

'Isn't a what?' she asked quietly.

Could he tell her the thing that he barely even admitted to himself? Then again, she probably already knew. She saw him more clearly than anyone ever had. Including himself.

Would she turn away from him if he said it? Or would she...? He decided to take a risk. 'Failing in me. Why I've always let women down in the past.'

'Let them down?'

'I'm not a cheat or a liar,' he said. 'But I always seem to pick people who don't want the same things as me. People who wanted me to give up climbing and the overseas aid work.'

'Then I think the failing was in them for expecting you to be something you're not. To expect you to change for them,' she said.

And how weird it was—as if she'd taken a huge load off his shoulders. All the guilt of his past. For the first time, she'd made him see that it wasn't just him.

'You're fine just as you are,' she said.

His mouth went dry. So was she saying she liked him, the way he was starting to like her?

He'd already said more than he'd intended. But he ended up blurting it out anyway. 'I like you, too.'

She went very pink. 'I...'

'That wasn't meant to be any pressure,' he said.

'I know.'

But the air hummed with sudden tension. The things neither of them were saying. The more time he spent with her, the more time he wanted to spend with her. She was like nobody else he'd ever met. But what did *she* want? She'd said before that she didn't want any complications. Did that rule him out? Could he become someone who wasn't complicated?

'Florence, I…' His words deserted him. He'd never had that happen before.

And she let him off the hook by moving the subject back onto safer ground. 'I might be completely wrong about the ADHD,' she said. 'Either way, it's a huge thing to take on. It'd knock anyone for six. Give yourself time to… Well, to let it sink in. Talk to your brother about it.'

All very sensible. And he was supposed to be sensible. Plus, much as he wanted to scoop her up and carry her off and kiss her until they were both dizzy, he was still feeling under par and couldn't actually do it. He'd told her he liked her. He needed to take it slowly and build on that. 'You're right,' he said. 'I will. Seeing as I'm being forced to rest all week, I've got the time to do a bit of research.' He grinned. 'My brother's going to love this. Especially as I talked him into making a pact with me.'

'What kind of pact?' she asked.

'He's going to "be more Rob" and do things outside his comfort zone, and I'm going to "be more Ollie". That way, we're both kind of bringing out the best in each other.' He shrugged. 'It's worked so far. If I hadn't nagged him to be more me, he wouldn't have told Gemma how he felt about her and they wouldn't be together now.'

'So he's kept to his side of the pact. Did you keep to yours?' she asked.

'Of course. The proof is that I'm sitting here right now,' Rob said. 'Being sensible and resting while I'm recovering from the infection.'

'I seem to remember having to pull rank and boss

you about to get you to stay here,' she pointed out. 'Which only worked because you were really ill—otherwise I don't think you would've been sensible.'

'I'm trying,' Rob said. 'And that's the best I can do.'

'That's enough,' Florence said. And her smile made his heart feel as if it had done an anatomically impossible backflip.

Florence was feeling decided out of sorts by the time she got home on Tuesday.

'Are you OK?' Rob asked.

'Yes,' she lied.

He simply raised an eyebrow.

She sighed. 'No. I had a case that really got to me today.'

'Want to talk about it?'

'I had a patient who'd gone out to lunch to celebrate her retirement, tripped on the stairs, and smacked her knee on the metal trim of the step.'

'Sounds nasty,' Rob said.

She nodded. 'There was a ten-centimetre laceration under her knee, about two centimetres wide—and it went down to the bone.' Though that wasn't what had upset her. She'd seen far gorier cases.

But Rob seemed to have worked out that talking through the medical stuff was giving her the space she needed to sort out her feelings, because he asked, 'So you treated it as an open fracture?'

'Yes. There was an arterial bleed, too. We managed to stem it, and I gave her prophylactic intravenous antibiotics and sent her for an X-ray to check if there was a fracture. Luckily there wasn't, but I had to send her to Theatre so the surgical team could close the wound.'

'Good call. A wound that deep gives a huge risk of infection,' Rob said.

'I asked her if I could call anyone to be with her, and she said no. No partner, no kids, her sister's in New Zealand, and she didn't want to burden any of her friends.' And that was the thing: would that be how her life was, in thirty years' time? No partner, no children, maybe not living near her sister any more and with the girls having moved away? She bit her lip. 'So I sat with her in my break.'

'That was kind,' he said.

Kind wasn't how she felt. At all. 'Sorry, I'm a bit...' She grimaced. 'I probably need to go for a run. Shake off my shift.'

'You're a runner?'

'It clears my head if I have a case that gets to me,' she said. 'Given that in Manchester you'd actually have to drive somewhere to climb, I'm surprised you're not a runner when you're at work.'

'I am, when I can't climb,' he said. 'I like to run by the canal or the river. Water works when I can't get to climb something. It's not quite as good, but it's better than nothing.'

She smiled. 'I like being beside the sea, when I'm out of sorts. I take the girls and we build sandcastles or look for shells.'

Another vision flashed through Rob's head of three little girls with his eyes and Florence's fine bone structure. The five of them building sandcastles by the sea, finding pretty shells, listening to the waves swishing on the shore...

Oh, for pity's sake.

He'd never had these sorts of fantasies. This was the second time in a week. What the hell was wrong with him?

He needed air.

'You know what? You've had a shift that's left you feeling a bit down, and I think we both need a change of scene. Let's go out for pizza or something,' he said. 'My treat, because it's my idea.'

For a moment, he thought she was going to protest. But then she nodded. 'Thanks. That'd be nice.'

'You don't have to dress up,' he said swiftly. Because he'd be in real trouble if she looked as incredible as she had at the departmental Christmas dinner. Dressed casually and with no make-up she was gorgeous enough; dressed up, she'd be irresistible. 'Just you and me, pizza and a taxi?'

'No need for a taxi. I'll drive,' she said.

'We'll do some car karaoke, then,' he said. 'Pretend I'm your nieces and sing along with me.'

That, to his relief, made her smile.

And somehow they ended up singing various Abba tracks on the way to the pizza place.

He noticed Florence smiling to herself as she parked the car. 'What?'

'I was just wondering about your teenage band. Which was better, your guitar playing or your singing?'

'Oh, my singing,' he said. 'By a long way. My guitar solos were right up at the screechy end.'

The corner of her mouth twitched. And then they were both laughing themselves silly.

'Sorry. I don't mean to mock you. But...' She trailed off, shaking her head. 'Singing might not be your forte, Rob. I hate to think what your guitar was like.'

'I did say our parents and our neighbours were all over the moon when the band broke up,' he reminded her, and grinned. 'Ollie can't sing, either. Imagine the pair of us doing harmonies round the house. You should've heard our version of "Bohemian Rhapsody".'

She grinned back. 'Well, hey. Nobody's perfect.'

'You're right. By the way, you sing flat, too. Though not *quite* as flat as I do,' he allowed.

It broke the tension between them, but when they were settled at their table in the pizza place Rob found himself wishing that this was a proper date.

Florence had said she was over her ex, but was she really? Did he stand a chance with her? He'd been trying to tell himself he should stay away; but the pull he felt towards her was so strong.

Then he became aware that she was asking him something.

'Sorry. I zoned out temporarily. Lack of carbs,' he fibbed, not wanting to tell her what he'd actually been thinking about. 'Would you mind repeating that?'

'I was just wondering how your research was going,' she said. 'The ADHD stuff.'

Brilliant. So he could avoid the emotional stuff he found it hard to deal with. 'It's hugely interesting,' he said. 'I went through some questionnaires, based on what I was like as a kid and how I am now.'

'And?'

'It looks as if I'm pretty much a textbook case,' he said. 'And it's probably why I like emergency medicine: everything's fast, I know what I'm doing and I thrive on—'

'—pushing yourself too hard,' she finished.

And it explained why his relationships had fizzled

out in the past. He got bored quickly and he wasn't good enough at paying attention to his partner's needs. And he suspected that both his brother and his parents had accommodated his behaviour because he'd never got into real trouble at school and he'd never struggled academically. Everyone had just assumed that he was a bright boy with a low boredom threshold. Rob the Restless. Rob the Risk-Taker. It had been good-natured teasing: but maybe if he'd had a clue earlier he might not have hurt past girlfriends by not being there enough for them. At least he knew what to watch for now.

'So where do you go from here?' she asked.

'I'm meeting Ollie for lunch tomorrow,' he said. 'I thought we'd throw a few ideas about.' And, given that Oliver was so happy with Gemma now, maybe he could point Rob in the right direction with Florence, too...

Florence was glad that they hadn't bothered ordering wine, on the grounds that she was driving and Rob was on antibiotics. She needed to steer well clear of anything that might lower her inhibitions even a fraction in the vicinity of this man.

He was good company. Charming, warm and funny.

He was beautiful, too.

And he kissed like an angel.

But he also thought he wouldn't make a good dad, which meant he probably didn't want children. So she'd just have to keep reminding herself that he was Mr Wrong.

CHAPTER SEVEN

ON WEDNESDAY, ROB took a taxi to Ashermouth Bay and met his brother outside the surgery.

'You look terrible,' Oliver said, giving him a hug. 'Have you been overdoing things?'

'No. I just had a bit of an infection. The antibiotics are working nicely, and I'm on the mend now,' Rob said.

'What? An infection? When did this happen? Why didn't you tell me?' Oliver demanded.

'Because you'd worry, you'd tell Mum, and she'd fuss.' Rob clapped his brother's shoulder. 'Stop worrying. I'm fine. *Really*. I felt a bit rough on my shift last week, and I was sensible about it and went to the renal department. No misplaced heroics.' Even though originally he had intended to wait until after the end of his shift, Ollie didn't need the worry of knowing that. 'They ran all the checks, decided it was an infection rather than the beginning of rejection, and gave me some meds.' He grimaced. 'And they signed me off for a week.'

'Why didn't you come and stay with me?' Oliver asked.

Rob squirmed. 'Look, I've already wrecked one engagement for you. I didn't want to wreck this one, too.'

'Apart from the fact that it wasn't your fault Tabby ended things, and Gemma isn't Tabby—Rob, for pity's sake, you're my *twin*. Next time something like this happens, you call me,' Oliver said, glaring at him. 'Yes, of course I'll tell Mum, because we need to keep her in the loop so she doesn't worry herself stupid, but I'll also be a buffer and make sure she gives you the space you need.'

Rob blew out a breath. 'Sorry. I know I probably should've said something earlier.'

'There's no "probably" about it,' Oliver said.

'I just didn't want to worry you. Or get in the way with you and Gemma.'

'You wouldn't get in the way. Gemma seems to like you, for some strange reason,' his twin said dryly.

'I like her, too. She's right for you,' Rob said. 'So, where are we going for lunch?'

'Pub?' Oliver suggested.

'Can we get a quiet table?' Rob asked. 'I'd like a bit of advice.'

'That sounds serious.' Oliver's eyes were full of concern.

'It's absolutely nothing to do with the infection or the transplant,' Rob reassured him.

Once they were seated and they'd ordered, Rob said, 'So, the advice stuff. As a GP, how would you go about diagnosing a patient with ADHD?'

'Why?'

'Humour me,' Rob said.

'All right. I'd start with talking to my patient's parents, go through the diagnostic questionnaires with them and maybe with the school with the parents' permission, then do a referral to a paediatrician specialising in spectrum cases.'

'What about if the patient was an adult?' Rob asked.

'Then I'd go through the diagnostic questionnaires with them. Why?'

'Has it ever occurred to you,' Rob asked, 'that *I* might have ADHD?'

'No. You're just you.' Oliver looked thoughtful. 'Though, now you've said it, you certainly fit the hyperactive side of the criteria. Mum always says you were the busiest toddler she's ever met. But we're identical twins, and I don't fit any of the criteria: so how can you have ADHD if I don't?'

'Because we're not *quite* identical,' Rob said. 'Remember when they tested us before they did the transplant? Bits of our genomes are different, which is why they put me on low-dose immunosuppressants. I've been reading up a lot about the copy variant stuff, this week, seeing as I've been off work—'

'—and you can't sit still and rest,' Oliver interjected.

'My point precisely,' Rob said. 'And it's possible that we're a bit more different than we thought.'

'So you think you might have ADHD.' Oliver looked him straight in the eye. 'Are you asking me to diagnose you and maybe prescribe something, Rob?'

'No, to both,' Rob said. 'I'll see my own GP for a proper diagnosis. I just wanted to know what you think. And apparently there are other ways to deal with it, not just medication.'

'A lot of undiagnosed adult ADHD patients self-medicate to manage how they feel,' Oliver said. 'Actually, now I think about it, that's what you do.'

'What? How?' Rob frowned. 'You know I've never

abused prescription meds or taken any kind of drugs. I don't smoke. And, although I appreciate good red wine, I stick to the limits.'

'That's not what I mean,' Oliver said. 'And not even your chocolate habit. It's the risky stuff you do. The climbing. The humanitarian aid stuff. I think that's how you manage yourself.'

'So are you saying that, if my GP put me on meds, I wouldn't need to climb any more?' Rob asked.

Oliver shook his head. 'I think climbing means too much to you for you ever to give it up. And you'd need to discuss treatment with your GP. But if my hunch is right and climbing's what you do to manage it, then you need to find something to challenge you until you're fit enough to go back to climbing. Something you can do while you're resting and healing.'

'I might have done that,' Rob said, thinking about the sewing and Florence. 'Or, rather, a friend might have found the answer.'

'Friend?'

Of course his twin would pick up on that. They knew how each other's minds worked and often finished each other's sentences. Rob wrinkled his nose. 'It's complicated.'

'You don't do complications.'

'I know. But I kind of want to.' He sighed. 'Which is even more of a complication, and I don't have a clue what to do about it. Where to start.'

'Be honest with her. Talk to her,' Ollie said. 'Don't keep stuff back.'

'The ADHD? She was the one who suggested it. There was a boy in the department with a spring stuck in his hand.'

Oliver grinned. 'That sounds like the sort of thing you would've done at school.'

'Yeah,' Rob admitted. 'The more she talked to the boy's mum, the more she thought he sounded like me. So she asked me if I'd ever considered it.'

Oliver thought about it. 'That makes a lot of sense. The way you need to be on the move all the time. The fact you're such a minimalist—if you don't have any clutter in the first place, that means you can't get overwhelmed by it. The way you hyper-focus, whether it's work or climbing or anything else you do. Actually, that makes you pretty amazing, because you've worked out how to deal with it all by yourself, without even knowing what the problem is in the first place.'

'I did get a fair bit of help,' Rob corrected him. 'Remember the teacher who got me into climbing?'

'That's a good point,' Oliver said. 'He'd probably seen quite a few kids who couldn't settle and discovered that the discipline of climbing helped them.' He frowned. 'I wonder why he didn't talk to Mum and Dad about it and suggest having you tested?'

'Maybe he did and they said no, I'd always been a busy child, and it was just a phase I was going through. Not that I'm criticising them,' Rob said swiftly, 'just trying to make sense of things.'

'Back then, ADHD and Asperger's weren't really understood,' Oliver mused. 'We still don't know enough about the spectrum, but back then a child who couldn't pay attention and never got homework in on time would've been labelled lazy—nobody would've thought about teaching them time management.'

'I never handed my homework in late,' Rob said.

'Though I did zone out in a couple of exams. The teachers assumed I was distracted by girls.'

'Which was also fair,' Oliver said, 'considering the number of them who fell at your feet.'

Rob shrugged. 'Right now I feel a bit of an idiot for not realising before why I was different.'

'Talk to your GP. Get the official diagnosis. And,' Oliver said, warming to his theme, 'you're right about stuff other than meds being able to help. For a start, there's exercise.'

Rob raised an eyebrow. 'Climbing?'

'Not just that. Something you can do anywhere. Gemma and I have been sorting out stuff for our elderly patients.'

Rob gave him a speaking look. 'I'm ten minutes older than you, not four decades.'

'I don't mean that. I meant the stuff we've been putting on the practice website about exercise for health. Mental as well as physical. There's yoga.'

Yoga—which Rob knew Florence did every week. Could he do yoga with her?

'A one-to-one teacher would probably be more helpful than a class for the mindfulness stuff. I found something called mindful walking, the other day, but I haven't got round to researching it properly yet. I'll add it to my list and see if it's something that might work for you.' Oliver smiled. 'And I'll do any or all of it with you, if you feel too self-conscious or weird to do it on your own.'

'Thank you, because right now I feel a bit stupid for not realising it before.'

'You're very far from stupid, and you're not the only one who should've picked it up.' Oliver clapped his brother's shoulder. 'We've got this. And you need to talk to your friend. Tell her how you feel about her.'

'What if she doesn't feel the same way?'

Oliver coughed. 'We've had this conversation before. Except it was me with the doubts, last time. Take your own advice. Talk to her and be honest.'

'But how do you know, Olls? When you meet The One?'

Oliver looked at him. 'It's that serious?'

'Answer the question.'

Oliver sighed. 'I got it wrong with Tabby, remember.'

'Yes, but you've got it right with Gemma. How did you know?'

'She made me feel as if the sun was shining every time she walked into the room,' Oliver said. 'The doubts were all in my head. If I'd be enough for her—because I wasn't enough for Tabby.' He looked at Rob. 'What's her name?'

'Florence.'

'How does she make you feel?'

'Still,' Rob said. 'I can be *still*, with her. It's…' He shook his head. 'But she's been let down, and I've never wanted to commit to anyone before. There's always been a mountain to climb and a world to conquer.' He paused. 'What if I hurt her? I can't trust myself to commit.'

'The old you—before the kidney—would never even have considered that,' Oliver said.

Rob flinched. 'Because I'm selfish and unthinking.'

'No. You were always honest and you never pretended to be anything you weren't,' Oliver said. 'But you sound different. You sound as if you want something else now.'

'I do.' And that particular revelation still shocked him. 'But, when I'm fully fit again, will I be like I was before?'

'Restless? I don't know,' Oliver said. 'But having to be still and wanting to be still are two very different things. One of them is your choice.'

'I guess.'

'How does Florence feel about you?'

'I don't know,' Rob admitted. 'I think she likes me.'

'That's a good start.' Oliver paused. 'The only way to find out is to talk to her.'

Talking. Which he was great at when it came to putting patients at their ease, and rubbish at when it came to relationships. But he knew his twin was right.

'What are you doing?' Florence asked, the next morning, when Rob walked into the kitchen wearing his work suit.

'Going to work. If you don't mind giving me a lift, that is.'

'I do mind,' she said. 'You were signed off for a week.'

'It's been *nearly* a week,' he said.

'Six days.'

'What's one little day between friends?' he asked with a smile. 'And I feel perfectly fine.'

'You're pushing yourself,' Florence warned.

'I'll pace myself. I promise,' he said. 'But I need to be back at work. I need to feel I'm doing something.'

'You were signed off for a week,' she repeated.

'And I'm feeling back to normal,' he said. 'It's Thursday. I'm not due in tomorrow. If I go in today, it eases me back into things.' He gave her a rueful smile. 'To be precise, it eases me back into the schedule that's meant to ease me back into things.'

'If you feel the slightest bit rough,' she said, 'then you say so and you *stop*.'

'I will. Promise,' he said. 'For me, believe me, this is taking it slowly.'

'Hmm.' But she drove him in.

And it was fine until the middle of the afternoon, when the paramedics brought in a young mum-to-be who'd been in an accident.

'This is Kelly. Thirty-four, five and a half months pregnant with her first baby, and she was rear-ended in a queue of traffic,' the paramedic told Florence and Rob. 'The airbag didn't go off, but she's worried because she can't feel the baby moving.' She lowered her voice. 'I couldn't pick up a heartbeat with a stethoscope, but that could be the way the baby's lying.'

Florence really hoped she was right.

The paramedic spoke normally again. 'No sign of contractions, no leaks of any kind of fluid, and obviously Kelly's worried so her pulse rate is a bit on the high side.'

Some good news, some not so good. 'OK. Thanks. I'll get a call up to Maternity,' Florence said quietly, and turned to her patient. 'Kelly, I'm Dr Jacobs and this is Dr Langley. I know right now you're feeling scared, and we're here to look after you and the baby. Before today, did you feel much movement?' With a first baby, Florence knew the mum might not even feel the baby moving until around twenty-four weeks.

'A bit. It felt like fluttering.' Kelly was pale. 'But there's been nothing since the crash.'

'That doesn't necessarily mean there's a problem,' Rob reassured her. 'Babies all have different rhythms. Are you booked in with the team here?'

'No, I live in Glasgow. I just came over for the day to see my gran. I… Oh, God.' She bit her lip. 'I can't lose this baby.'

'Can we call anyone for you?' Rob asked.

She shook her head. 'My partner's on his way. And my mum's called Gran to say I…' Kelly shuddered, and her words ground to a halt.

'That's fine. He'll be here soon,' Florence said soothingly. 'We'll give you an ultrasound scan so we can see how the baby's doing.' And so she could check the placenta; an impact, even if the jolt wasn't that severe, could make the placenta shear away. 'I'll examine you as well, if that's OK.' She took Kelly's hand and squeezed it. 'I know right now everything feels incredibly scary, but you're in the best place.'

Kelly was shaking and crying too much to reply.

Please let the baby be all right, Florence begged silently. And she was glad Rob was here. He was the perfect person to help her, right now. Those blue eyes and that smile of his would go a long way towards helping calm Kelly down.

'Do you know your blood group?' Rob asked.

'A positive,' Kelly said shakily.

Florence exchanged a glance with Rob. That was one complication they could avoid, then. If Kelly had been Rhesus negative, there was a risk that if the baby was positive and the baby's blood mixed with hers, Kelly's immune system might become sensitised and attack the baby's red blood cells. Rhesus disease was the last thing Kelly needed right now.

'That's good,' Florence said. 'Do you have any pain—anything that feels like a bruise, or any feelings of tightness?'

Kelly shook her head. 'I don't… I can't…just… Please, is my baby OK?' she begged.

'I'm going to get the portable scanner now,' Florence said. 'I'll be gone for five minutes tops.'

'And I'm going to stay right by your side,' Rob said, his voice full of reassurance. 'Try and breathe slowly for me—three counts in, three counts out—and I promise that will help with all the scary stuff. I'll count you through it. Count along in your head with me. And that's in, two, three…'

Florence knew she was leaving Kelly in the best possible hands. Rob was excellent with patients, calm and kind. He'd be the perfect anchor. Once she'd closed the curtains round the cubicle, she grabbed the first person she saw. 'Ranj, I've got a woman in from an RTA. It's her first pregnancy and she can't feel the baby move. Can you grab someone from Maternity, and tell them it's urgent? Rob's with her now and I'm getting the portable scanner.'

'I'm on it,' Ranj said.

'Thanks.'

She wheeled the scanner through to the cubicle. 'How are you doing?' she asked.

'The baby's still not moving,' Kelly whispered.

Please, please let this be just panic and a first-time mum not yet used to feeling her baby's movements, Florence begged silently. Please let it all be OK.

She gave Kelly a reassuring smile, and talked her through what she was doing as she set up the scan.

'We wanted this baby so much,' Kelly said. 'It took

us three attempts at IVF. All I want is to be a mum—
and this is all my fault. If I hadn't come to see my gran,
then I wouldn't have had the accident.'

'It's absolutely not your fault,' Florence reassured
her. 'Apart from the fact you were stationary when the
other driver hit you, accidents happen anywhere.'

Florence knew it was true, but it put a lump in her
throat. This could so easily have been her, if Dan had
agreed to try for IVF with a sperm donor. She knew
how it felt to be so desperate to have a baby. The waiting and the hoping and the disappointment that grew
sharper every month.

That little catch in Florence's voice right now: Rob was
pretty sure something was very wrong indeed. Had
something like this happened to Florence, and maybe
her ex hadn't been supportive enough?

He glanced at Florence, but her expression was that
of a concerned doctor; the woman was hiding behind
the job. Though he noticed a moment of anguish when
Florence stroked the transceiver head across Kelly's
stomach. 'I can see the baby's heart beating,' she said,
and turned the screen so Kelly could see it for herself.
'Look. The baby's kicking. And the heartbeat's there.
Nice and strong.'

Kelly sobbed in relief, and Florence held her hand
tightly. 'It's going to be all right,' she soothed.

Though that wasn't strictly true. Rob could see a
blood clot on the screen—something Florence clearly
wasn't making a big deal of it because it would terrify
their patient. It looked to him as if Kelly might have
a concealed placental abruption, where the blood was
trapped between the wall of the womb and the placenta

rather than showing as a vaginal bleed. He exchanged a glance with Florence and knew her clinical judgement mirrored his.

'Kelly, may I examine you?' Florence asked gently.

'Yes, of course.'

'No sign of blood or any tears,' she said.

But then Kelly said, 'My back aches a bit now. I didn't really notice before, because I was so scared about the baby and that's all I could focus on.'

'What kind of ache?' Florence asked.

'Like when you catch the back of your hand on the corner of a desk and about three days later it's sore,' Kelly said.

Like a bruise. That definitely wasn't a good sign, Rob thought.

'I'm going to ask someone to come down from the maternity department to see you,' Florence said carefully. 'It might be that they decide to keep you in overnight and keep an eye on you, because the symptoms you're describing mean it's possible that a bit of your placenta has come away from the wall of your womb.'

'My placenta's come away?' Kelly's face paled. 'Is my baby going to be OK?'

That depended on the severity of the abruption, but Rob knew they needed to keep Kelly as calm as possible. 'We'll do our very best to keep your baby safe,' was the best he could promise.

Ranj came in to tell them that Naz Mahmoud, one of the senior registrars from the maternity unit, was on her way down. A couple of minutes later, Naz arrived and Florence had a quiet confab with her outside the cubicle to fill her in on the situation before bringing her in to introduce her to their patient. 'Naz will look after you now, Kelly. All the best,' Florence said.

'You're in good hands,' Rob reassured her.

He intended to grab Florence and whisk her off to the hospital canteen for a coffee and a quiet chat, to see if she was OK, but the red phone shrilled again with news that the paramedics were bringing in someone with a suspected stroke; there just wasn't time to leave the department.

'Are you OK?' he asked.

'Of course,' she replied.

He knew she wasn't telling the truth, but right then there was nothing he could do to help.

At the end of their shift, when their patient with a stroke had been admitted, Florence said, 'Give me ten minutes before I give you a lift?'

'Sure. I'll get some hot chocolate to go. Meet you by the car?'

'Thanks.'

Whenever was upsetting her, it went deep. And Rob knew he was going to have to tread very carefully indeed to make sure he didn't make things worse.

When she met him at the car, she was all smiley and chirpy. And Rob could see straight through the act. 'Hot chocolate,' he said. 'And cake.' Cake made everything better. 'Do you want me to drive?'

'No, it's fine. Thanks for the hot chocolate.' She took a sip, almost as if she was trying to prove to him that she was fine, then slid the cup into the holder in her car.

Rob fell back on the doctors' old trick of waiting for the patient to fill the silence. But, with Florence also being a doctor and knowing the same trick, it backfired on him; she didn't say a word. And she had that brittle smile on her face all the way into her flat.

He knew he wasn't great with emotional stuff, but no way was he going to abandon her. 'I'll cook. There's pasta in the fridge and a pot of sauce.'

'I'm not hungry,' she said.

'You've had a tough shift,' he said. 'And you're not okay. Florence, I'm a guy and I'm not great at talking about feelings, but even *I* can see you're upset, and I'm pretty sure that it's to do with Kelly. Talk to me. I'm here, and it's not going any further than me.'

When she still said nothing, he sighed. 'Just ignore the fact I'm six feet tall and male. Imagine I'm your ballerina sister,' he said, 'because I think you really need a hug.' He wrapped his arms round her and held her close. He wondered if she was going to pull away again, or if she'd actually talk to him.

And finally he felt the tears judder through her.

He rested his chin on Florence's shoulder and kept her wrapped in his arms until she'd managed to stop shaking. Then he settled her at the kitchen table and made her a mug of tea. 'Talk,' he said. 'Was it Kelly?'

She nodded. 'Naz said we were right. It was a concealed abruption. Kelly was asleep when I called up.'

'Rest—' much as he hated it personally '—can do a lot.'

'Yeah.'

Why had this case got to her so much? Had something like this happened to her? He knew he'd be twitchy if they had someone in with a burst appendix or a transplant rejection; he'd be cool and calm in the department, but afterwards—when he was on his own and had had time for it to sink in—it would definitely get to him.

'Forgive me for asking,' he said softly. 'I don't mean to hurt you or bring back bad memories. But is that what happened to you? You had an abruption and lost a baby?'

She swallowed hard and whispered, 'I didn't even get that far.'

He remembered what else Kelly had said: she'd had IVF. 'You had IVF that didn't work?' he guessed.

Florence shook her head; when she looked up at him, her huge brown eyes were filled with pain.

He didn't understand. 'What can I do to help?'

'Nothing.'

He couldn't just sit here and watch her suffering.

He scooped her out of the chair, sat her on his lap and held her close. He could feel her shaking with the effort of trying not to cry.

'No judgement,' he said softly, 'and nothing you tell me will go anywhere. Just the same as you haven't told anyone about me and my kidney.'

'I told the head of the department I'd taken you to the renal team.'

'That's different. The head of the department already knew about my kidney, and it's the kind of thing that managers need to know.' He stroked her hair. 'If you don't want to talk, that's fine. But sometimes getting the words out stops things hurting quite so much.'

She was silent for so long that he thought she was going to close off on him.

But then she sighed and rested her head on his shoulder. 'Dan—my ex—we tried for a baby for three years. When we didn't get anywhere, we saw our GP and went for tests. I was fine but Dan wasn't. There was a problem with his sperm; he had a really low count and the motility was poor.' She bit her lip. 'Apparently he had mumps when he was about thirteen. Nobody paid any attention to it at the time, but clearly that affected his fertility.'

'So IVF didn't help?'

'It might've done. But he absolutely refused to do ICSI, where they'd extract his sperm under a microscope and inject it into my egg, or IVF with donor sperm.' She closed her eyes. 'I desperately wanted a baby, Rob.'

But her husband had been infertile; and he'd refused the medical treatment that could have helped. She'd said the divorce was because they'd wanted different things. Now he was beginning to understand.

'I'm sorry,' he said, stroking her hair. 'That's tough.'

'And that poor woman today... It could so easily have been me, if Dan had agreed to the IVF.'

They were taught to maintain professional distance at work, but every so often a case resonated with you. Really hurt. Clearly this was one of those for Florence. 'Just remember, you were there to help her. You got her admitted so she's under close observation.'

'There's no guarantee the abruption won't get worse and she could lose the baby.'

'There's no guarantee the abruption *will* get worse,' he said gently, 'and if it does she's in the right place to get the help she needs immediately, and that'll make all the difference. You did your bit, Florence, and you *helped*.'

'It doesn't feel enough,' she whispered.

Her misery felt bone-deep and he ached to comfort her. 'It's enough. *You're* enough.'

'It doesn't feel it,' she repeated.

Had this affected her so personally that it made her doubt her own medical judgement?

Before he could find a way of asking her and reassuring her, she said, 'It's not just that he refused IVF or adoption. He said they wouldn't be his kids biologically.'

'It takes more than biology to be a parent,' he said, furious that the guy could've been so selfish and hurt her so much. 'And I'm sorry he let you down.'

She looked away. 'It turned out that he did want kids, after all. Just not with me. He—he had an affair. And he didn't have a problem with his mistress already having kids who weren't biologically his. He just didn't want kids with me.'

Rob bit back the harsh words that rose to his lips. She didn't need his anger. She needed comfort.

'Because there's obviously something wrong with me,' she finished.

'There's absolutely nothing wrong with you, Florence Jacobs. You're bright, and you're kind, and you'd make a brilliant mother. Any man would be proud to love you.' That included him. Though he'd never talked to her about love, and now absolutely wasn't the time. How could he tell her that he was more than halfway to falling in love with her, and he didn't have a clue what to do about it because he'd never felt like this about anyone before? 'He didn't value you the way he should've valued you, and that's *his* fault, not yours. Never yours.'

'Thank you.' But she still didn't look as if she believed him. He didn't know what to do, what to say. He just held her close.

And he meant to give her a reassuring kiss on the cheek; but somehow their mouths connected.

Somehow his eyes were closed.

Somehow he was really kissing her, as if they were both drowning and needed each other for air...

And then she broke the kiss and slid off his lap. 'My head's not in the right place for this.'

He'd stepped so far beyond the boundaries, it was untrue. 'I'm sorry, Florence. That wasn't... I shouldn't have done that. I was trying to... I don't know, show you how much I want you. That you're *enough* for me. I got it wrong, and I apologise.'

'It's not you. It's me.' But she wouldn't meet his gaze.

'It's *not* you,' he said. He paused, feeling awkward. 'Look, I understand if you want me to go. I'll get my stuff together and call a taxi.'

'No—it's fine.'

But it wasn't. It wasn't fine at all. 'I...um—look, let me cook you that pasta.'

'I'm not hungry,' she said. 'I just need an early night.'

'I'm so sorry.' It was very English, he thought: apologising, apologising for apologising, and both of you going round in circles while you stuck up a protective wall. And he didn't know how to deal with this. How to make it better.

'Not your fault.'

'Can I—? Do you want a drink of anything?'

'You already made me tea.'

Which she hadn't drunk and there was a skin forming on the top.

Anything he said now would just make things worse. 'If you need anything...' Oh, and how did that sound? Of course she didn't need him. Mr 'I can't commit, and I blame it on my itchy feet when it's really just my own failings'.

She just gave him a wan smile. 'Nobody in the department knows—about…'

The words were clearly sticking in her throat. 'They won't hear anything from me. It's nobody else's business,' he reassured her. He rather wanted to pay her ex a visit, dangle him off a narrow ledge and make him admit what a worm he was. But that wouldn't solve anything. 'See you tomorrow,' he said.

But he sat up late, thinking.

Now he knew the truth about her marriage break-up, it proved that, even though he was falling for her, he wasn't the right one for her. She wanted children, and he'd never been in a relationship to the point of wanting to settle down and have children. Florence Jacobs wasn't like anyone he'd dated before; but he wasn't dating her. She was his temporary colleague. Until tonight, he would've said they were becoming friends. But he'd made things awkward between them, responded in completely the wrong way.

He was only staying with her until he recovered. And he should've left a couple of days ago, when he'd started feeling better. He shouldn't have given in to the temptation to stay. Shouldn't have responded to her warmth. *Shouldn't have kissed her again.*

Was she asleep? Probably not. But he could hardly knock on her bedroom door and ask to talk to her. Quietly, he packed his things. Tomorrow, he'd get a taxi to the hospital, pick up his car, and go…well, not home. Back to his flat.

And he'd have to be bright and breezy with her in future. Treat her as nothing more than a colleague, not even a friend. It wasn't want he wanted—he wanted *her*—but he couldn't give her what she needed. She deserved a chance to find someone who'd love her, someone who'd give her the family she dreamed of.

And how he wished it could've been him. That he was different. But if he stayed, he'd let her down, and she'd already been let down enough.

The next morning, she'd clearly decided on the same tactics, because she was bright and breezy with him. 'Toast?'

'Thanks, but I'm fine,' he said. 'And I wanted to say thank you for looking after me so well, this week.'

'You're very welcome. You look a lot better,' she said.

'I feel a lot better,' he said. 'So it's time I got out from under your feet and went back to my own flat. I've stripped the bed and put everything in the laundry basket. I've got a taxi booked for—' he glanced at his watch '—any minute now, so it makes sense for me to wait outside. I'll see you at work on Monday.'

'OK.' She gave him a super-bright smile that didn't fool him in the slightest. He knew she felt just as awkward as he did. But she'd been the one to call a halt, and he wasn't going to push.

Back at his flat, he contacted the local florist and arranged for a hand-tied bouquet to be delivered, with a message.

Thank you for looking after me. You were a good friend and I appreciate it. Rob

And then, with nothing better to do, he cleaned his flat. Twice.

* * *

The flowers were spectacular. Large roses, spray roses and stocks, all in delicate shades of pink, set off with pretty foliage.

Florence knew who they were from before she opened the card.

Pink. He'd chosen that deliberately. Like the flowers she'd taught him to stitch.

But the message made her heart sink.

Thank you for looking after me. You were a good friend and I appreciate it. Rob

It was perfectly polite—and very distant.

Which was her own fault. She'd been the one to call a halt when he'd kissed her, last night. He'd been comforting her when she was upset. That sweet, gentle kiss on the cheek had been comfort. And she'd kissed him back on the mouth. Instigated it. Stopped it. Given mixed messages.

Of course he'd backed off.

How could he possibly have stayed here after that?

Never had flowers made her feel so miserable.

And her flat felt so empty, without Rob. For the last week, she'd been sharing her space and she'd enjoyed not coming home to an empty flat. To sharing the cooking—well, in his case he'd organised a takeaway, made a very quick stir-fry and taken her out for pizza. But sharing her space. Sharing her time. Getting to know what made him tick. The sewing lessons. She'd loved every minute of it.

Now he'd gone, it felt as if all the colours had dimmed.

She blew out a breath. The flowers were lovely. And she needed to thank him.

Quickly, she tapped a message into her phone.

Thank you for the flowers. They're stunning.

Had they been just a polite thank-you? Or was he using them to try and connect with her again? Should she say something about the sewing, maybe even tease him a little? Would that get their connection back, or would it make him back away even more?

Or perhaps she was overthinking it. In the end, she finished with a safe:

See you Monday.

He didn't reply.

Which told her the flowers had simply been polite. If he'd wanted to take their relationship further, then he would've used the excuse to keep the conversation going. Weeks ago, Lexy had advised her to ask him out. To tell him her dating skills were rusty and suggest maybe going for a drink after work.

But she'd pushed him away. And she'd told him the whole story about Dan, about how she'd so desperately wanted a family. Rob had made it clear that he was only here for a few more weeks. He was leaving. And, even though Florence thought she might be halfway in love with him, she knew that wouldn't be enough to make him want to stay. She hadn't been enough for Dan and she wouldn't be enough for Rob. So she'd stick to being colleagues and having professional boundaries.

But her flat still felt empty. And she couldn't even

go and spend time with her sister, because Lexy would ask her about Transition Man and she'd have to explain what a mess she'd made of things.

Nothing felt right. Nothing distracted him. He couldn't even lose himself in research.

And that text Florence had sent him was so polite it set Rob's teeth on edge. 'See you Monday' clearly meant 'Please don't contact me over the weekend'.

If only he could go climbing.

A walk on the beach didn't help much, because he remembered she'd said she liked the sea when she was out of sorts. He liked water, too, but this time it didn't help.

Nothing helped.

And he didn't have a clue how to make things right with her.

If only he'd kept his mouth to himself. If only he hadn't given in to the impulse to kiss her. That was where it had all gone wrong. He should've just comforted her, moved out over the weekend so he was ready to go back to work, and then asked her out.

But no.

He'd kissed her.

And she'd told him straight that she wasn't interested.

He managed to get himself in full charm mode for lunch with his parents, Oliver and Gemma on the Sunday. His twin insisted that they keep the tradition of the two of them doing the washing-up, though Rob knew it was an excuse for Oliver to grill him.

'So did you talk to Florence?'

He couldn't admit, even to his twin, how badly he'd messed up. 'No.'

'That advice you gave me was sound,' Oliver said.

'Yeah.' No, it wasn't. 'I'll talk to her.'

And if Oliver knew it was a big, fat fib, at least he also knew not to press it.

CHAPTER EIGHT

IF THE WEATHER was meant to reflect your mood, Monday morning should've been filled with endless rain and fog. But of course it was sunny, with the sun sparkling on the frost. Rob scowled, and stamped through the corridors. Somehow he had to regain his equilibrium before he saw Florence again. Treat her as if she was just another colleague, when she was actually the first woman he'd ever wanted to settle down with.

By the time he reached the double doors to the department, he'd managed to put a professional smile on his face.

The bit he was longing for and dreading in equal measure was seeing Florence. How would she be with him? He'd take his cue from her, he decided. His conversation with Ollie had clarified things in his head: he wanted her to see him as someone safe. Someone who wouldn't let her down. And he needed to find a way of doing that—once he was sure that was what she wanted, too.

The roster showed that they were in Resus together. Which meant they'd have to work closely, but at least they'd be busy and completely focused on their patients. At least that was one area where they were in tune.

The red phone shrilled, and Florence's face was grim when she put it down again. 'Builder, forty, fallen ten feet off a ladder. The paramedics say his GCS was ten at the scene, dropped to eight, and he's had a seizure and isn't communicating. His partner's on his way in.'

With any fall from that height, Rob knew, there was a worry about head injuries; and the seizure hinted that there might be a possible bleed in his brain, which would need surgical intervention.

They set up, ready to receive the patient. Once the paramedics had brought him in, between them they lifted the patient off the trolley and onto the bed, leaving his neck brace in place. There was blood trickling from his nose and his left ear; Rob caught Florence's eye, seeing the slight worry in her face. Like him, she recognised it as a sign of potential problems.

She shone a light in his eyes. 'Pupils equal and reactive,' she said.

That was better news, Rob thought.

He could hear the man whispering. 'What's happened? Where am I?'

'You're at the hospital,' he said. 'You fell off a ladder and we think you hit your head. I'm Dr Langley, and this is Dr Jacobs. We'll be looking after you.' He paused. 'Can you remember your name?'

'Tim,' their patient said. 'My head hurts.'

Conscious, talking and lucid. That was a really good sign, even though the pain in his head might not be.

'Tim, we're going to send you for a scan and see what's going on,' Florence said, holding his hand. 'Your partner's on the way in.'

A tear trickled down Tim's face. 'Can't move my head.'

'You've got a neck brace on to protect your spine,'

Rob said. 'Once we've done the scan, we'll know if we can take it off.'

'Ash will kill me. Said be careful, it's icy.'

'These things happen,' Florence said gently. 'He'll be here soon. And we're here to look after you.'

The scan showed pockets of air in Tim's skull.

'I don't like this,' Florence said. 'I'm going to call the neurologist to review the scan.'

'Good call. Looks like a possible fracture,' Rob said. 'And large pockets of air can compress the brain. I've seen that in people who fell when cl—' He stopped, realising what he'd just been about to say. Given what his favourite occupation was, that wasn't tactful. And it wasn't the way to convince Florence that he was a safe bet; it'd make her think he was someone who'd fill her future with worry.

'Climbing,' Florence finished. 'And you wonder why your mother worries about you.'

Yeah. She knew he'd cause her worry. 'I wear a helmet.' Wore. Who knew when he'd get the chance to climb again? 'And I don't climb in poor conditions,' he added, to make sure she'd understand that he was restless, not reckless. There was a difference.

'Good.'

But she didn't meet his eye.

How was he ever going to get things back to normal between them? How was he going to persuade her to give him a chance?

'I'll do a couple of checks on Tim while you call the neuro team.'

'And I'll go and find his partner on the way back to join you,' she said.

Thankfully Tim seemed even more lucid than he had

earlier, and Rob was able to reassure him a bit and run through a few checks before Florence and Tim's partner joined them.

'Ashir, this is Dr Langley, who's helping me look after Tim. Rob, this is Ashir, Tim's partner,' Florence introduced them swiftly.

Ashir shook his hand. 'Thanks for what you've done.' Then he turned to Tim. 'So falling ten feet off a ladder is your idea of being careful?'

'Could've been worse. Could've been twenty feet,' Tim said.

'I'm glad you're talking. When I got that call, I thought...' Ashir shuddered and held his partner's hand.

'You always said I was bone-headed,' Tim said, clearly much more relaxed now his partner was here.

'I swear I'm going to glue that safety helmet to your head in future,' Ashir said.

It was the same kind of banter he'd started to have with Florence, when he'd stayed with her. And it made his heart ache that it wouldn't happen again.

Later that morning, the neuro team admitted Tim for observation, but a second scan had been more promising.

'Watch and wait,' Florence said.

Was she going to tease him about 'wait' being his second-favourite four-letter word? Rob wondered. But she didn't. And that threw him. They'd become friends over the last few weeks. If she didn't even see him as that, how could she ever see him as anything more? He wanted her to see him as more. He'd been thinking about it for days.

And he didn't know how to reach out to her.

* * *

'Come over for dinner,' Oliver said on Wednesday evening. 'You sound as if you could do with Gemma's lasagne and some cake.'

'Hang on—you're starting to appreciate cake now?' Rob teased.

'Gemma's a cake fiend. I have no choice,' Oliver said. 'Seriously, though. You sound a bit low. And it'll be more fun than sticking something in your microwave.'

'Yeah.' And maybe his twin would have some insight into how to fix this impasse with Florence. Something other than 'talk to her', because Rob knew he'd already made a mess of that.

He called in at the supermarket on the way to his brother's, buying flowers and wine. Gemma was at a dance aerobics class—though Rob could smell the lasagne bubbling in the oven.

He was halfway through explaining the situation with Florence to Oliver. 'I want to prove to her that I can stick at something,' he said.

At that moment, Gemma came into the kitchen, kissed Oliver hello and hugged Rob. 'Hey, Rob the Risk-Taker—planning your next climb?' She tried to ruffle his hair; when that didn't work, because his hair was so much shorter than Oliver's, she laughed. 'Sorry.'

'No, you're fine.'

'Tell Gem what you were telling me,' Oliver said. 'She has the advantage of two X chromosomes, so she understands how women's minds work.'

'What can I do to help?' Gemma asked.

'I feel a bit bad, talking about someone else's private life,' Rob said.

'It's not going any further than us,' Gemma said. 'Talk.'

Rob explained about how Florence had been hurt before and didn't want to take any risks. 'And with me being what I am…' He grimaced. 'She's the first woman I've ever felt like this about. I need to find a way to prove to her that I'm serious about her.'

'Try telling her exactly what you just told us,' Gemma said.

'Words aren't enough. I need something physical.' He thought about it. 'She likes needlework. She taught me to do cross-stitch. Maybe I can make her a picture.'

'That's not something you can do like snapping your fingers, Rob,' Gemma said. 'Even a bookmark, if you did a proper one with a few different colours and back-stitch, would take you about ten hours—plus unpicking the bits where you've gone wrong, because everyone has to unpick things.'

'I know I've got a reputation for being impatient—' Rob began.

'You *are* impatient,' Oliver interrupted.

'But I can be patient for this. I can focus. Because it's important.' He spread his hands. 'I guess there's a benefit to only working three days a week, after all: it means I have time to do it.'

'Putting your feelings in stitching instead of words. Well, that'd definitely show you mean it and it isn't just a whim,' Gemma mused. 'Though don't stitch all day without a break, or your hand will hurt for a week.'

'She said something like that when she taught me

how to stitch,' Rob said wryly. 'And you sound as if you know about stitching.'

'I know a bit because my best friend Claire's mum Yvonne has a craft shop. She runs workshops and I sometimes help out. What do you want to make?'

'I don't know,' he admitted.

'She'd be an excellent person to ask for ideas, plus she can sort out what you need to make whatever it is when you decide,' Gemma said. 'When are you free next?'

'Tomorrow,' Rob said.

'Right. I'll call her tonight and tell her about you. Meet me at the practice at lunchtime and I'll introduce you to her,' Gemma said.

'Thank you, Gemma.'

She smiled. 'You're welcome. That's what family's for. Well, I'm not *quite* family.'

'You're engaged to my brother. You make him happy. You're definitely family,' Rob said, and hugged her.

'So that's the thing she did to challenge you? Taught you to sew?' Oliver asked.

Rob knew his twin wasn't mocking him. 'Yes. It's weird. I would never have believed it would work.'

'Counting stitches. I guess it'd have the same effect as counting reps at the gym,' Gemma said. 'Mentally, that is. Not physically.'

'It's weird,' Rob said again.

'What I can't get my head round is that it means you actually sit still. That's almost unheard-of,' Oliver said with a smile. 'I know how much you miss climbing, and I'm glad you've found something that grounds you. Better still, something that doesn't involve dangling off a mountain.'

'I'm trying to be more Ollie,' Rob teased.

'Yeah? There's one thing that pact of yours doesn't take into account,' Oliver said.

'What's that?'

Oliver patted his arm. 'I love you for who you are. You're worth the risk. If she understands you, she'll get that.'

'I hope,' Rob said, 'you're right. Because at this precise moment it feels impossible.'

'Think of your climbing,' Oliver said. 'You'd do a risk assessment and work out how to scale a crag. This is the same thing.'

'He's right,' Gemma said.

Except, if he miscalculated this, the hurt would go much deeper than just a broken bone...

The next day, Gemma introduced him to Yvonne, and he explained what he wanted. 'This is what she taught me to do,' he said, and brought out the bookmark. 'I want to sew something for her that tells her I love her.'

Yvonne drew up a file of photographs on her laptop. 'There are a few patterns here. There's this one.'

A heart, filled with rows of different sorts of hearts. It was pretty, but... He shook his head.

'It's pretty, but it's generic. I want something personal.'

'OK. Give me a bit more detail. What do you want to tell her?'

'That with her I'm not restless any more. I can be still.'

Yvonne thought for a bit. 'So she makes you feel grounded, as if you have roots?'

'That's it exactly.'

She scrolled rapidly through the file of patterns, and brought up another one: a tree, whose trunk was made out of the word 'love' in a very fancy script; the branches made a heart shape, and the leaves were hearts. 'How about this?'

'It's almost perfect,' he said. 'How do you add something to a pattern?'

'It depends what you want.'

'I want the tree to have roots that spell out her name.'

Yvonne put a hand to her face. 'Oh, that's so romantic! Well, I can tweak the pattern for you. Do you have a laptop and a printer?'

'Yes.'

'Then I'll sort it out for you over lunch and email you a PDF,' she said. 'Now, I assume you need the fabric, threads and everything else?'

'Yes, please.'

'Come and see me when it's done, and I'll frame it before you give it to her. On the house, as you're Ollie's brother and Gemma's like family to me.'

'Thank you,' Rob said. And he called in to the chocolate shop on the quayside on his way home, choosing a special assortment to be delivered that afternoon to thank Yvonne for her help.

He started work on the project as soon as he got back to his flat. He knew it would take time and he couldn't rush it, but hopefully this would show Florence what was in his heart. Tell her what she meant to him. Prove to her that he could manage his itchy feet, with her by his side.

And then maybe she'd agree to try to make a go of things with him...

* * *

On Friday, they were both rostered in Resus.

And again, Rob was aware of the awkwardness between them.

He'd never wish ill health on anyone, but he was glad of their first case, that morning: Michael Winters, who'd been brought in by his grandson.

'Grandad wouldn't let me call an ambulance,' the young man said. 'He just didn't look right this morning. I checked his pulse and it was sky-high, and his breathing's not good, so I bundled him in the car and brought him in.'

The triage team had sent them straight to Resus.

'Good call,' Florence said. 'How long has your grandad been like this?'

'Since I saw him this morning. Maybe overnight—I was late in, last night,' he said.

'Has he ever had anything like this before?' Florence asked.

'Not as far as I know, though I could check with my dad.'

'Are there any medical conditions we need to know about?' Rob asked.

'If stubbornness is a medical condition,' the grandson said wryly, 'he's definitely got it.'

Rob was very aware of Florence looking straight at him.

Was she calling him stubborn, too? She was one to talk.

'Nothing,' the young man said. 'He doesn't smoke. He likes his glass of whisky before he goes to bed, but it's not a huge one. He takes the dog out every day, and he eats properly because I live with him and I do the cooking.'

'OK. We'll assess him now,' Florence said, 'so if you

don't mind waiting in the waiting room, we'll come and get you as soon as we've finished.'

The young man nodded. 'Do what they tell you, Grandad,' he said, squeezing Michael's hand. 'I want you back home with me. And I want you well.'

'You fuss too much, Dylan,' Michael wheezed.

Rob wasn't happy with Michael's heart rate—more than double the norm—or his oxygen saturation levels.

'Oxygen,' he said to Florence, 'to help with his breathing.'

'And beta-blockers,' she said, 'to get his heart rate down.'

The longer the over-rapid heartbeat went on, the more stress it put on the ventricle, the lower pumping chamber of the heart, and it could lead to heart failure.

But the beta-blockers and oxygen seemed to have no effect, and Michael complained of feeling sweaty.

'I think we should do cardioversion,' Rob said.

'Agreed,' Florence said, looking grim.

'I'll go and have a word with Dylan.'

He found the younger man in the waiting room.

'Is everything all right?' Dylan asked.

'As you know, your grandad's heartbeat is too fast—something called superventricular tachycardia or SVT for short. There are lots of different causes for it,' Rob said. 'The most common one is an electrical problem with the heart. We'll be able to sort that out, but for now we need to get his heart back into a normal rhythm and he isn't responding the way we'd like to medication. So we want to give his heart a small electric shock.'

'But—isn't that what you do when someone has a heart attack?'

'Sort of,' Rob said. 'What it'll do is bring his heart

back to a normal rhythm. It'll only take about ten minutes. Your grandad will be under sedation so it won't hurt; he might feel a bit dizzy afterwards and might have a little bit of chest pain, but we'll keep him in for a few hours on the cardiac ward to keep an eye on him. The cardiac ward can also run tests to find out exactly what kind of electrical problem caused the SVT and how to treat that so he doesn't get this again.'

'Just make him better,' Dylan said. 'Whatever it takes.'

'I'll come and get you when we've done it,' Rob promised, and headed back to Florence.

Between them, they sedated Michael, put the sticky pads on his chest and attached the electrodes to the defibrillator.

Things might be a bit strained between them personally right now, Rob thought, but they were in tune at work.

'And clear,' Florence said, and administered the shock.

The results were dramatic: from the scary one hundred and eighty-five beats per minute, Michael's heart rate dropped straight down to a more normal seventy-five beats per minute.

'Result,' she said. 'Go and fetch Dylan, and I'll ring the cardiac team to get Michael admitted.' She smiled. 'It's good to have a good outcome.'

'Definitely,' Rob said.

And if only he could make sure that things between himself and Florence had a good outcome, too…

CHAPTER NINE

IN THE MIDDLE of the following week, Florence had to drag herself out of bed when her alarm went off.

Maybe she was going down with some kind of bug; as a morning person, she never usually struggled getting up for work. Washing her hair didn't make her feel any better. She made herself a mug of coffee, but couldn't quite face drinking it because the smell made her feel slightly queasy; and her toast tasted odd. Metallic.

Some viruses affected your sense of taste and smell, she knew. If she was going down with something, the last thing she wanted to do was to spread it among her colleagues.

She checked her temperature; it was normal.

But she still didn't feel right.

She was about to call work, saying that she felt rough and didn't want to spread whatever it was, when it hit her: she hadn't bought any tampons for more than a month.

And her periods were normally so regular that she could practically set her watch by them.

She counted back swiftly. Her last period had been just before Rob had started at the hospital, and her current period had been due on the week that he'd stayed with her. She'd been so busy concentrating on fighting her attraction to him that she hadn't noticed her period was late.

She wasn't sure whether she was more excited or apprehensive. Three years ago, she would've been trying to contain her excitement—and at the same time wary of getting her hopes up, only for them to be dashed again. Now... Now, she wasn't even in a relationship. And the idea of being pregnant was terrifying. Her whole life would be tipped upside down.

Could she be pregnant?

Or maybe she was overthinking this. Maybe because her routine had been slightly disrupted, her body had followed suit and she'd just skipped a period.

Although the night she'd spent with Rob had been smack in the middle of her cycle, her most fertile time, they'd used contraception. OK, so a condom could fail; but even if that was the case, she knew that he was also taking immunosuppressant drugs to stop his body rejecting his brother's kidney. It wasn't her area of medicine, but she was pretty sure she'd read studies showing that immunosuppressants affected fertility.

Which meant the chances of her conceiving were infinitesimally small.

Sipping a glass of water made her feel a bit better.

And that in itself was worrying. The symptoms were all starting to point away from a bug and towards...

Oh, help.

She didn't have time to worry about it now. She'd be late for her shift, if she didn't get a move on. She pulled herself together and headed for work. And she was seriously glad that Rob was off duty that day, because she couldn't have handled working with him—not with this weighing on her mind.

Thankfully they were so busy that she didn't have time to think about it during her shift; but there was only one way to prove to herself that her missed period was just a blip, caused by a change in routine or stress or whatever. She couldn't be pregnant.

Once she'd done her handover, she drove to an out-of-town supermarket, put a magazine in her shopping basket and then slid a pregnancy test underneath it, so if she did bump into someone she knew they wouldn't see the test and jump to conclusions.

She knew the drill and she was pretty sure that this test would be the same as every one that had broken her heart when she and Dan had been trying for a baby and her period had been a couple of hours late. When she'd taken a test, full of joyous anticipation, hoping that this would be the month their dreams would come true. She'd pee on the stick and wait for a minute; the line would show up in the first window to say the test was working; and then…

With every test, the other window had stayed stubbornly blank. And each one had sucked away a little more hope, until the point where they'd gone for testing. They'd expected that the problem was hers; the doctor had dropped the first bombshell, but Dan had dropped the bigger one.

She shook herself. That was then. This was now. And the test would just confirm that of course she wasn't pregnant. She performed the test, set the stick on the sink on the ledge between the taps, washed her hands, and glanced at the stick. It was all exactly as she expected: one window with a line to show that the test was working, and one blank window.

So she wasn't pregnant.

She stared at herself in the mirror. 'See? You were just being paranoid and stupid and ridiculous. Of course you're not pregnant.'

She knew she should have felt relieved. But she felt the echo of all the failed pregnancy tests from before, and it made her sad. She'd thought her life would be so different. That she, like her sister, would find it easy to get pregnant. That she and Dan would have children. Be a family.

There was nothing wrong with being single. You didn't have to have a partner and children to be fulfilled. She had a family she loved, a job she loved, good friends.

Except, deep down, she was lonely. Sharing her flat with Rob for a week had reminded her that she enjoyed living with someone else.

Though Rob had made it clear that person wouldn't be him. That he didn't want to settle down.

Tonight, she decided, she'd start looking for a flatmate.

She was just about to wrap the test and drop it in the bathroom waste bin when she realised that the second window had changed when she wasn't looking. It wasn't blank any more.

There was a line. A faint line, but it was definitely there.

She stared at it.

No way. This had to be some kind of mistake.

She blinked, and stared again. The line was still there. And now her certainty deserted her. Did that mean it was a positive test—or was it a false positive? Was she actually pregnant, or was it just a hormonal blip?

If she was pregnant, then she'd need to tell Rob. He had the right to know that she was expecting his baby. But she had no idea how he would react. Would he decide he had to do the right thing, and then resent her for trapping him? Or would this make him want to leave even faster?

When she'd asked him if he wanted kids, he'd said he thought he'd be a terrible dad. But would he really? Children needed to know they were loved. Rob was impulsive—but he'd been unfailingly good with their patients, paying attention and listening to them. The way he spoke about his family left her in no doubt that he loved them dearly. She was pretty sure he'd love their child.

What she wasn't sure about was how he felt about her. He'd comforted her when she'd let that case get to her—but then it had turned to kissing. So was it just all about the sex? And was that enough for a relationship? Or would she fail as badly as she had with her marriage to Dan?

Though she could hardly call Rob and talk to him right now, not when she wasn't certain.

Even two and a half years ago, the prospect of doing a second test to check it was a definite positive and not a mistake would've filled her with elation. Right now, she just felt confused: as if her world had tilted and she was sliding towards the edge.

Pregnant.

A baby.

The thing she'd wanted so much for so long, and thought wasn't possible.

Wasn't the saying, be careful what you wish for?

Because now it looked as if she might have her wish.

She wanted a baby. She wanted a child with a deep, visceral longing. Yet, at the same time, she was terrified. Being a parent wasn't easy; being a single parent was even harder, even though she knew her family and friends would be there for her.

Right then, she didn't have a clue what to do.

She could call Lexy—of course she could—or her mum. They'd both support her.

But Rob was the one she wanted to talk to most. And, until she was absolutely certain it wasn't just a blip, a false positive, she couldn't call him.

The obvious thing to do now was a second test. She headed back to the supermarket, and this time bought a different test—the all-singing, all-dancing sort that could be done even before you missed a period and told you in writing how many weeks pregnant you were. And this time she bought a double pack, in case something went wrong with the first test.

Back at her flat, her chest felt tight and she could hardly breathe.

And she couldn't squeeze out a single drop of urine to do the test.

She drank a glass of water. Paced up and down her flat. Waited. And she still didn't need to pee. 'Oh, for pity's sake. Don't be so wet,' she told herself. She made herself a mug of coffee, on the grounds that caffeine irritated the bladder and made you want to pee more quickly. This morning—and in fact all day at work—

she hadn't wanted coffee; but, if need be, she'd hold her nose so she could drink the stuff. She added enough cold water so she could drink it straight down, and paced the flat again. Yet still she didn't have the slightest urge to pee.

It was driving her crazy. She needed to know the answer, and she needed to know now. Was she or wasn't she pregnant with Robert Langley's baby? Just how long did it take liquid to go through your system? Was this how Rob felt all the time, twitchy and edgy and scattered? How did he cope, short of heading up the nearest mountain?

'Argh,' she said. Distraction. That was what she needed. Something to take her mind off it. Sewing was usually her answer, but this time she couldn't concentrate. She kept thinking of Rob when she'd taught him to sew: his beautiful blue eyes, his nearness, how she'd been tempted to steal a kiss. And that really, really, wasn't helpful.

OK. Chores, then. She vacuumed the living room, then glanced at her watch. Surely more time must have passed than that?

What next?

Maybe some yoga would help her settle. She tried some of the moves she'd learned at class, but they didn't help. She couldn't concentrate. Not until she had the answer.

Then finally, finally, she was ready to take the test.

Every nerve-end prickled. Would it be positive—or would it be negative?

She took a deep breath, did the test and capped it. As before, she left it on the ledge of the sink while she washed her hands. She could feel her pulse speeding up as she waited for the result to show; or did her pulse only feel faster because the seconds were dragging?

A line appeared in the first window, so the test was definitely working.

Now for the bit she needed to know. Pregnant or not?

She wasn't aware that she was holding her breath until the words actually appeared on the screen; and then the noise that came out of her mouth was the kind of wail that shimmered between joy and despair, everything all mixed up together.

She was pregnant. More than two weeks. Which fitted with her dates and the night she'd spent with Rob.

She sank down on the floor, drew her knees up to her chin and wrapped arms round her legs.

What now?

One thing she was definite about: she was keeping the baby, whatever happened. All those years of longing meant there was no way she'd choose a termination or to carry to term and have the baby adopted. This baby might not be planned, but he or she would most definitely be loved. She knew her family would support her and so would her friends.

But she had to tell Rob that she was expecting his baby.

It was the kind of conversation they needed to have face to face. Even a video call wasn't good enough. She didn't want to leave any room for misunderstandings.

She grabbed her phone and texted him.

Need to talk to you about something. Are you free this evening?

He didn't answer immediately, but she tried not to be unreasonable about it. He might be busy doing something with his brother or his parents. His phone might be accidentally on silent so he wouldn't know he'd got a text; or it might not even be switched on at all. The battery might have run out. There were all kinds of reasons why he wasn't answering.

There was still no answer after half an hour.

This wasn't something that could wait, because it would weigh on her mind. Though it was definitely not something she wanted to discuss at the hospital.

She'd have to bite the bullet and call him. Taking a deep breath to calm herself, she went into her contacts list and pressed on his name. She could feel her pulse accelerating as the line connected; but after two rings the call went to voicemail. She waited for the beep to leave her message. 'Rob, it's Florence Jacobs. I'd appreciate it if you could call me this evening, please. It doesn't matter what time. Thanks.'

Then she groaned when she ended the call; she must've sounded so snooty. *Florence Jacobs.* How many Florences would he know? But she could hardly call back and gabble something else now.

'Robert Langley, you are the most annoying man in the universe,' she muttered. 'Why is it so hard to get hold of you?'

It could be hours until he returned her call. And she needed to eat—for the baby's sake, if not her own. Plus she needed to work out what she was actually going to say to him. She made herself an omelette, grabbed a pen and paper to make notes about how to tell him, and just taken the first bite of her dinner when her phone rang and Rob's name flashed up on the screen.

She gulped the mouthful down and hit 'accept'; but

the food went the wrong way so she was coughing like mad when her phone connected.

'Florence? Are you all right?'

She swallowed a mouthful of water and coughed a bit more. 'Yes.'

'I just got your message,' he said.

'OK.'

'You asked me to call you. Which I'm doing.'

'Thank you.' But everything she'd meant to say went out of her head. Why hadn't she written it down before she'd even called him the first time?

'Florence? Are you still there?'

'Uh…yes.'

'What did you want?'

She took a deep breath. 'I need to talk to you about something.'

'I gathered that.' She couldn't tell if he was irritated or amused. 'I'm listening.'

'I… Not on the phone.'

She could practically hear the frown in his voice. 'Are you all right?'

That rather depended on your perspective. 'Yes.'

'Then what…?'

He sounded confused. Yeah. She knew how that felt. 'Can we meet?'

'Do you want me to drive over to you?'

'No. I'll come to you.' If, when she told him the news, and he decided that he didn't want to be involved—which was what she was expecting—then at least she could walk away with her head held high, rather than be the one left behind.

'What time?' he asked.

'I'll leave now. See you in a bit.' She ended the call

and forced down the rest of her meal; then she brushed her teeth, stuck the pregnancy test in an envelope and the envelope in her handbag, and drove over to his flat.

The only time she'd been to his flat before had been the day he'd come to stay with her. She hadn't taken in their surroundings as he'd packed an overnight bag.

Bearding the lion in his den. Or would Rob be a lamb rather than a lion?

She had absolutely no idea how he was going to react to her news. He'd kept his distance from her over the last week or so, not even suggesting grabbing a coffee or lunch together on the days when they were both rostered in Minors. So did that mean he'd back away even further when she told him about the baby?

There was no point in trying to second-guess him. And as for how to tell him... She was beginning to think that the best way was to be blunt.

She flicked on the stereo, and switched it off when she recognised the song as one of the ones she and Rob had caterwauled along to, the day he'd taken her out for a pizza when she'd been feeling low after her shift. He'd teased her into a brighter mood, and they'd laughed until they'd hurt.

It had felt so right.

But then it had gone so wrong...

She parked outside his flat. There weren't butterflies fluttering in her stomach; it felt more like a stampede of panicking dinosaurs.

She rested her hand on her stomach. 'You can do this, Florence Emily Jacobs,' she told herself. Then she hauled herself out of the car, walked up to the entrance to the block of flats, and pressed his intercom button.

He answered immediately. 'Hi, Florence. I'll buzz you in.'

And he met her at the door, looking concerned. 'Can I offer you a drink?'

'No, thanks.'

'OK. Come and sit down.'

His flat was super-neat and very minimalist; there was almost nothing on any of the surfaces, other than some framed photographs on the mantelpiece. It felt more like a show flat than a home.

She perched on the edge of one of the chairs.

'So what did you want to talk to me about?' he asked.

'There isn't an easy way to say this.'

'Say what?'

Oh, God. Why hadn't she practised this? In the end, the words came blurting out. 'I'm pregnant.' When he said nothing, panic filled her. 'I'm telling you simply because you have the right to know, but I don't expect anything from you.'

He still said absolutely nothing.

Which told her everything. He wasn't interested. And she couldn't take him rejecting her the way Dan had. She needed to leave. Now.

'That's all,' she said, and stood up. 'I can manage everything on my own, so don't worry that I'll demand anything from you. It's fine.'

She was pregnant.

With his baby.

Rob couldn't think straight.

He'd had no idea what she might want to talk to him about. His focus over the last few days had been entirely on trying to work out how to persuade her to take a chance on a proper relationship with him.

Now she was telling him she was expecting his baby.

He shook his head to clear it; it didn't work.

But then she stood up, ready to walk out of his life.

He couldn't—wouldn't—let that happen.

'Florence. Don't go,' he said. 'We need to talk about this.'

'There's nothing to say. I know you don't want kids.' She shrugged. 'It's not a problem.'

'No,' he said. 'That's not true. I've never said I don't want kids. And I don't…' He shook his head. 'Please. Don't go. Let me process this. Let me get my head straight so I don't say something stupid. And if I do say something stupid, cut me a bit of slack. Because all it means is the words are coming out wrong.'

For a moment, he thought she was going to leave anyway.

But then she nodded.

'Can I get you some cof—?' He stopped, mid-offer. Were pregnant women meant to avoid coffee? Would the smell upset her? 'Tea? Water?'

'No, thanks. I'm fine.'

'Forgive me for pacing. I'm not— It's not you, it's *me*,' he said. 'I need to move about when I'm thinking.'

'OK. I get that.'

To his relief, she sat down again.

He took a deep breath. 'First of all, are *you* all right?'

She looked surprised, as if she hadn't expected him to think of her welfare. 'Yes. At least, I think I am,' she qualified. 'I'm still getting my head round this.'

'So when you did find out?'

'This morning. It's not like me, having to drag myself out of bed.'

'No.' He looked at her. 'Then what?'

'My toast tasted funny. I didn't want my coffee.' She took a deep breath. 'And I realised my period was late. Normally it's really regular.'

'So you did a test at work?'

'After work. I bought one on the way home. And then I went out for another one.'

He raised an eyebrow. 'Why?'

'The first was just to prove to myself that I was being ridiculous. I couldn't be pregnant. Apart from the fact we used protection, you're on immunosuppressants with your kidney, so that affects your fertility—doesn't it?' She frowned.

'I don't know. It wasn't even an issue at the time,' he said. 'I was single when I went abroad. When they offered me the transplant, my focus wasn't on when or if I planned to start a family with a girlfriend who didn't exist, it was on getting fit enough to work again and be able to go climbing. So, actually, I'd need to look at the meds I'm on and check the details.'

She looked at him. 'So if you're on meds that don't affect your fertility…'

'…and the condoms in my wallet, even though I'm pretty sure they were in date, were old,' he said, 'then that would explain it.'

'With the first test, the line was very faint,' she said. 'It was the first time I'd ever actually seen a line appear in the second window.'

He remembered what she'd said about trying for a baby for years with her ex, and discovering that he was infertile. The disappointment every month when her period arrived must've been crushing—and even more so on the occasions when it had been late.

'I couldn't be sure it was a truly positive result, and I couldn't tell you about the baby unless I was absolutely sure. So that's why I went out and bought a second test—and a spare, just in case.'

Rob wanted to wrap his arms round her and hold her close, tell her that everything was going to be all right; but he knew that he needed to resist the impulse. Right now he needed to give her the space to tell him what was in her head.

'And this time the line was stronger?' he prompted.

'This time it was one of those that actually say it in words, and how many weeks pregnant you are.'

That night was the only time they'd slept together. 'So, if that night was in the middle of your cycle, then you're six weeks now?'

'Yes.' She took an envelope out of her bag. 'The test says three weeks plus. But I calculated the same as you did.'

He took the envelope, removed the test stick and stared at it.

Something he'd never thought he'd do.

And, instead of making him feel trapped and as if he'd been stuck in a little box, it filled him with joy. Pure elation.

They were going to have a baby.

He wanted to pick her up, twirl her round and cheer.

But she—despite the fact she'd told him that she dearly wanted a baby—didn't seem to be very happy about it. Had she changed her mind about babies? Or was *he* the problem?

He needed to know what was in her head. And there

was only one way to find out. He damped down all his impulses, and asked, 'So we've established we're having a baby, next summer. What do you want?'

'I already told you, I'm not going to make any demands on you,' she reminded him.

'Leave me out of the equation for now,' he said. 'I want to know what *you* want. Do you want the baby?'

'Yes.'

'And to make a family?'

'I keep telling you, I don't expect you to do anything.'

So did she want to be with him, or not? He was going to have to ask her straight out. And he was probably going to have to be the one to tell her that he wanted to make a go of things between them, because if she *did* want to be with him she clearly didn't want to be the first to say it.

He gave her a wry smile. 'My nickname in the family is Rob the Risk-Taker. This is the one time I really, *really* need to take a risk—and I'm absolutely terrified. Will you promise you'll hear me out and not back away?'

'I...'

'Please, Florence,' he said. 'It's important.'

Finally she nodded. 'All right.'

'So here's the thing. I don't have a proper diagnosis yet, but thanks to you picking it up I think the fact I can't settle is all down to the way my brain is wired, and not just pure selfishness on my part, which makes me feel a bit better about it, but...' He took a breath. 'I'm babbling. What I'm trying to say is that now I know I'm going to be a dad, and that changes everything. I'm absolutely terrified that I won't be very good at it—but I'll do my best to learn *how* to be a good dad, because even though I haven't had much time to get my head round the news I'm thrilled.'

Disbelief was etched across her face. What didn't she believe—that he was going to try to be the best father he could be, or that he was thrilled with the news?

He tried again. 'I know we've done this the wrong way round. You're supposed to date someone, then sleep with them, then decide you want to make a family together. We still haven't even got round to dating properly. We slept together and we made a baby. But things have changed for me since I met you,' he said. 'For the first time in my life I've met someone who actually makes me want to settle down. Someone I can be *still* with. Someone who understands me.'

She still didn't look convinced. Then again, now he knew what her ex had done, how he'd denied Florence her dearest wish and then rubbed her nose in it… 'Your ex,' he said softly, 'is an idiot who didn't recognise what he had with you, and I hate the way he treated you. I have my faults, but I promise I won't ever deliberately hurt you or deny you. I love you, Florence.'

'You love me?' She still didn't sound as if she believed him, but was that a glimmer of hope he could see in her eyes? He'd take that for the win.

'I love you,' he said. 'We haven't known each other for long,' he said, 'but it's been long enough for me to know. I *like* you. The doctor I see at work who's kind, who listens to her patients and takes the trouble to wash someone's face or sit with them in her lunch break because she knows they're lonely. The woman who saw

I was ill, and who looked after me without making me feel shut in and smothered. The woman who fitted together the pieces of a puzzle I would never have managed to solve for myself. The woman who taught me how to just *be* instead of having to move all the time.'

'That's liking, not love.'

'I haven't finished,' he said. 'Because I believe liking's the basis of real love. My parents like each other as well as love each other. Ollie and Gemma like each other. And I really like who you are. I like the way you can be brisk and efficient—but at the same time you'll take the trouble to stitch a picture of a dinosaur in a tutu for your niece just because you know she'll love it.

'I like the way you kiss like an angel and you don't mind that I sing flat—you laugh with me, not at me. I like *you*. But, more than that, you make my pulse skip a beat when you smile. Those huge brown eyes of yours turn me to mush. And every time I see you I want to kiss you until we're both dizzy.'

Her eyes glittered with unshed tears.

'And I'm growing to love you a little more every day. I've been going crazy, this last week, trying to work out how to tell you how I feel about you without making you run a mile.'

'But you've avoided me at work.'

'I've been trying to give you space,' he said. 'I was kind of hoping you'd miss me and then I could show you how I feel about you. That I'm serious.'

'Show me?'

'I finished this tonight.' He headed to the sideboard, took the thing he'd been working on all week out of a drawer and handed it to her. 'This is for you.'

* * *

Florence stared at the piece of material.

Rob must've been working on the cross-stitch for *days*. It was way too complicated for a beginner.

And it was absolutely beautiful: a tree, whose branches were in the shape of a stylised heart. He'd added heart-shaped leaves to the branches; the trunk contained the word 'love' in a fancy script; and the roots also made a name.

Her name.

'That's amazing,' she said.

'I made it for you,' he said, 'to try to tell you how I feel about you. You ground me, Florence. You're my roots. And what's growing is love.'

Tears filled her eyes. 'I think that's the nicest thing anyone's ever said to me.' Or done for her. She couldn't believe he'd made something so beautiful.

'I mean it,' he said. 'I did have some help finding the design and customising it—Ollie's fiancée is very close to the owner of the local craft shop, and she helped me. But it's from my heart.'

'It's stunning. I can't believe you've put all that work into it.'

'And sat still for so long,' he said with a wry smile.

'It's amazing.'

'So here it is,' he said. 'I'm not offering you something easy. I'm always going to have a restless side, even though now I know what's behind it I can do more to keep that under control. And there's the whole kidney thing, and the possibility of the transplant rejection will always be in the background. But I love you, Florence, and I want to be with you. I want to make a family with you. I want to help you bring up our baby—and maybe more babies in the future, if we're lucky. I'm hoping that maybe I can stay here permanently, but until a permanent job comes up here I'm happy to commute, or do whatever it takes to make this work. I know you've been hurt, and I know I'm asking you to take a huge risk—but I love you and I think we can make this work if we do this together. Will you marry me?'

He loved her.

He wanted to marry her.

He wanted to be there for the baby, make a family with her.

'You don't have to answer just yet,' he said. 'Think about it. I'll give you all the time you need.'

'You love me,' she said.

'And I'm not asking you to marry me just because of the baby, or because I think it's the right thing to do. I'm asking you because I want *you*. Because with you the world finally makes sense.'

'I've been so scared of letting myself fall for you. That's why I left your hotel room, that morning. I thought you'd be gone again in a few weeks and I didn't want to fall in love with you, only to lose you,' Florence said. 'But I don't think my heart was listening to my head, because I fell in love with you anyway. The way you danced with me. The way you made me feel.' She swallowed hard. 'I love you, Rob. You're right. It's not going to be easy. But we can make this work because we'll be together and we're on the same side. So yes. I'll marry you and make a family with you.'

He whooped, picked her up, and swung her round. And then he put her down hastily. 'Sorry. I need to treat you with kid gloves.'

'Says the man who can't stand cotton wool,' she pointed out.

'I seem to remember someone recommending bamboo cloths,' he said with a grin.

She spread her hands. 'Works for me.'

He kissed her. 'I love you, Florence. I'm going to be the best partner and the best dad I can be—and I know I'll be my best self with you by my side.'

'I love you, too, Rob.'

He kissed her again. 'And I think we have some family meet-ups to arrange. My family's going to love you.'

'And mine's going to love you. Especially if you tell three certain flower girls that they can have pink floaty dresses.'

'With an accessory of dinosaurs,' he said. 'Yeah. Works for me.' He kissed her again. 'And we have a wedding to plan.'

EPILOGUE

August, nine months later

FLORENCE AND GEMMA stood still as their matrons of honour did up the zips at the back of their dresses, then came round to the front.

'Beautiful,' Claire pronounced.

'Perfect,' Lexy agreed.

'And we're all ready, girls?' Rupa, Florence's best friend and chief bridesmaid, asked.

'Yes!' Margot, Anna, Scarlett—Gemma's goddaughter—and Darcey chorused, doing a curtsey.

Even baby Iona, cradled in her grandmother's arms, cooed a kind of 'yes'.

'It's a perfect day for a wedding,' Stephanie Baxter, Gemma's mum, said.

'Doubly perfect for a double wedding,' Heidi Jacobs, Florence's mum, added. 'Isn't that right, Iona?'

The baby gurgled again.

Stephanie glanced at her watch. 'Looks as if we're about ready to go. Who's going to hold my hand?'

'Me!' Scarlett said.

'And me!' Anna said.

'I'll let the photographer know we're coming,'

Claire said. 'I can't believe you found a house with a double staircase.'

'One side for each bride, and all our bridesmaids and matrons of honour in the middle,' Florence said gleefully. 'Just be glad we didn't make you all dress in Regency outfits.'

'Olls would look lovely as a Regency gentleman,' Gemma said. 'Though Rob would have to lose the stubble and wear a wig.'

'He would've grown over-the-top whiskers, if we'd suggested that,' Florence said with a grin. 'They'll look good enough in top hat and tails.'

'And you look amazing,' Stephanie said. 'Gemma, your father's so thrilled.'

'Me, too,' Gemma said softly.

Florence reached across and squeezed her sister-in-law-to-be's hand; Gemma had told her about how Oliver had helped heal the breach with her parents. 'Hey. No crying allowed, even if they're happy tears.'

'Yeah.' Gemma gave her a broad smile. 'The only one allowed to cry is Iona. And I get first dibs on cuddles.'

Florence saw the sudden brightness in Gemma's eyes, and wondered. When their mums and attendants had all left the room, she said, 'Would I be right in guessing you're just past the morning sickness stage?'

Gemma blushed. 'That's the problem with having medics in the family. They notice things. Twelve weeks.'

'You look doubly radiant—a bride and a mum-to-be,' Florence said. 'Ollie's going to fall in love with you all over again.'

'And Rob's going to fall at your feet. How do you

manage to look so gorgeous when you haven't had a full night's sleep in weeks?' Gemma asked.

'Because it's our wedding day,' Florence said, 'so I think there's just a bit of magic everywhere.'

'This place is pretty spectacular,' Rob said, gesturing to the beautiful double staircase in the hall of the Georgian house. There was a stained-glass dome in the ceiling, and the sunlight shone through so that the black and white marble floor was full of colour.

'Given that Gemma loves all the Austen stuff as much as Florence does, we should consider ourselves lucky they were satisfied with a Regency ballroom and didn't want us dressed up as Mr Darcy,' Oliver said with a grin.

'You know what? I wouldn't have minded if it made Florence happy,' Rob said.

'I wouldn't have minded either,' Oliver said. 'Though it's not how or where you get married that matters, it's having your family and your friends there.'

'Agreed,' Rob said. 'Look—here come the girls. I can't believe how many bridesmaids we've got between us. And look at Mum. She looks so happy.'

'Of course she does. It's the wedding day of both of her sons—and she's cuddling her first grandchild,' Oliver said. 'Getting in a bit of pract—' He stopped abruptly. 'Um...'

Rob's head whipped round. 'Are you telling me...?'

'Twelve weeks. Don't tell Gem I told you,' Oliver warned.

'I won't,' Rob promised, and grinned. 'That's brilliant. Welcome to the never-sleep-again club.'

'Thank you. I can't wait,' Oliver said. 'If I look as good on it as you do, bring on the sleepless nights.'

And then they both fell silent as their brides walked out from opposite sides of the gallery to the middle, hugged each other, then stood at the top of the double staircase.

The string quartet in the middle of the hall began to play 'The Flower Duet' from Delibes' *Lakmé*, and Florence and Gemma walked down the stairs towards them.

'It doesn't get better than this,' Rob whispered.

'Oh, it does,' Oliver said. 'We get to kiss our brides. And the first dance.'

'And then,' Rob said, hugging his brother, 'we get the happy ever after.'

* * * * *

COMING SOON!

We really hope you enjoyed reading this book.
If you're looking for more romance, be sure to
head to the shops when new books are
available on

Thursday 16th September

To see which titles are coming soon, please visit

millsandboon.co.uk/nextmonth

MILLS & BOON

THE HEART OF ROMANCE

A ROMANCE FOR EVERY READER

MODERN

Prepare to be swept off your feet by sophisticated, sexy and seductive heroes, in some of the world's most glamourous and romantic locations, where power and passion collide.

HISTORICAL

Escape with historical heroes from time gone by. Whether your passion is for wicked Regency Rakes, muscled Vikings or rugged Highlanders, awaken the romance of the past.

MEDICAL

Set your pulse racing with dedicated, delectable doctors in the high-pressure world of medicine, where emotions run high and passion, comfort and love are the best medicine.

True Love

Celebrate true love with tender stories of heartfelt romance, from the rush of falling in love to the joy a new baby can bring, and a focus on the emotional heart of a relationship.

Desire

Indulge in secrets and scandal, intense drama and plenty of sizzling hot action with powerful and passionate heroes who have it all: wealth, status, good looks...everything but the right woman.

HEROES

Experience all the excitement of a gripping thriller, with an intense romance at its heart. Resourceful, true-to-life women and strong, fearless men face danger and desire - a killer combination!

To see which titles are coming soon, please visit

millsandboon.co.uk/nextmonth

MILLS & BOON

Coming next month

REAWAKENED AT THE SOUTH POLE
Juliette Hyland

Helena Mathews put Kelly Jenkins's shoulder X-rays on the light box. Carter still couldn't believe his eyes. If it hadn't felt ridiculous, he'd have pinched himself. Not that it would do any good. This wasn't a dream.

She was truly here. At the Amundsen-Scott South Pole Station. The odds were astronomical. This was a situation that one saw in cheesy movies. Not actual life.

Time had been exceedingly kind to Helena. Her features were more refined now, but the beautiful young girl had transformed into a stunning woman. The long blond hair she'd worn in braids was shorn close to her head in an adorable pixie cut. It was a cut that her parents—particularly her mother—probably would have hated, just like she probably disliked the small diamond stud in Helena's nose. But both seemed to suit the woman standing next to him.

And some things hadn't changed. Like her jade eyes or the full lips that barely stuck out in a pout. Kissable lips.

Carter shook himself as he stared at the light box. He needed to pull his shaken core together. Seeing Helena was a shock, but it changed nothing. He wanted to believe the lie, but his heart hammered against his chest, denying that anything about this winter assignment would be the same.

For the first time since he'd ended his engagement, he felt like he was at a crossroads. In those broken moments he'd sworn he'd never step off the isolated path he'd chosen, and nothing was going to change that. Yes, Helena was here, but that didn't have to mean anything significant for him. She was just another medical professional wintering at the research station.

Except…

His brain cut that thought off before he allowed it to wander.

Crossing his arms, he studied the X-ray. It was Kelly's shoulder that mattered right now. Not the soft woman standing inches from him.

"I don't see any breaks, Carter."

His name on her lips sent a wave of unwelcome emotions through the darkened corners of his soul. Light poured into places that had been dormant for years. Home…it felt like home. Warm, welcoming, supportive. All the things he'd taken for granted. All the things he did not need.

Home.

Continue reading
REAWAKENED AT THE SOUTH POLE
Juliette Hyland

Available next month
www.millsandboon.co.uk